T0041914

WHAT A DOG KNOWS

ALSO BY SUSAN WILSON

The Dog I Loved

Two Good Dogs

The Dog Who Saved Me

A Man of His Own

The Dog Who Danced

One Good Dog

Summer Harbor

The Fortune Teller's Daughter

Cameo Lake

Hawke's Cove

Beauty

WHAT A DOG KNOWS

SUSAN WILSON

ST. MARTIN'S GRIFFIN
NEW YORK

This is a work of fiction. All of the characters, organizations, and events portrayed in this novel are either products of the author's imagination or are used fictitiously.

Published in the United States by St. Martin's Griffin, an imprint of St. Martin's Publishing Group

WHAT A DOG KNOWS. Copyright © 2021 by Susan Wilson. All rights reserved. Printed in the United States of America. For information, address St. Martin's Publishing Group, 120 Broadway, New York, NY 10271.

www.stmartins.com

Designed by Donna Sinisgalli Noetzel

The Library of Congress has cataloged the hardcover edition as follows:

Names: Wilson, Susan, 1951– author.
Title: What a dog knows / Susan Wilson.
Description: First Edition. | New York : St. Martin's Press, 2021.
Identifiers: LCCN 2020057512 | ISBN 9781250077264 (hardcover) | ISBN 9781466889224 (ebook)
Classification: LCC PS3573.I47533 W48 2021 | DDC 813/.54—dc23
LC record available at https://lccn.loc.gov/2020057512

ISBN 978-1-250-07727-1 (trade paperback)

Our books may be purchased in bulk for promotional, educational, or business use. Please contact your local bookseller or the Macmillan Corporate and Premium Sales Department at 1-800-221-7945, extension 5442, or by email at MacmillanSpecialMarkets@macmillan.com.

First St. Martin's Griffin Edition: 2022

10 9 8 7 6 5 4 3 2 1

To David

for more than a hundred mornings of walking the dog

so that I could get to work

PROLOGUE

Back in the day, Ruby Heartwood—fortune-teller, seer, psychic—seemed exotic, mysterious, slightly dangerous. Now, for someone who dresses in a gold-brocade caftan and reads tarot cards in a conical tent with a pennant flapping in the breeze, she looks, well, dated. Madame Ruby isn't drawing them in like she used to. The trouble with setting up at these Renaissance Faires is that it has become more *Game of Thrones* cosplay than an homage to the era of Camelot. Nowadays people seem to like seers with pyrotechnics. Today, one customer, dressed like a cross between a barbarian (as imagined) and Jared Leto, offered to let her read the chicken bones from his order from Ye Olde Pub Grub. Complete idiot. She declined, asked for his hand and read him a completely bogus fortune that included attracting a woman who would appear gnomish at first, but then be revealed as a femme fatale. Happily, the hairy jerk planted a sticky twenty in her hand and sloshed his Ye Olde Pub authentic "mead" all over the rug she had beneath her table. Even if she had actually been able to glean a real prognostication from his palm, she would have lied to him anyway.

Ruby tries not to dwell on the fact that for the past few months it's all been bogus readings. Her powers of interpretation seem to be on the decline—as in gone.

The truth is, Ruby is ready to move on. If this had been a more lucrative gig, she'd stay through the rest of the weekend; but, really, there is no point. Another hundred bucks, and that's being optimistic, won't make or break her budget. It's more imperative to listen to her instincts. This Renaissance Faire is tapped out. Time to go. The itch to be gone has evolved, as it always does, from a niggling idea to a compulsion.

As she always does when it's time to go, Ruby pulls out her atlas and opens it to the next state from where she happens to be. It's not quite as random as, say, closing her eyes and dropping a finger on a page, but not too far off. Some would suggest that a fortune-teller might consult her tarot cards or tea leaves, but Ruby prefers a degree of planning over allowing fate to take the wheel. Forty years on the road, and she has learned that it's better to move one hop at a time than take big strides. Better to have at least an idea of where she's going. Both she and her VW Westfalia have aged out of eighteen-hour drives.

Ruby packs up her tent, stows everything into the camper van that has been her home on the road since it was almost new, ever since her daughter, Sabine, went off to college and never returned to their wayfaring lifestyle. A decision that made it possible for Ruby to quit any pretense at needing a stationary place to call home. As she has said before, if you have a van you aren't homeless.

Since the advent of direct deposit and ATMs, cell phones and online bill pay, Ruby hasn't spent more than a few weeks in any one place. She could. She could take up her daughter Sabine's offer to use the little garage apartment attached to their house; settle into grandmother-hood and being useful to Sabine and her busy family. Those few times when she'd done that, made a concerted effort to be a normal mother, the claustrophobia descended. Not the kind of claustrophobia that would make one nervous about elevators, but the kind that gives Ruby the sense that she is being followed. Observed. As if she's an object of someone's curiosity. Not in the way that as a psychic she has cultivated curiosity. That kind of curiosity she stops attracting simply by taking off the gold brocade caftan, sweeping her hair back up into a twist and throwing on jeans and a T-shirt. Poof, just your average lady. Nothing to see here.

This sense of being watched is neither ominous nor benign. Not comforting; not frightening. It is more a shadow or a glint in the corner of her eye. A presence that keeps Ruby's hands on the steering wheel and her foot on the gas. *Don't catch me.* When she was a kid, a runaway, she sometimes thought that it was her unknown mother looking for her, a fantasy only a little different than the imaginary reunions she and her fellow orphans indulged in. Different in that, even as a teenager, Ruby was pragmatic; her survival required her to focus on the here and now; keeping ahead of the law. Now that feeling of being sought has evolved into a simple habit—keep moving.

Last night, for the first time in many a year, Ruby had a dream about her mother. She had no face, no voice, no *presence,* but Ruby had awakened knowing that the dream had been about the woman who left her behind.

Ruby doesn't bother to let the management know of her retreat. Some people call it an Irish goodbye, but for Ruby it is what she has always done. To simply vanish. Even on paper, Ruby doesn't exist.

PART I

1

Ruby can barely see the road in front of her beyond the smeary path left by the worn-out wipers. She's on a back road, having gotten off the west to east highway an hour ago when the rain started coming down. Neither her wipers nor her nerves can take highway speeds in weather like this.

In the random way of many rural roads, there is suddenly a stop sign in front of Ruby. She has run out of west to east road. Her choice is now left or right, North Farms Road or South Farms Road. The only vehicle on the road, Ruby can take her time deciding. She glances to her left, and there is the prettiest little house she thinks she's ever seen. A perfect hobbit house of a place. Even in the downpour, the yellow of its clapboards and the bright white of its gingerbread trim glow. Maple trees with their new pale green cauliflower buds bounce in the gusts, framing the view. If there was a B&B sign hanging out front, Ruby thinks she'd stop, see about spending the night. But there isn't. Press on. She signals to the empty road that she will be taking the South Farms Road turn. Within a few feet she spots a sign: HARMONY FARMS 10 MILES.

At this point, Ruby has been on the road for most of the day and right now she just needs a place to pull the Westie off the road, eat her dinner and regroup. If the rain subsides, she'll make a few more miles to her, as yet, undetermined destination. If the rain doesn't let up, she can lock the van and go to sleep.

A sudden streak of lightning and she sees a brown state park sign directing her to Lake Harmony. Perfect. She pulls the van into an empty parking lot, notes the restroom facility and the scattered picnic tables. It's too dark now to see the lake, but she can make out the lights of homes sprinkled around the edges. Another lightning bolt, immediately followed by the boom of thunder, and she backs the van out from under a pine tree. No sense getting crushed if a tree should get struck and topple over.

In the van she eats the leftover grinder from a rest stop Subway, cracks open a little screw top single serve bottle of wine. Home sweet home.

Are you nervous? Being all alone, a woman, and all? How many times has Ruby had to deflect that question with a wave of her hand and a laugh? A thousand? A million? She doesn't tell them that it's being in company that makes her nervous. It would seem rather odd to admit that being around people who want to be with her is far more frightening than bunking down alone in her automotive tiny house. Besides, like a Victorian lady, she does keep a little peashooter under her pillow at night, no bullets, but it's a comfort. And, in forty years on the road, she's never had occasion to use it. Ruby is a recluse with an active social life. Just don't try to tie her down. Even her daughter can't do it.

As if conjured by her thoughts, Ruby's phone buzzes with Sabine's FaceTime alert. Time to bid the grandkids good night and endure another round of where-are-you-and-where-are-you-heading-now-and-why-don't-you-come-here?

"Hi, Ruby!" Two faces crowd the screen. Molly and Tom. Plain names, what Sabine likes to refer to as *normal*. Where so many of her mommy-peers are giving their kids trendy monikers, Sabine, who has had to explain her exotic name too many times, chose to give her kids what Ruby thinks of as plain vanilla names. But they suit them.

"Hello, my darlings." Ruby is fortunate in that she doesn't have to do much heavy lifting in these satellite-powered versions of face-to-face conversation with her grandchildren. They are happy to give her a thumbnail sketch of a busy kid's day, talking over each other as they bring Ruby up to speed on the last days of school and the intransigence of their parents in refusing to consider going to Disney as a summer vacation.

And then they're gone and the face on the screen is her one and only child. "Do not encourage them in this demand we be like everyone else's parents."

"Now, Sabine, when have I ever chosen to be like other people?" Ruby smiles. "I will go to the mat for your right to rebel against societal norms."

"Yeah. So, where are you now?"

"Come on, Sabine, use your talents." Like Ruby, Sabine has the gift. A gift she has spent most of her life suppressing. A gift quite different from Ruby's, not just as a reader of signs and portents, but as a medium; seeing ghosts, interpreting the astral plane. Nonetheless, Sabine is pretty good at reading psychic vibes.

"Right now, my talent is pinning you someplace near a lake."

"Yes! See, you still have it."

"What I have is Find Friends."

Ruby's concession to Sabine worrying so much about her wandering lifestyle was to agree to let Sabine add her to the app. "I have no idea where I am, somewhere between here and there." It's her old dodge of a joke. "Hey, it's really coming down now and starting to thunder. I have to hang up."

"Go. Be safe. Call me in a couple of days."

"Love you."

"Love you too." A statement Ruby had despaired of ever hearing while Sabine worked through her adolescent rebellions. "Hey, Mom, quick question."

"Shoot."

"How old was I when I, you know, started *feeling* things?"

"You had flashes of it by the time you were eight or so." Ruby would ask Sabine why that particular question, but she already knows the answer. "Molly?"

It seems as though it is an inherited trait, this business of sixth senses and visions and clairvoyance. Like the distinctive single freckle located at the corner of Ruby's mouth, Sabine has the same small blemish. Once Molly had grown out of babyhood and her features become more of a little girl, Ruby had seen that she, too, bore this tiny hereditary marker. It simply stands to reason that Molly would grow into the other distinctive family marker.

"I think so." Sabine's face on the tiny screen betrays a maternal blend of worry and acceptance. "And you, when did you get yours?"

"About the same age, although it wasn't until I was older that it became a problem." It is a conversation like the one most mothers have with their daughters, except that the topic isn't menstruation but psychic powers. "And, Sabine, the good thing is that Molly will never have to figure it out on her own."

"Like you did."

"Like I did."

She saw Karen fall on the playground, except that they weren't on the playground, they were in the chapel, hands clasped in proper reverence for the morning's prayers. She felt the burn of a skinned knee even as her own, bare between knee sock and plaid skirt, felt the smooth fabric of the kneeler. She wanted to reach over to Karen and comfort her friend even as Karen dutifully recited the prayers, oblivious to her upcoming accident. The feeling was so strong, so *inevitable*, that when Karen joined the queue to head out for their ten minutes of play before school, she grabbed her hand and jerked Karen back from going outside. "Mary Jones, what's the matter with you? Let me go." Karen yanked her hand out of Mary Jones's and ran out of the chapel onto the playground and promptly tripped in exactly the way Mary Jones had seen in her mind's eye. And Karen, knee bleeding and tears running, blamed Mary Jones for her fall.

Ruby shuts off the little battery lamp on her pop-up table, pushes the curtains to the side, the better to enjoy the light show nature has provided for her entertainment. The storm is moving northeast and streaks of lightning illuminate the wind-roughened lake water in front of her van. She can hear the sloppy chop of water against a wooden pier jutting out away from the beach. A split second of brilliant lightning and an almost immediate crack of thunder and suddenly all of the lights across the lake are out. Within seconds, a second thunderbolt and the fine hairs on Ruby's arms stand up; her whole body tingles. The darkness is complete. Then a searing brightness that lasts for a full five count. Ruby closes her eyes against it. When she opens them, she fumbles for her lamp and turns it on, pulls the van's curtains across the windows. Squeezes through the space between the two front seats and sets up the folding privacy screen against the windshield. It's a weak measure against the brilliance of the electric show outside, but she feels better. Except that the tingling is not subsiding.

Another person might be concerned, but Ruby sits and listens to this phenomenon, studies it for meaning. A normal person might think she's been lightly electrocuted, but Ruby doesn't. She may not have gone beyond an eighth-grade education, but she knows that the van, on its four rubber tires, sitting in sand, out from under trees, and with its aerial long gone, is grounded.

Auguries and signs. Portents and forebodings. The ozone is thick in the air. She can smell the pine, the water, the very sand and where it changes from beach to loamy trail. She can hear beyond the heavy rain the sound of a fish jumping. This has happened before—a literal recharging of her senses. Whether it simply manifests itself as a better sense of smell or as renewed extrasensory powers, she won't know until she is tested. But one thing Ruby is certain of, something is about to change.

2

Ruby dreams again of her mother. This time she hears her voice. Of course, she cannot possibly know what her mother's voice sounded like as she has never heard it. Or seen her face. Or felt the touch of her hand. Nonetheless, someone is speaking to her, a faceless entity. *Please open the door. Let me in.*

Ruby opens her eyes, pushes back the café curtain in the Westfalia. The light gracing the lake shimmers in the dawn. The blue sky above the lake's surround of green pines is cloudless. It's a pretty day. The dream has dissipated, but not the sense of hearing a voice.

Open the door.

"Oh geez."

Not her dream-mother, but some stranger outside her van asking for admittance. Jumping up, Ruby slips a sweatshirt over her T-shirt, pushes open the café curtain on the door side of the van, and looks out. No one there. Then she hears a rough scratching against the side of the van, too rhythmic to be a branch. She slides the heavy door a few inches and looks out, then down. Looking up at her is a small black and white dog. It has a goofy grin on its face, as if it's brought her a surprise. *Please let me in.*

Ruby sinks back onto the bench. Scowls. She slips the derringer into the palm of her hand, then pulls aside the café curtains on the other side of van, looks out. Still no one. No one human.

In, please.

Ruby jerks open the van door to its fullest and steps out, looks for the ventriloquist who has woken her with his foolish parlor trick. But it is only the dog. Taking her silence for permission, the dog jumps into the van, jumps onto the bench, circles three times and is instantly asleep.

"Hey, you can't do that. Out."

The dog opens one eye. "You invited me in."

It's not like the dog's mouth is moving, or even that she's hearing its voice with her ears, it's more like she's being inhabited by some kind of auditory mist. It's all in my head, she thinks. And yet it doesn't feel entirely unfamiliar. It is almost exactly the same misty sense that she gets when she has an actual intuitive moment with a client. Or when she was a child, just finding out about her clairvoyant powers, and would *see* the future or the pain or the conflict residing within a person. In this case, she is *hearing* what the dog thinks. It's not even that what's bouncing around in her mind are actual words, it is the language of images and senses, not speech. Gingerly, she reaches out and touches the dog on its furry back. There is a mild vibration, a tingling that courses up through her fingertips and suddenly her mind is filled with sounds which feels like she's breathing them in. It's like a sudden onset synesthesia, where scent translates into colors. In this case, the olfactory becomes visual. She hears grass and macadam; the way a child's skin is soft; the way loss is unspeakable. She pulls her hand away. Her heart is racing, her hands shaking. Ruby is suddenly dry-mouthed. She leaves the van, leaving the door wide open and runs to the park's restroom. Scooping water from the faucet, she drinks and then splashes her face. Catches her breath. "This is crazy."

If she can understand what this dog is thinking, what does it expect of her?

Refreshed from its brief nap, the dog greets Ruby outside the van, bows and stretches. Shakes. Squats, and Ruby sees that this is a little girl dog. Ruby sits down, pats her knee and the dog bounds over. "What do you want?" She doesn't touch the dog, wanting to see if this phenomenon will happen without a physical connection. She leans down, and the dog gives her a tiny kiss. "I want to be with you."

"Why?" Ruby hopes that she is truly alone in this state park; she would hardly like to be observed asking a dog questions as if she expected answers.

"You are alone."

"I'm not looking for a companion."

"Yes, you are."

Okay, this is all in her head. Ruby is certain that she's never been psychotic before, but maybe that's what all this fortune-telling has really been; all this seeing the auras of other people. The way the *gift*, as her first mentor called it, rises and ebbs like the tide. Maybe she really is just plain crazy. Although, to be accurate, she's never before heard voices in her head. Voice, singular, and, to be clear, she's not hearing a voice, but hearing images. Oh, yeah. Totally not normal, not even for a psychic.

Ruby pushes the sliding door fully open and sits on the ledge of the van's carpeted floor. The dog snuggles up to Ruby, shoving her little black nose under Ruby's arm so that she can press herself against Ruby's side. The dog's white ruff is as soft as down and Ruby feels herself calming as she runs the fur through her fingers. She can practically hear her own pulse slow down. They sit, neither one speaking, and that overused phrase, *companionable silence*, seems to describe the moment just about right. The morning air is spring flavored. The calm beyond the storm. The calm of capitulation for sure. The lake surface ripples as a fish somewhere leaps for joy. Where the heck am I, Ruby thinks, in what rabbit hole have I fallen?

"With me," says the dog. "Place. Stay."

It had been a horrible night. I regretted my impulse to bolt from where I had been even though I had been there without food and water for

so long. The rain and the thunder and the searing lightning were terri-
fying, until I saw that van. I have been in many a van in my short life,
always in a crate. I expected that the person in that van might have a
crate I could crawl into, and maybe food too. The problem was that in
all that storm noise, she couldn't hear me ask for help. So I hunkered
down beneath the vehicle, waited until it was safe to come out and
then asked for what I needed. Thankfully, I had happened upon the
only human I have ever encountered who understood me.

An hour later and Ruby is dressed and ready to move on. She needs
coffee and the van needs gas and now she's got this little hitchhiker
ensconced on the bench seat as if Ruby wants her there. "What am I
going to do with you? Who's your person?"

No answer. The dog wiggles her expressive eyebrows and settles
her chin more comfortably on the seat. Ruby sits beside her, places her
left palm against the dog's skull. A mild stimulation tickles her palm.
"Home with you."

"This *is* my home."

"Mine too." The dog's mouth cracks open in a happy pant. "Now."

"I can't complicate my life with you."

"I'll be good." She rests her chin on Ruby's arm. "I'm a good girl."

This audible scent of good intentions floods Ruby's mind with a
strange mixture of hope and comfort. Without a doubt, she understands, this dog is as rootless as she but hasn't always been. No one will
come looking for her, any more than anyone has ever really searched
for Ruby.

Ruby cups both hands against the sides of the dog's head and feels
the increasing tingle. "Where did you come from and why did you
choose me?" It may be a far too complex question for a dog's thoughts,
but she asks anyway. A moment later, the scent of rotting flowers, that
peculiar nasty odor of forgotten vases. No. It's not flowers. This dog

has lost her former owner to death. A lingering, lonely death. Ruby jerks her hands away.

For nearly eighteen years Ruby traveled with her daughter, Sabine. Encumbered first by pregnancy, then by an infant, then by having to make sure her daughter was educated, even if it meant settling for a school year in a dozen different places, Ruby missed Sabine, but as an empty nester, or, in her case, an empty Westfalianer, she'd quickly grown used to, was maybe even happier, going solo. She and Sabine had knocked heads so often over Ruby's wandering lifestyle that not having a glowering teenager in the passenger's seat was, in some ways, a blessing. Happy and settled, Sabine was a lot more fun now when they saw each other.

So, at least a dog wouldn't complain about being constantly on the move. A dog might even be useful. A dog whose thoughts she could interpret might even lead to something interesting. What if Ruby is now open to other dogs' thoughts?

"Okay. You can stay." Ruby strokes the dog's head, noting that the tingling is gone. But the contented look on the animal's face is plain. Ruby has made her happy.

3

The gas station is attached to a Cumberland Farms convenience store. A large man in a baggy New England Patriot's hoodie over stained Carhartt pants is leaning against the side of the Cumberland Farms building, paper cup in one hand and the other stuffed in the kangaroo pocket of the sweatshirt, a cigarette dangling from the corner of his mouth. He looks like someone you'd avoid. Beside him is a well-made yellow Labrador retriever. The man's eyes are focused on nothing, but the dog's are on Ruby. Even from the distance between the pumps and the building, Ruby feels the intensity of the dog's gaze. It isn't a hostile intensity; she doesn't feel threatened as the yellow Lab leaves his master's side and heads toward her. Inside her van, little forepaws balancing on the dashboard, the black and white hitchhiker barks twice, communicating in her own language that this van is already occupied by a dog. No need for another.

Ruby finishes gassing up the van, hangs the pump nozzle back in place. As the yellow dog meanders over to Ruby, she clears her throat and then her mind. This might be as good a time as any to see if this bizarre new ability is authentic.

"Hey, fella." Ruby pats the dog's blocky head and instantly feels a prickle of connection as if she's touched something faintly electric, not dissimilar to the feeling she may get when she holds a client's hand for a reading. A charge, not so much electrical as emotional. She puts both hands on his head and now it feels more like the vibration she'd gotten this morning with the black and white dog. The yellow dog sits, leans his weight against Ruby's legs. He lifts his eyes to hers and Ruby is suddenly aware of a humming sound like wind across a wire, vaguely musical. She takes her hands off the dog's head and the humming stops; the prickle stops.

"Get over here, Duke." The man half-heartedly calls the dog over. "Come on, leave the lady alone. Come 'ere."

"He's fine. He's a good boy."

The dog presses his head into Ruby's thigh. When she touches him on the shoulder, the sensations are back.

"My name isn't Duke."

A slow smile spreads across Ruby's face. This must be what it's like to understand a foreign language without having to study it. Or to suddenly be able to play the piano when you actually can't. Ruby leans closer to the dog's face, her eyes holding his over his boxy muzzle. "Too much anger word."

Ruby rubs her hands together, replaces them on either side of the dog's blocky cheeks. She closes her eyes and touches her forehead to his skull. Instantly dreadful images flood her mind, pain, darkness, hunger. She pulls away. Let's go of the dog. "Who hurt you?" She's ready to confront the guy who has dropped his cigarette onto the ground, is crushing it out with the toe of his boot.

"Other man."

She can smell whiskey, cigar, and pond water and what she thinks might be the odor of gunpowder.

Ruby gestures toward the man with her eyes. "Him?" The guy looks so rough that she half expects the dog to ask for asylum with her.

The hum grows louder. "He's my friend." A new image, a shared bed, the taste of cheese.

As with the little hitchhiker, this canine's thoughts are very clear; although not in actual language, more like waves of thought. Beams. Like sunlight or radar. Images that seem like she's breathing them in.

"What name do you want?"

"Boy."

"Why Boy?" she asks, but Ruby understands, the dog associates the generic "Boy" with kindness.

"Please." The dog points his nose toward the man, wags his tail. "Tell him my name." The dog shifts his body away from Ruby, and the humming begins to fade away; the prickle in the tips of her fingers is gone. The dog trots back to his person who gives him a loving thump on the ribs.

"Okay." Ruby says this under her breath. "Why not?"

She shoulders her purse, tells the dog in her van to wait, and heads toward the door.

"Sorry about Duke. He's real friendly, just not so good with manners." Up close the man's face looks like he's done a lot of living in it, but it's open and friendly, not unlike an overgrown ten-year-old.

"He's fine. I like dogs." To prove her point, she fondles the dog's triangle-shaped ears. He licks his dewlaps and offers a paw. No prickle, no humming. Maybe it *was* all in her head. The dog sneezes, woofs, gives Ruby a meaningful glance. "By the way, he says that his name isn't Duke. He'd prefer to be called Boy." Ruby pulls open the heavy glass door and, without so much as a sidelong glance to judge the dog owner's expression, goes into the convenience store, keeping her self-satisfied smile to herself. She doesn't do it often, but when she drops a bomb like that on the unsuspecting, it is kind of fun.

A large Farmhouse Blend flavored with vanilla nondairy creamer just cries out for an accompanying pastry, and she lingers a bit over the array in a clear plastic box. Sighing, Ruby allows herself only the fantasy of a doughnut, grabbing a less satisfactory but wiser granola bar for breakfast. Then she heads to the grocery aisles and tracks down a bag of kibble. And a box of Milk-Bones.

"Do you know that guy out there, the one with the dog?"

The clerk, a skinny pale-cheeked boy sporting long skater hair, shrugs. "Bull. Bull Harrison. He won't bother you. He's harmless. He's not supposed to hang around, but he does."

"He's fine, I just wanted to know his name. Thanks." Ruby picks up her purchases and the cup of coffee and pushes the heavy door open with her shoulder. Bull Harrison grabs the handle to help.

"Thank you."

"So, how'd you know that? About his name?"

Ruby likes that he isn't trying to deny the message like most men would or tell her that she's full of it. "He thinks that 'Duke' has too hard a sound to it. He doesn't like hard things. He's afraid of them."

"Well, considering his background, that makes sense." Bull scratches at a grizzled cheek. "So, you some kind of an animal whatchacallit?"

"Psychic. Not really." He's been open-minded about all this; she should be honest with Bull. "I usually read people." Ruby knew that there were ladies, and they were most often ladies, in her line of work who specialized in animal communication, but she had never, before today, experienced the phenomena. Food for thought.

"So, Duke, umm, Boy is your first?"

Ruby points to the black and white hitchhiker staring out at them. "Second."

Bull bends to kiss his dog on the head. "Okay, Boy. Boy it is."

The dog, Boy, thrashes his back end around in joy.

"Good. He'll be happier. Goodbye, Bull." Ruby heads toward her car slowly enough that she'd give him enough time to twig on the fact that she'd said his name and call out to her to ask how she knew. But he doesn't; he doesn't even look curious. Maybe everyone around here knows who this semi-vagrant is.

Ruby grabs a cereal bowl from the tiny overhead cupboard in the van and dumps some kibble into it. The Hitchhiker looks at the food, then at Ruby's granola bar, then back to the food in the bowl.

"That's all they had. Sorry."

The Hitchhiker nibbles at the dry food, throws Ruby a baleful look.

"Oh, come on," Ruby says. She pours the coffee from the paper cup into a mug, unwraps the granola bar. "The first pet store we pass, I'll get you something better. I promise."

On impulse, Ruby touches the dog again, wondering how temporary or fragile this new gift might be. Will it last for a day or become a part of her repertoire for years to come? Will it disappear in the next thunderstorm? Taken away. "How long will I be able to understand you?"

"I stay. You stay. Hear me. Here with me." She wags her white tail, which fans out like a banner behind her.

The nuns at Sacred Heart School for Girls, located in a tiny village in Ottawa, were the last of their kind, their wimples soon to be replaced with short modern veils and their voluminous black habits with street clothes. The knuckle rapping and ear grabbing would fade to history. But when Ruby Heartwood, known then as Mary Jones, a name assigned to her upon her newborn arrival at the orphanage, grew up in that foursquare brick edifice, the nuns looked like nuns. Pale faces framed by starched white bands, heads veiled in black, female bodies uniformly draped, and any spirit they might have been born with suppressed. Most of them had been given to Jesus by families too poor to feed them. Only one of them had come to the convent through her own volition, Mother Superior.

Mary Jones was considered an orphan because, she was told, she had been left on the convent's doorstep. In those days, it wasn't an entirely unusual event and Ruby has always imagined that the sister who found the cardboard box with the day-old infant only sighed with annoyance, not shock. Mary would be settled in the nursery with two other babes recently arrived. The girls would remain, the boy child would soon be transferred to a city orphanage. The girls would repay the kindness of the nuns with sixteen years of work. And, if either of them showed any inclination, they too would be brought into the fold.

It wasn't an entirely awful life, only a bit Dickensian. The nuns were not warm and fuzzy, but nearly all of them were kind. Firm but not unfair. Two were well educated and Ruby flourished in their classrooms. On the cusp of puberty, Ruby began to receive the visions that changed everything. Still a child, she wasn't guarded against revealing this gift to see into the futures of her classmates and teachers. Soon enough, she was considered in league with the Devil and punished for predicting Sister Anne's cancer as if she had caused it herself.

Clairvoyant, psychic, seer, fortune-teller, all decidedly against the Rule.

4

You can't plan these things. That's what years of a nomadic life had taught Ruby Heartwood throughout her late teens and early twenties. Sometimes you think you're moving on and sometimes the One in Charge has other ideas.

First, Ruby misses the sign pointing toward the highway and keeps going along a local route for about fifteen minutes before realizing that she is headed away from the highway. It isn't until she passes the yellow Hobbit house that had caught her eye yesterday that she realizes her mistake. She doesn't have GPS. In her mind there is something antithetical about a psychic using a disembodied voice for directions. Even Dan, her son-in-law and early adopter of navigational aids back in the early days of Garmin, has given up badgering her about her stubborn unwillingness to use this one, to his mind, vital travel convenience. To Ruby, giving in and using Waze would take away the beauteous sense of adventure that getting lost affords. What next? They're already touting driverless cars. Would the human race eventually lose its ability to navigate, to drive, to be one with the machine? Such thoughts always bring that dire Zager and Evans song "In the Year 2525" to mind. We won't use our legs or arms. Even now the ability to parallel park is on its way to extinction. Unlamented.

Second, she realizes that, in turning around, she's just arrived back at the point where she started, the state park at the lake. "Apparently

I'm going around in circles." She's had the company of the Hitchhiker for what? Two hours? And already Ruby finds herself talking out loud to her. There is some pleasure in that.

If there is a third sign, Ruby will stop trying to escape Harmony Farms. Given her profession, Ruby is a firm believer in signs and portents.

And just like that, a third sign that the place is calling her to stay.

A bright poster nailed to a telephone pole:

FARMERS' MARKET AND MAKERS FAIRE
SATURDAYS 10–2 TOWN GREEN

Ah, "Faire." So perfect. "Well, why not stop for a couple of days and set up the old tent?" People always brought their dogs to these sorts of outdoor venues; could be a good chance to see if this new skill set extends beyond the Hitchhiker and Boy, who are a couple of dogs who have had traumatic events, which could be what has made them so open to her.

The Hitchhiker agrees, so Ruby dials the contact number on the poster and reserves a spot for herself at the Faire.

Ruby pitches her conical tent with a practiced hand and the fresh June breeze takes hold of the pennant at its apex. She then goes inside the tent and closes the flap, tying together the ribbons that hold it shut. Quickly, she slips on her caftan and slides off her jeans from underneath. The caftan is a ground-sweeping gold brocade perfection of everyone's idea of a fortune-teller or a seer. Putting it on, Ruby is instantly in character. Sometimes she thinks that there is true magic in the cloth, that, like Mickey putting on the Sorcerer's hat, she *becomes* what she pretends to be. She may have the gift of prognostication, but it is, after all, mostly acting. Ruby zips up the robe, pulls out her hair clip and shakes out her hair. Once upon a time she'd worn a curly red wig to look the part. Now, her own graying locks give her enough cred as a crone to bring in the curious. Adding a little more mascara and eye shadow complete the look Ruby has cultivated over the years. She kicks off her comfy Skechers and pushes her feet into the pointy-toed boots that look more like the footwear of a fortune-teller. Just a little witchy.

Dressed, Ruby pulls the tent flaps wide, revealing her square table and two folding chairs. A crisp white cloth covers the table, long enough to hide the ugly card table legs. The finishing touch to the staging is a decorative teapot and matching cups. Her most precious possession. Her purloined tea set. She has never used it without first muttering a curse on the man whose mother she stole it from. The man who raped her.

The final touch is the sandwich board with what Madame Ruby offers: PSYCHIC READINGS, TAROT, TEA LEAVES, OR PALM. There is room at the bottom of the board to add Animal Communicator, if, indeed, this gift extends beyond the Hitchhiker and Boy. She's hoping that someone with a dog will venture by and she can test the waters.

Okay. All set. Bring on the crowds. Ruby pulls one of the two folding chairs into the sunlight, sits down, and busies herself with a knitting project she's picked up and put down a million times over the past year. The knitting performs two purposes. One, it gives her something to do besides blankly stare at the slow-moving crowd, and two, by focusing on the work in her hands, it gives the impression that reading your fortune today isn't the most important thing on Madame Ruby's agenda. The cable-knit cardigan is. Not the twenty lovely bucks that she'd discreetly take from your hand. Never look hungry. Never look like the outrageous fee you've plunked down for the privilege of setting up a tent has depleted your ready cash to a concerning level.

The Hitchhiker settles herself right into the scene, as if she has been Ruby's familiar forever, not for two days. Ruby has sprung for a dog bed and the dog is curled up in it, just inside the tent. If Ruby had thought that she might bark, or otherwise be a nuisance, she's pleased to be proven wrong.

There is only one wrinkle. There are only a handful of strollers passing between the two rows of nonfood tents, the "Makers" tents where her neighbors offer wooden boxes and woven place mats, wind chimes and the ever-popular hand painted floor cloths. Everyone else on this June Saturday morning is intent on the fresh-baked pastries and the free trade coffee and the suspiciously out of season organic tomatoes and sunflower stems.

Ruby lifts her eyes from her knitting and nods to anyone passing by, a knowing nod, not quite friendly, not quite hostile, very mysterious. Most avoid eye contact, but that is natural. She begins to play a game with herself, seeing if she can intuit which one of a trio of teens will pause long enough to laugh with her friends and say she'll do it for fun. Ruby doesn't really enjoy giving teenage readings, it's too easy. It doesn't take a fortune-teller to know that there will be body issues, parent issues, boy—or girl—issues, and the raging hormones sometimes broadcast things she really doesn't want to mention. It was said that the girls of Salem fame were afflicted not by demons but by group think. The power of suggestion. Not only that, but if a reading takes place within sight of a teen's companions, they telegraph the information that Ruby uses. Easy peasy but never pleasant. Jealousy. Bullying. Lost virginity. Plus, in recent years, they wanted to get a selfie with Ruby and she really detests that.

The giggling trio, arms linked together, keep going. The central girl, built on the lines of a lacrosse player, is the one Ruby thought might be the most likely candidate. Indeed, the girl looks back over her shoulder at Ruby and smiles but does not try to break loose from her companions.

The lovely scent of apple turnover wafts on the light breeze right into Ruby's face. Well, no harm dashing over to Betty's Blessings and then to Bob's Free Trade Coffee. It isn't like she's going to keep anyone waiting. Ruby pulls her coin purse out of her knitting bag. The ground hasn't yet dried from the night's heavy mist, and the heels of her boots sink into the turf. Maybe it is time for a different style of footwear. Besides, these old boots are pinching her feet. The Hitchhiker leaps to her feet and toddles along beside Ruby, happy to be moving.

The turnover is still hot and when she takes a bite, she burns her mouth. The coffee is hot as well and no help. She's standing there, willing herself not to spit out the bite of pastry, waiting for the pain to lessen when a woman comes up to her. She has a faux smile on her face, as if she's about to take great pleasure in imparting bad news. "Are you the one with the psychic tent?"

"Ah, ah." Ruby tried to mime that she's in a bit of a crisis, but the woman doesn't seem to notice.

"I don't think our policy is to have something like that. It's not a craft."

The mouthful of hot apple has gone down. Tears in her eyes, Ruby shakes off the pain, dashes a finger beneath her heavily made-up eyes, and wipes away the tears. "Actually, it is a craft. Like being able to sing or build boats. Not everyone can do it." She thinks, but doesn't add, *and the tent isn't psychic. I am.*

"Cynthia Mann. Selectperson and member of the Farmers' Market and Makers Faire committee. I disagree."

The Hitchhiker sits, points her nose at the woman, narrows her eyes. She's too small to look aggressive, but she clearly is taking offence at the selectperson's umbrage. "I don't like this one."

Ruby hears the thought and agrees with the dog's assessment. "I'm Ruby Heartwood and I paid my money."

"That was an oversight."

"That's absurd. And, if you'll excuse me, I have customers." Ruby makes herself walk away from Cynthia, dignity and hauteur intact. Sometimes the magic works, and, miraculously, there are two twenty-something women in front of her tent.

"I'm here. Sorry to keep you waiting."

"Oh, we weren't . . ."

"Of course you were." Ruby's tone is carefully modulated to calm the reluctant client, much as one would speak to a frightened little bird not quite confident the crumb in the palm of her hand is worth the danger. "May I surmise that you are a soon-to-be-bride?"

The shorter of the two nods her head vigorously; as if of their own accord, her little hands with the ginormous engagement ring clap together. "How did you know?"

Points for the professionally observant. "You have a certain aura."

"That's what everyone says. That I glow!"

The bride's companion, just behind her, grimaces slightly. A little jealous, perhaps? Or, no, she's the pal who has already seen six of her closest friends walk down that aisle. She has the jaded look of a perennial bridesmaid, trying loyally to gin up enthusiasm yet again.

"And you?" Ruby directs her attention toward the second young woman. "Glad your friend has found happiness and wondering when it will be your turn. Oh, no. Wait, am I sensing that there is," dramatic pause, "someone on the horizon?"

The second girl, blessed with a highly readable porcelain skin, shrugs even as her cheeks grow patchy with redness. "No."

"Still early days?"

"Yes."

"You didn't tell me!" Bride-to-be smacks her companion's arm. "You're holding out."

"No. Maybe." Little fireballs of emotion appear on her cheeks, but she's smiling.

Enough of giving this away free. "Why don't you decide which one of you would like a reading. Or I can do both of you." Ruby steps aside to let them talk about it. "Twenty for tarot or tea leaves. Or, I'll do you both for thirty-five."

"Together?" they chorus, and Ruby can see that there are some details each would prefer to keep from the other.

"No. That's not possible."

"Okay. Thirty-five and don't tell Rodney."

Presumably the groom.

"What is foreseen in Madame Ruby's tent stays in Madame Ruby's tent."

After a lost three minutes of deciding who should go first, the bride enters Ruby's tent.

A slow trickle of customers becomes a respectable flow as the morning wears on. After the bride-to-be and her pal, Ruby counseled the jobless, the childless, and the tired; the hopeful, the confused, and the skeptical. All in all, a typical day in the life of a fortune-teller. The apple turnover is long since forgotten and Ruby thinks that a break is in order. There is a food truck parked on the perimeter of the grounds, a fairly long line suggesting that it's a decent choice beyond the organic whatever the vendors are serving.

Ruby slips off her boots, puts on her Skechers, and closes the tent flap. She is surprised to see that it's already one o'clock. The market only goes until two, so maybe it's enough that she's had a good morning, maybe she can break early and treat herself to a nap. Reading stories fabricated out of body language is an exhausting pursuit. But a taco first.

"Not yet. Talk to him." The Hitchhiker is standing, her boxy little spaniel nose pointed toward a man with a golden retriever pulling him along.

The Hitchhiker bounds out of the tent and right up to the golden, effectively stopping the dog in his tracks.

"Nice dog," Ruby says as the guy tries to get around the Hitchhiker.

"Oh, thanks." He gives her one of those half-smirk smiles that so many give her. The unbelievers.

"I can read him, if you'd like."

"What do you mean?"

"You're having trouble with him." Not a question, it's pretty obvious.

"He's just a little rambunctious."

No time like the present to practice a little persuasion. Ruby flicks the long skirt of her caftan aside and squats to put her hands on both sides of the dog's large head. He smells of having just been bathed. "I want to go swimming."

Bam. That was quick and ever so clear. Ruby stands up. "When was the last time you took him to the lake?"

"Um, I don't. He stinks if he gets wet."

"Well, he'd like to go swimming."

The guy roars with laughter.

"He'll behave if he gets the kind of exercise he's bred to have."

"Thanks. I'll keep that in mind."

Like a sled dog heading for Nome, the golden yanks the man back into motion.

"I tried."

"I know." The Hitchhiker pokes her nose into the back of Ruby's knee. "Trouble here."

"Not only isn't this a craft, but your dog should be on a leash." Cynthia Mann is fairly crackling with moral authority.

"Ees not my dog." Ruby wonders if this cranky lady remembers that Inspector Clouseau bit. Evidently not, as Cynthia looks pointedly at the dog in the tent and then at Ruby. In no way does Ruby feel like a dog owner. This dog is nobody's pet. She's an independent sort of beast. "I'm closing now, so I'll bid you good day."

Cynthia, believing that she's won the skirmish, marches off.

Ruby is ready to call it a day, but first she'll find the committee treasurer, Ariel Hippy Chick or something, who runs an essential oils booth, and pay for next week's spot. She isn't going to let that pretentious long drink of water with the sour puss derail her train. Even if it means staying in Harmony Farms for another week.

With the Hitchhiker by her side, Ruby hands the dreadlocked white girl her fee for next week's market. "Same spot if I can have it."

"Of course, we always like to have our vendors feel comfortable in their location. I'm so happy it worked out for you." She has that wide beaming smile of a person who wants oh so sincerely for you to feel you have her entire attention.

"Oh, it has. Very much."

Go ahead, Cynthia Mann, Ruby thinks, *try to push me out now.*

5

Thanks to a surprisingly lucrative morning, there is enough now in the coffers, that is Ruby's cigar box, to afford a cheap motel. Ruby loves her van, but she has come to require the relative luxury of hot showers and standing upright, the mechanism for raising the pop-up roof long since failed. Of course, now she has the Hitchhiker and she may not be able to find a place willing to allow pets. Not that HH is a pet. A quick check on her smart phone suggests that Harmony Farms prides itself on keeping the long reach of Corporate America outside its boundaries, so the nearest chain hotel is ten miles away in another town. Ruby, having settled on making Harmony Farms her temporary destination, isn't about to commute into it. That leaves a whitewashed motel, a vestige from the era of motoring vacations, when a family would pile into a Buick and go in search of fresh air. A circular drive curls around a garden that looks like it's just been freshly mulched. Begonias and impatiens also look freshly planted, no blooms yet, with sufficient space between each plant to allow for a massive display in a few weeks. Standing tall in the center of the garden is a signboard: The Dew Drop Inn. It too looks freshened up, prepared for a new and hopeful season of lake visitors.

A tiny central office is flanked on each side by six rooms, each of them boasting a picture window offering a stunning view across the busy road of a freight company and a used car dealership. Ruby pulls the Westie into a parking spot. She's a little encouraged; so far, she hasn't seen a NO PETS sign. Just a VACANCY sign. "Okay, Hitch. Why don't you stay here, and I'll do the talking?"

The Hitchhiker wags her tail.

A young brown-skinned man is sitting behind the reception desk and leaps to his feet as soon as Ruby pushes on the door.

"Welcome to the Dew Drop Inn." His accent is east Asian, but Ruby can't tell if it's Indian or Sri Lankan or something else altogether.

"Do you have anything available for a few days?"

"Of course." He smiles and clicks a computer key. "Double or queen?"

"Double will be fine. It's just me." Ruby toys with the idea to smuggle the dog into the room but thinks better of it. The young man's aura is pure kindness and she would hate to take advantage of it. "What's your policy on pets? Well-behaved small dogs?"

The aura deflates a tad, and Ruby senses that he's balancing the equation of a paying guest in an empty motel versus a small dog.

"I could pay a little more."

"As we do not have a pet policy, I think that there is nothing to say against having a pet. As long as it's quiet, of course." He smiles at his own cleverness.

"Perfect. She's very quiet." Ruby, of course, has only a couple of days' experience with the dog, but so far she hasn't been a barker. "She listens very well." *Speaks well too,* she thinks with a smile.

"I will put you on the end, closer to the woods."

"And I will clean up after her."

The room is clean, and the taps don't drip. Ruby puts underwear and pj's into the drawers, hangs up her caftan, and aligns her toiletries on the shelf above the sink. The moisturizer promptly falls over, and the flat case holding her blush slides off and into the sink. She looks around and notes that the awful landscape over the bed is crooked. She taps it, and it tilts right back into its dejected slump. The Dew Drop seems to be built on an angle or maybe is sinking into the earth, giving in to gravity. Nothing is plumb, which kind of increases its charm in her eyes. Her life has been out of plumb recently and a crooked little motel is just the perfect place to sort it out.

The Hitchhiker has made herself comfortable on the double bed, nose between paws as if daring Ruby to scold her. The last couple of nights the dog has spooned herself against Ruby, a feeling not unlike having a toddler snuggled close. Ruby doesn't make the dog get off the bed.

Ruby takes the ham and cheese sandwich she picked up at the local deli, a place called the Country Market, and goes outside to sit in the afternoon sun. Each room is provided with a plastic chair and round table outside the door, and that's where she settles. She picked up a copy of the local free weekly. It's always been one of the first things Ruby does when pausing in a new place, read the local rag. She has a wonderful memory for names, and an instinct for detail, so often when a client, as she likes to call them, visits, she has a little insight already into their lives. An engagement, a funeral, a scandal. She takes in the news about funding the elementary school, the repairs scheduled for the town athletic fields, and the ongoing debate about whether a Subway franchise is truly considered a chain or an asset for the harried, hurried soccer moms in town. It isn't quite put that way, but it doesn't take a psychic to read between the lines. Harmony Farms certainly styles itself as special. In Harmony Farms proper, the pretty little main street sports pennants remind the slow-witted that it's now summer. This other end of town sports one of those hideous flopping men reminding people that Watkins Motors offers the best deals in pre-owned cars.

The Hitchhiker stares at Ruby, or more accurately, at the sandwich. Ruby makes her wait until the last bite, then "accidentally" drops a sliver of cheese. She's pretty sure it's a bad idea to encourage begging. She should make the dog work for the prize. Ruby folds up the paper, clears off the table, and checks her watch. There's no Staples in town, so she'll go visit the local print shop and get a few flyers made advertising her services. On her laptop is a template of her flyer, she just needs to add "animal communicator" to the list. Ruby isn't sure that the term fits as, so far, it's only dogs who have burrowed into her consciousness, but why be self-limiting?

After lunch Ruby spends an hour on the internet—thank you, Dew Drop Inn, for free Wi-Fi—just seeing what animal communicators offer as services, how they describe their skills. The first word that pops out is *telepathic*. Good word. Another is *translator* and this feels right to Ruby. One claims to hear actual words, and maybe, with practice, that's what Ruby will be able to do. Some help owners through their animal's death, connecting later with the animal's afterlife. Behavioral problems. Tracking lost pets. It's a bit surprising that so many of them, the telepaths, don't need to be anywhere near the beast. That one is confusing, given that it's in the touching of the dogs that Ruby has "heard" them. The websites are pretty sophisticated, and Ruby suffers a brief moment of doubt that she can pull this off. Then she looks at the fees. Oh, yeah, this she can do.

Ruby is suddenly aware that the Hitchhiker has her chin on Ruby's knees. Ruby strokes the dog's head, fingers her long ears, takes a slow cleansing breath and listens.

"I would really like a walk now. Can we walk now? Outside now?"

"Yes, we can." Ruby closes the laptop. If she and this pup are going to be out and about, she definitely needs to get a proper leash and collar. Cynthia Mann's rules notwithstanding, Ruby very much wants to keep this dog safe from harm.

I really enjoyed the trip to the place where the scent of toys and food and chews and toys and food and chews is so exciting, I almost forgot myself and pulled hard on the new leash and harness. Almost pulled my Ruby off her feet in a rush to find the right toy and chew and food. And treats! Life is good. I do not think anymore about what was. Only about what is.

A bright-as-dawn full moon lances through the space between the half-drawn curtains, waking Ruby. In the shadows she sees the shape of a woman. She knows that it's a woman, and that it's a phantom because Ruby also knows that she's dreaming. The woman-shape rises, floats, reaches out and touches Ruby's face. Leans down and kisses her. A mother's kiss. Ruby sobs and wakes herself up. The dog is there, looking at the shadow space where the phantom woman had appeared in the dream. As loud as words, Ruby hears the Hitchhiker's thoughts as the dog looks back at her. "Don't fret. She'll come again."

The taste of the dream lingers into the morning. Ruby has never been an interpreter of dreams as much as of cards or palms, but she knows that some dreams are messages that should be heeded. The question, of course, is what that message might be. Was her absent mother trying to reach out from beyond? And another question would be, beyond what? Ruby really doesn't know if her mother exists in this world or the next, except that Sabine has never suggested that the woman who would be her grandmother was anything but still in this world. Not once has she sensed a revenant shadowing Ruby. They talked about it, years ago. Ruby had asked if Sabine would consider reaching out and trying to contact the nameless, faceless woman. "What makes you think she's passed?" Sabine had said. "If she has, she's not hovering around you." She was still young and had no idea how painful those words were. Ruby had never asked again.

It was more the kiss, the ultimate maternal gesture, that kept the sense of warmth, of safety, of a certain coziness, percolating through

Ruby's body all morning. Almost the same kind of coziness, security, and pleasure she finds herself enjoying when the Hitchhiker is settled on her lap. "You aren't my mother, are you? Come back to life as a dog?"

"No. I am not a mother. I would like to know yours."

"So would I. So would I."

Cynthia Mann resembles nothing so much as a grasshopper as she strides across the grassy area toward Ruby who, on this second Saturday of the Farmers' Market and Makers Faire, is standing patiently in line at the taco truck. Cynthia's green Wellington Hunter boots, waxed jacket, and khaki pants scream out for a pith helmet to complete the look. Stress sometimes brings out the best in Ruby's abilities and suddenly she is smitten with conflicting auras. She sees Cynthia's lime green aura of an outsized self-importance and beneath it, the grayer, grimmer aura of insecurity and old rage.

Ruby has had a good morning, reading four humans and two dogs. Whereas she had fudged the human fortunes a bit, it was easy as pie to read the two dogs. One was willing to quit chewing on furniture if she understood better which things she was allowed to chew on (Ruby suggested more rubber toys), and the other, a sad little terrier, believed that his person was never going to come back every single time she went out the door. Ruby counseled finding a good trainer to help with that. Now she's just looking for a good lunch.

Cynthia puts herself between Ruby and the person in front of her. "I thought that I had made it abundantly clear that you can't rent space here." There is nothing of the faux friendly look on her face this time, her upper lip is fighting against the dermo-filler and threatening to crumble into lines. Twin dots of red sit just above the hollows of her cheeks. "We'll happily refund your money."

"I think not." Ruby steps around Cynthia, moves one step closer to the taco truck window. She's not going to give in and she's not going to miss out on a nice food truck lunch because this woman, who, yes, seems to have a little spittle in the corner of her mouth, wants her gone. Ruby is all too used to the prejudices of the skeptic against the psychic professional. "But I'm happy to do your cards next Saturday. Or, perhaps your dog's." Dang, now Ruby's committed herself to another week in Harmony Farms.

"I would never!" Cynthia again puts herself between Ruby and the person next in line. "And I certainly do not have a dog." She says this as if she'd been accused of a cardinal sin. As if the idea of having a dog is tantamount to admitting a drug habit. "You are a fraud and a charlatan."

"So you say. I am a practitioner of the gentle art of reading cards and tea leaves. Not the Antichrist." No, that was the accusation so many years ago. The one that set her on the road toward her own unknowable future.

"It's the Devil in her."

"Nonsense, Sister. It's a teenage girl acting out." The Monsignor set his teacup down on the polished surface of Mother Superior's desk. He ignores the flash of annoyance in the older woman's eye. She knows her place. He addresses the younger nun who has brought this complaint to them. "Little Mary Jones, rebelling against authority. She's always been different."

The younger nun, Sister Clothilde, closes her eyes, squeezing them shut so tightly that the priest thinks that she's fighting a rebellious spirit of her own. "She divines, Father. She sees things that haven't happened. She told her classmate Jeannie that she would soon hear from a distant family member. Things like that get a child's hopes up."

"And, indeed, Jeannie's deceased mother's sister did come." Mother Superior slides a sheet of paper beneath the teacup. "She took her."

The third nun in the room, Sister Margaret, chimes in, "Surely Mary Jones heard something; she's a listener. You find her skulking in the hallway when she should be in class. She probably overheard Sister Nanette talking too loudly about Jeannie's situation. Took it upon herself to tell the child."

"Perhaps." Sister Clothilde folds her arms across her midsection, tucks her hands into her sleeves. "But how do you explain Mary Jones predicting poor Sister Anne's cancer?"

Mary Jones had touched the old nun's face, an invasion and yet a tenderness the sister hadn't ever experienced. A warmth had come to her cheeks and she couldn't say if it had been the child's hands or her own heat. "I'm sorry you're sick," Mary Jones had said.

"But I'm not."

"You are." The girl had burst into tears. Sister Anne was a favorite among the girls, known for fairness and generosity with sweets.

"Having a sensitivity isn't the same as being in league with the Devil." Monsignor LaPierre shrugs, reaches for another cookie from the plate on Mother Superior's desk. "Send her to me."

6

"I'm sorry, but Ms. Mann has said I shouldn't rent you space." The essential oils purveyor's brows are dragged south in an effort to communicate her Hippy Chick deep empathy for Ruby's being thrown out of the Faire. "I really can't . . ." She lets the thought drift.

"Is this private property?"

"Uh, no. Town property."

"Public space?"

"I guess so."

Ruby is making this up as she goes along, but Emily—the Hippy Chick's actual name, although Ariel would suit her better—seems gullible enough to bite. "Then she can't exclude me. I can set up my tent on the edge of the park and not pay a fee. I'd rather pay and do this the right way."

"She'll kill me."

"Or not."

On Monday morning, Ruby will see about getting a proper busker's license from the town office. There is precedent; she's dropped a buck into the open guitar case of the guy who busks in the library park. The other evening there was a string trio playing for tips in front of the post office. Ruby will use her aforesaid foresight to go to the town hall when Selectperson Mann will likely not be in the building. With that license in hand, she has the legal right to perform for tips. And if one thinks of palm reading as a performance—which, admittedly, it is most of the time—and the customary tip is twenty or twenty-five bucks, well, put that in your pipe and smoke it, Miz Select Mann.

As she heads back to her tent for the last two hours of the Faire, Ruby really has to ask herself why she is so determined to stay put when her whole life has been based on the determination to get away. What is it about Cynthia Mann that gets her back up? The Hitchhiker is truffling for spilled popcorn, dropped bits of doughnut. She's sporting a new green collar with a matching leash so, at the very least, Cynthia can't say anything about the dog. Back at the tent, Ruby closes the flap, eats her lunch, and then calls the dog over. With the Hitchhiker's head in her lap, her hands cupping the small skull, Ruby asks: "What do you think about that angry lady?"

The scent of dark gray fills Ruby's mind. Ruby lets the moment grow until she pictures an amalgam of guilt and sorrow with an overlay of ego.

"So, she's carrying a lot of baggage, then?"

"I don't know what that means. She bites because she needs to. No one likes her."

It isn't clear whether the dog means humans or canines. Both maybe. She lets go of the dog and clears the table, uses a wet wipe to clean her hands and then opens the flap of her tent. She takes up her knitting. Back in business.

Back in the day, in her carnival life, Ruby sometimes paid a roustabout to act as a shill, paying him a sawbuck to act like he was getting his fortune told, drawing the curious closer. Now she has the dog, who is a magnet, attracting oohing and aahing young and old, who just seem compelled to give the little dog a hug and a cuddle. It's only a moment before the conversation turns to a reading.

By the time the last client takes the plunge, Ruby's only managed a couple of rows on the sweater.

"Please, take a seat." As always, Ruby directs her clients to the seat on the south side of the table. The north side is hers. She gives her client a professional scan, pulling what details she can from appearance, level of anxiety, and expression. Dressed in Saturday chic of skinny jeans and a drape-y T-shirt, the woman—maybe early thirties, maybe a tad over—has a massive handbag, the kind that eliminates the need for a suitcase on weekend getaways. She sets it down on the grass at her feet and immediately a tiny head pops out. Ruby's first thought is that she had inadvertently attracted a Kardashian to her tent. It has a furry face, silvery fur blended with a color Ruby could only describe as a mauve-brown. Two brown button eyes gaze up at her from the bag with intention. It sneezes. Without thinking, Ruby bends down and pats the little critter gently on the dome of its skull. Instantly, she feels the tingle of connection.

"Your dog does not like being in that bag. She feels embarrassed. No, more like humiliated. She says that she doesn't like being treated like a stuffed toy."

"What?" The woman's professionally designed eyebrows shoot up. "What?"

"Sorry, let me pour the tea."

"No, go on, tell me more." The woman fishes the tiny dog, a Chihuahua perhaps, out of her bag. "What's she thinking?" She looks both avid and a little relieved. "She's been grumpy lately. Maybe you can help."

Twenty minutes later, the woman is smiling broadly, and the dog is wagging her tail. As her client hands a twenty-dollar bill to Ruby, she says, "I have loads of friends who would be interested in getting their dogs read. Would you be interested?"

Ruby has never been one to avoid the signs. A sure sign that she's meant to stay where she is for the moment.

"Yes." She takes the woman's twenty. "Let me give you my card."

Mary Jones has been called to see the Monsignor in his office. There are only two reasons for a girl to be summoned. The first, rarest, is because a relative willing to take her has been found, or a willing set of adoptive parents has chosen her. The second, most common, is that the girl in question is to be punished for something beyond the jurisdiction of the nuns. Back talk, cheating, even theft are dealt with at the lower levels. By the women. To be sent to the man in charge, a girl has to have done something egregious, vile. Sinful.

At the end of the hallway, opposite the Monsignor's office, is a statue of Christ. It stands nearly life-size and was a gift from the family of a former Mother Superior on her elevation. Carved of wood, more cigar store Indian than work of art, it's been at the school since the end of the last century, and the paint of its sandaled foot has been worn off by generations of girls touching it for luck or hope or even faith. Mary—Ruby— notices only the drops of thick red paint that signify the bleeding Sacred Heart. If this man could be so mistreated, what hope does she have? He, at least, had a father, God.

Real fear dries her mouth, her tongue sticks to the roof of it. She can hear her own heart, its percussive thumps growing louder and almost painful. The hallway telescopes out, then retracts, and her feet in their donation bin Keds squeak as she makes her slow way to the opposite end of the corridor. The smell of Butcher's Wax and snuffed candles. Her intestines cramp. Mary Jones pauses, leans a hand against the wall. Yesterday she had told Sister Gertrude that she was sorry for her loss. The old nun exuded the aura of one in mourning, and as Mary has always been fond of the old woman, it seemed wrong not to acknowledge her grief. "What are you talking about?"

"Your brother."

"What about him? What do you know?"

Mary Jones turned and fled. Afraid both of the power of her vision and how dangerous it was.

In the second before Sister Gertrude could snatch Mary

Jones's braid and haul her back to explain herself, the nun was called to the Mother's office.

Mary was in the stairwell when she looked out to see the street door open and Sister Gertrude leave the convent, getting into a car. As if sensing that Mary was looking down, the nun, face crumpled with true grief, raised her eyes to seek out Mary's. With slow deliberation, Sister Gertrude made the Sign of the Cross and kissed her crucifix.

7

It was such a good Saturday that Ruby has reserved what she is now thinking of as "her room" for another week. Ravi, the owner/operator of the Dew Drop Inn, is clearly pleased and even offers to take the surcharge for the Hitchhiker off the tab. For her part, the Hitchhiker has behaved impeccably.

After arranging for her busker's license at the town hall—well before Cynthia Mann might drop into the selectperson's office—Ruby heads to the Country Market to pick up a few groceries. The restaurants in Harmony Farms tend toward the overpriced.

Ruby is wandering the short aisles of the Country Market with a basket dangling from her arm; in it a box of cereal, a quart of two percent milk, a bag of kibble, and a small box of medium-size Milk-Bones. She's been in here often enough that the little store has become familiar to her; she can find most everything, but she's damned if the canned fruit isn't eluding her. Once in a while, Ruby gets a hankering for the only kind of fruit she knew when she was a little girl in the convent orphanage. She remembers the giant no. 10 cans of Del Monte fruit cocktail or pears or, her favorite, the peaches. Soft, sweet, and thick with syrup. One would expect the canned peaches to be near the canned vegetables but they're not. Elvin, the elderly proprietor of the market, is jawing with a couple of work pants–wearing, flannel-shirted locals sucking down paper cups of coffee from his limited—but cheap—coffee bar. One of them is Bull. They guffaw and all three of them end up coughing, laughing, coughing. *Har har hack. Har har hack.* "Shoulda seen the look on his face." Ruby suspects that half of their stories end up with that phrase. After years of living among old carnies, she's familiar with the dynamics of old men and their stories. Well, she won't interrupt their confab, so she trots toward the single attended checkout station where a teenage girl in an uneven bob with fuchsia highlights stares blankly out into space and chews contemplatively on a wad of gum, punctuating her mastication with snaps every few seconds.

"Can you tell me where I can find the canned fruit?"

"Umm, like, over there." The girl points at an end cap with canned pumpkin, well in advance of the season, and other pie fruits.

"No, like peach slices, in syrup." Maybe, in this suburban Mecca, kids don't eat canned fruit.

"Aisle four." A short but well-endowed woman of a certain age, filling out the contours of a dark green uniform, comes up to Ruby. "Between the flour and the maple syrup. Don't ask. Country Market is stocked with no rhyme or reason."

"Thank you."

"Are you Ruby?"

"I am." Ruby is a little surprised to be identified. She's dressed in jeans and a striped tee, not her caftan; her hair is tidy in a normal everyday twist. "Are you Polly?" No tricks, the woman does have a badge with her name, Polly Schaeffer, pinned to her ample chest. The Harmony Farms assistant animal control officer. "How'd you know me?"

"It's my job to know every dog in town and yours is waiting for you very patiently outside. Process of elimination, you're the only one with dog food in your basket. Plus, you do have that nice tag on her with your name and number."

"Nice work." Ruby can only admire Polly's deductive powers as well as her delivery.

"Hey, ladies, how're my two favorite girls?" Bull Harrison, aged adolescent.

Ruby and Polly share a look and Ruby knows that she's got a new friend.

"Ruby reads dog minds."

"Really?" Polly doesn't look skeptical, she looks interested. "You're an animal communicator?"

"So far only dogs, but yes. I guess that's what you call what I do."

"Can they tell you who their owners are if they're lost?"

"Maybe not by name. But I get images, like with my pal out there. I *know*," and Ruby air quotes the word, "that her former owner died. What she can't tell me is if she ran away or if they dropped her off in the country figuring, as cute as she is, she'd find a new home."

"Which, if you think about it, worked." Polly laughs, a ringing laugh suitable for a woman with her dimensions.

Bull has wandered back to Elvin, a new cup of coffee in his meaty hand. He sets the cup on the top of the meat case, hitches up his pants. Goes back to gabbing with his cronies.

Polly catches Ruby's eye. "I know, he's a piece of work, but every town needs a Bull."

"You ready to check out?" the gum snapper asks, and Ruby sets her purchases down on the counter along with her cloth carry bag. She won't realize that she's forgotten the peaches until she gets home.

Ruby has the dream again. The phantom woman touches her cheek, brushes aside her hair. She wakes, not in a cold sweat, but feeling as though she's been nurtured.

There was nothing nurturing in Ruby's early life. Food enough. Clothed adequately. Never cold. Untouched except for an occasional smack. Sitting up in bed, dawn's rosy fingers heralded by a cardinal in the highest treetop, Ruby wonders for the millionth time why she was left with the nuns. Why she was unwanted. Most of the other girls in the place had some cursory knowledge of their parents, knew *why* they had been left in the care of the nuns. There was an assumed sinfulness about Ruby's—Mary's—genesis in that place. Child of sin. Bastard. Where the other toddlers were there because of some family tragedy, or inability to care for them, Mary Jones was tainted. The others in her infant group were eventually adopted out. But not Mary, who didn't arrive with a name.

"Who left you?" The Hitchhiker is standing with her feet on the edge of the bed, her spaniel eyes focused on Ruby's. The question is loud and clear. Ruby has been the one asking questions of dogs; this new development, of being questioned, is a little frightening.

To say, *I don't know* in answer is wrong. So Ruby tells the dog, in plain English, "My mother."

"Find her."

Perhaps she dreamed the dog's question and her own answering of it. Ruby wakes again, the red dawn giving way to a rainy day. She pushes aside the bedclothes and reaches for her laptop. She types in the convent name, Sacred Heart Convent and School for Girls, and the little town in Ottawa. Closes her eyes and prays without knowing if she hopes it still exists or has burned to the ground.

Monsignor LaPierre resembled nothing so much as a cannonball, a spherical form dressed in black. Folds of pink flesh cascaded over the band of his clerical collar. His smooth pink cheeks suggested a boyish lack of beard. Tussocks of gray blond hair were interspersed with the shiny pink of his scalp, a sparsely planted wheat field. Someone who had not met him might have thought he looked jolly. Benign. A roly-poly doll in a black suit.

"Mary Jones, please stand before me." The priest was sitting in a soft chair. His legs, encased in the dull fabric of his trousers, were widespread to accommodate his belly. His short plump fingers gripped the arms of the chair.

She hesitated. She had never been this close to him in his street clothes, only at Mass, where his bulk was shrouded in the cassock and chasuble of his priestly authority, where his sausage fingers placed the Host on her tongue.

"I said to come here." He was breathing in truncated bursts. Puffed from the action of moving from desk to chair.

Mary took a slow step toward him. A soft hum began to tease, more sense than sound. The hum was fluid as it rose and fell with each step. The closer she got to him, the more intense the sound until she was sure he must have heard it too. Images: A man. Pain. Thin wrists gripped, crossed like a martyr's. The hum became a high-pitched squeal and yet the priest did not flinch. His pale blue eyes did not move from hers.

"I haven't got all day."

"He hurt you." The words could not be contained.

The Monsignor pushed back into his chair. "What did you say?"

"I'm sorry."

"What did you say?" The priest pushed himself awkwardly out of his chair. Took one step and grabbed Mary's chin. "Tell me." His puffing breath is foul with the smell of unclean dentures.

"He hurt you. That's all I know. You were a boy."

"No one knows. Not even my confessor." Fat snail trails of tears leak from the corners of his eyes. His pink cheeks are florid, wobble with anguish. Anger. Disbelief. "You are a witch." With the hand not gripping Mary's chin, he vigorously crossed himself.

"No. I'm not. I just feel things. I mean no harm." Mary wrenched her chin out of his hand. "I won't do it again."

Monsignor LaPierre stepped away, leaned heavily against the edge of his mahogany desk. "You will have to be isolated."

"I'm not sick."

"Kept away from the others, from everyone. Until I can pray upon this affliction. Beg for an answer."

Mary Jones stood where she was. Her fingers clutched at the pleats of her school uniform. For a fourteen-year-old girl, isolation was frightening. The companionship of her class-mates, three or four friends in particular, was the only thing that made life worth living. "Please, Sir, don't lock me away."

"I don't know if you have the devil in you, or if you are adept at discovering secrets, but you cannot be allowed to mingle with the others."

"May I go?"

"Tell Sister Clothilde that you will be in the unused sick room until further notice." He had his back to her, the tight broadcloth outlining the ridges of fat of his back. The great secret and determiner of his life was evident in the dark pur-ple shimmer of the grim aura that surrounded him. She knew that she looked upon a man at once broken by an event in his youth and made by it.

In the hallway, Mary Jones looked at the bleeding heart of the wooden Christ and touched its foot. She was sorry for frightening people with this unwanted gift, but she wouldn't accept that it was something from a malevolent source. She couldn't see that it was anything other than God given and she just needed to learn how to use it. She wished that she could see into her own future, but all she could envision was the low metal bed of the unused sickroom, the dusty curtains blocking the sun through never-opened windows. The legend was that if your fingers touched the statue's foot and the wood felt warm, you would get an answer to your prayer. Mary Jones opened her hand, laid her whole palm across the instep of the sandaled foot. When she had touched Sister Anne, and then Sister Gertrude, it had been like she was touching flame. The wooden foot felt only like wood—smooth, neither warm nor cool. She lifted her hand to the Sacred Heart where it protruded from the cavern of the opened chest. The heart is where the power is. If it burns me, I will know that I am evil. Mary Jones placed her right hand on the carving. Please help me. There was no burning, no heat. And yet, one word seemed to come through her fingers from the carved heart and straight into hers. Go.

It had only taken a few keystrokes to discover that the Sacred Heart Convent and School for Girls hadn't burned down. The orphanage was long gone, and a token number of nuns remained to teach at the Parochial school. Featured on its barebones website was the statue that had brought Ruby Heartwood into existence.

8

Ruby has a house call to make today. After almost two weeks, her flyer—with the addendum of "animal communicator"—tacked to the notice board at the Country Market has hit pay dirt. Although many of her peers do this sort of thing over the phone, Ruby really wants a face-to-face, or, rather, face-to-muzzle reading. She knows, even as that sounds more authentic, it's really because her abilities are nine tenths intuition, not second sight. She's got to get a read not just on the cards, but on the face and hands of the client. A scrim of sweat on an upper lip, the slight vibration in a hand as a palm is turned over for her examination. Voices can be controlled, but "tells" not so much. With the dogs, the clearest messages are when the vibration she feels in the palms of her hands intensifies and the cross connection between scent and image develops in her mind's eye. She can't imagine being helpful without touching the dog.

With the Hitchhiker ensconced on the double bed, fresh water, and light air-conditioning making her hours of waiting for Ruby's return quite comfortable, Ruby makes sure she's got her tarot cards with her just in case the client decides that she needs a reading of her own, and locks the door behind her.

The van gives Ruby a moment's hesitation before starting. "Come on, old girl, we aren't done yet." Ruby cranks the ignition, tickles the gas, prays to whatever goddess rules over tetchy machinery and is relieved when the engine shakes into life. Ruby has signed up for another Saturday at the Faire, not just to tweak Cynthia Mann, but because the van needs attention. If she's to keep moving, she's got to keep the Westie in shape and, with an ancient vehicle like this one, that doesn't come cheap. Her son-in-law has broadly hinted that maybe it's time to retire the van. By which he means retire herself. Well-meaning but unheeded advice.

The address of the client is Poor Farm Estates. She's toured around the outskirts of town often enough now that she has passed Poor Farm Road and assumes that this may be some modern affordable housing development, and also thinks that the name is a tad insensitive. Driving past an ancient wreck of a house, she thinks she spots Bull Harrison. She slows down, waves. He's outside hacking at the lilac bushes, a cigarette in the corner of his mouth, wielding a pair of hedge trimmers that look like they'd been new in the nineteenth century. His dog, Boy, is in a Sphinx-pose just at the edge of the driveway. Ruby slows down, pulls over. Recognizing her car, Boy jumps to his feet to amble over, tail swinging. Rising to his hind legs, he pokes his head through the open passenger window. She gets a nice image of meat from the dog's mind; the image is so strong, for a moment she thinks she's smelling it, and then realizes that she is. Bull's got something on the grill.

"Hey there, Ruby, what brings you to my neck of the woods?" Bull tosses the cigarette butt into the road in front of her van.

"I have a client in the neighborhood." She's already thinking that she can't possibly charge anyone living in this neighborhood her new fancy price for having a dog read. "Poor Farm Estates?"

"Down the hill, quarter of a mile. Can't miss it."

"So, was there a poor farm?"

"Oh yeah. Back in the old days. Town took care of its indigent. Put 'em to work on the farm."

"And now?"

Bull chuckles, pats Boy on the head. "You'll see."

The address is 259 Poor Farm Drive, and the house is absolutely the antithesis of a poor house. Talk about tone deaf. Whoever the developer was certainly had either a warped sense of irony or a mean streak. Acres once set aside for hay fields and rows of vegetables now boast two- and three-acre lawns and landscape architect–designed flower gardens, oh, and Olympic-sized swimming pools. And this. A house that looms over the landscape, not so much a part of the scenery as the focal point. Glass and half timbers, columns and gables—a hybrid between Tudor and Frank Lloyd Wright. Not a hybrid, Ruby thinks, a hydra. The garage is bigger than an average house. No doubt bigger than the original poor house.

Well, a client is a client. A reading is just a reading. She has no urge to discriminate against more money than taste. And any impulse to reduce her fee is gone, replaced by the thought that she isn't charging enough. Sliding scale, that's what she should charge. Slid all the way to the top of the meter in this case.

The massive front door resembles what the door to the Magic Kingdom would look like if the Magic Kingdom had a front door. Predictably, and it didn't take special powers to do so, the doorbell rings with the distinctive notes of Big Ben. Ruby has to put her hand over her mouth to stop herself from laughing. It's so trite. This is going to be fun.

The lady of the house herself opens the door. "Ruby, hello, thank you for coming." Her client is Jane Turcott and her dog is a pale fawn-colored Great Dane. Said Great Dane is in the kitchen, in a crate the size of a playpen, which would be intrusive if the kitchen hadn't been the size of an airport hangar. Ruby doesn't even have to try; this dog is thinking right at her. "Let me out!"

"Does he have aggression problems?"

"Oh, no. He's as sweet as can be with everyone."

"Then let him out. I need to touch him to get a good reading."

Jane does, and Gulliver eases himself out of the crate. Stretches, walks up to Ruby who, sitting straight in her chair, can look the dog in the eye without having to lean down. "He's a big one, isn't he?" She takes the dog's muzzle in her hands, ignoring the drool. "Tell me again why you called me." This to Jane, although she's pretty sure she'll get the real answer from the dog.

"He has started pulling on the leash and he's never pulled before, not even when he was a puppy and in training. And he," a pause for proper terminology, "pooped where he shouldn't."

"In the house?"

"Oh, no. Outside, but not where he should."

"Have you consulted his trainer?" Ruby is certain that the trainer is probably on retainer.

"Of course. And we went through a refresher course. But the minute the trainer is gone, it starts up again."

"Why'd you call me?" Ruby thinks that Jane isn't a likely candidate for reaching out to a psychic to figure out her dog problem. She looks more like a woman who would trade the dog in for a better-behaved model.

"My housekeeper saw your poster. She's a dear, and I didn't want to discourage her wanting to be of help so, in all honesty, against my better judgment, I called you."

Ruby gets a better picture now: Mrs. Turcott wants to keep her housekeeper happy, and surely it's the housekeeper who's doing all the doggie cleanup. What's that phrase? Good help is hard to find.

Jane slides onto one of the high-backed counter stools, rests her elbows on the high-gloss slab of Carrara marble. She looks a little embarrassed, a little tired. "I never wanted a dog. My husband, Mr. Turcott, said that a house like this should have a good-sized dog."

"As ornament?"

"As guard dog, but, as you can see, Gully is anything but fierce."

Ruby thinks, no, that's not what *Mr. Turcott* intended. Big house, big dog. Probably has a big car. Freud, anyone?

"Play with me," Gulliver thinks, and Ruby hears it loud and clear. Images of ropes and balls.

"Do you ever play with him? Say, tug of war?" The Hitchhiker loves nothing better than to tug on her rope toy with Ruby on the other end.

"He's too big, he'll pull me down."

Fear. Probably not an unreasonable reaction given that this dog certainly outweighs his mistress. "Will he fetch?"

"Chase the ball. Chase the ball," thinks the dog. Ruby can practically taste the bright red scent of a rubber ball.

"I don't know. I don't let him loose. I'm afraid . . ."

"That he won't come back?"

"That he'll wreck the gardens."

"You've got how many acres here? Surely there's enough area for the dog to run, get some exercise, be a dog."

"I thought you were going to read him, that he'll tell you what the matter is. Why he's being so naughty."

"He is telling me. He wants to get out of that crate, to play, to run. He's not a bibelot you take out to show off and then put back in its box."

Jane stands up, huffy now. "He *told* you that?"

"Not in so many words,"—especially *bibelot*—"but in images. He wants to run. He's a big athletic dog."

"You're just putting your own spin on it." Act II in the play. Doubt and accusation.

"What do *you* think?" Turnabout.

Jane Turcott moves a vase of freshly cut lilies from one side of the marble counter to the other, adjusts the positioning of the three blooms so that they are displayed to perfection. A light orange dust of lily pollen sprinkles onto the black surface. Jane stares at it. "I cannot get that gardener to remember to cut the stamens." Ruby notes the nonanswer to her question.

Gulliver leaves Ruby and marches over to his mistress. He cocks his head, which sports cropped ears, giving him less of an aggressive appearance than one of mistreatment. He whines softly. Jane doesn't acknowledge his presence until she points. "Go to bed."

The big dog is a portrait of despondence as he does what she says. "Don't lock it."

"He can't roam free. I mean, what if he *does* make a mistake in the house?"

"Then find a new home for him or he'll continue to be a problem, maybe even develop worse behaviors." Ruby has no idea what she's talking about, but she knows that this dog deserves better than what he's got.

"He was a very expensive dog. We can't just give him away."

"Sure, you can." It would be a far better thing for this giant dog to live in a two-room hut with a loving family than in a crate in this ostentatious house. Ruby stands up, gathers her bag. Gives Jane a moment to realize that this isn't a social call. "Ahem."

"That was it?" Jane's face is a mask of civility. She won't let her annoyance show. But Ruby sees it, feels it.

"I've read him, given you the results and that's what constitutes a session. One hundred twenty dollars, if you please." Twice what she planned on asking.

"Fine." Jane finds her purse, hands Ruby the cash. "You can go out through the garage." Ruby has the sense that Jane is hustling her out. She thought she'd heard a car door slam a moment ago.

Predictably, there is a giant Hummer in one of the three car bays. Ruby bets that Mr. Turcott also smokes Cuban cigars.

As Ruby comes out of the garage, she spots Jane's visitor. Cynthia Mann. Jane perhaps didn't want Cynthia to see that she'd employed a psychic, an animal communicator, especially one who has stuck in

Cynthia's craw. "Hello, Cynthia. Lovely day, isn't it?" Ruby twiddles her fingers in Cynthia's direction and climbs into her van. Cynthia waves a flaccid, queenly hand.

It's a darn good thing that Ruby charged the delightful Mrs. Turcott double the price for her poor dog's reading because the Westfalia has chosen to take a break. The dodgy starter can no longer be charmed into turning over. As a professional road warrior, Ruby has never been without AAA. She watches as the van is ignominiously hauled onto the back of a flatbed and she fights the urge to wave goodbye. Of necessity, with her mobile home in the shop, Ruby has booked another few days at the motel.

Ravi stands beside her. He has taken a slightly filial tone with her, consoling and at the ready to help her find alternate transportation. "I have the number of our local taxicab company. I would be more than happy to make a call for you."

"My daughter would tell me to download the Uber app." Ruby has on her Skechers and is planning on a walk to town. Once she gets past the sidewalk-less industrial area, it's only a mile or so into Harmony Farms proper. Besides, the Hitchhiker is up for a nice walk. The day is seasonably warm, the sky a tad overcast.

It's amazing how different things look on a casual walk; Ruby notices things otherwise invisible as they are sped past in a car. An otherwise nondescript white vinyl-sided house has a charming picket fence against which old-fashioned roses climb; a stone cherub appears to bless the blooms. A black and white cat sits on a porch step, eyeing their progress with disdain. The Hitchhiker stares but makes no hostile move. Ruby pauses long enough to see if the cat says anything to her, but without the tactile element, she gets nothing more than what anybody would expect a cat to think, and she moves on.

The proletarian outskirts of Harmony Farms quickly become

patrician as the houses go from shabby mid-century to historic an-
tiques restored to within an inch of their lives. Gardens are designed
and driveways paved with smooth blacktop, delineated in granite
blocks. Most are Federal style; all are white. Probably some arcane rule
against individual style, Ruby thinks. Another block and she's down-
town.

"Is that you, Ruby?" a female voice calls out from a white truck. It's
Polly Schaeffer on her rounds.

Ruby feels like a townie as she leans an elbow on the open truck
window. "Catch anything?"

"Actually, I'm on the hunt for a missing dog." Polly chews the
inside of her cheek for a moment. Ruby can tell that she's debating
whether or not to ask Ruby for help. Weighing the outlandish novelty
of recruiting the help of an animal communicator versus what her
boss might think. Her boss, being, of course, the Town of Harmony
Farms and, by extension, Cynthia Mann, selectperson.

Ruby helps her out. "I'll see what I can do."

"Got time now?"

"Sure."

"Hop in."

As they pull away from the curb, Ruby reminds Polly that she has
only ever communicated with dogs through touch. She's not sure she
can pinpoint a missing dog via telepathy, but she's willing to try. Other
pet psychics do and with professed success. "I'll need to start where
it was last seen."

As they pass Bull Harrison's unkempt house, Ruby has a genuine
flash. "This isn't that poor Great Dane, is it? The Turcotts' dog?"

"Ruby, you really are a wonder. Yes. What told you that?"

"I read him the other day and the poor animal is miserable. I'm
glad he got away."

"Well, I can't not look for him. It's my job."

Yes, Ruby thinks, and that Selectperson Cynthia, buddy of Mrs.
Turcott, would not take kindly to such a failure.

As if she's fallen into a dream, Ruby gets an absolutely clear image of the animal's whereabouts. He's found a family, near the lake. Probably vacationers. Probably won't keep him but will turn him in when they leave. She startles out of the vivid vision. "Let him be. You'll be getting a call in a day or two and he'll be turned in. For right now, he's having a good time. He's being loved. Don't take that away from him."

Polly gives Ruby a slight nod of agreement, of compliance.

After a stop for a quick cup of tea, Polly drops Ruby and the Hitchhiker off at the Dew Drop Inn with a wave and a thank-you for Ruby's help. Ruby waves back, smiling, thinking that it has been a long time since she felt a kinship with another person beyond Sabine and her family. Rootlessness has a cost, and even when they spent a school year in one place, Ruby wasn't inclined to develop friendships, knowing that friends have to share histories or forever remain at arm's length. She has left behind a whole host of arms-length acquaintances. Only fellow carnies ever came close to becoming friends, and that relied on a tacit agreement to keep personal histories vague. The other problem with friends is that they expect that they can persuade change in you. See a flaw—transience, for example—and they have a solution. Even Sabine, with her firm offer of a garage apartment, thought that she, of all people, could affect a change in her mother.

Polly is different. She's a bit like a dog herself, very much living in the present. She speaks of what's in front of her, not behind. Ruby likes that, and it's easy to lose an hour chatting about town doings and pet owners following best practices. Polly's aura is warm and caring, but there is a definite haze of something underlying it. It's an unusual shade of lilac, suggesting that Polly fights every day to avoid something she really wants.

When Ruby lived in the convent orphanage, she and her friends all had one desire in common. Each of them told a version of her own history, some more accurate than others, but they all had a common hope for their future: to be embraced by a family. The girls who had arrived at an early age, under two, had no words for this desire. This convent life was all they knew. But a day would come when their imaginations flickered into life. A Sister might read them a story featuring an intact and loving family and a little girl would feel that longing take hold of her heart, growing like an unrelieved pain. Another might catch sight of a friend leaving the building with an aunt and uncle or with a childless couple whose life was now fulfilled with the addition of a little girl. It wasn't an empty desire but a solid burden on the heart. Not being wanted.

The older girls made up stories about inevitably being reclaimed by parents who were on the stage, or spies, or traveling through Europe; surely, they were misplaced princesses. No one made up stories of death or illness or despondency or carnal mistakes. Someone, somewhere, they all said, loved and remembered them and would be back. "When my parents come . . ." Words whispered in the gloaming of the dormitory.

Everyone made these claims, except the girl who would become Ruby Heartwood.

The seasonably warm, slightly overcast morning, has settled into a thick humid summer day. Ruby sits down at the small business desk squeezed in between the dresser and the mini-fridge. The window air conditioner hums with an occasional rumble of protest as Ruby pulls out her tarot cards and shuffles them. It was, perhaps, cowardice, seeking guidance from a well-used set of cards. Procrastination certainly. Even as she shuffles, Ruby knows that she will not get an answer to a question she is having a hard time forming.

The Hitchhiker jumps down off the bed and sits beside Ruby. She puts both forepaws on Ruby's leg, sets her black-tipped nose between them. She has little spots on her eyebrows, just the color of a woolly bear caterpillar's brown parts. They give her face with its bandit's mask of black a curiously human expression. Ruby doesn't need to touch the dog to know that the Hitchhiker is thinking she should just put down the cards and . . . and what?

The dog drops back to the floor, then rises on her hind legs to touch the edge of the motel desk with her forepaws. With utter conviction, the Hitchhiker sniffs the closed laptop that Ruby has shoved aside to give herself room for the cards. Ruby's mind is filled with the odor of earth, of molecules rising and leading. She sees a trail, but it isn't a path, more like the cartoon wafting of the scent of apple pie. "Follow the scent. Seek." The dog drops to the floor again, shakes herself vigorously, and jumps back onto the bed where she curls herself up into a tight ball. She opens one eye, blinks, and settles into an instant nap, satisfied that her instructions will be followed.

Ruby gently taps the deck of tarot cards back into shape, slides them into their wooden box. Snaps the closure. Opens her laptop and recovers the Sacred Heart website. Contact info. *Ask the question, Ruby.*

"Dear Mother Superior. . . ." Now what? If they knew nothing about her origins back then, what could possibly have changed in the intervening forty years? Should she be apologizing for running away?

"I was an infant placed in the care of Sacred Heart . . ."

"I was an orphan placed . . ."

"I was an inmate . . . resident . . . student . . . child . . ."

"I wonder if you know where my mother is? Who my mother is? Was?"

Ruby closes the lid of the laptop gently. Pushes the computer aside. Reaches for her cards. Sets them aside. The Hitchhiker, fresh from her nap, nudges Ruby, asking to get into her lap. She buries her nose in the dog's neck, letting go of her tension. "Why am I suddenly thinking about these things?"

"You want to remember. You want to know what makes you." None of this in words, only the stimuli of scent and grayscale images. The look on the dog's face.

Vividly, Ruby remembers the moment she knew that she needed to leave, to run away. The feel of the wooden heart beneath her hand, the certainty that remaining would lead to a most difficult consequence, although Ruby couldn't imagine what the Monsignor might do to her. Something more than rap her knuckles, that was for sure. Isolation was just going to be the beginning. What next? Exorcism? Hanging? "Go," the Sacred Heart had said, and go she had. And forty years later she is still moving.

Her heart was pumping hard as Ruby emptied her book bag of school materials and loaded it with underwear and socks, her toothbrush, and her only cardigan. She took her almost-too-small coat from its hook in the coatroom. She ate the dinner that was brought to her in the sickroom. A slice of boiled ham, a baked potato, and a helping of canned peaches. The nun, a novitiate, handed her the tray as if she was afraid that Ruby would cast a spell on her. Backed out the door, closed it gently. Other girls had run off. Some had returned, others vanished forever. Sometimes Ruby thought that it was divine inspiration to name herself Ruby Heartwood, taking her first name from the color of the garish red paint on the statue, and her last from the statue itself. In the middle of the night, Ruby slung her book bag over her shoulder and unlocked the window of the sickroom. If the intention was to punish her by putting her in this room, the Monsignor had inadvertently given her a gift. A fire escape.

All of this feels as fresh to Ruby at this moment as it did forty years ago. She tastes the fear on her tongue, she feels her heart rate go up; she tastes the peaches. The Hitchhiker reaches up and licks Ruby's nose. "That's done with. Be present. Be with me."

Where do you go when there is no place to go? Into the presence of strangers. Moving away from Sacred Heart as fast as she could, Ruby hitched her way south toward the U.S. border into New York State, her instincts—or her second sight— keeping her out of danger, as she knew when to accept a ride and when to refuse one after reading the negative aura of the driver. Once over the border, she found shelter in the company of other transients, learning from them how to find the local soup kitchens and Salvation Army shelters. For a week or so, she might join a pair of teenage runaway girls. Inevitably one or the other would find an easy way of making money and Ruby would split, wanting no part of prostitution, even if it meant a warm bed and a meal. Most often she'd befriend an older woman, one willing to act as if Ruby was with her, keeping the authorities from recognizing that she was a solitary runaway. She begged for coins. She lied to everyone: She was waiting for her dad, or her mother. She just needed the change to make a phone call, let them know where she was. They'd be here in a moment. No, she wasn't a minor, she'd just left her purse at home so she couldn't prove it. She was on a school trip. The transit police saw right through her, and more than once Ruby had to slip out of the grip of a well-meaning officer's hand.

Maggie Dean spotted Ruby huddling in an alcove, warming herself over a vent. "You need to eat?"

Ruby nodded. "I can't pay."

"No need. They don't ask for anything but a contribution, and if you ain't got one, they don't make a fuss." Maggie, hobbled by arthritic feet, asked Ruby to take her arm and led the way to a church basement. In the past six months Ruby had gotten over avoiding churches. It wasn't like there was an ecclesiastical network of orphan chasers. Ruby had come to believe that, on this side of the border, no one was looking for her. Likely no one was on the other side either. It should have made her feel free, but it just made a lonely existence lonelier.

The room was warm and funky with the gathering of the unwashed and unwanted. Mostly men. Mostly bearing the damage of their lives on their faces. Maggie pointed out a few of the regulars, muttered "Served in 'Nam" or "Alcky" under her breath. "What do you call yourself, girl?"

"Ruby."

They stood in line, each with a plastic tray. The scent of soup and bread teased at the hunger deep in her belly. Ruby couldn't remember what she'd had to eat since arriving a day ago in this town. An apple picked out of the trash? Water from a dripping spigot? The server gave Ruby extra bread. "Come back if you want more," she said.

Ruby smiled and thanked her. "Your daughter will be fine." It came out, and the woman behind the counter tilted her head.

"Maggie, what did you tell this kid?"

"Nothing. What would I tell?"

"How does she know?" The server looked from Maggie to Ruby. "What do you know about my daughter?"

Ruby felt herself break out in a sweat, chilling her beneath her thin sweater. "I'm sorry. I just got the sense that your daughter is in trouble and I wanted to tell you that things will be all right." Ruby knew that, once again, her second sight was calling attention to her, and it would probably end poorly. She set her tray down, grabbed the bread, and made a dash for the door. Except that, for a crippled-up old woman, Maggie Dean was pretty strong and the grip on Ruby's donation bin jacket relentless.

"Sit down and eat."

"You were a teacher? Weren't you? And then you couldn't be anymore." Ruby could see the old woman's past as if it was her own. A scandal. A child. A rejection so painful that it altered her physical self.

"And you've got a gift. I can help you make the most of it."

Ruby set down her tray of soup and bread. "I don't. It's not true."

"It's nothing to be ashamed of. It can maybe save your life." Maggie Dean took Ruby's hand, tugged it until the girl sat. "You're right about her daughter; she's running with a bad crowd." Maggie sniffed at the soup on her spoon. "Uck. Vegetable soup again."

"And you? I'm right, aren't I?"

"Close enough. I was a teacher and that's all I'll say."

Those with secrets are the best at keeping them. The currency of trust between outcasts.

9

On this third Saturday of the Farmers' Market and Makers Faire, it's hot in the tent, the air decidedly summer-like, so Ruby moves her table under a small canopy she's rigged up so that the breeze keeps her cool, that plus not wearing anything beneath her caftan but undies. It's too hot to knit so she just keeps shuffling her cards, fanning them out, fanning herself and then reshuffling the cards. By eleven-thirty, the crowds have thinned out, the flower vendors are making bouquets out of the leftover stems, the pie bakers have sold out, and the guy selling the artisanal coffee is dozing in his camp chair, hardly a good advertisement for strong coffee. These things are sometimes better in lousy weather. Best if the morning starts out iffy and plans for the outdoors are put off till afternoon. Stragglers pass her booth, barely giving her neatly chalked board a look. Palm Readings, Tea Leaves, Tarot. Animal Communication. Some people, Ruby has noticed over the years, won't look her in the eye, as if she can read their minds and seduce them into sitting down, learning something about themselves that they don't want to know. Others scoff. Those are the ones most likely to circle back if they can ditch the husband or the kids. One teen tried to drag her girlfriend into speaking range, but the other girl balked with such actual terror that Ruby waved her away. "I don't read anyone under eighteen." Not exactly true, but not a bad policy. She watches the pair of teens slope off toward the scented candle tent. With adolescent girls it is like trying to catch sunbeams to get a read on their auras. Clearly the girl has some serious trepidations. Probably religious. While with carnivals, lo those many years ago, she'd had Bible thumpers praying over her immortal soul while she was in the middle of a reading. According to some, Ruby is in league with the Devil. After fleeing from the convent school, Ruby almost believed it of herself. Almost. Until the perfection of her imperfectly conceived child.

As hard as it was being a teenage mother, Ruby never once felt that Sabine had been a punishment. Motherless, Ruby had poured all her heart into making sure that her baby would never feel the lack that she herself had grown up with, even if it meant slipping away in the night to avoid child welfare services, even if it meant pretending to be her daughter's babysitter to avoid scrutiny.

As if she senses Ruby's thoughts, the Hitchhiker gets up from her little bed, stretches fore and aft, and shakes. She noses Ruby's clenched fist. Ruby strokes the Hitchhiker's silky head, presses a thumb in the declivity between the dog's black eyes. Finds a quietness

"You should look."

"I should introduce you to my daughter."

"You have her. You need the other."

These interior conversations are becoming almost routine. Like thinking about men landing on the moon, suddenly a new normal flattens out the magic. Of course men had once been on the moon; of course the Hitchhiker has an opinion.

The Westfalia is still in the shop, a hard-to-get part keeping Ruby stuck in Harmony Farms for at least another few days. When the mechanic had said that, yes, it was the starter, not a big problem, Ruby had a flash of hope, until he went on to say that he'd subsequently diagnosed six other problems for the geriatric foreign car. *Ka-ching. Ka-ching.* Ruby has had three other calls for canine interpretation, but she only charged one of them her top rate. The second one was just a little kid with a puppy. She accepted his two dollars for advice with grace.

The last one, she actually gave away for free. The elderly dog asked ever so clearly to be allowed to die. Everyone cried.

Ravi at the Dew Drop Inn has been kind enough to offer her a discounted rate as a "regular" customer. She wonders if he knows what she does for a living. This morning Polly transported Ruby and her tent and table to the green. "He got turned in, just like you predicted. The Great Dane."

"I wish they'd kept him."

"Interestingly enough, they asked me if I would ask Mrs. Turcott if she'd keep them in mind if she ever wanted to re-home him."

Ruby smiled, pleased. Hopeful.

It's been a fun morning. We got a ride in a truck that smells of dogs, but there weren't any in it, so I think that they are now all happy back with their people. There was another scent in there too, an objectionable scent of feline. Then we met lots of people. My job is to greet them and bring them closer to Ruby's tent so that they can talk about deep things while holding hands or sipping stinky tea. Sometimes they cry, and then I have to comfort them.

It's really too hot to be sitting out here. The air beneath the canopy is almost hotter than outside, trapped by the impervious nylon. "Want to pack it in, Hitch?"

The dog wags her plume of a tail, yips.

"I'll take that as a yes."

Closing the tent flaps, Ruby does a quick change of clothes, puts her cards in their case, and wraps the teapot in its protective Bubble Wrap. She's got to wait for Polly to come back, so she'll close up shop but not fold up the tent. They'll head to the Country Market and get an iced coffee and then sit in the library park where it's nice and shady. Polly, working on a Saturday, has planned on meeting Ruby at two, so she'll head back a little before then. Sometimes just making a little decision feels like a conquest.

"Oh, are you leaving?" The voice is that of one of the teenagers who had passed by earlier.

"I don't have to."

"I'm eighteen, so, it's okay, right?"

"Sit." Out of the corner of her eye she sees the Hitchhiker sit, as if she'd been given the command, not the girl. That makes Ruby smile, and the girl, who is visibly nervous, smiles back. Ruby, no longer dressed as a fortune-teller, asks if the girl wants cards or palm. The teapot is packed away and she won't be brewing more.

"Palms?"

"Okay. Hold out your hands." Ruby places her hands palm up under the girl's. It's a hot day, and it's no surprise that the girl's hands are hot to the touch, but this is a different sort of heat. A pulsing heat. The heat of distress. Ruby can feel the heat of the girl's aura, the flicker and flash of being female, of being young. Of being sexual. Ruby can't bring herself to incant the usual long lifeline, meet a man, success in business claptrap she gives those with whom she has no actual connection. This girl warrants something like the truth. A guarded truth. She needs to find actual help. Ruby closes her eyes and lets the wash of connection take over. It has been such a rare event in the past year, and she knows that this is only possible because of the girl's agitation, her distress. It's more similar to how she's been interpreting the dogs, images flood across her mind's eye, grayscale, but vivid. Ruby sinks into a borderline trance. "I see a shadow behind you. Is someone following you?"

"Sometimes."

"Someone who is familiar to you?"

"Yes." The girl's pulse quickens and the image in Ruby's mind clarifies. Hardens.

"There is a predator in your life."

A tear slides out from the corner of the girl's left eye, traces a path on her ruddy cheek. She nods.

"Someone close?"

She nods again and Ruby's angry heat rises, flushing her cheeks and bringing her back to a moment in her own young life when she was prey. She turns the girl's hands over and grasps them in her own. "I'm not speaking as a psychic now. I'm speaking as an adult who also suffered at the hands of someone I knew. You must promise me to go to a trusted adult." She shakes the girl's hands, makes her look Ruby in the eye. Then Ruby releases her grasp and turns the girl's hands over again. She traces a line. "This line tells me that you are a strong woman." She touches another, close to the thumb. "You will act, and in acting on this, not just survive but thrive. No one can take your future away from you if you don't let them."

"Who should I talk to?"

Ruby lets the last image in her mind fade before answering. "You have an aunt. Go to her."

"How did you know?"

"It's what I do." Ruby lets go of the girl, waves off her proffered twenty-dollar bill. "Just talk to her. Now."

"Thank you, um, Madame Ruby." She shoves the twenty into her pocket, a lock of hair falling over her eyes. She shoves it away and looks at Ruby. There is a flicker of resolve in her expression. "I will."

Ruby reaches out to touch the dog, gathers a handful of fur between her fingers. She's too shaky to get to her feet. The images coming from the girl overlay her own memories of being young and vulnerable and alone. And afraid. The Hitchhiker jumps into Ruby's lap, shoves her head beneath Ruby's chin, and a long strand of taste and scent fill Ruby's mind with calm. *If you suckle you are filled with good feeling.* To the dog, the memory of being a puppy is her comfortable place. The dog's memory comforts Ruby.

"Come with me and I'll help you use that weird skill of yours."
Maggie Dean looked like a helpless old woman doomed to
freeze to death on the streets, but in fact, she was a bit of a
Fagan among the children that lived in those Hartford projects. A kind enough Fagan, and her criminal encouragement
wasn't to become deft pickpockets, but to introduce them to
certain gentlemen who could make good use of their fleet-
ness of foot and innocent eyes. As a former teacher, she also
expected them to learn to read and do arithmetic.

Ruby followed Maggie home, home being a squat in the
projects. The only comfort in the room, which had no running water or electricity, was a fetid armchair. But it did have
books. Hundreds of them, stacked like dolmens blocking the
windows, serving as stools or footstools. The pervasive scent
of kerosene, which Maggie used for her lantern, and a touchy
space heater. Ruby closed her eyes and saw tragedy. Old tragedy. Tragedy to come.

"Over there, second stack from the left. Third book
down. Fetch it."

Ruby did as asked, pulling a how-to book on tarot from
the pile.

"And that one, top book." Maggie pointed to the tallest
stack. "You should know a little astrology. I have nothing on
the more occult art of reading tea leaves, but this will get you
started. You do read, don't you?"

"Yes." Ruby had smiled. "I read secrets."

"You've already got it figured out, don't you? The mys-
tique of the psychic."

There was no longer any point in lying. "It's not fake, you
know. I really do see things."

"What you need is an act, or maybe it would be better to call it a performance that frames your talent. Carerra
Brothers Carnival is back here from Florida in about a month.

I bet they'd be interested in a psychic. A young, very young, psychic."

A wave of cold fear dried out Ruby's mouth. Then anger. "Are you a white slaver?" The term had been a useful warning to the young girls at Sacred Heart, what would happen to you if you should speak to strangers. Abducted, enslaved. Of course, no nun ever said what they would be enslaved to do. They all pictured farm work in rags.

"No. I just try to find purpose for kids like you, a safety net, if you will. Otherwise, you might be taken up by the wrong kind. There are plenty of predators out there, but if you can make your own way, you may stay alive."

Predators indeed. And Maggie Dean's tutelage into the psychic arts and subsequent introduction of Ruby into the carny world almost guaranteed that Ruby would encounter just such a man.

10

The Lakeside Tavern, which is less lakeside than lake-overlooking from the opposite side of the road, offers a reasonably priced pub menu and a nice selection of craft beer. Ruby orders the eggplant parm special and a local brew. She grabs an outside table, a little damp but mostly protected by the porch overhang, and ties the Hitchhiker's leash to the leg. It had been raining so heavily this morning that the Farmers' Market and Makers Faire had been canceled and Ruby had enjoyed what felt an awful lot like a snow day. She pulls her atlas out of her satchel and flattens it against the tabletop. "Okay, where to?"

The Hitchhiker rests her chin on Ruby's knees. Sighs. Eyes up, worried eyebrows. Ruby places a hand on the dog's head to listen.

"Here is now."

"Nope. Time to go. The van is back and I'm ready to find new adventure." Ruby looks around, thankful that there is no one within earshot of a woman having a one-sided discussion with a dog.

"Here is now."

"That doesn't even make sense."

The worried eyebrows. Spaniel eyes.

"Why not?"

"No go."

"Don't worry, little one. Travel is fun. I won't leave you behind."

The dog sighs but does not look any less worried. "More work left."

What Ruby "sees" in her mind's eye is the scent of unhappy animals. "There are dogs everywhere that I can help."

"Here is now."

Frustrated, Ruby is glad when the server comes with her meal. The Hitchhiker's thought processes remind her all too much of a truculent toddler's. *No go. Well, let's remember who's in charge here.*

"Hey, Ruby, what brings you into Harmony Farms' best kept secret?" It's Bull Harrison with Boy.

"Bull, hi. Probably the same thing that brings you here." Ruby gestures toward her mostly empty plate and the beer.

Boy and the Hitchhiker perform their greeting routine, tails wagging. Both flop down on the porch floor, noses directly in line with anything that might fall from the tabletop.

Without being invited, Bull sits down opposite Ruby, taps the atlas with a forefinger. "Going someplace?"

"Looking for the next stop."

"I thought you'd be staying."

"No. I've about tapped out the Faire. Besides, Cynthia is being a pain in the tuchus. Gets in my face every single week."

"That's just her. Full of herself. She's got something against everybody."

"That's no surprise. That woman is attitude on a stick."

Bull rubs his whiskery chin in a gesture Ruby recognizes as a tell. She has an urge to grab Bull's meaty hands and turn them over. She doesn't, but she can read his thoughts in his expression. Not unlike his dog's, Bull's rumpled face gives away a lot of emotion.

"How come she's angry at you?"

Bull makes that noise that might be choking or laughing and then stops. "We have a rocky history."

"Former girlfriend?"

He shakes his shaggy head and Ruby gets why he might be nicknamed Bull. "It's a long story, but everything worked out in the end."

"Now you have me intrigued. Give me a short version."

Bull gets a moment to decide if he wants to tell the story as Ruby's server has wandered back to clear the table and ask about Ruby's desires vis-à-vis dessert. She asks, "You want something to eat, Bull?"

"Naw." He looks at the server. "Just the usual, Deb."

"Seltzer and lime. Got it." She scoops up Ruby's plate, glances at her glass. "Another beer?"

"No. Thanks." Ruby stops her. "Yeah, maybe another." She's intrigued by the wavering aura that now floats around Bull. She wants to have an excuse to examine it. "Go on, Bull. What happened?"

"A couple of years ago her ex-husband, although he wasn't ex then, was arrested for animal abuse."

"Whoa. Let me guess, Boy was the dog."

"Yes, ma'am, he was." Bull takes a long moment. "Anyway, it was my son who arrested him." A beat. "My younger son."

She keeps getting flashes of sharp grief, panic, and profound cold. Something deeply personal and yet not quite connected to the story that Bull has told her. His apparent need to clarify which son performed the arrest.

"Anyway, her husband, Don, went to prison for a bit. She liked having his money, but apparently so did he, so she didn't get a ton of it in the divorce."

"Kids?"

"One. I forget his name, but he was already in college at that point."

Ruby gets it. Cynthia is one of those people for whom loneliness becomes bitterness. She is aggrieved and will make life miserable for anyone in her path. She also senses a hole within Bull Harrison. More than one. Not aggrieved, grieving.

She would ask but Deb has arrived to place a tall glass of seltzer in front of Bull. He sets aside the straw and takes a long drink
and bends the conversation away. "So, tell me about where you're
headed?"

It's a fair question. "I'm thinking Newport maybe, or the Cape.
Look for street fairs, that sort of thing." Even as she says this, Ruby
realizes that she's not as hot to pack up and venture blindly off as she
had been an hour ago. The Hitchhiker noses her foot. Boy sighs and
flops over on his side. The air is cool here, the breeze off the pretty lake
ruffles her paper napkin. The sun has disappeared behind a scrim of
fair-weather clouds, and the fairy lights hanging from the porch roof
have come on. *What's the hurry?*

"Polly will miss having you around. She says you've been a help."

"That's kind of her to say." The fact is, Polly has been a help to
Ruby. Letting her read the dogs in her care to some success gave her
confidence that this canine communication phenomena is sticking
with her.

"If it's staying in the Dew Drop, well, you're welcome to stay with
me. Free. No strings."

Ruby has no words for this offer. She's seen the outside of his
house; she can't imagine what the inside must look like. "Um, that's
kind of you, but it's not that. It's just time to go."

Bull sucks down the rest of the liquid, spits an ice cube back into
the glass. If he's disappointed or relieved, she really can't tell.

"Stay stay stay." Ruby hears Boy's plaintive request. Even in her
mind's ear, his voice is distinct from the Hitchhiker's.

Ruby closes the atlas, motions to the server that she's ready to pay
up. Bull digs into a back pocket for his wallet.

"No, I've got it. You can buy me a drink some other time."

"Deal."

"Do you need a ride home?"

"Nah. Got my trusty Raleigh. It's not far."

"It's dark."

"Got a good light. Coop bought me one of them LCD things. Real bright."

"I think you mean LED."

There's a little goofy in his grin, the gaps where his front teeth should be giving him an oddly innocent expression. "I always get that mixed up."

Ruby watches Bull pedal off before she starts her van. He's got an uphill ride. She wonders at the effort he has made to go get a drink of fizzy water.

I do not understand why Ruby thinks it's a good idea to leave here. Doesn't she know that this is our territory? That we have marked it? That no good comes of wandering?

"I am so sorry to say goodbye and I hope that, when you are back in the area, you will make the Dew Drop Inn your home." Ravi gives her that heartbreakingly melty smile of his and takes both her hands in his. She is unaccustomed to having her hands held rather than being the holder of hands. She momentarily expects him to read her and is surprised at the slight warmth rising in her cheeks.

"I will. I promise." With the Westfalia back on the road, the summer weather absolutely divine, there is no reason not to camp. So, why does she feel like she's wrong-footed?

As Ruby loads the rest of her stuff into the van, the Hitchhiker sits with her back toward Ruby, her nose pointed down and the term *abject* comes to mind. "Hey, girlie, hop in."

The dog doesn't move.

"Hitch, get in." Ruby points toward the interior of the van beyond the wide-open slider. "Up. Up."

Nothing. A sigh. A yawn. Her cheerful little companion is pouting.

Ruby swoops down, encircles the dog with her arms and hefts her onto the bench seat. "I'm bigger than you are. Ha-ha."

The Hitchhiker circles three times and curls up, tucks her nose beneath her hind leg. Closes her eyes.

Ravi waves from the office door as Ruby pulls out of the empty parking lot. The weekends have been busier, but the weekdays she's had the place pretty much all to herself. The begonias and impatiens have fulfilled their promise of huge happy blooms in the time she's spent residing in this humble motor lodge. Ruby bangs a left, which will take her through town and on toward the highway entrance. Except for Ravi, she's told no one goodbye, as is her habit. She's got Polly's number; she'll stay in touch. She's enjoyed Bull's unique company, and he knows she's going. As with pretty much everywhere else she's been in her life, Ruby leaves without leaving a wake.

A quarter of a mile before the highway access there is a large modern church, far enough away from town proper as to not be in architectural conflict with its more traditional peers of the Protestant persuasion. St. Sebastian's RC Church boasts a bright pebble-dash façade interspersed with tall wide windows and a bell tower surmounted by a gold cross. It also boasts a massive black-topped parking lot, in the western corner of which is a fleet of flatbed trailers bearing the unmistakable burden of carnival rides. Ruby slows, pulls in to read the church's signboard. St. Sebastian's Days will open on Friday at five with the traditional feast of all things Italian. Bands! Contests! Traditional dancing! A Kids Parade on Saturday with fireworks Saturday night! And, most tempting for a psychic on her way out of town, the featured Benini Bros Carnival! Holy Exclamation Point!

Three more days in Harmony Farms but no need to deal with Cynthia Mann. For a cut of the take, she knows that old Angelo Benini will let her read cards out of her van unless he's found himself a fortune-teller willing to travel under his banner. Ruby vastly prefers to be a subcontractor than an employee.

"What do you say?"

The Hitchhiker has jumped down from the backseat and is standing between the front seats, her tail wagging in triple time.

"I haven't changed my mind, but this could be a good reason to put the travel on pause." Ruby doesn't put her hands on the dog because she isn't interested in any comment from this furry peanut gallery.

Ruby finds Angelo Benini the younger coming out of his camper. She remembers him from when he was just a tyke, following his dad around the various empty lots where the carnival would set up. He and Sabine were sometime playmates and once even classmates when they both overwintered in North Carolina when Angelo, Jr.—called Joe by his peers—and Sabine were in third grade.

"Ruby Heartwood as I live and breathe!" Joe trots over and throws his arms around Ruby in a joyful embrace. "You look great, you haven't aged a bit."

"And you are a flatterer or need glasses. But thank you."

"And Sabine, is she here with you?"

"Nope. Happily married and firmly rooted in Moose River Junction."

"She always did talk about finding a place to call home."

"Your dad? Is he around? I'd like to talk with him."

"He's in Florida, semiretired. He remarried after Mom passed and his new wife isn't carny."

That is, one of us. Itinerant. Transient. It was always a bad sign when a carnival worker married outside of the culture; either the marriage failed or they found other, less transient employment. Even though an outsider might flirt with the life, it is a rare thing for them to stick with it.

"But he's happy." Statement of fact, not a question. She can read Angelo the younger without too much effort and interprets that he's pretty okay with being in charge. "You're happy."

"We both are. He joins us for part of the year, so he gets his fix."

"Well, I expect you know what I wanted to talk to him about."

"You are more than welcome to set up with us. Let me check the layout and find a good place for you."

The carnival is more just an edited-down version of itself, consisting of games of chance and rides, not the full-bore midway that Benini's was known for a decade or so back. Joe notices Ruby noticing. "This is the local amusement division. Our big stuff is waiting for the big fairs coming up at the end of the summer—Topsfield, Freyberg. I'd love to have you there."

"I'd like that. It's been awhile since I did a big fair. I've been mostly doing little places. I like it. I can pick up and go when I want." Except that she can't seem to get out of Harmony Farms.

Because it's asphalt, Ruby can't set up her tent. Joe grabs a stack of traffic cones and delineates a space for her van, writes "Madame Ruby" in chalk in the rectangle. "All set."

Time to deal. "Sixty/forty?"

"We're more into fifty/fifty these days, but, hey, you're family. Sixty/forty is fine."

It feels so good to be among folk who get her.

Maggie Dean found a gaudy robe in a thrift shop in Newington; Ruby filched a box of hair dye from Caldor along with a home perm kit. Her holey Keds were set aside for a Goodwill pair of boots Maggie spray painted gold, then glued sequins to. Every day they practiced Ruby's schtick. Ruby studied the tarot cards, memorizing the suits and meanings until it felt like she was prepping for exams. And just as if she was prepping for a big test, Ruby began to balk. She had never gotten the psychic feeling from props, only by touch and proximity. It was all intuitive, although she didn't have that word in her vocabulary. "I can't do it, Maggie. I just don't feel it. I don't know what to say if I don't have a connection."

"You only have to act, to pretend that you know what the

cards mean. When you get a real feeling, then go with it. Otherwise, just play like you're seeing something in the distance."

Ruby would sit in Maggie's book-crowded squat and shuffle and deal; shuffle and deal over and over until she had softened the edges of the cards. Curled up under a Salvation Army sleeping bag, she dreamed of laying out cards, of the Wands dancing, of the Fool wagging his finger at her. She learned the language of "cups" and "swords" and "arcana" and "wands" and on and on. Storytelling based on an occult mythology. And each time Ruby shuffled and dealt and interpreted cards from their position, upside or reverse, she thought of her life in the convent school and the fear in the nuns' eyes when she displayed her gift of second sight; the anger and humiliation of Monsignor LaPierre in the face of her knowing his past. How she was considered the Devil's tool and here she now was, handling the mysteries of the occult. Sometimes her fingers burned.

And it got easier. Maggie Dean reminded Ruby that she didn't have to make up more than a half dozen readings; no one would ever know that she was passing out the same tales of future glory or past pain over and over. It wasn't accuracy, it was the skill with which she would weave the tale, inexact but believable. The details would be left to the client; her job was to guide them into revealing enough to suffice. Improvisation by any other name.

The caftan was hemmed, and the boots were properly glittery; Ruby's strawberry blond hair was now curly and as dark red as the jewel of her name. Maggie, her black trench coat belted tightly around her waist, took Ruby's arm and the odd pair walked the six blocks to where the Carerra Brothers Carnival had set up. As if she were Ruby's grandmother, Maggie kept up a litany of do's and don'ts, mostly don'ts . Don't tell them your real age. Don't give them your real name. Don't let anyone touch you. And then, when they met the brother who hired acts for the sideshow, Maggie actually did introduce Ruby as her granddaughter. One with extraordinary abilities who would draw a crowd. The brother shrugged, having no illusions about their relationship or Ruby's so-called abilities, and said no thank you.

Ruby felt Maggie Dean's ragged fingernails dig into her forearm, reminding her of their plan. In a pathetically thin voice, she offered: "Let me read you." A free sample in the face of refusal.

Ernest Carerra laughed, shook his head, and waved them away from his trailer office. "Just beat it. Fake psychics are a dime a dozen. This isn't that kind of show."

"We both know that's not true." Maggie laughed. "It's all fake."

Ernest Carerra slammed the door of his trailer. End of discussion.

"Never mind." Maggie renewed her grip on Ruby's arm. "It's a second-rate carny anyway. I'll get you in with a better one."

Ruby felt stupid dressed in the flowing robe and the glittery shoes, and the permanent wave curls in her dyed hair were beginning to frizz. Building within her was the urge to move on. She'd been too long in one place. Enough with Maggie Dean's vision of her future. The next afternoon when Maggie was out panhandling, Ruby shoved the props of her untested profession into her schoolbag and slipped away.

Her unplanned route out of the city took her past the carnival. She skirted around the gate and marched up to Ernest Carerra's trailer. Knocked. Dressed in jeans and a T-shirt, her Keds on bare feet, her hair scraped back into a ponytail, he didn't recognize her at first.

"I need a job, Mr. Carerra. I can sell tickets or popcorn or sweep up. Whatever you need."

"You're that psychic kid. Maggie's protégée."

"No. I'm Ruby Heartwood and I need a job." She watched his hands, the way they flexed as he thought about hiring someone who clearly didn't fit the legal parameters of an adult. Someone who he would take on the road, farther away from whomever or whatever she had run from. Ernest Carerra had been a long time in the business and knew trouble when he saw it. But Ruby could see in his weary-looking blue eyes that he had a soft spot for trouble.

By the time the carnival had moved across the state, Ruby was plying her trade, paying Ernest six of every ten dollars she took in.

11

Because it's only Thursday and the feast doesn't open until to-morrow night, Ruby doesn't want to set up camp on the overheated asphalt of the St. Sebastian's parking lot. The rest of the roustabouts, rides and games people, have air-conditioned campers and have al-ready commandeered the available outlets from the carnival gener-ator. It'll be a long day sitting around if she sets up now and a longer night hoping her laptop battery lasts long enough to watch a movie. At another venue Ruby might be more inclined to set up and hang out, but with these folks, not so much. She's basically an interloper, an unknown. Except for Joe, there isn't anybody she knows from pre-vious associations.

Remaining within the boundaries of Harmony Farms doesn't pre-clude camping instead of enjoying the Dew Drop Inn's relative luxury. Despite Joe Benini's generous offer of only 40 percent of her take, Ruby really needs to start economizing. The question becomes where should she set up her modest camp tonight? The state park isn't an option; no overnight camping. Her one and only night there, the stormy night she discovered her new and extraordinary powers—and the Hitchhiker—had happened under the radar. It now being full summer, she just doesn't dare park there and hope for a second helping of grace. When she hasn't indulged in the Dew Drop's hospitality, Ruby has camped at a little family campground on North Farms Road, but a quick call lets her know that they're full up for the rest of the week. "It's the Feast, you know," says the host.

With her little camp toilet, all Ruby needs is a place to plug in. If this town had a Walmart, she could, as she has done many times over the years, dock at one of the camper-friendly parking spots and use their bathrooms. Buy a cheap dinner at the in-store Subway. Alas, this is tony Harmony Farms.

The Hitchhiker seems to know that they are no longer leaving town because she's hopped up on the passenger seat and is cheerfully gazing out the window, the frond-like tip of her tail beating a happy tattoo against the back of the seat.

"Okay, where do we go?"

"Boy boy boy."

It takes Ruby a second to realize that the dog is thinking about her pal, the dog self-named Boy. Bull's yard. It wouldn't be the same as staying with him. Just hooking up to his power source. He did offer, after all. Ruby points the Westie in the direction of Cumberland Farms. Even without psychic powers, she knows that the best place to find Bull Harrison at this time of day is at Cumbie's.

Sure enough, there he is, leaning against the wall like some kind of 3-D mural. Boy is flat out on his side but lifts his head at the sound of Ruby's van as if he recognizes the puttering engine. His rudder tail beats time against the hot cement, and he hauls himself up to his feet to go greet her halfway across the parking lot.

"Thought you blew town." Bull drops his cigarette butt. Steps on it.

"I was practically gone and then I spotted the St. Sebastian's Days. Friend of mine is the amusements guy. I couldn't pass up the opportunity."

"Shaking off Cynthia?"

"Something like that. But, hey, I've got a favor to ask of you."

"Shoot."

Ruby lays it out: She'll spend the next couple of nights parked in his yard. Nothing more than space and an outlet to plug into. She won't get in his way, won't need anything else.

Bull sweeps his trucker hat off his head. "I'd be honored."

Boy beats time with his tail and the Hitchhiker dances on her hind legs.

Never have I ever been so happy to see a friend. When I was in my former career, I had many acquaintances, but few with whom I could share a joke, ramble around a property, play tug-o'-war. Boy is a pushover in that game. He thinks that he has to be gentle with me, but he's mistaken. All to my advantage, I can tell you. I could hold on to that knotted end for the whole day and he would only tire out. He and I have something in common that makes our friendship different. We have both endured difficult times.

The Hitchhiker is all played out and sound asleep on the fold-out bed. She snores lightly. She and Boy have been chasing each other around Bull's ragged yard all afternoon. Ruby has tucked the Westfalia up against the hedge, and a long yellow extension cord ties her into Bull's only outside outlet. She's pulled the café curtains almost closed, leaving a crack so that she can see the yellow light of his kitchen. Beyond that, a half moon, bright in a clear night sky. She's set up the screens in the windows so the sound of insects and the muted hiss of the few cars that pass by are playing as background music. On the table in front of her, an array of tarot cards. It's not often that Ruby reads her own cards, but it's a little like testing the brakes on the van—pump and see if they hold. Since the early days of Maggie Dean's insistence that she learn the tarot, Ruby has come to believe that the cards do, on occasion, hold clues to the future. It's not the same as the intense feeling of connection that she sometimes gets with physical contact, but there's enough of a vibe to detect a narrative. Tonight they tell her nothing more than she will move on. Well, duh. Although she's been thinking of heading in a more southerly route, the cards suggest that north is the best direction to take.

She taps the cards into alignment and puts them away. Pulls out her laptop. That Bull has Wi-Fi is a bit of a surprise, and he was quick to hand her a scrap of paper with his password on it. "In case you wanna watch TV or something."

Ruby has received no response from the convent. After much dithering, she had finally sent off a brief query: Does the convent keep permanent records of the girls once in its care? She didn't identify herself as a former Sacred Heart girl. She might have implied that she was writing a novel. Nonetheless, she has gotten no response.

What she needs is a contact person. Ruby pulls up the Sacred Heart website once again. Studies the bare-bones information there, doesn't recognize the Mother Superior, whose smiling photo on the website suggests a cheerful middle-aged woman, only her short cropped gray hair and a large pectoral cross suggesting a vocation. A staff list allows for first and last names, none of the married-to-Jesus made-up names of the nuns of her youth. If one of these ladies is a survivor of Ruby's days at the orphanage, she can't tell by their names. No Sister Gertrude or Sister Martha Joseph; no Sister Clothilde. The staff list includes an office administrator. If anyone knows where things are, it's always the chief of the clerical staff. Ruby opens a blank email document, types in the office administrator's email, B. Johnson. Betty? Barbara? Ben?

"I am writing to ask if you have records of the girls who would have been put into the care of the order in . . ."

Ruby puts in her year of birth, which she knows; the month, which she estimates; and leaves off the day as she has never known the exact date of her birth. Anytime she's been forced to use a birth date, she uses what she considers her best in terms of numerology. She types in her assigned name. Not for the first time does she think that the nuns betrayed a remarkable lack of imagination in naming her Mary, and with such a generic last name. If there was ever any doubt that she'd been dropped on the doorstep, nameless, being called Mary Jones was proof enough of that. She supposes she should have been grateful that she wasn't called Jane Doe.

What kind of mother drops her kid off at an orphanage nameless? The very least she could have done was pin a tiny note to the swaddling: Please take care of my baby Victoria, or Renata, or what have you.

Unless. Unless it wasn't her mother who left her on that doorstep. Ruby lifts her fingers from the keyboard. She can feel her heart pounding in her chest. In all these years, it has never occurred to her before that someone else might have done the deed; an angry and embarrassed grandparent, or a kidnapper with second thoughts. In all her life, Ruby has been stuck with the origin story she had interpreted for herself from the scant clues offered to her by the nuns. *Left with us. No one to claim you.* Always, always assumed it was her mother.

". . . If you are willing, please let me know as soon as you can. It means a great deal to me."

First step. Find out if there is a slip of paper somewhere in the bowels of that redbrick building that has her name, however generic, on it. And, if there is something there, will it be enough to start a search she should have begun eons ago?

As the first of the St. Sebastian Days doesn't begin until five o'clock, Ruby decides that a quick trip to the local Laundromat is a good use of her time. She loves the Tons of Suds for its unabashed utility. Nothing froufrou here. Good old-fashioned coin-op washers that don't require an engineering degree to operate, a temperamental dollar-bill changer, and only three kinds of detergent in little boxes. It smells wonderful.

The attendant is a tiny Asian woman whose English is limited but who manages to keep the customers in order, admonishing against ignoring the lint traps and taking too long at the folding tables. Cheerfully opening the cranky bill changer to fish out coins. Somehow she knows that Ruby is a fortune-teller and each time Ruby comes in, says: "You tell my fortune. I give you extra dry time."

Ruby doesn't know how much the little lady understands of what she tells her, but she always smiles and seems pleased to hear that only good things are in store for her. A visit from a daughter, a grandson's good grades. She prefers the tea leaves over the cards. Prefers green tea over black.

Ruby is just folding her laundry when Polly Schaeffer comes through the door. She's toting a basket of towels and blankets and the smell from across the room is very animal shelter.

"Damned washer quit on me. I'm not looking forward to begging the town for the money to get a new one." Despite her title of "assistant," Polly is actually the only animal control officer. Paid as an assistant, she is also expected to manage the office as if she was in charge.

Polly has long complained that the town considers its animal shelter extremely low on the scale of need against that of playgrounds and fire trucks and office personnel. "Tax office has plenty of paper, I can tell you that. Me, I have to buy my own or wait till the budget is passed. If I don't anticipate a need, it has to wait maybe a whole year. And I didn't figure on a broken washer."

"When does the budget get passed?"

"Spring."

"Oh."

"I'm doing this on my own dime." Polly shoves a massive armful of stinky towels into an empty washer. The Asian woman frowns, turns her back, and goes into her office. Shuts the door.

Polly slams the washer lid, remembers the detergent, opens it, dumps in half a box. She jams coins into the slots and rams the mechanism in. Turns. "Hey, I thought you left town." Polly throws her arms around Ruby.

"How could I pass up the opportunity to read cards at the St. Sebastian's Days?" Ruby extricates herself from Polly's exuberance.

"To say nothing of the fact that the world's best food is served there."

"It will be nice not to have to think about what's for dinner for a couple of days."

"Are you back at the Dew Drop?"

"Not exactly." Ruby tells Polly about her temporary campsite, waits to see if Polly is appalled, or jealous.

"You know, he's one of the good ones. Nothing in his life has been anything close to a fair shake."

Ruby instantly imagines self-inflicted losses. Bull has all the aspects of a man who has long ago lost control of his own life. And that generally means the loss of control over the lives of others. "What's his story?"

Polly shifts in her seat. "His wife was killed when her brakes failed, and he was left with two young sons. One of them, Cooper, turned out okay. Cooper was our dog officer here a couple of years ago. He's the one who arrested Don Boykin for animal cruelty. You know, Cynthia's now ex-husband."

"And Boy was the dog. Bull did tell me that." More precisely, Boy told her about it. The taste of abject fear had filled her mouth, and with it the sensation of exquisite pain. She didn't feel the pain in herself, but in her mind. She had run her hand down the length of the dog, along his flanks, and felt the lumpy scars of shotgun pellets. She had heard the blast of the double barrel in her ears, and endured in a touch the long weeks of suffering.

"Cooper suggested me for the ACO job when he left town to go back to the Boston PD as a K-9 officer."

"And the other son?" This is the one she knows is gone, the one that throws Bull's aura into a smudgy gray.

"The other son, Jimmy, well he was just bad news from the beginning. Jimmy was running drugs or something and ended up going through the ice on the lake trying to get away. Drowned."

"Oh, that's awful. Poor guy."

"Between you and me, I think Bull's better off without him; but that's just me."

With their laundry done, Ruby and Polly grab lunch and then head to the animal shelter with the basketful of clean blankets and towels. Polly has a couple of dogs in house, and asks Ruby to "take a look" and see if there are any clues she can give toward locating the animals' owners.

The Hitchhiker seems reluctant to go into the building; she pulls back on the leash. Ruby scoops her up, presses her face against the dog's head. "It's okay, Hitch."

"They are not happy in there."

"They need to find their owners."

"If you go in there, will I lose you?"

"Hitch, you belong to me, don't worry. You won't lose me."

Inside the building Polly brings Ruby to where two dogs are in separate pens. One is a bulldog type, the other more of a terrier. "Where did they come from?"

"The big one was wandering around the state park; some picnickers called me. He was scaring the kids. The other one was rooting around garbage cans on Maple Ave."

"They want to be together. I think they're a pair." Ruby squats in front of the cages. Presses one palm against one door, and the other palm against the other. Both dogs sniff and at the touch of their noses, she gets a good blast of connection. "Something happened to their person. He didn't come home. They dug out of their pen, not for the first time. They sat in the driveway for a long time, and then forgot to wait."

"Can they tell me their address?" Polly is only slightly joking.

"How long have they been here?"

"Just since yesterday."

"So, hypothetically if their person had gone away and their dog sitter didn't show up, then their person might not even know that they're missing."

"Hypothetically. Yes."

"Or, if they were gone when the supposed caretaker arrived, he or she might have figured that the person took the dogs with him or her."

"Again, hypothetically."

"That's the best I've got. What happens if no one comes to claim them?"

"We work with rescues to re-home."

"How long before you do that?"

"We'll give them a week, ten days if we don't get crowded."

Ruby pulls herself up to her feet. "I bet they get claimed sooner than that."

"Psychic vibe?"

"No. Just a hopeful hunch."

The Hitchhiker has discovered that being free in a place where all others are behind bars is energizing and she's also discovered Polly's store of treats. The dog presses her nose between the links in the kennel separating her from the other two dogs. "The treats are good. You should try some."

The two dogs bark in plain language to get back.

Ruby pulls her van into the rectangle delineated by the traffic cones and slides open her door. She pops up the folding table, pulls the café curtains, adds an array of fairy lights, and pulls on her caftan. Loosens her hair. Ready for business.

The feast has wound down for the night. Ruby closes the van door, gets behind the wheel. Her cell phone is on the dashboard and she reaches

for it. No texts, one email. She is really tired, and almost doesn't look
at the email but then does.

> Hi, Ms. Heartwood. Yes, we do have an archive. As the rec-
> ords are not digitized, there is no way for me to take the time
> to go through them for you. You are welcome to visit.
> Best regards,
> B. Johnson
> Office Administrator
> Sacred Heart Convent and School

12

Ruby's first impulse is to hit the road, point the Westie northwest, and book it toward the convent. Then she remembers that Joe Benini has been kind enough to allow her to work his carny at a fair price and she has too much integrity to simply drive away without a fare-thee-well. She's no dope; Ruby knows that she'll need Joe's good graces another time, especially if she hooks up with the larger divisions of Benini Brothers Carnivals at the several big New England fairs this fall. No sense burning bridges to pursue something that has been moldering in a basement for decades. Her quest can wait another twenty-four hours. Besides, she's made bank today and prudence will always overrule impatience. Ruby takes them back to Bull's yard. One more night and she'll be on her way.

Ruby feels the pressure of a small black nose against her elbow. It emerges from beneath the crook of her arm, followed by the raccoon mask and floppy ears of the Hitchhiker. Chocolate drop eyes meet hers. "What do you think?" Ruby isn't sure exactly what she means by the question, but the look on the dog's face suggests that she is, indeed, thinking about something.

"Happy here. Can we eat?"

"You can." Ruby has enjoyed the fulsome offerings of St. Sebastian's ladies' guild. She's packed three days' worth of food into her little fridge. For the dog she pulls out the bag of kibble and a leftover meatball. Earlier in the day, a black-attired nearly toothless old woman, cottony white hair subdued by a headscarf, had pressed a baggie of broken meatballs into Ruby's hand. "For the dog." When Ruby tried to demur, she squinted. "You give me free fortune."

"Deal. Come to my van when you get a chance."

"No. Now."

In her career, Ruby had encountered many a true believer who had no doubts at all about Ruby's skills; no hesitation. "Okay. Palms up."

The little lady's hands were as soft as pigeon breasts, but the lines told of a hard life. Burns from decades of cooking; hardened fingertips from needle pricks working on traditional embroidery. A line that described great sadness early in life; another that suggested a lifestyle change was coming soon.

The woman's face screwed up at that. "Yes. My children want me to go into a rest home." She curled her lip. "Assisted living." She said it like the words tasted foul. "They don't want me to cook anymore." The old lady dabbed at the corner of her eye with the edge of her apron. "Who am I if I don't cook for my family? None of them can cook."

"You are their matriarch. Their North Star."

"My mother taught me to cook." The hand in Ruby's grew warm, as if the old woman had just taken her hand away from a hot skillet. Memories not her own flooded Ruby's mind; at once the *idea* of mother-love forced her to close her eyes and grasp both the old woman's hands.

"You lost your mother early in life, didn't you?"

She nods. "I was a young bride, newly pregnant. She never saw her firstborn grandson."

"What was her name?"

"Guiliana."

"Did you name your son for her?"

"Julian."

"She has loved him his whole life." Ruby was sure of this. "What's your name?"

"Josephina Bartolotta."

"And your son named his after you."

The old woman, Josephina, smiled in spite of herself. "Joey. He's almost old enough to have his own child."

They stood there like that, hand in hand for a moment. Silent. Josephina turned her hands over and looked at Ruby's. "Is your mother still with you?"

"I have never had a mother."

"So, no one taught you to cook?"

Ruby laughed. "No. But I manage. My daughter is by far the better cook because she decided to become one."

"I think my problem is that I never had a daughter. Just sons. Daughters-in-law aren't interested in keeping the old mama around. Not interested in learning how to cook properly. All vegan this and tofu that. How are my sons supposed to work all day on that kind of food?"

Ruby desperately wanted to be able to change the course of this lady's future, but that wasn't ever in her power. She wanted to catch the ear of one of her sons and say: Don't you know you're sentencing her to life imprisonment by asking her to give up cooking? What if you were told you could never golf again? She realized that she was making some assumptions based on the very Harmony Farms description of the daughters-in-law nutritional choices. But then again, half her job was to make assumptions, and most of the time she was spot on. "Children always think that they know best. They don't understand that we're not children, that we know what's best for ourselves." It was the case Ruby had made over and over to Sabine regarding her own preferred lifestyle. Her need to keep moving.

"You are the same age as my Julian. Wait till you turn ninety. Then you'll see. They won't let you say what's best."

What will Sabine say about this quest of hers?

Ruby Heartwood had traveled with the Carerra Carnival as they moved from New England curling toward the middle of the country. She was getting farther and farther from her origins and with each mile she began to convince herself that she was no longer of any interest to the authorities. She lied about her age and stuck to it, not that she was ever challenged. She thought that having the presumed custodianship of a group of adults, even adults as offbeat as carny folk, offered a modicum of protection from the law.

At first Ruby bunked in with the rest of the unattached women, sharing a tiny caravan towed behind a roustabout's Hemi in which the four women rode. There was nothing more in the trailer than four bunks and a series of pegs to hang the bags with their clothes. Highway rest stops served for hygiene. Food. The three others were as varied in size and temperament as three women could be. Ruby thought of them as the Large, the Medium, and the Small. With herself trending toward the second smallest and certainly the youngest and always stuck in the middle of the backseat of the truck's crew cab. They ran the kiddie games of chance, each hoping to move up to food vendor someday, selling fried dough and Italian sausages, cotton candy and overpriced sodas. As a group, they were pleasant enough to Ruby and were happy enough to let her take a shift encouraging over-sugared toddlers to take a "prize every time" chance at the magnetic fishing pole or one of the other games that guaranteed a kid would walk away with a noisemaker or a cheap plastic inflatable. Like Ruby, they were quiet about their origins, if voluble about most everything else, especially insults real or imagined from the carnival goers or the other women who fancied themselves above these single ladies by virtue of a husband or boyfriend in their campers.

When the Carerra Brothers Carnival set up in a cornfield on the outskirts of a middle-sized town in the Midwest, a

newcomer joined the caravan. Ruby was scrubbing the outside walls of the cotton candy truck, scraping off the filth of
road dust stuck to sugar dust when a massive state-of-the-art
camper pulled onto the grounds towed by what looked like
an off-the-showroom diesel truck all tricked out with decals
suggesting the driver was still fighting the Civil War and was
a rabid Steelers fan. By the way the roustabouts waved as the
rig moved through what would become the midway by four
o'clock this afternoon, Ruby could tell this was no stranger
venturing by. The rig slipped past the cotton candy truck and
Ruby got a good look at the driver rolling by, one arm hanging out the window, cigarette dangling between thumb and
forefinger. Ruby thought he looked like Wolfman Jack. At
least how he was portrayed in *American Graffiti*. He saw her
and smiled, the same kind of smile a celebrity might have at
being recognized, and Ruby, sticky with the filthy work she
was doing, thought she'd die of embarrassment.

A magnetic sign was attached to the driver's-side door:
MADAME CELESTINE, PSYCHIC. Indeed, there was another person in the truck, and as they drove by a woman leaned across
the wolfman and looked right at Ruby. "Stop." The driver did as
he was told, flicked the burning cigarette onto the corn stubble
at Ruby's feet. Shocked at the carelessness, she stepped on it.

"Come to see me tonight."

Ruby had no chance to answer as the woman, presumably
Madame Celestine, smacked the driver on the shoulder. "Go."

Ruby emptied the bucket of nasty water onto the ground
where the crushed cigarette lay.

Having enjoyed the meatball garnish to her regular kibble, the Hitchhiker licks her lips, then attends to her front paws, works her way south
to her undercarriage. Ruby idly strokes the dog's back, staring at the black
words fashioned against the dull illumination of her cell phone screen.

Ruby is surprised to find that the records from her birth year still exist. In some fatalistic, or perhaps pessimistic leaning, she had fairly convinced herself that this bit of ancient history would have long ago been burned with the day's trash in the scary incinerator that lived out behind the school. She remembers the custodian dragging barrels out there as the last task of his day, tipping them into the maw; the foul-smelling smoke that issued from the chimney. As a little girl, in second grade, she conflated the election of a pope with the burning of trash. This thing about black smoke, white smoke. What came out of the school's chimney was neither white nor black, just a foggy gray color and stinky.

And yet, no one saw the need to haul boxes of records out of the basement and heave them into the incinerator. Ruby laughs at her own train of thought. In this day and age, there was likely no incinerator anymore. No longer considered an environmentally sound practice. She pictures instead a dank basement with bankers' boxes stacked one upon the other, sagging with moisture and furry with mold. She sighs at the anticipation of struggle. "What do you think? Should I really bother with this?" Ruby has taken to speaking to the dog, which feels better than talking to herself. At least it's out loud and conversational, not the agitated mutterings of a half-mad crone. Sometimes she gets a little back and forth, but those times tend to be when eating or walking are involved. The dog doesn't demand to have her explain the context of her ramblings, so as to be a help to her, rather than a living sounding board. She just cocks her head and expresses some hope that another meatball might appear.

"I guess that I was hoping that they'd have kept those records neatly filed in alphabetical order in a well-lit file room."

"You can sniff around for what you want. Use your nose."

In answer, Ruby boops the dog on her nose. "I think that your nose is like my psychic ability. A magical thing."

The last day of the St. Sebastian's festival starts off with fine weather, and by noontime the skies have darkened and most of the festival

goers have bailed. The food is mostly leftovers anyway and the fireworks are canceled when a tornado watch is announced. The Hitchhiker has been restless and even got in the way during one of Ruby's
few sessions, slipping beneath the table and resting her chin on Ruby's
feet. All in all, a good time to tell Joe Benini she's packing it up. His
crew have already begun dismantling the rides.

The rain begins in earnest just as Ruby pulls out of St. Sebastian's
parking lot. It's a monsoon-level cascade and her windshield wipers
cannot keep up. Except that it is broad daylight, it reminds her of the
night she met the Hitchhiker. The night she was graced. She is suddenly afraid that this new storm will take that grace from her. She pulls
off the road and grabs the dog, lifting her onto her lap. She presses her
forehead against the dog's and whispers, "Talk to me."

"*This is scary. I don't like thunder. We need to find shelter. Go to
place with bed for us go inside.*"

The image in Ruby's head is the Dew Drop Inn. She is taken with
the wisdom of a small dog. *Seek shelter.* Ruby turns the van toward the
Dew Drop and inches her way through the deluge toward that safe haven. Ravi is delighted to see her as she and the Hitchhiker dash through
the rain into his office. In minutes they are back in their little, slightly
askew room. Ruby showers and even though it's barely three o'clock,
pulls on pajama bottoms and a sweatshirt. The rain continues, but the
tornado warning is lifted. She's got the spoils from her sojourn among
the Italians in the dorm-room fridge so there's no need to go out again
today. The Hitchhiker is on the bed, nose beneath tail, a tiny package
of contented fluffiness.

Tomorrow is another day. Tomorrow, she promises herself, she will
reverse her lifelong trajectory and return to where she began.

13

As the old saw says, what a difference a day makes. Ruby awakens to a clear, dry morning, a perfect day for a road trip. She quickly dresses and heads out to get enough ice to hold the leftovers awhile longer. The Hitchhiker trails along, tail waving in salute to a beautiful day and a cheerful companion. Ruby is cheerful. After dwelling on this idea of finding out where she came from, or at least trying to, she is content with her decision to head back to Sacred Heart Convent and drill down through whatever boxes she needs to in order to find out her real origins. The idea of knowing who she is, who her mother was—or is—has begun to take on a bucket list feel.

Last night she called Sabine. Told her what she was up to.

"Are you sure you want to do this?"

"She's been coming to me. In dreams."

Dreams and portents, signs and auras, the stuff of their lives. Sabine wishes Ruby good luck. "And try not to be disappointed if nothing comes of it. You'll still be you."

Sabine is right, and Ruby understands that knowing if she was left by a mother or a stranger won't change her life; it won't really matter in the long run. She will still be Ruby Heartwood, self-invented. But doing nothing, not trying to find out, has become an unacceptable choice.

·   ·   ·

All is quiet at the Dew Drop Inn this early in the morning. There are cars enough to suggest that there are occupants in six of the twelve units. Ravi doesn't discuss his economics, but Ruby has figured out that the Airbnb phenomenon and other do-it-yourself rentals are taking a toll on the traditional accommodations. The guests she's encountered before have all been older, mainly couples, mostly just interested in a place to rest before continuing on to their actual destinations. A way station, that's what the Dew Drop Inn is. A motor court between Boston and the Berkshires or Vermont or Canada.

One half of one of those couples is sitting in the plastic Adirondack chair outside his room. He's wearing Madras shorts of a style Ruby hasn't seen worn without intentional irony in years. Loafers with tassels but no socks. A turquoise golf shirt with a popped collar. He's either got an angry resting face or something is troubling him. Ruby doesn't pause as she walks by but does give him a civil nod to acknowledge his presence. He looks right past her. It's nothing to her, she's just being polite. Nonetheless, she notes his aura, and begins to sense his expression isn't anger but something else, perhaps grief or melancholy. It's rare enough to get vibes from a man, rarer still to see such a defined aura surrounding one.

"Are you okay?"

He does see her then. Gathers himself enough to give her a smile. "Oh, fine. Just waiting for the wife."

The wife. Boy does Ruby hate that two-word identifier.

The door opens and The Wife comes out. She's maybe half a decade younger than he is and sports a massive engagement ring aligned with a wide gold band thrust on a long finger with a gel coat manicure in a shade of deep purple. She's tan and trim and wearing high-tech athletic pants and a sweatshirt with St. Augustine emblazoned across her chest. Ruby smells second wife all over her. She has no particular aura surrounding her. Just a cloud of curly auburn hair that Ruby finds herself pining for. It's kind of like her hair was thirty years ago. Which was, of course, a wig. Her costume. Her disguise.

Under the woman's left arm is a bundle of white. At first Ruby takes it for laundry, or a towel, maybe she's headed to the seldom-utilized pool. Then the bundle shifts to reveal two brown eyes and a black nose. It arfs at her. Wiggles.

"Zelda, that's not polite. So sorry." The bundle's carrier chides the dog in a fairly pro forma way. Like she has to do that every time the dog encounters another human being.

Ruby recognizes a yappy little dog when she sees one. Except that this one, like just about every other dog she's met during her stay here in Harmony Farms, has spoken to her, mind to mind.

"Zelda. Cute name."

Zelda wriggles harder, nearly launches herself out of the woman's arms. "I'm not cute. I want to walk."

"She doesn't like to be carried."

"Excuse me?"

Ruby wonders why it is that all these dog people have to be excused when she first interprets for their dogs. "She thinks it's undignified. To be carried. She's a dog, she wants to get down and sniff the grass. Meet other dogs."

"I hardly think that's appropriate."

Ruby reaches out to stroke under Zelda's chin. "I tried."

Zelda's little head sags, but her tail wags gently, the long hairs on it tickling her owner's bare skin.

"She'd get dirty."

"I suppose she would. But she'd enjoy it."

Zelda raises her tiny head to stare at her bearer. If ever a dog could plead for clemency, it was Zelda.

"It's nice and grassy out back. She could run around, get some exercise."

The mister of this odd couple has said nothing, just continued to stare out across the parking lot as if there was a nice view. "Doreen, put the goddam dog down and let her be a dog."

Ruby realizes that his aura is the ashy color of regret, and she knows that it isn't regret for being snappish.

"Well, nice meeting you." Not.

The Hitchhiker is waiting at the room door as if she has deliberately ducked the opportunity to meet the couple and their unhappy arm candy of a dog.

"Consider yourself lucky."

"I do. Especially if cheese is going to happen." Hitch is quite single-minded about cheese.

Once again Ruby bids Ravi adieu, and once again he reminds her that she is always welcome at the Dew Drop.

And once again, the van doesn't start.

"It's almost like I've been bewitched or cursed; like I can't get past the borders of this town because of some spell." Ruby takes a bite of her dill pickle.

"Have you thought about consulting someone?" Polly, who has already finished her sandwich, is now at work on one of those individual servings of pudding. She points her spoon at Ruby.

"I've been consulting my cards. Thank you for not being skeptical."

"The man who acts as his own lawyer has a fool for a client." Polly sticks a finger into the plastic cup, drags up the last of the pudding.

"You may have a point."

"Have you ever thought that if you leave Harmony Farms, you might lose your animal communicator abilities?"

"No. Maybe. But . . ." Ruby wraps the other half of her sandwich. She's lost her appetite. ". . . I have had the feeling that the whole thing is temporary."

They are sitting at a café table outside of the Country Market. The Hitchhiker rests her chin on Ruby's foot, adds a paw to remind Ruby that she's there, holding her in place.

"Well, as long as you're still here, would you be willing to do a consult?"

"Another guest of the town at the shelter?"

"No. Actually, it's not a dog. I'm hoping that you're interested in advancing to large animal communication."

"How large?"

"Pretty big."

"I thought you only dealt with dogs and cats."

"Don't forget the occasional bunny. But no, I also do farm inspections."

"I repeat: How big?"

"Fifteen hands."

Ruby knows this means that Polly's consult request is for a horse. "I have no idea if I can connect with a horse, but hey, like you said, I'm still here."

"I'll call the owner."

Ruby figures that communicating with a horse might help pay for the van's latest illness. Maybe she can charge by the pound.

An hour later Ruby and Polly, with the Hitchhiker in the backseat of the truck, are on their way to Far Piece Farm.

If Ruby was expecting the whitewashed fences of Kentucky, she was bound for disappointment. Far Piece Farm boasts a three-strand electric fence delimiting a collection of paddocks. Polly leads Ruby through a Butler building barn, behind which a riding ring has pride of place. They walk toward it, watching three women trot around a fourth who stands her ground, planted dead center in the ring. She never flinches as the trio change direction, zigging and zagging and circling around her. Each of the riders wears sunglasses against the midday glare, and the appropriate gear of helmet, tall boots, and riding tights; they are distinguishable from one another only by the horses upon which they ride. A chestnut with flashy white legs, a dark horse whose ears keep flicking backward, and a mottled-looking creature Ruby will learn is called a red roan.

Polly motions for Ruby to take a seat on a bench to wait out the lesson. "The horse in question is the black one."

Ruby keeps her eyes on the animal, hoping to get some intel on the creature's troubles. The pinned ears and the fact that the rider looks tense is a pretty good indicator of problems.

"Who's its rider?"

"I can't tell with the helmet and sunglasses. The horse is a schoolie, a lesson horse, so it could be anyone on her."

As Ruby watches, even she can see that the horse is resisting its rider's orders. There is a tension in its—her—eyes, and Ruby has to wonder how safe an unhappy horse could be for a student rider.

"Okay, everybody. Cool them out for ten and then bring them in and untack." With a wave, the instructor finally acknowledges Polly and Ruby sitting on the bench. While her riders walk their horses slowly around the ring, she comes out. "I'm Carrie Farr." She sticks her hand out for Ruby to shake.

"Farr, ha. So, the name of your farm then is a wink."

"And a nod." Carrie is also dressed in riding clothes but wears a frayed ball cap rather than a helmet, a straggly ponytail coming through the gap in the back, and clogs on her feet. She's wiry, giving off the impression of contained power, kind of like a stick of dynamite. She could be forty or sixty.

As they head into the barn, Ruby says, "Polly tells me that you've got a problem with that black horse."

Carrie shrugs, picks up a dropped hoof pick, tosses it into a box. "Sometimes. Not always. That's what's weird. I've had all the usual things checked out when a perfectly lovely animal starts to go off. You know, teeth, feet, back, health check. Blood tests for Lyme. The whole shooting match. The thing is, she's a school horse, which makes her valuable in her job, but if she won't do her job, well, it's my way or the highway."

"Got it."

Leading their horses, the riders have entered the barn like a little parade, one after the other, and Carrie takes the reins of the horse in question from the hand of her rider, who turns and walks away without a word. The other two start untacking their mounts, chatting about their lesson, commiserating over errors, verbally slapping each other on the back for a good canter or trot. They finally pull off their helmets and Ruby can see that they are just girls. Teenagers. They offer handfuls of carrot chunks to their horses. The other rider, having disappeared into the tack room does not come out to treat this horse. Carrie quickly untacks the mare, who stands calmly on her cross ties while Ruby observes.

Carrie pats the animal on the neck. "I just want you to know that this isn't something that I, um, believe in, animal communication. I mean, I communicate with my animals, but it's through touch and aids and food and, well, sometimes some inspired swearing, but not mind to mind."

"And if I'm to be honest, I'm not sure I can do anything anyway, but hey, it can't hurt, can it?" Ruby looks toward Polly's truck, where the Hitchhiker is standing on the armrest, her head out the window. Two big farm dogs are staring up at her.

Carrie sees where Ruby is looking. "Is that your dog?"

"More like I'm her person."

"My dogs won't bother her if you want to let her out of the truck."

"I'll go," Polly offers.

Ruby stands to the left side of the horse, who lowers her head so that human and horse are eye to eye. The animal's eye is soft, deep brown, and her lashes are remarkably long. If the eyes are the windows to the soul, this creature seems quite soulful to Ruby. "Can I put my hands on her face?"

"Sure, she's not head shy at all. Or, at least wasn't until recently. Don't be surprised if she lifts it away from you. And watch for getting clunked in the head with hers."

As Ruby lifts her hands, the horse does bob her head, then shakes it. This isn't the same as when the Hitchhiker shakes her head, which is a sign she wants to play. Ruby lowers her hands, then reaches slowly to stroke the animal on the cheek. Immediately, the connection is there, not as electric as with the dogs, more a soft humming. The mare lowers her head and closes her eyes. Ruby moves to stand in front of her, lays her hands on either side of the horse's muzzle. Leans in instinctively to breathe into the mare's nostrils, breathe in the mare's breath. Pictures of greenness come to mind, images of what speed feels like.

"You've been around horses, I take it." Carrie is standing aside, arms folded. "You've read a lot of them?"

"Nope. She's my first one."

"But you know about introducing yourself that way, breath to breath."

"Not a clue. I'm just listening to her."

The curious thing is, the contented vibe that Ruby is getting begins to harden, she tastes tension in her mouth. The switch is so quick it makes Ruby feel as though she's being hunted. As if there is a predator lurking.

"Carrie, I want to book a lesson for this weekend. Private, if you can." The third member of the class walks up to Ruby, Carrie, and the horse, who now jerks her head out of Ruby's hands.

Cynthia Mann.

It all makes sense.

"Hello, Cynthia."

Is Ruby imagining it, or does Cynthia's lip actually curl before struggling into a smile? "Oh, hello, Ruby. Practicing your dark arts here now?"

"Helping figure out what's spooking this poor horse."

"If you ask me, she just needs to keep working with an experienced rider, fewer children letting her get away with murder." Cynthia clearly means herself as the experienced rider.

Carrie bends to give the Hitchhiker a pat, and Ruby can see she's biting her tongue.

"Carrie, a lesson?" Cynthia does that arms akimbo thing she must have learned from her first-grade teacher.

"Sure. Let's go look at my book."

As the two women walk away, the horse drops her head, nudges Ruby with her muzzle. *Predator predator get away.*

"I know. She's after me too."

Carrie returns in a moment. "So, what's the verdict?"

Ruby sees Cynthia's Land Rover speed away. "I think that she would very much like to go back to being a children's mount. She doesn't like bossy people."

"Well, that's kind of what her purpose is, to be asked to do something and to do it. Besides, I have more adults than children."

"Then she needs to have a nicer adult on her. Right? Someone who isn't convinced of her own infallibility. One who asks more nicely."

Carrie gets it. "Yeah, I see what you mean."

"Exactly."

"I've got a nice older lady this mare might work well with."

"What's her name?"

"Eleanor Something. Dorsey."

"I mean, the mare. What's her name?"

"Bella."

Ruby places her hands against the horse's muzzle, finds herself drawn to kiss that soft nose. "Bella, life will be good if you'll give Mrs. Dorsey a chance. No more predator."

14

"When you gonna call it?" Bull has joined Ruby at the Lakeside Tavern, his usual glass of seltzer and lime in his hand. A Cuban sandwich on his plate. "Put that poor thing out of its misery?" Bull is referring to the Westfalia. Which is still in the shop.

"I don't have a lot of choice."

"Bet you could sell it. Get something decent I'd think for a classic like that."

"Then what would I drive?"

"Buy yourself something from this century."

"Ha-ha." Ruby tucks into her artisanal grilled cheese sandwich. Three cheeses, locally sourced, only one of which is familiar to her. Still, it's pretty darn good. A gooey string dangles between the sandwich and her lip. She reels it in. "I'm essentially spending every penny on keeping the van going—and the Dew Drop—so I haven't got much in the old savings account."

"Guy across the street from the Dew Drop? He'll cut you a deal."

"And trade in my semi-reliable Westie for a risky used car? A beater I couldn't even use for a camper? Nuh-uh. No, thanks."

This is the same conversation she's had with herself for years. It's kind of nice to have someone else take half of the dialogue.

"You got kids, an ex? Someone who might help you out?"

"A daughter. No ex. And, no. I couldn't do that."

Bull shrugs. He's done his bit to try and solve her automotive problems.

The fact is, she'll stay put—hopefully only a little longer—in Harmony Farms. Long enough to do one more Makers Faire and maybe scratch up enough private animal consults that she can get on the road to Canada before the big fall fairs start up. Otherwise, she's going to have to postpone her search for her origins until almost winter. And that idea doesn't appeal. She may have fled Canada when she was very young, but she still has vivid memories of deep cold and snow. The Westie is much more a fair-weather vehicle even when in top form.

Ruby emailed B. Johnson, Sister Beatrice as she turns out to be, first telling her that she would come to Sacred Heart to root through the archives, and then to let her know she wouldn't. No reply. A second email came back with an out of office stamp. Which, considering her delay in leaving Harmony Farms, almost made Ruby feel relieved. It would have sucked to get all the way up there only to find out that Sister B is away and there is no one else willing to help Ruby out.

Ruby spots Carrie Farr at one of the other outside tables and waves. Carrie grabs her beer and comes over.

"Bull, do you know Carrie Farr?" Ruby feels like she should do hostess duties.

"Of course I do." An unkempt gentleman, Bull gets to his feet and gives Carrie a hug.

The Hitchhiker scrambles to get Carrie's attention, paws up, sneezing, fluffy tail waving like the lap flag at the Indy 500. As soon as she's attended to, Boy, Bull's placid Labrador, gets to his feet to get his share of petting. Carrie squats to accept the Hitchhiker's greeting and gets Boy's nose right in hers. Upon rising, she pats Ruby on the shoulder. "You might want to know that I fired Cynthia the other day."

"Fired?"

"Yeah, told her I wouldn't be her riding instructor anymore."

"Why?" Ruby points to an empty chair at an empty table. "Sit. Tell."

"Well, after your, um, diagnosis of Bella's behavior, I put Cynthia on another school horse. Big gelding with the patience of a saint. I fudged it by telling her that I thought she needed a taller horse. She liked that. Long story short, old Bud started pinning his ears and acting exactly like Bella had been. Case closed. Some riders have what we call an electric seat, and I think that Cynthia is one of them. I don't want to ruin every horse in my barn, so I told her I wouldn't be her instructor anymore. She needs to find a new hobby."

"And how did she take it?"

Carrie smiles behind the lip of her beer mug. "About as you'd expect."

"With grace?" Bull chimes in around a mouthful of sandwich.

"If you call threatening me with losing my business license grace, then yeah. Sure."

"Oh, Carrie. I'm sorry." Ruby says this but can't disguise the bubble of mirth fighting its way up.

"I'm not. She's never going to be a good rider. She just likes the equestrienne look." Carrie gets up to go back to her table where two of her students are finishing up their lunches. "I have to look out for my animals." She dips down to give the Hitchhiker another pat. "Cynthia doesn't intimidate me, but Ruby, you might want to keep a low profile because, for some reason, she's blaming you for my *attitude*."

"Not a chance. I'll be in my usual spot on Saturday at the Makers Faire. She's been trying to get me thrown out of there since the first week."

Bull drags a wad of paper napkin across his mouth. "Someone forgot to tell Cynthia that she has no power anymore."

"Well, she is a selectperson."

Bull grunts. "Yeah, that and a quarter won't even get you a cup of coffee."

Ruby isn't really sure what he means but laughs anyway.

A moment later her phone rings, the repair shop number coming up. "Wish me luck." Ruby holds her breath, crosses her fingers, and answers.

The Westfalia is ready, the hard-to-get part found and installed, the cost only exactly what Ruby had made at the St. Sebastian's Days.

"You wanna plug in at my house?"

It's Thursday, and now Ruby is stubbornly committed to staying on to Saturday to plant her flag at the Makers Faire. Having her weekend's profits wiped out and with a long trip north in the works, she really should economize where she can. So she nods. "That would be nice, thank you." The Hitchhiker will be happy to be around her pal, Boy, for a little while longer.

As neither of them have a vehicle, Ruby and Bull and the two dogs take an amiable walk along the lake edge to their respective destinations. He to Poor Farm Road, and she to the auto repair shop.

All this sense of leaving is very disturbing to me. Ruby wants to leave; she has a destination in mind that I cannot see. All I see is that we should be here, in our territory. Not roaming. I have tried to tell her, but she is like so many of her kind, deaf to entreaty.

A pale shimmer of moonlight leaks through the space between the curtains, drawn hours ago against the night. It is a spirit-shaped shimmer, and it reaches out to touch Ruby on the face. Her eyes open and she sees the suggestion of an apparition before her. Once again, she knows that she is dreaming and is more curious to see where the dream will lead than she is afraid of the shimmering spirit. She sits up and, instead of the dog sleeping soundly at the end of her camper bed, Ruby sees a woman sitting there. She might be the Holy Mother or Ruby herself many years ago, a visitation from her past. The spirit woman holds up one finger, either keeping Ruby from saying anything out loud or as a caution. Ruby's dream self wants to reach out and touch that finger, but she is incapable of moving. It is as if she has become an inanimate object. Before the shimmer dissolves into the fading moonlight she withdraws that cautionary finger and Ruby regains motion. She lunges forward, hands grasping nothing but air.

Ruby awakens to the Hitchhiker licking her face.

Before the dream can dissolve away as all dreams do, Ruby jots down the basics of it. She's had enough of these—what she calls her mother dreams—to warrant seeking a professional dream interpreter's opinion if she knew one that she could trust. The fact is, it doesn't take a professional interpreter or even a psychologist to link her waking desire to find her mother with her dream world. She's finally looking for her. It makes sense that, in her dreams, she would encounter her.

His name was Harold, but everyone called him Buck. Although he looked like a rough approximation of a grown man, he was only nineteen. His entire life had been spent living among carny folk. In some ways he'd grown into the roustabout profession as if it had been predetermined that he be big, strong, and none too bright. Others had gravitated toward the games of chance, or the mechanics of building and breaking down rides, but Buck had no interest in anything that required a skill beyond scoring girls and drugs. And his good looks guaranteed the first, his bullyish behavior the second. His mother, Madame Celestine, doted upon him with all the blind love a lonely carny worker could give. Ruby had one thing in common with him: he too had no idea who his father was.

As ordered, Ruby knocked that evening on the tin door of the RV belonging to Madame Celestine. The woman who pushed open the door to stare at Ruby barely resembled the woman in the truck. Without her wig, and dressed in comfortable sweats, she could have been a housewife. Anyone's mother. A strong waft of fried chicken tickled Ruby's nose and her stomach growled.

Celestine, without a word, stood aside and motioned Ruby to enter the RV. Much bigger than the camper that Ruby was sharing with the other single women, this one boasted a kitchenette, a flush toilet, and shower. Two sleeping spaces, one up a little ladder and the other in the back. Ruby knew that a third bed could be made up in the space where a fold down table was now set for dinner for two. It was an efficient space, uncluttered.

"He doesn't live here; he has a girlfriend."

Ruby noted the demonstration of psychic ability, the expectation that she would be amazed and ask how Madame Celestine had guessed her thoughts. The truth is, Ruby was only interested in if the second-place setting was intended for her.

"Sit down."

Celestine was a very good cook. It had been a long time since Ruby had had a real meal that wasn't carnival food. Perhaps since she'd run away from the orphanage. Over dinner Ruby had given Celestine a thumbnail and very edited version of her travels, if not the why of them. Finally, dinner over, Ruby was offered a cup of tea. Madame Celestine cradled the teapot with both hands as she brought it to the table. It was a lovely teapot, a deep pink color with a frieze of hand-painted ivy in varying shades of green. Gold edging on the tip of the spout and the finial of the lid. Madame Celestine set a tiny matching cup and saucer in front of Ruby in such a manner that Ruby understood this to be her opening and she took it. "I can read the leaves if you'd like."

"I was going to offer that to you."

"I have some ability."

"I know. I intuited that about you the moment I laid eyes

on you. You have the aura." This was the first time Ruby had heard the term, and immediately she understood that she had been seeing auras her whole life, that much of what she divined about people came from them. That was the first lesson Madame Celestine offered, and suddenly Ruby felt juiced with the idea that here was someone who could help her hone her skills. Not in the clumsy way of poor Maggie Dean, but as a professional in the art.

As Ruby helped wash up after dinner, the two psychics came to an arrangement. That night Ruby gathered her few things from the single ladies' camper and became Madame Celestine's boarder and student. In exchange, most of what Ruby would make would be turned over to her mentor. It seemed like a fair deal to the fourteen-year-old. A roof and a job. And real food.

What she couldn't have foreseen was Buck breaking up with his girlfriend.

"I didn't think we'd see you here again, Ruby," Emily, the essential oils seller/treasurer of the Farmers' Market and Makers Faire, says as she takes Ruby's money. "Cynthia said you'd left town."

"Well, I can't say that I haven't tried, but here I am." She flashes the girl a bright smile. "Same spot still available?"

"Sure. People are starting to drop out, so take whatever space you want."

Ruby has deliberately arrived early, mostly to be well dug in by the time Cynthia showed up to flaunt her imagined authority. As she sets up the tent, she notices a rent in one of the panels. The poor old thing is really showing its age. "Come on, pal, hang in there till winter." Ruby pinches the edges of the tear together, wondering if some fabric glue or super glue would hold it long enough to get through fall fair season. Otherwise she'll have to use her van. She didn't mind so much for little venues like the St. Sebastian's Days, but at the bigger affairs it's a lot like inviting strangers into her home instead of her office.

The Hitchhiker, trailing her leash, is sniffing around, tail swishing from side to side as she meanders in a vaguely serpentine pattern. Her black ears dust the ground as she goes. Every night Ruby has to clean debris tangled in her floppy ears. Her head pops up from the ground and she makes a dash toward Polly Schaeffer, who is ambling along with a white bag Ruby just knows has something warm in it from Betty's Blessings, the bakery tent.

"Why don't you brew us a little tea in that fancy little pot of yours?" Polly sets the bakery bag on Ruby's round table and plops herself down on one of the chairs.

Ruby has a souvenir mug from the Great Smoky Mountains and another from the Berkshires and she puts them on the table, produces a paper plate for the goodies. "I already got a Thermos of coffee from Bob's Fair Trade Coffee. I need to reserve my tea leaves for readings."

Ruby has offered to do a reading for Polly any number of times, but the assistant animal control officer always demurs with: "I don't think I want to know." Ruby has gleaned enough of Polly's history from actual conversation to know that the woman is in recovery from an animal hoarding habit, and that she has found her emotional equilibrium in taking care of the town's lost and homeless animals, receiving great satisfaction in effecting happy reunions and finding others new homes instead of keeping them in her own house.

In a normal friendship, Ruby would offer up selections from her own troubled past, but Ruby has never had a normal friendship. She isn't quite sure what part of her life is of equal currency to Polly's revelation that she's had difficulties with her son because of her sometimes overwhelming compassion for the beasts of the earth, particularly cats. Like a prized jewel, Ruby plucked the story of her running away from the convent as her contribution to this friendship, not telling the story well, and not embellishing it. Polly listened as Ruby told it. Told it with dispassion. As if the story belonged to someone else. In the end, Polly had taken Ruby's hand in hers and patted it, and that was enough to let Ruby know that if she remained in this town much longer, she would be tempted to reveal a lot more about herself. Already she has mentioned this idea of heading north, of getting her hands on those buried files. Polly has been encouraging but not enthusiastic. Like Sabine, she has asked: "Are you sure you want to know?"

15

It's a slow morning at the Makers Faire, by noontime Ruby hasn't given one single reading. Plenty of folks who want to pet the Hitch-hiker, but no one wants to have her cards read. The Hitchhiker is a draw, getting people to come close to the tent, but this particular Saturday even her magic aura doesn't attract anyone into the seat. Ruby is beginning to come to the conclusion that, Cynthia Mann be damned, this gig is over. Unless she gets a rush before two o'clock, Ruby figures that the day represents a total loss. She's spent more on the vendor's fee and coffee than the full afternoon of readings it would take to turn the day profitable.

A zephyr swirls through the grounds, catching dust and debris in its rotation. Ruby feels the breeze on her cheeks and the walls of the tent swell and deflate. The dog barks. What's that quote from *Macbeth*? *Something wicked this way comes.* One of the witches foreshadowing the tragedy. Despite her limited education, Ruby has long been a fan of the Bard.

And, as if conjured, there's Cynthia. She's striding toward Ruby's tent. Today's outfit features a flowy black sweater over a black T-shirt, skinny black jeans, and a pair of pointy-toed black booties. The drift of the long sweater only enhances the overall impression of a witch in search of a broom. Ruby motions for the Hitchhiker to hide under the table. No sense taking chances.

Before Cynthia can close the distance between herself and Ruby, a middle-aged man with a middle-sized dog steps up to Ruby's tent. As with most, he tries to look like he's not quite interested. She flashes him her most welcoming smile and gestures to the other chair. "And what can I help you with?" She's not going to let him dither around before he finally decides to ask for help with his dog, because, of course that's what she immediately intuits about the pair. "Your dog has some questions, perhaps?"

"Well, no. I mean . . ." And dither he does, but Ruby is holding his eyes with intention, holding his hands, using the guy as a wall between herself and the grimy aura of Cynthia as she approaches. If Ruby had hoped that Cynthia would be deflected from her purpose by the presence of another human being, she is disappointed.

"Hello, John."

"Cynthia."

Because his hands are still in hers, Ruby gets a quick flash of history between this guy, John, and her nemesis.

Cynthia turns her attention to Ruby. "I don't recall seeing your name on the list of vendors this week."

"It wasn't. Pure availability of space. Now if you don't mind . . ." Ruby nods toward the guy, John, who is unsure where to look. He's clearly a little embarrassed to be seen with his hands in the hands of a psychic, but he's man enough not to bolt.

"Of course I mind." She reaches out to touch Ruby's client on the shoulder, leans in conspiratorially, and stage whispers, "She's a fake. And she's a whack job."

Ruby lets go of the guy's hands. Stands up. The Hitchhiker is beside her, pressing both of her forepaws onto Ruby's instep in a doggy version of *I've got your back*. She growls softly, a little fear, a little offer of protection.

"Cynthia, that is uncalled for." It's John, now on his feet. "Why don't you just shuffle off? I've got business here."

"I can't believe that you're falling for this, this nonsense." Cynthia laughs a particularly barky laugh and wheels away.

"Sorry about that. She's never been much of a charmer. Especially since . . ." John lets his remark drift off, unfinished.

"Since?"

"You know, or maybe you don't. Her husband? The dog?"

"I'm a stranger in town, John." She smiles. "But yeah. I know a little about that. I guess that she didn't like being the subject of the kind of gossip that incident must have generated. Surely she felt like her own reputation had been ruined."

"More like people stopped talking about her. Which was worse. Shunning is such a popular New England–style punishment." John smiles. "She certainly seems to have it out for you."

"I have no idea why, but I have been a hair across her posterior ever since I showed up. Some people have a fear that I'll perceive their deepest secrets and throw up a shield. In Cynthia's case, she uses animosity." Ruby doesn't mention that she influenced Carrie Farr's rejection of Cynthia as a riding student. "So, to the business at hand. What can I help you with?"

John puts a hand on the head of his middle-sized dog, a mongrel if ever there was one. "He's not happy and I don't know why."

The dog, a mottled brown, long-bodied creature with upright ears and a docked tail, sits, sighs. He does indeed look unhappy. He's sniffed the Hitchhiker, who has also taken his measure and gone back under the table.

"We got him . . ."

Ruby holds up a finger. "Let me get a read and see if he can tell me." The dog seems happy enough to let this perfect stranger put hands on his head. Immediately that tingling vibe that she got with the Hitchhiker all those weeks ago, and then with Boy, begins to fill her hands and then her mind. She's had decent connections with most dogs—and with the horse—but this one is stronger than that. This dog has something important to say. She takes a breath of fear and sorrow and confusion. She hears the scent of loudness and distance. Ruby closes her eyes and knows that this dog has come from afar, that he was never beloved, that he doesn't understand kindness. She opens her eyes and meets the eyes of the dog; the connection is almost painful, and she removes her hands. They still tingle and she rubs them together to try to stop the zizzing in her palms. "He's a rescue from someplace rather far away. Down South, perhaps?"

"Yes. We saw his picture on the web and just fell in love with that face."

"I see. So, he probably was in a kill-shelter."

"That's what we were told. He was one of the lucky ones, pulled out by the rescue team."

"He's never had people of his own, so he's confused. It's not that he's unhappy, he's just uncertain of how to be."

"Doesn't he know that he's never going to be homeless again?"

"No, not yet." Ruby touches the dog once more, simply running her hand along his spine. She gets a whiff of a deeper confusion, an empathic grief. "He's picking up on some unhappiness of your own."

When John doesn't respond, she looks up at him and sees for herself that what the dog is absorbing from his new forever home is this man's own despair.

"Let him help you."

"I thought getting the dog would help. That he would fill a hole for me."

Ruby doesn't have to read John's tea leaves or palm to know that the "we" he had used was really a force of habit. There was no longer any "we" in his life. Except the dog. So much pressure on an animal.

"It takes time. Patience. He doesn't know how to help you."

John squats and takes the dog's head between his hands. "You are helping, Roscoe. Just by making me get out of bed."

Roscoe's stubby tail begins to tick tock and he gives John a quick, shy kiss.

"Oh! He's never done that before! Good boy, Roscoe."

It has been one of the unexpected benefits of this odd new talent, witnessing the wonderful care people have for their animals. Most of them, that is, with a couple of notable exceptions like the Great Dane woman and that other woman who wouldn't let her little dog touch the ground. Ruby leans down and swoops up the Hitchhiker. The dog licks her face and the warm contented feeling of companionship soothes away the last of the vibrations.

Each time that tall skinny woman approaches, it feels like the air is being sucked out of my body. I am a lover of all humans, I have made a career out of being nice and friendly, cheerful and available, but I swear, this *Cynthia* woman is more wolf than dog. I fear her feet. I fear a kick that would send me into oblivion. I sense Ruby's distaste for her, but I don't detect fear, which is all I can take courage from. If my person is unafraid, then I am too.

It's after six o'clock when Ruby pulls into her little space at Bull's house. She's been to the Country Market and to the wine shop. She's ready to settle in for a pleasant evening of Netflix. Things had picked up after John and Roscoe so she's feeling a little better about her prospects. She opens the side door of the van and the Hitchhiker jumps out to greet Boy heading in their direction, goofy Labrador grin on his face and feet failing to keep pace with his tail. Except for her grandchildren, Ruby doesn't think anyone has ever greeted her with such enthusiasm as this dog does. Ruby gives him some love and then hunts around for the extension cord that will keep her—brand-new—battery from draining as she uses her laptop and the interior lights. She spots the yellow cord a few feet away. Bull waves from his kitchen window like a friendly neighbor as she picks it up. She waves back, equally neighborly.

After dinner Ruby makes a quick phone call to Sabine, checking in as she has promised her daughter to do, asking after the kids, listening more than talking. Sabine is living the life Ruby had long ago rejected—that is, utterly established. Sabine sits on committees and carpools with other moms. She has a permanent address in a house that is one of the oldest in the town. Married to a man whose antecedents founded the place. She is carefully growing a root system. Ruby thinks, more power to her. She tries not to think of it as a commentary on her own life of perpetual motion. Her chosen lifestyle.

Ruby opens up her laptop and moves to click open Netflix but hits the email icon first. Two emails. One is a come-on from an online retailer. The second bears the address of the Sacred Heart Convent and School for Girls. A moment of true psychic inspiration washes through Ruby, jolting her enough that the dog jumps up and presses her nose into Ruby's neck. *Opening this message will change everything.*

PART II

16

From the way that she sat there staring at the machine she consults when she isn't consulting me, I knew that there was something of great portent in its message. If we canines like to communicate through scent, both the leaving of it and sniffing of it, I also knew that this black box was Ruby's primary way of communicating with those out of sight. Her other method, the littler box, at least made some sense to me as I could discern the other voice, its pitch and quaver a little harder to comprehend than if I could see the speaker and read his or her expression, but comprehensible all the same. I especially liked it when there was a picture on the screen, much like the moving pictures on the TV. Yes, I am one of those dogs who watch television. I especially like the animal programs. I like to bark at them. Although I am in what my people have referred to as a "small package," I am all field dog.

As Ruby seemed to be locked in some human-style point, I got to work, jumping on the bed, shoving my nose into the crook of her neck, which never fails to tickle. She pushed me aside. Her hands hovered over the machine, and I could smell the excitement and nerves and fear and other luscious human scent markers emanate from her into the air, thence into my nose as I sucked them in, the better to understand what, exactly, was going on here. Giving up on shaking her from this odd torpor, I settled for crawling onto her lap and going to work licking my forepaws as if I had no particular interest in anything other than hygiene. I was rewarded with an embrace, her cheek against my head, a whisper of praise, reminding me not only am I a "good girl," but I am essential to my human's well-being.

Ruby pulls her hands away from the keyboard, quelling the temptation to reply instantly before thinking. Fortunately the Hitchhiker is on her lap and that's where her fingers land, stroking the soft fur, pulling gently on the floppy ears. She hopes for the vibration of psychic communication, but all she gets is the comfort of a small dog on her lap. And then she realizes that the dog *is* communicating, but in a more normal fashion. While Ruby has been able to read the dog, she realizes more and more that the dog also reads her. Opting to speak out loud, Ruby asks: "So what do I do?"

The dog studies Ruby's face with gimlet eyes, her pink tongue darts out and gives Ruby a kiss.

Ruby pulls the curtain aside, stares out at Bull Harrison's house. There's a light on in the kitchen and she can see the blue flicker of his television, visible through the naked window of his living room. She thinks about calling Sabine back, letting her know what's possible.

> Hi, Ruby,
> I need to let you know that the file that you are interested in is on my desk. Ironically, just as I replied to your query, the board of trustees voted to dispose of the boxes in the basement. Timing is everything in life, isn't it? I remembered your hoping to find out something about yourself and I went down to see if I could find anything. It felt wrong to let you

miss the opportunity to get some answers. Luck, or God, or Providence, was with me and the file wasn't buried too deep. Almost as if it was waiting for me, if you like. You see, I wasn't completely up front with you. I was in your class or maybe the one after it. I remember you warning me about skinning my knee and then I did. It was weird, but it kept you lodged in my memory after all these years. I wasn't Sister Beatrice then. I was Karen.

At any rate, let me know what you want me to do with this file. I haven't looked in it. But I will if you want me to. Yours in faith, Sr. Beatrice Johnson

A tingling starts in Ruby's palms. A zizzing. The Hitchhiker presses her skull more firmly into Ruby's hands. Images flood; she sees the world as if a child looking up at a chair she cannot climb up into. She sees knees, table legs. This is the Hitchhiker's world view, always looking up, until she looks down and suddenly Ruby is filled with the idea of grass and water and the scratchy feel of pavement. "You want to go out?"

"Yes, please."

"Why don't you ask me like a normal dog? Go to the door and bark?"

"I don't have to."

"I love you."

"I love you back." The Hitchhiker jumps off Ruby's lap.

This last exchange is both spoken—her—and scented with something vaguely stinky but clearly pleasant in the dog's mind.

Boy meets them outside, greets them exuberantly as is his habit, as if he had had no hope of ever seeing them again. The summer evening has become cottony with humidity, Ruby can taste it on her tongue. The dogs disappear into the darker reaches of the cluttered yard and she stands by herself, possessed by a kind of inertia. She should call the Hitchhiker to her, prop the bed back into its couch position, unplug the cord connecting her to Bull's outside outlet. Check her wallet to see if she has to make a quick ATM run and then turn toward the highway. These are actions that she has executed a million times; she has almost no need to think about them, they are reflexive, comfortable even. But the thick night air holds her still.

A tiny button of red appears on Bull's back porch. She can hear his deep inhale, his noisy exhale, his cough. If she stands very still, he won't know she's out here, but Ruby moves toward the porch. "Evening, Bull."

"Hey, Ruby. Just givin' Boy last call."

"The Hitch is out there with him. I'm just hoping it isn't a skunk they're so interested in." Ruby joins Bull on his porch.

"They're smart enough to stay clear."

There is so much on her mind that Ruby has a hard time keeping up the gentle banter, the neighborly chitchat. Ruby feels the buildup of emotional steam rising past being able to keep her news to herself. In a weak moment Ruby had found herself telling Bull and Polly about her sudden interest in finding out more, about her origins. "I got an email tonight. My file is sitting on a nun's desk right now. In Canada. I need to go get it."

"That's good news, isn't it?"

"Don't I sound like it's good news?"

Bull sails his cigarette butt to the dirt at the foot of his steps. "What do you hope will come out of that file?"

"I don't know if *hope* is the word. Maybe *fear* or *worry* is better."

"When I was eighteen, and they were pullin' numbers for the draft, I found myself hopin' that they'd pull mine; it would be my ticket out of here and away. And in the same breath I was knee-knockin' shaking that they would. I didn't want to die, but I didn't want to stay here."

"You were called up?"

"Nope, my number was so high there was almost no way I'd be drafted. So I joined up."

"And you survived."

"I suppose. Point is, sometimes things are scary. But necessary if you want to get on with life." Bull shakes another cigarette out of the pack. "This is your draft number. Or your chance to volunteer. I think that you'd regret leaving that file on the desk."

"You were desperate to leave Harmony Farms, but you came back."

"Lots scarier things out there than having a crazy old man. Plus, I had a girl waiting for me here."

"At least you knew who your old man was."

"Well, there may have been a paternity test involved, but he did the right thing in the end. Just never really accepted me."

Ruby studies Bull in the gloaming, sees the youth he might once have been. "Mine never tried."

"Go get that file."

Ruby nods, calls the Hitchhiker, and heads down the porch steps

"Hey, you want me to go with you?"

Ruby pictures Bull's bulk in the passenger seat, the yellow dog and the Hitchhiker sharing the back bench. Not since Sabine has she traveled with anyone. Oddly, the idea doesn't appall her as much as it should. "I'm good, but thanks."

"Let me know if you change your mind." He snaps his fingers and Boy bounces up the steps and into the house. The door closes.

Ruby flips up the laptop cover, opens her email with every intention of replying to Sister Beatrice that she will be heading north, when she sees that there is a new message from the former Karen Johnson.

If you'll give me your address, I'll FedEx the file to you.
+ Sr. Bea

Ruby starts to laugh. So simple. So logical. So obvious. Maybe a quest requires a journey, but in this day and age, FedEx will suffice. And any concern Ruby had that a runaway Canadian with not quite legitimate papers might find it difficult to get across the border—and then back—has been neutralized.

Bull's kitchen light is still on, so she dashes across the yard to knock on his door. "If I can stay a bit longer, and if you're willing to let me use your address, that file can come to me."

"I'd rather take a road trip, but sure: 1806 Poor Farm Road." Bull shrugs, pulls open the screen door. "And you know that you're welcome to stay as long as you like."

That settled, Ruby trundles back to her van, and the excitement of knowing that there is a file slowly evolves into wondering what in the world she will find in it.

In exchange for a place to sleep that is far more comfortable than the single girls' trailer or any Salvation Army bed Ruby has slept on in the past year, Madame Celestine expects chores done and a cut from every reading Ruby does. The two fortune-tellers do not compete against each other for clients; they take turns. Madame Celestine likes her nap in the afternoon, and her cocktail in the evening, so Ruby has begun taking those hours in Madame Celestine's place. It's a workable situation: Madame Celestine loses no opportunity to make a buck, and Ruby is gleaning everything she can from the woman's routines. Ruby is still young, but her psychic senses are as strong as they ever will be. So strong that Madame Celestine begins to fret that Ruby is stealing her thunder, that clients who have heard of this child wonder are waiting for her to vacate the tent and for Ruby to enter it. In the end, Celestine figures that she can certainly capitalize on Ruby's talent and popularity with very little effort. She begins to introduce Ruby as her protégée. She begins to say things like: "I've never had a daughter, but if I did, I'd hope she would be like you." Even the suggestion that Celestine feels a bit maternal toward her is enough to relax Ruby's guard. She doesn't ask if Celestine is referring to herself or to her talents.

From county to county, the carnival moves, an erratic wagon train with no certain destination. In each location, Ruby helps Celestine set up her booth, and makes sure the tea-pot is clean and the tea leaves are within reach. The tablecloth smooth, the chairs aligned perfectly so that Madame Celestine can comfortably reach across the table to grasp a client's hand. Ruby shills for Madame Celestine, sometimes beckoning to passing carnival goers to hear their fortunes, sometimes pre-tending to be having her fortune read. "Oh, Madame Celes-tine," Ruby would say, reaching into that actor's bag of tricks Maggie Dean taught her. "A boyfriend and a winning lottery ticket? How wonderful." Sometimes Madame Celestine had to whisper to Ruby to take her acting down a notch. "You don't get any Oscar nominations for this. Just look happy."

As fall became early winter the carnival wended its way toward Florida. "What happens when we get there?" Ruby is ironing Celestine's better caftan.

"We stop."

Ruby's pressure on the flimsy fabric increases. Madame Celestine notices and comes up beside Ruby. She touches her on the chin, turns her head to meet her eyes. "If you're wondering, no, I don't have any intention of giving up my protégée."

If only Ruby's real mother had felt the same way. The Hitchhiker leans her whole weight against Ruby's back as she thinks about that long-ago part of her life, of that brief period when she thought she had found her place in the world. Images and memories she rarely allows herself to visit.

The psychic vibe coming now from the dog is pleasant, commiserative. A comfort as Ruby cuts the reverie off before she falls off the dark edge of how it ended.

"Be present," says the dog with her nose pushing against Ruby's shoulder. "Be with me now."

17

In the dream Ruby is standing outside of a door. It is an interior door, perhaps a bedroom door or the door to a cellar. She knows, in her dream, that her mother is standing on the other side of that door. She can hear a quiet rustling, as if her mother is wearing crinolines or taffeta. Every time Ruby's dream-self reaches for the doorknob, it moves. She tries to catch it in both hands, and it disappears. She wakes, realizing that she needed to dream her mother into opening the door.

"Hi, Ruby," Granddaughter Molly has liberated her mother's phone and called her. She does this occasionally, usually with some whim that needs satisfying. A game or a must-have fashion item for the tween set.

"What's up?"

There's the sound of Molly clumping up the stairs of their antique house, a door shutting. "I have a question."

Maybe it's being a psychic, maybe more being a blood relative, but Ruby hears the question before Molly can ask it. *Is it normal to know things before they happen?*

"Is it normal for me to know things about people before they do?"

"Have you asked your mother?" Sabine has always been close-mouthed about her skills in front of the children.

"She said that sometimes people get feelings. It doesn't mean anything."

"Did she say, 'people like us'?"

"Not exactly, but I don't know anyone else who knew that my friend Grace would get sick. I saw, Ruby. I saw her blood in my mind. It was bumpy."

"She's very sick?"

A sigh. Maybe a sniffle, and Ruby wishes Molly had FaceTimed instead of calling. "Luke something."

Leukemia. Disease of the blood.

"Molly, the important thing to understand is that you might have predicted Grace's illness, but it was already there. You didn't cause it."

"I know. I just got scared when my mind told me this and then it happened."

"I'm glad you called me. You know that both your mother and I have the same . . ." Ruby almost says affliction. ". . . gift."

"Kind of. Mom gets kind of weird if you call her on it."

"And you do know what I do for a living."

"You tell fortunes. For real. Like in fairy stories."

"Yes. Well, not exactly like in fairy stories, but at fairs and carnivals and even parties."

"Ruby?"

She knows the question before Molly asks. No big deal for a woman blessed with second sight. "I was your age when I knew. Your mom was too. It's who we are."

"No, I knew that. I just want to know if we're witches."

"Heavens no!"

Ruby hears Sabine hollering up the stairs for Molly to get a move on. Off to some organized activity no doubt. Molly signs off with a quick thank-you and I love you and is gone. The phone against Ruby's cheek is hot.

At the very least, Molly will never have to figure out this "gift" for herself.

Assuming that Sister Bea will send the file off first thing Monday morning, and assuming that she won't send it overnight but by regular business, Ruby won't allow herself to become anxious about the file's arrival until Wednesday morning. In the meantime, it's Saturday and the Makers Faire awaits.

Over the past few weeks, the number of booths set up has begun to increase and Ruby's tent is now flanked by a hat maker and yet another herbalist. This one specializes in lavender, and Ruby can smell it even before she arrives at her spot. It reminds her of the scent of old women, but she supposes that's only because of the connection to the play, *Lavender and Old Lace.*

She greets the milliner, admires her array of hats, many of which are wide-brimmed and decorated with dried flowers. Very hippy, Ruby thinks. The milliner also has cloches on display and Ruby sort of wishes that she was a hat person, someone who could carry off wearing a cloche. Someone who wore the right coat and had the right shoes for such a hat. On her other side, Ruby says hello to the lavender lady and tries not to inhale too deeply.

Ruby gets the tent up, admires the little row of stitches she's put into the tear in the tent wall, satisfied that it should hold up awhile longer. She's been looking online for a new tent, feeling a bit like a traitor. This old girl has been a part of Ruby's life, her routine, for so long, she fancies it is an old friend, a guardian. The holder of secrets. How should she honor it when the time comes to replace it? She feels the same way about the Westfalia. It's sentimental, not logical. There's no explaining it, no excusing it. Ruby runs a finger down the length of the repair and sighs. If her old tent and her old bus quit on her, she'll be bereft.

The Hitchhiker bumps up against the back of Ruby's knees. "You have me."

"Yes, I do." She scoops the dog up into her arms, never mind the dog hair embedding itself against her brocade caftan. She'll wear it with pride.

The air seems lighter, the atmosphere around the tents and trailers and canopies cheerier somehow, and Ruby realizes that Cynthia Mann is nowhere to be seen. She will not invoke the name of her nemesis for fear of making her appear in a puff of brimstone smoke, but she does wonder where the heck she is. It doesn't feel like Cynthia will suddenly jump out at her; it feels like a delightful absence. As if in recognition of that, her booth has been busy all morning, the cup of coffee she started with is untouched and cold. Fully half, maybe more, of the clients have been there for their dogs. She's done more translating of canine concerns than predicting of future love. A nice change. She's come to love touching these animals, feeling the soft fur, the bony skulls. The hiss and zizz of thought and feelings. The basic necessities they all come desiring—affection and kindness. A human hand laid out in hers never feels as accurate. The things she envisions for the dogs come to her so much more easily than the forecasting images she gets for humans. Maybe because dogs live so much in the present; humans, not so much.

Finally Ruby gets a break, slips off her caftan, hangs up her decorative BACK SOON sign and snaps the Hitchhiker's leash to her harness. The pair circumnavigate the grounds, stretching their legs, letting the dog relieve herself, deciding which food truck to patronize. Ruby sees Polly's animal control truck alongside the western edge of the park. Polly is in line at the burger truck. If Ruby knows anything about her friend, she's pretty certain Polly will be asking for leftovers for her guests at the shelter. She joins her in the line.

Lunch in hand, the two ladies snag a park bench. The Hitchhiker keeps making little muttering sounds, trying to look like she's not begging, but willing to be a help cleaning up leftovers. Ruby has been firm about not feeding the little dog people food, but sometimes a bite of hamburger just happens to fall to the ground.

Around a mouthful of burger, Polly says, "Got a call the other day. Missing dog."

"Can I help?"

"Possibly." Polly swallows, wipes her lips with her paper napkin, doesn't look at Ruby.

My life is in what happens in front of me, not behind. I don't think about what came before, how it made me feel. I think about the here and now. The closest I come to understanding the future is knowing that if Ruby puts on her big dress, we go to the place where she touches other people and dogs and makes them feel good. If the sun is gone, I know that dinner is possible. If the lady who smells like lots of other dogs and even cats shows up, something usually happens.

But having said that, I can admit that I remember the past. I remember it in images that sometimes come to mind because of a scent or a sound or the sight of a crate. I remember grooming and trotting alongside a tall man who taught me how to "stack," how to tolerate long rides in a crate. How to be a winner. The humans all say that we know when we've won. It's true. There's a pleasant air of approval that comes with winning. And sometimes special treats. Then it starts again. But we also know when we haven't won. And the air around that is heavy with disapproval. That first tall man went away, and a short fat woman began to show me. But she had no stamina for the long trots around the ring and soon handed me over to yet another human. This one made some mistake and we were sent from the ring even before the ribbons were handed out. And that's when my life changed.

Polly says, "Ruby. The dog described sounds a lot like your dog."

Ruby crumples up the remains of her burger, now just bun, and jams it into the paper bag. "Her person is gone."

"I know, she told you." Polly doesn't sound the least bit cynical.

"Whoever had her died. Of that I am certain."

"You are correct. That's the story the caller gave me."

The Hitchhiker has jumped onto the bench, made herself comfortable on Ruby's lap. Her muzzle is draped over Ruby's arm. She sighs. Ruby is filled with florid images, bright clouds of an unfamiliar odor, part perfume, part offal. She almost puts the dog off her lap; it is almost too much to receive this kind of information. Within a moment, the images resolve to a deep sense of needing to run. Of needing to be gone. She isn't sure if it's the dog's thoughts or her own.

Polly doesn't seem to notice that Ruby isn't listening as she relates a story about adult children finding their elderly mother dead on the kitchen floor in her house, where she had been for some time. Apparently there was a clause in the adoption agreement stipulating that the dog go back to the breeder if the owner was unable to care for her. Unfortunately, the dog had vanished in all the drama.

"Ruby, the Hitchhiker might be this dog."

"What evidence do you have?"

"Tricolor Cavalier King Charles spaniel. That's what's gone missing; that's what you've got."

"And I imagine that there are any number of similar dogs circulating." Ruby sets the dog back on the ground. Stands up, brushes off her front.

"Gone missing pretty much the same week that you arrived."

Ruby gathers the leash into both hands. "You don't know that."

"I do. You've told me."

"No proof."

"She's microchipped."

Ruby sits back down. How come she hadn't seen this coming? Why hadn't she consulted her own cards? She had, but it had been in such a narrow way, focused on what direction to take, when to leave, when to stay. She hadn't seen loss.

18

The Carerra Brothers Carnival had one more stop before they headed to winter over in Florida, like migratory birds, or retired northerners. It was only mid-October, and they were far enough south that the air still held a summer feel to it. Sticky. Charged. Ruby is alone in the RV, washing the lunch dishes, when Buck bangs open the RV's screen door and walks in. At over six feet and with a thick body builder frame, he fills the available space. His muscle shirt is drenched with sweat from the heavy lifting of setting up the rides. He is pungent and Ruby wrinkles her nose as he reaches above her head to take down a glass from the cupboard. Does she imagine that he leans closer to her than necessary?

Buck is back to living in the RV, his girlfriend of the season having given him the heave-ho upon discovering she could no longer tolerate his serial flirting with the other carny girls or the hot-to-trot carnival goers all dressed in their short shorts and flouncy midriff-baring tops. This has meant that Ruby has moved from the alcove bed to the couch, that her night is often interrupted by Buck coming in late or finding his way to the miniscule bathroom, where she can hear every sound he makes. She hopes that he finds a new girlfriend soon. She likes living with Madame Celestine, but Buck's presence has altered the dynamic. She is no longer the favored child; she is back to being the boarder. Celestine dotes on her son and makes no apology for it. He is the son of her long-lost lover, her constant reminder of a short period of happiness in her life. Ruby is uncertain if the man died or if he, like so many of these carny types, just vanished.

"How's it going, Ruby Tuesday?" Buck thinks it's funny to call her that, humming a few bars of the Rolling Stones song. "Who could hang a name blah blah blah."

"Fine."

"Girl of few words, aren't you, Ruby Tuesday?"

Ruby has watched the other girls enjoy Buck's teasing, using it as an excuse to touch him, to go all Southern Belle, and giggle. It's something Ruby views with disdain. She cannot see herself acting demur, acting like a brainless Barbie doll just to attract gross attention. What man falls for that anyway? At some point this year she turned fifteen, but Ruby feels more like she skipped right over youth and has landed in adulthood.

"My mom treating you okay?"

"Yeah. Good."

"Teaching you a lot?" Buck reaches into the tiny fridge and pours himself a glass of milk. He leans against the counter where Ruby stands over the sink. His hip touches hers and she moves away. "You making her some good money?"

"I guess."

His hip follows hers. He stinks of sweat and cigarettes. When his hip touches hers again she sees him as he will be in a few short years and it isn't a pretty picture. Like some men, he has peaked too soon. Too early for his essential good looks to last. She sees in her vision a Buck who still thinks he's beautiful when in fact he will be a caricature of what he is now. A man who will never get it that women not only don't find him attractive, but he has slid into repulsiveness. As Ruby pulls the sink stopper and rinses her hands, she is filled with the certainty that his degradation from hunk to has-been will be the outward manifestation of a disturbed act. He will forfeit his beauty with his already extant inner ugliness.

And, already, she understands that she will be the instrument.

Ruby's first impulse is to pack up her tent and blow town. There's no way she's going to give up her dog. Yes, her dog. It's been weeks, most of the summer, and Ruby can't imagine not having the companionship of the Hitchhiker. If she had a permanent address, she would even have gotten the dog a license. Maybe she can fudge things a bit and use Bull's address to establish her residency. Lie a little. Something that Ruby is quite good at.

Polly's hand on her arm keeps Ruby seated on the park bench. "Let's just confirm things at the vet's. Maybe she isn't the dog they're looking for. . . ."

"They lost her. They left her out on the street to fend for herself." This is a rough interpretation of the story the dog herself told her. A story without words, only images and scents.

"Possibly. But the important thing is that you have taken good care of her. Maybe the breeder will let you keep her." Polly's tone is hardly convincing.

"You really believe that a breeder with a return stipulation will let an itinerant fortune-teller keep this dog?"

Polly doesn't give Ruby an answer.

"All right. Better to be fully informed than operate out of ignorance." Ruby stands up, lobs her crumpled paper bag into a trash receptacle. "But I've got to finish out the day here. I'll meet you at, where?"

Polly gives Ruby the address of the local vet, Dr. Amanda Davios. "I'll let her know that you're coming. Right after two, okay?"

It feels like Polly has her hands around Ruby's throat and is squeezing. "I'll be there."

Needless to say, Ruby can't concentrate enough on her clients to get any kind of authentic read, so she spends the rest of the afternoon making stuff up, relying on forty years of telling fortunes, most of which are the psychic's equivalent of "take two aspirin and call me in the morning." Yes, good luck will follow bad. Yes, the future object of your affection is just around the corner. No, don't take that trip.

The Hitchhiker doesn't retreat to her bed as usual but tucks herself up under Ruby's floor-length caftan and on Ruby's feet. Of course the dog knows something's up. Something is not right. Ruby's mind is filled with good-case scenarios and bad. Mostly bad. Even while running her forefinger along life lines, shuffling her deck of tarot cards, brewing tea, Ruby's thoughts are running toward the "what ifs": what if she just runs off? She certainly has a history of being successful doing that. Then again, what if the dog isn't the one who's gone missing? Would she then feel like a fugitive (again) and for no good reason? Should she get confirmation that the dog *is* the dog being sought and then run away? Ruby recognizes that she's getting wound up. Why can't she put her psychic powers to good use for herself and give herself some advice?

Ruby closes up shop before anyone else can approach her booth. As fast as she can, she folds the tent, packs up the table and the teapot. Shoves everything into the van without caring where it goes. She can straighten things up later. The dog is already inside, sitting upright on the bench seat, spaniel eyes following Ruby's every move. She keeps yawning, a dog's way of releasing anxiety. Is it Ruby making her anxious, or is it some canine intuition that she is vulnerable? That their partnership is vulnerable?

As soon as Ruby gets into the front seat, the dog hops onto the passenger seat, places her forepaws on the dashboard. Barks. It's as if she's urging Ruby to get going. Ruby's hand actually trembles as she pokes the ignition key into the slot, missing it twice before inserting it. Twisting it. Hearing the rear engine grumble. Her heart is pounding and suddenly it feels exactly like it did in that moment so long ago when she picked up her schoolbag filled with socks and underwear and little else and ducked out the window and down the fire escape to run away from the convent.

No, this is more like that desperate moment when she slipped out of Madame Celestine's trailer and took off into the night. A runaway again. And, this time, a thief.

How serious will this breeder be about recovering the Hitchhiker? Will she press charges, incite a manhunt? It's one thing to be able to blend into a population alone; a distinctive, attention-attracting dog at her side might make that impossible. Ruby slips the van into neutral. Shuts it off. "Talk to me." She gathers the dog onto her lap, presses her cheek against the dog's skull. The little dog presses her muzzle against Ruby. The zizzing and vibrations start immediately. Clouds of flavor and scent; pine and red. The confused senses eventually coalesce into thoughts, pixels becoming images.

The first memory/image that comes to mind is that of the nice lady. She is different from everyone else I know, and I instinctively know not to jump on her. She is fragile. But very, very happy to have me in her house. I have not been a dog in a human house. I have been a dog in a crate going from one place to another until that day when we left the ring. I have a memory/image of the scent of that handler, that day. The scent of anger and disappointment. This day I get the scent of a new job. Although I am brushed, I am not groomed. There is a distinction. Although I am walked, I am not required to stack. The old woman teaches me new tricks. I learn to sit up and beg. Humiliating, perhaps for some, but I get a kick out of it. I listen endlessly to words that have no meaning to me, but understand that it is my job to take them in. My chief job, though, is to be *with* her. This does not have to be taught.

Having no sense of time, I can't say how long we were together, long enough for several seasons to pass. Long enough for me to observe that there were changes with her that did not bode well. My nose identified internal problems, a subtle whiff of trouble against which I could not warn her. So, when she cried in the night, I simply pressed myself closer.

The second memory/image that is provoked out of my mind as Ruby holds me is the old woman, but her body is down where it shouldn't be. We are there together for enough time to pass that I am pretty sure I will also die. My water bowl is empty. My food behind a door I cannot scratch open as hard as I try. I am humiliated in having to relieve myself on the rug in front of the back door. Moment by moment the air around me thickens with decay. The sounds that signal the passing of the days continue: the sound of the bus that takes the children from the neighborhood. The sound of it returning them. The sound of the mail dropping through the slot once a day. I bark, hoping that the mail carrier will understand that I'm not defending the house, which is what I was usually doing, but asking for help. The voices from the television endlessly repeating words I do not understand.

The third memory/image is of the front door opening, a voice calling, a shriek, and so much confusion that I don't even greet these people. I stand aside until someone notices me. I can feel the rush of air behind me as my tail takes on a life of its own. But they don't speak to me, shove me aside. In all my life I've never been ignored so thoroughly. I did the only thing I could do: I ran. I went in search of you.

If the story lacks clarity, which being constructed of the gossamer threads of senses and instincts, it does, it is still clear enough in Ruby's mind that she weeps into the soft fur. She is filled with the illusion that she herself had been in that house, knew that woman, couldn't comprehend her death and was trapped until unthinking, grieving children arrived and she made her escape. Ruby pulls her cheek away from the dog, wipes her eyes. The images shimmer and fade. The dog shifts on her lap and jumps across to the other seat. Shakes, sneezes.

It is a little after two o'clock. Ruby knows that Polly will text her in five minutes if she doesn't show up at the vet's office, which is less than half a mile away. Even taking her time packing up she would still have to work hard at being late. She wonders a little that Polly hadn't specifically sought her out with this information, that it had been a—presumably—chance encounter at the Faire. Or maybe Ruby's just reading a little too much into Polly wanting to have lunch before dropping a bomb on her friend. Friend. Okay, those have been few and far between in her life. It's been one of the high points of this unscheduled sojourn in Harmony Farms. Not quite on the same scale as suddenly being able to read the minds of animals, but pretty nice.

"Okay. No sense running off if this is a false alarm." But Ruby is certain that it is not.

The office of Amanda Davios, DVM, is an unassuming clapboard-sided one-story building painted white. Green shutters flank the picture window and a green and white-striped awning hangs over the double front door stenciled with the business name, Harmony Farms Veterinary Clinic. Polly's truck is parked in the first space by the walkway and Ruby pulls her Westfalia alongside it. There are no other cars in the parking lot. There will be no wait. The Hitchhiker noses the ground, darts for the shrubbery planted alongside the pavement and adds her signature to the invisible collection there. She's willing enough to go through the door, no hesitation; apparently she is not a dog who's afraid of the vet. No cowering here, no anticipatory dread. It's Ruby who has the heebie-jeebies, a dread of outcome.

"Ruby." Polly sounds just a touch surprised to see Ruby walk through the door.

"Let's get this over with." Ruby has never been a crier. A weeper. But right now she feels on the verge of bursting into tears. She pushes the urge down, hands the leash to Polly because she doesn't want to telegraph to the dog how upset she is. She needn't have bothered. The dog plants her feet and Polly has to pick her up rather than drag her into the examination room. The Hitchhiker throws Ruby a baleful glance, her confusion writ large upon her face.

Dr. Davios takes the Hitchhiker from Polly. "What a pretty little girl you are." She makes friends with the dog, all the while giving her a quick exam. "Spayed?"

Polly answers, "Don't know for sure, but if she was a retired show dog, most likely."

"So you really don't know anything about her?"

Ruby thinks but doesn't say, *Enough. I know enough.*

"I'm going on a tip that this might be a missing dog. We're really only here to see if she's got a chip. If the town would ever spring for a reader, I wouldn't have to be a bother."

"Oh, Polly, you're no bother." Dr. Davios grins. "The town would be wise to get a reader for you. I bill them. It adds up."

Ruby wishes they'd stop talking. Get on with it. Is this how death row prisoners feel while the executioner chats up the warden?

The vet picks up the microchip reader and points it between the dog's shoulders. The Hitchhiker and Ruby lock eyes. Ruby suddenly gets a whiff of roast beef, of cheese. The dog is imagining a reward at the end of this examination. A prize for being a good girl. And then the Hitchhiker reacts to Ruby's own thinking. She begins to scramble on the slippery surface of the exam table, nearly launches herself off except that Dr. Davios is an experienced hand at keeping little dogs on the table. "Easy there, little one." She nods. "Yep. Got a number."

Ruby thinks she's going to be sick.

19

Polly hands Ruby a cup of water. Rests her other hand on Ruby's back, rubs it a little, like a mother might rub the back of a heartbroken child. "I wish it hadn't been so."

Ruby nods. She's got the Hitchhiker, whose name is actually Cross Cut Roundelay, on her lap and the dog is pressing herself into Ruby as if she is trying to hide. Ruby is getting no vibes from her, no thoughts, no scents or images. It's as if hearing her real name has broken the spell. She'd cocked her head when Polly said her name, Roundelay. Daughter of Champion Cross Cut Roundabout by Champion Cross Cut Round Robin out of Champion Delta Dickens. The Hitchhiker, as Ruby will continue to call her until the moment the dog is wrested from her care, is not a champion. All of this Polly has gotten from the dog's breeder in a six-minute phone call. Polly had made the call immediately, and Ruby knew that it was the old rip-the-band-aid method of getting it over with rather than anything more protracted. In a less than charitable notion, she wondered briefly if Polly was throwing up a deterrent against Ruby running off with the dog. Now the breeder knows who has her.

"What happens next?" Ruby crumples the paper cup. Tells herself to pull herself together and does.

"I don't have the budget to drive all the way across the state to deliver the dog so I'm not sure."

"Across the state? I thought someone local had her."

"Yes, she was here in Harmony Farms, but the breeder . . ." Polly checks the note in her hand. "Mrs. Cross." She pauses. "Huh, hence the Cross Cut kennel name. The breeder is in Stockbridge. Well, Mrs. Cross will have to arrange something."

This gives Ruby a flicker of something that's not quite hope. "But she will stay with me until such time. Right." Not a question.

Polly nods. "I don't see why not." But even as she says it, Polly grasps Ruby by the wrist. "And you'll be staying in Harmony Farms until such time. Right."

Ruby has been a professional liar for so many years she knows that she can lie, even to this friend of hers, and not only be believed, but not even feel badly about it. But there is something else that keeps her from lying to Polly and bolting for parts unknown. Her FedEx package. "I will."

If the package with her file arrives before the breeder can arrange for the Hitchhiker to be picked up, well then, all promises are null and void.

The Hitchhiker is as subdued as Ruby and doesn't even sniff at the shrubbery as they head to the van. She hops in, jumps onto the bench seat, circles three times and tucks her nose under her tail as if exhausted by far more than a visit to the vet. Ruby wishes she could curl up beside her there. Instead she grinds the gearshift into reverse and pulls away without saying anything more to Polly.

Ruby holes up for the rest of the day in her van, now back in its spot in Bull's side yard. Despite the warmth, she keeps the door shut and puts the screens in the sliding windows to catch the breeze. She shuffles and reshuffles her second-best set of tarot cards but doesn't lay them out. She googles Cross Cut Cavaliers. The Hitchhiker leans over her shoulder as she studies the charming images of adult dogs and the adorable ones of puppies. The dog woofs softly, acknowledging

the photographs in the same way she identifies dogs in television programs. Ruby doesn't for a single moment entertain the notion that the
dog is recognizing individuals as her littermates or her parents. She
always barks at pictures of animals. Ruby clicks on the contact button, pulls down the email address, a phone number. Polly didn't say
anything about not talking to Mrs. Cross. In her role as dog officer, of
course Polly would assume that she would be the contact person. What
if? Ruby sits back and the Hitchhiker climbs onto her lap. What if she
pleads her case to the breeder directly? Would a woman with a name
like *Cross* be receptive to Ruby's heartwarming tale of falling in love
with this dog? For, Ruby realizes, that is exactly what has happened.
With the exception of her family, this is the only sentient being Ruby
can honestly say she loves.

Ruby's cell phone chimes, pulling her away from her thoughts.
Sabine calling a day earlier than usual. Their conversations tend to
occur on Sunday nights, just before the kids are bustled off to bed.
What Sabine calls that golden hour between intensive weekend activity and starting to think about what needs to happen in the upcoming
week. She never sounds exasperated.

Sabine, never one for prevarication, jumps right in. "I'm getting a
pretty strong sense that all is not well. Are you okay?"

"I love it when you think of me."

"Mom, what's going on? I keep getting vibes about discovery. But
today I'm hit with a sense of loss." Sabine must be really concerned;
she almost never addresses Ruby as "Mom."

"You are very good at what you are. How's Molly coping with her
new skills?"

"Stop. Talk."

The Hitchhiker shoves her head under Ruby's chin, kisses her
cheek. "Something wonderful and something not so much. There is
a file with my name, well, my old name, on it winging its way to me
here from Sacred Heart, and Polly Schaeffer, my friend the dog officer,
has discovered that my dog . . ."—yes, the Hitchhiker is *her* dog—"is

supposed to go back to her breeder because the person who had her died." Ruby feels herself choke on the words and isn't sure she's actually gotten them out of her mouth.

There is a pause, a breath. "Okay, first things first. What's in the file?"

"I don't know. I'm not even sure what I'm hoping to find, except that it might bring me a little closer to understanding how it is that we all have this, for lack of a better word, talent."

"Okay. Second thing. Can't you just keep the dog? I know how much she means to you."

Over the weeks the dog has been in her life, Ruby has sent Sabine and the kids pictures of her posing in front of the van, or in the van, curled up. Sitting in the passenger seat like she's giving directions. Bright eyed and photogenic. Sabine once remarked, a little acerbically, that she could never recall Ruby ever having taken so many candids of her. Ruby reminded Sabine that cameras weren't quite as handy in those days, and film was expensive. "You're right. I'm going to talk to the breeder myself. It's just that I'm afraid that my lifestyle might not work for her."

Another pause, another beat. Ruby knows where this will go. Any time that Ruby encounters a difficulty, or makes a complaint about something, Sabine's default is to say *Stop. Stop traveling; stop being the roaming fortune-teller. Stay put. Stay here.* Maybe this time she'll say yes.

Indeed, Sabine does say, "You know the answer to that problem. Listen, I don't have any advice, but I'm here if you want to talk. Well, actually we're heading out to dinner with friends, but you know what I mean."

"I do. And, Beenie, thank you for calling. For knowing that something was off kilter. You really don't have to worry about me, but I'm glad you do."

"Let me know what you actually find out from the file. After all, whoever she was, your mother was my grandmother."

"Did I say that's what I was hoping for?"
"You didn't have to."

It is so warm that Ruby just throws a light sheet over herself and settles
on the bench seat without unfolding it into a proper bed. She's short
enough that she can stretch out. Despite the heat, the dog is beside her
and Ruby falls asleep stroking her soft fur.

In the dream Ruby is waiting for the arrival of a Greyhound bus.
She is in a cavernous space, and she needs to find the right dock. She
is walking down the middle of a ramp. She is a young girl and is wearing tattered Keds on her feet. Bus after bus pass her by, stopping and
disgorging its passengers. Ruby doesn't know who she's meeting but
knows that none of these people, all of whom are dressed in business
attire, is the one. Finally a bus moves past her, close enough she feels
a draft of air. Suddenly she has to run, desperate to catch the fast-
moving vehicle. She knows that this is the right bus. That whoever
gets off of it will be the one she is looking for. She is out of breath,
running with arms flailing, Keds falling off her feet. The bus comes
to a stop. Masses of people debark, more than any real bus could ever
hold. Ruby approaches the door and it closes with a snap. The dream
Ruby bangs on it and it creaks open. Standing on the stairs is a woman's
shape. Faceless, it drifts toward Ruby, glides over her. Vanishes.

Ruby wakes in a sweat. Gathers herself, grabs the glass of water she's
set on the table. Says out loud, "If I were an interpreter of dreams, I'd have
to say that one was pretty significant. Although . . ." She strokes the dog,
who is clearly puzzled at this midnight wakefulness. "It was a pretty trite
one." She slips back under the sheet, closes her eyes, and hopes that her
mother will begin to take a more substantial shape once that file arrives.

It had been such a good day yesterday, at least until Polly showed up
with her disheartening news, that Ruby decides she'll spend the next

couple of days at the Dew Drop. She can use a shower and a change
of scenery. She knocks on Bull's back door to thank him and let him
know where she will be and asks if she can come back on Tuesday just
to wait for her package. Tuesday being optimistic, she knows.

Boy pushes past Bull's legs to get outside to greet the Hitchhiker.
Noses meet, tails swish, the little dog practically crawls under the
big one to gain the best sniffing advantage. Greetings accomplished,
they bound off to where the edge of Bull's property meets the scrubby
woods.

"Yeah, that's fine. Great," Bull says, scrapes his Red Wing boot
against the step trying to dislodge something. "I heard what happened, what Polly did."

"She's only doing her job, Bull. I don't blame her."

"She's pretty upset by all of it."

Ruby shrugs. "Yeah. Me too."

With an awkward but gentle pat on her shoulder, Bull conveys
his sympathy and Ruby finds herself comforted by his shy gesture.
"When I was going through a rough patch, back when the boys were
little, Polly was very good to them, to me." Bull coughs, reaches for a
cigarette, and then thinks better of it.

"I'm not mad at Polly. She's still my friend." Ruby is just going to try
to avoid her for as long as possible, but she doesn't say that.

Ravi was thrilled to see her back, and also offered his thoughts on Polly's actions.

"How did you know?" Is Ravi a psychic as well as a concierge?

He gives her one of his sweet smiles and laughs. "Polly has been
talking to anyone and everyone. I heard it at the coffee shop from
Carrie Farr."

Ravi bends over to give the Hitchhiker a pat. "You should see if you
can keep her. She belongs to you."

"She does." As if they have agreed to a pact, Ruby sticks out her hand to shake on it. Ravi takes hers and then covers it with his other hand. "Go for it."

If everyone seems to think this will work, who is she to believe otherwise? Even if her own psychic senses are telling quite another story.

A long shower beforehand soothes away the tension from Ruby's shoulders. When she comes out of the tiny bathroom, the dog is ensconced on the bed, always happy to be at the Dew Drop. "Okay, no more waiting. Let's make a call." The dog's feathery tail beats an encouraging tattoo on the coverlet.

The kennel may be located in the last town in Massachusetts, but it is not all that far if she thinks about it. Sixty, seventy-five miles, if that, from where she is now. A couple hours' drive. What if, instead of making her case over the phone, Ruby just showed up? Presented herself as the dog's best option. There's no way that file folder with her history is going to show up before Tuesday, at best. If she started now, she could be there and back by dinner tonight. Assuming the Westie holds together.

A dark vision clouds her mind. A long drive home without the dog.

20

The carnival moved one more time before packing in the season and everyone heading to Florida to their winter homes. At the last location, Madame Celestine had Buck pull the RV a little ways away from the rest of the carny trailers. She'd had a tiff with two of the midway vendors, complaining that they were encroaching on her space with their noisy games of chance. "How am I supposed to give a discreet reading when all anyone can hear is their bells and whistles?" Management, as she always referred to the Carerra brothers, was of no help. It was bad enough to hear all that ruckus in the midway, but she was damned if she was going to suffer with their rowdy after-hours noises too.

On her way back to the RV after her own session in the tent, Ruby was stopped by one of the girls she had shared a trailer with back before Madame Celestine's arrival. Judy, fair-haired, a few years past youthful beauty, was a freelance shill, attracting passersby to any ride or game of chance whose operator was buying her beer. "Ruby, just a word to the wise." Judy took Ruby's elbow in a hand slightly sticky with the filth of working in a carnival.

"About?"

"Buck. Don't find yourself alone with him." A recommendation that was, given her living arrangements, totally impractical.

"Hard to avoid but thank you. I'm fine."

Judy let go of Ruby's elbow. "Seriously, he can be a charmer. A snake charmer."

Ruby took Judy's hand and turned it over. Ran her forefinger along Judy's life line. "I see a turning point for you. The choice you make now will open a new path for you."

Judy pulled her hand out of Ruby's. "Hokum. But thanks. As it happens, I am thinking about not moving on with the carnival."

"I don't think that you'll regret it." Ruby clapped her hands together as if she'd been doing manual labor. "I'll be careful." As she walked toward the RV, Ruby reflected on how worldly she'd become since that moment she decided to run from the orphanage. Maybe worldly isn't the word; maybe it's having lost her naïveté. The facts of life had been parceled out in increments, and the overarching lesson was that the human female body was treacherous and sinful. Now in the company of rougher folk, she understood that pleasure in whatever form it takes is a reward for life's struggles. She no longer felt shocked by anything she saw or heard. And she knew that Judy was right—Buck could become a problem if she didn't have the protection of Madame Celestine. Buck might be a Romeo outside of the RV, but inside, he was his mother's little boy.

The RV was empty. Madame Celestine nowhere to be found and Buck still on the grounds. Ruby was sweaty beneath her heavy caftan and decided that she'd sneak in a shower. Madame Celestine was a nag about using too much water. Ruby would make it quick. Her benefactor would never know. The tiny bathroom was stinky. The holding tank was nearly full, and the septic odor wafted up. Ruby didn't wait for the water to get hot before jumping into the shower stall. She soaped, shampooed, and rinsed in less than five minutes. She carefully wiped down the walls. It wasn't late, but Ruby pulled on her only nightgown, the label inside the collar declaring it the property of the Sacred Heart Convent and School for Girls.

Settled on the banquette with a peanut butter and jelly sandwich, Ruby thumbed through an outdated *Newsweek* until she couldn't keep her eyes open any longer. Madame Celestine was still out, so she left a lamp on and made up her bed, climbed into it. Buck had been nosing around one of the food vendor girls whose boyfriend had broken up with her so Ruby didn't think she'd hear from Buck. All in all, it felt nice to be alone.

It was the scent of alcohol that woke her. Fumes and the weight of the man who breathed them into her face. Ruby fought Buck as he took her hand and put it on his erection. "Girls like that. You should like that."

"No. Get off. Stop." Ruby thrashed, but that seemed only to make Buck more aroused.

"You can't tell me I'm your first." Buck's glee was evident. "Lucky me!"

"You're hurting me. I can't breathe." And she finally figured out that if she just let it happen it would be over with and she could breathe again.

A couple of thrusts and it was all over. Buck pulled himself away and buttoned up.

"You need to practice."

"And you need to watch out. Your mother will kill you."

Buck laughed, leaned over, and smacked Ruby gently in the face. "Don't bet on it. It's better for you if you don't say anything because she'll throw you out."

Ruby pushed herself upright and got to her feet. There was something powerful moving through her, more powerful even than fear or anger. She could feel the blood on the back of her nightgown. She throbbed where he had penetrated her. A sensation like rushing water rose from her deepest parts to her heart. She felt as if she was filling up with a potency stronger than any psychic vision she had ever experienced. Buck's malignity had caused something to be released in her. She barely reached Buck's shoulder, but she drew herself up as if she towered over him. She pointed. "I curse you. I curse you. I curse you."

"I'm the fortune-teller's son. I know bullshit when I hear it and all of it is bullshit."

"Not this time."

Monday morning. Does Ruby dare to email Sister Bea and ask if she's sent the file yet? Would she be perceived as being pesty? Should she offer to pay for next day shipping? Patience, she counsels herself. After nearly fifty-five years of not knowing anything, what's another forty-eight hours?

She has been expecting Polly's call, dreading it, so when her phone rings, Ruby feels like she's going to have a heart attack. She has been unable to bring herself to make that call to the breeder. Therefore, there is nothing left to do but wait for Polly to tell her what will happen. She pictures Polly sitting by her phone in the animal control office, also reluctant about making a phone call.

"What if I just don't answer the phone?" she says to the dog, who blinks slowly, as if considering the suggestion. But she does, looking first at the caller ID. Not Polly. It's not a number she recognizes. But she absolutely knows who it is. Ruby's mouth is as dry as paper as she answers the call.

"Is this Ruby Heartwood?" The voice is female, a little crusty. Ruby senses a woman who does not beat around the bush, and when she doesn't wait for confirmation but gets out the next sentence, Ruby knows she is right. "I'm Martha Cross and I believe you have one of my dogs."

"I love her." Her own voice croaks like an adolescent boy's.

"How'd you get her?"

"She came to me."

"There's been some suggestion that you took her."

"No. The Hitchhiker met me at Harmony Lake. The dog was look-ing for asylum. She asked to stay with me." Ruby deliberately phrases it the way it happened, despite knowing that doing so was not doing her any favors. Mrs. Cross will think she's nuts.

"Asked?"

"You know what I mean."

"I do. Cavs are particularly good at getting what they want." Mrs. Cross coughs, although it might have been a laugh. "What do you call her?"

Ruby takes a smidgeon of comfort from the way the conversa-tion is going. "The Hitchhiker. It felt like she was hitching a ride with me that day, and she's been my buddy ever since. Please let me keep her."

"My policy is that any of my dogs who need to be re homed come back to me. I've only ever had two come back, both times, like this one, because the owner passed away. I don't know you."

"I'm happy to give you references." Polly, for sure. Ravi? Carrie Farr. Maybe even Bull if Mrs. Cross doesn't meet him face to face.

"What's your living situation? I require that my dogs have healthy environments. Preferably fenced-in yards."

It would be so easy to lie, to say that she was living in a tiny house but with plenty of safe space for a dog to run. The little yellow house on North Farms Road she has so admired comes to mind. She could embellish with details borrowed from Sabine's place. Picket fence, two nice kids. Stable environment. Although Ruby has never been a phone call psychic, she's getting very strong vibes from Mrs. Cross, to the point she can almost envision her. But what she senses most is that this woman would see right through her lies. "I travel for a living, which is why the Hitchhiker is such a great companion. She's my navigator."

Well, sort of, given that Ruby has been seemingly unable to cross the
border out of town.

"The animal control officer, Ms. Schaeffer, said something about
you being psychic." The crusty tone hardens. "Working out of your
car?"

"Yes. My Westfalia, a camper. But I'm also an animal communicator. I don't know what your experience is of that, but I can tell you . . ."

"Not a believer. And I require all my dogs to have stable homes.
Flitting about the country is not conducive to a healthy environment."

"Any more than traveling from dog show to dog show? Being
passed from handler to handler? Hitch and I are very good together.
I groom her every day, including brushing her teeth. She's never left
alone. We have wonderful long walks." Ruby feels the tears build, her
voice thicken.

"I don't give my dogs away."

"I don't expect you to." Actually, she hadn't expected that keeping
the Hitchhiker would involve a monetary transaction. Could kindness
of heart be enough?

"I'll need two references, one from a veterinarian. I'll need you to
sign my contract and," Mrs. Cross adds, "I'll want a bank check for
two thousand dollars."

"Oh."

The object of the conversation jumps off the bed and shakes herself. Scratches behind an ear. Ruby is dry-mouthed. Where is she going to get that kind of money? "Could I use a credit card?"

"No. No credit cards, no personal checks, and no layaway." Mrs.
Cross laughs at her own joke.

Ruby wants to cry. "I'm not sure how quickly I can come up with
the money, but yes, please sell her to me."

"Roundelay should come back to me while you figure out how to
come up with the money. I'll hold her for you."

Hold her hostage, Ruby thinks. "She's been with me all this time;
I think it would be very upsetting for her to be separated from me."

"I'm sure you can explain it to her, what with being an animal communicator and all."

"How do you expect to pick her up?" Ruby hopes that the logistics will discourage Mrs. Cross from her plan. She is certainly not volunteering to take the dog back to Mrs. Cross, even temporarily.

"I have a litter about to be whelped, so I've asked my son. He's willing to pick her up. You can hold on to Roundelay until he gets there."

"When will that be?"

"Well, he probably can't get free until the weekend, so I guess you'll have her till then."

There it is, the flicker of hope that Ruby has been looking for. "If I have the money by then . . ."

"He'll have the papers with him."

Ruby knows that she sounds a bit like an adolescent again, this time one whose had her wish fulfilled even with restrictions. "Thank you, Mrs. Cross. It's the right thing to do."

Mrs. Cross harrumphs. "We'll see. Get those references." Hangs up.

The Hitchhiker jumps into Ruby's open arms. "Now all I have to do is figure out how to earn a couple grand in five days."

Ruby has a little more than $600 in cash. Her checking account has enough to cover daily expenses and this stay at the Dew Drop. She'll check out today, save on tomorrow's rate. Ravi will just have to understand. Maybe she can set up the Westie someplace and do some readings in town; even a hundred bucks will help. Ruby snaps the dog's leash to her harness and takes her for a long thinking walk. Ultimately, as painful as it will be, it will likely come down to calling Sabine and seeing if her daughter will front her the remainder of the money for the dog. This puts a new tent and new tires on hold, but who cares? And maybe it won't come to that. Maybe she should buy a lottery ticket using her psychic powers. Ruby makes herself laugh, and for the first time since Polly's bad news, there is a return of optimism in her heart.

"You look cheerful." Polly pulls the animal control truck over to where Ruby and the Hitchhiker stand on the sidewalk. "Good news?"

"Pretty much." Ruby fills Polly in on her conversation with Mrs. Cross.

"Please let me be one of your references."

"That would be great. I know that will help, having your thumbs up," Ruby says. "Now all I have to do is raise the money."

"Why don't you do one of those personal social media donation things?"

"I don't know. I'm a little squeamish about asking strangers for money to buy a dog. So many other people out there, like those with serious medical problems, deserve help."

"There's so much money floating around this town. We just have to figure out how to tap into it."

"Says the woman the town doesn't even pay equitably. Got that shelter washer fixed yet?"

"No."

"Well, I'm not going to fund-raise and I'm not going to beg. I'll earn it."

"In five days."

"You bet."

21

Tuesday afternoon and still no delivery from FedEx. It's almost five o'clock and Ruby debates the wisdom of calling Sister Beatrice and simply asking if she's sent the file. She'd promised herself not to get concerned until Wednesday, but it's a promise she can't seem to keep. Instead she calls the FedEx depot nearest Harmony Farms. Just in case it got misdirected. Alas, she is told, without a tracking number, yada, yada.

Ruby sits outside on one of Bull's lawn chairs to make the call to the convent. The dogs are playing behind her, some kind of rough and tumble "I'll chase you if you chase me" game of their own design. Abruptly, the Hitchhiker ends the game and joins Ruby in the side yard. Boy wanders over to his water bowl and laps noisily. Flops onto his left side in the overgrown yellow grass, instantly asleep. His yellow coat blends in so well with the grass that Ruby, seated across the yard, can hardly make him out.

Hundreds of miles away, the convent office phone rings and rings. Each buzzy repetition sounding increasingly like someone giving Ruby the Bronx cheer. "Come on, Karen, Sister, whoever you are. Answer the phone."

If the nun cum office manager has sent the file, Ruby wants the tracking number. If she hasn't, well, Ruby will handle that politely but firmly.

Finally, just before the answering machine clicks into action, someone picks up the phone. "Sacred Heart Convent and School for Girls." The voice is different, older sounding.

"Bea?" Ruby quickly corrects herself. "Is this Sister Beatrice Johnson?"

"No. This is Mother Superior. How may I help you?"

It must be hardcoded, this instant sense of fear. The thought of speaking to a Mother Superior again, despite all the time that has passed, gives Ruby a chill. Of course, the woman who sent her to Monsignor LaPierre, the woman who accepted his cruel order of isolation to punish her without protest, is long gone. Ruby recalls the far more benign face of the current Mother Superior on the convent's website. Finding her voice, Ruby politely asks for Sister Beatrice. "She's sending me something and I haven't yet received it."

"What is it?"

The Hitchhiker noses Ruby's elbow, almost shakes the phone right out of her hand. Behind her, Boy jumps up and barks at something she cannot see.

"Some information about the school."

"Well, I'm sure she has. She's very responsible. Patience is a virtue." The head nun chuckles as if she's coined a new joke. "What did you say your name was?"

"My name *is* Ruby Heartwood."

"Were you a student here?"

The sound of an engine, slightly squeaky brakes. A transmission thrown into park.

Ruby pushes herself out of the lawn chair. "Maybe." She thumbs off the phone. With the Hitchhiker by her side, she meets the FedEx man halfway.

It's a most curious thing. My companion is as excited as if she was about to give me a special treat, but she is also afraid, as if she is expecting pain. I can't quite suss out what's going on except that I maybe should have kept that strange man away, not let him give her that flat object smelling of many hands. But she seems to like this thing, holds it up against her as if it was as precious as I know I am to her. She is talking, but none of her words are part of my collection of human utterings. First we go back to sitting outside, and then we go into our little mobile house. She closes the door, then opens it. Stares out at the big house where Boy's man lives. Boy has followed us to our mobile house and is waiting patiently outside for me to rejoin him. He's napped and now he's interested in playing. Still she holds the flat object in her hands, not doing anything with it. This is not a book. I know what a book is, and yet she seems to be staring at it like she does those. Finally, she sets the thing down and picks up her phone. Taps it. With my excellent hearing, I can discern the little whoosh sound she causes it to make, almost immediately followed by a ding sound.

"For God's sake, Ruby, open it." Sabine doesn't bother texting back. She calls her mother.

"Will you stay on the line?"

"I will."

The Hitchhiker watches as Ruby pulls the cardboard tab to open the mailer. Her little nose is wriggling, taking in the history of its journey from a convent to a VW bus. Ruby slides a manila folder out. It is crisply new, no doubt a replacement for the one the good sister had taken out of the box of files. She's attached a bright pink sticky note: *Hope you find what you're looking for. Blessings, Sr. Bea.*

"Me too." Ruby pulls the note off, sticks it to the table. She lays the folder on the table beside it and places her hands on it. It is fuller than she'd imagined. Almost like there is something other than paper in there.

"Mom, hey, you there?"

Ruby had forgotten that Sabine was listening in.

"Just looking for a vibe."

"Oh, for goodness sake, open it."

Ruby can hear the sound of Beenie's refrigerator door, the *click click click* of the ignition of the gas range. She's getting dinner started. The kids are probably on their way back from some activity. Her life is busy.

"Okay. Here goes." Ruby flips the cover, and the first thing revealed is a stack of report cards in kraft envelopes. Kindergarten through eighth grade, in order. Ruby randomly selects one, third grade. She wasn't a bad student. Remarks are generally favorable. She pulls the report card out of the last one, her eighth-grade year. She was still a solid B student, but the remarks are less favorable. The last quarter of that year is blank. A note at the bottom in black ink: *Left without permission. Fail for the year.* Ruby looks at the signatures of the various teachers and is surprised that she can call most of them to mind, that their faces framed by their wimples are vivid. "Report cards."

"That's all?"

"No. That's what's on top."

"Keep going."

Health records come next. Inoculations, colds, a bout with chicken pox. Nothing extraordinary, nothing that would distinguish her from any of the other children there. Ruby remembers having the chicken pox. The itching. The warnings by the exasperated caretakers to not scratch if she didn't want scarring. The way Sister Clothilde fed her chicken broth and laughed when Ruby asked if that's how she got the chicken pox in the first place.

"Maybe you should flip to the back of the file," Sabine says.

Ruby doesn't want to. Doing it this way, piece by piece feels more correct, as if she's peeling the layers away and at the end she will find the heart of the matter.

Beneath the medical records Ruby is surprised to find drawings that she had made in the early grades. Imagine the nuns keeping those, keeping them in a file. Crayon drawings illustrating the life she was leading—a big building, a group of small people, a couple of stick figures wearing something that must represent a habit. Scrawled black crayon a little beyond the edges of the garment. Behind that picture, another of the life she had wished to have. A house, two big stick people and two small ones. A towering tree with bright red apples dotting the green. No Westfalia, no carnival rides, no conical tent with a banner. Ruby is unaccountably saddened by the hopefulness of her child self. When did she stop wanting a normal family? When did a Volkswagen become her home?

"Ruby? You okay?"

"Fine." She sets the drawings aside. "Fine."

She lays her hands flat on the next of the documents within the folder. She can feel the raised texture of an imprint. She waits, knowing that if she is patient, she might see something, as if this last piece of her history was a tarot card or a palm open to interpretation. Some truth. Some explanation.

"Open your eyes, Mom. Get the truth the easy way. Read the last document." Leave it to Sabine to know what Ruby was doing.

Three sheets of legal paper stapled together are next. There is rust bleeding from the staple, like dried blood. The heading on the first sheet is in both English and French. It is a pro forma intake form. This is the legal document that put her in the care of the Sacred Heart orphanage, giving them custody of a female infant, surrendered on May 3, 1964, date of birth, May 1, 1964. Surrendered by . . .

A shaky signature, almost illegible. Ruby stares at it. In the same way her clearest psychic visions reveal a plain fact, a name appears. Estelle Williamson. *Surrendered by.*

Can you die of finding out the basic fact of your life? Ruby sits back, pulls the dog into her arms and rocks. She doesn't know whether to laugh or weep. Breathless is how she feels, nearly out of body. Could this Estelle Williamson be her mother? Is it remotely possible that it would be this simple? She looks closer at the signature line, reaches for her reading glasses. No. Faded but distinct is a printed word beneath the signature: *agent*. Not parent. Not mother. Surrendering agent.

The out of body sensation quickly descends into a common garden variety disappointment.

There is one last piece of documentation in the file. A Baptismal certificate dated May 10, 1964, presumably a week after her surrender.

Name of Child: Mary.

Two nuns stood as godmothers and the custodian as godfather. She remembers him. He was always kind to the girls and now she knows why; he was probably godfather to half of them.

The dog licks her nose, presses her head beneath Ruby's chin. "I love you," she thinks. Ruby cuddles the dog, then remembers her daughter still listening in. "Well, it's a start."

"Start to what?"

"Finding my mother." Ruby closes the file folder. "I've got a name. If I can find this Estelle person, I know that I'm that much closer to finding my mother."

"And at least we can now celebrate your real birthday," Sabine says, and signs off.

22

"I have an opportunity for you if you're interested." Ruby has bumped into the milliner at the Country Market. "I know it's short notice, but would you be interested in doing a party?"

"What do you mean?"

"Do readings at a bridal shower."

"Sure. When?"

"Well, that's the thing, it's tomorrow."

"Even better. I've never heard of a bridal shower on a Thursday before."

"It was the only day we could get the restaurant." The milliner, Rachel Bergen, flutters her fingers. "Besides, it was cheaper on a Thursday than a Saturday. This is a budget event. But we have no entertainment. I mean, we couldn't get a, you know." She flutters her fingers again.

Ruby takes a stab at Rachel's meaning. "A male stripper? Kind of an odd choice at a bridal shower."

Rachel nods. "This is kind of a combined shower and bachelorette party."

"Sign me up."

Birthday parties, bridal showers, baby showers, retirement parties have all been a part of Ruby's job description over the years. When she was raising Sabine, these were her bread and butter. It's been a few years. Ruby's preference for being on the road has mostly precluded such

events. Having been in Harmony Farms far longer than she had anticipated, and being a fixture at the Makers Faire, has allowed her to become
something of a town presence. People know her. Like Rachel here, now
asking for a favor. Ruby asks how many readings she might be asked to
do. Rachel really has no idea, so Ruby offers her terms, guaranteeing that
she'll walk away from this Thursday-night party with nothing less than
$250 and possibly more. Chipping away at the Hitchhiker's price tag.

Ruby plugs the yellow extension cord into the Westie's outlet, puts
away her few groceries. Bull is out in the backyard tossing a tennis
ball for the yellow Lab. Bull is a pretty good pitcher, and in a wave of
insight, Ruby sees him as he might have been many years ago. Trim,
clean, athletic. As quickly as the vision came, it dissipated, leaving the
real Bull in her sight line—shaggy, stained, and puffing a little with
the effort of lobbing the tennis ball.

The Hitchhiker has gone out to join in the game. Her banner tail
is waving and she yips in excitement. Imagine being that enthusiastic
about a tennis ball, and one that is pretty gnarly with dog spit. Bull
leans over, out of breath. The dogs, sensing that the human participant
in the game is done, play a little "catch me if you can" by themselves.

"I bought lemonade. Want some?"

"Wouldn't mind." Bull pulls himself upright and joins Ruby, who's
dragged over two sagging lawn chairs from Bull's collection.

"You know that you should give up the cancer sticks, right? You
want to be around for that dog, don't you?"

Bull shoots Ruby a look that says this isn't a new suggestion. "I
gave up drinking."

"That's good. So giving up smoking should be easy."

"They don't arrest you if you smoke too much."

"Fair enough." Ruby hands Bull a glass of lemonade. They both
look up as Polly's animal control truck pulls into the yard.

"You speakin' to her yet?"

"I was never not speaking to her, Bull, she was just doing what she's paid to do." Ruby pushes herself out of the lawn chair. "Besides, it's going to work out." This gig tomorrow night will push Ruby over the thousand mark. With no word yet from Mrs. Cross as to when to really expect the arrival of her son, Ruby is almost complacent about the fact that she can pull together much of the second thousand with another few days of busking around town. There are just enough tourists that she has a good supply of potential customers. And, God bless her, the Hitchhiker is the best shill of them all, attracting anyone who has left a dog behind while traveling. That, plus the steady stream of "pet parents" wanting Fido's psyche read.

"Greetings all." Polly grabs another lawn chair. Ruby hands her a glass. Bull pours the lemonade. The three of them sit quietly for a few moments, content to simply be sitting down and enjoying the lemonade. The weather today is sultry; August has arrived.

"You know who that bridal shower is for?" Polly plunges in as if they had been talking about it.

"Rachel Bergen signed me up. I figure it's a friend of hers."

"Her cousin, well, her cousin's daughter. A little bit of a rush job, if you know what I mean."

"Do people even care about that anymore?"

Polly waves a dismissive hand. "Apparently some people still do."

Buck left her alone in the RV. Ruby dragged herself back into the shower and scrubbed herself until the water ran out. She put on clean underwear. Jeans and a T-shirt. The bloodied nightgown she left in a heap on the floor. Knees to chest, Ruby waited in the dark. It was midnight before she heard Madame Celestine open the door to the trailer.

"What's this, then?" Madame Celestine flipped on the lamp and looks surprised to see Ruby sitting there. "Why up so late?" It was such a maternal thing to say that Ruby's breath catches in her throat and the tears begin to run.

"Buck . . ." Ruby found that she had no words to describe this thing that had happened to her.

"What about him? Is he all right?"

"He hurt me."

Celestine glanced at the heap of nightgown on the floor. "I'm sure it was an accident."

In the single women's trailer, romance novels were passed around from girl to girl. Ruby had read her fair share, and it was with that vocabulary that she finally spat out what Buck had done. "He forced himself on me. He penetrated me."

"He would not. You must have done something to make him think it was all right. He's rough around the edges, but he's a good boy. I didn't raise him to hurt women."

"He's rough, all right. Look." Ruby grabbed the nightgown off the floor, twisted it until the blood stain on the back appeared. "Tell me he didn't hurt me."

"You got your period. That's all that is. Rinse it in cold water."

"There is no more water. I used it up trying to get clean."

The sense of power that had coursed through Ruby's body in confronting Buck in the moments after his assault returned in that moment. It was as if she was transforming from youth to crone, limbs stretching, heart beating. Anger fueling her metamorphoses from child to adult.

Celestine abruptly turned around, wobbling a tiny bit, and Ruby realized that she was half drunk. Ruby sniffed the air and caught the scent of booze. "We'll discuss this in the morning. Good night." She grabbed the handrail and hoisted herself into her bedroom. The metal door clicked shut.

Ruby shook her head. *No, we won't*, she thought. *No, we won't*. Ignoring the breaking of her heart, Ruby stuffed her schoolbag with her belongings. She had been so happy with Madame Celestine, letting herself believe that the woman was a mother figure, someone to admire. Someone who would care for her. This new version of herself realizes that the old woman owes her. Owes her for letting her monster of a son back into the trailer. For taking his side over this girl who would love her like a daughter. Ruby's conscience was clear as she opened the drawer with the day's take. She's owed it. She stuffed the bills into her pocket. As Ruby moved toward the door, she spotted something else. The beautiful hand-painted teapot. She's going to need it to start the next chapter in her life. As carefully as if it were an infant, Ruby liberated the box containing the teapot and slipped it into her bag. Opened the door and took off.

In the years to come, that teapot would help her support the child who was both penalty and prize.

Even as she goes through the motions of daily life, Ruby is dwelling on the inconclusive nature of what she has found out. Inconclusive because she doesn't know the *why* of her abandonment. Had it become too much for her mother to keep her? Had her mother wanted a fresh start? Had she been coerced into giving her up? The custodial papers offer little more than Ruby's intake into the orphanage. Every possible scenario spins in her imagination as Ruby grooms the dog, purchases loose tea for the bridal shower readings, showers, brushes her teeth, and looks herself in the eye in the mirror and wills herself to understand. To see.

She lines up the facts. Rearranges them. There is no dot-to-dot solution. She's even dealt herself a hand of tarot to see if, armed with this information, she can discern the truth.

Ruby wakes up Thursday morning with the dog standing on her chest, nose to nose, her round brown eyes fixed on making Ruby open hers. Barely awake, Ruby is defenseless against the dog's thoughts. The Hitchhiker is growing impatient with Ruby's distractedness. Ruby feels the touch of grass and the taste of a rubber ball. She isn't quite saying: "Play." It's more she's thinking that Ruby needs to stop chewing on the hard bone of her new knowledge. "It doesn't taste good," thinks the dog. "Give."

"You're right," says Ruby. It doesn't taste good. It tastes like the ashes of disappointment. "I wasn't expecting anything, and yet, with all this information, I can't get it out of my head that my mother gave me away. I worked so hard to keep Sabine. Is that because I had some latent memory of the moment my mother handed me over?" She hugs the dog to her, breathes in the doggy scent of her. "And here I am struggling to keep you."

"Thank you. I love you. I want always to be with you."

"Then let's go earn some money."

Ruby has two clients with dogs today. She won't need a teapot or a set of tarot cards unless the owners suddenly decide to get their own fortunes read. The first is a pit bull type dog, a rescue. The second, the owner proudly mentions, is a rare breed, a Mexican Xoloitzcuintli. He spells it out and then gives Ruby a quick tutorial on pronunciation: Sho-lo-itz-QUEENT-ly. Sho lo for short. Both dogs are exhibiting depression.

Because the Hitchhiker's thoughts have been so pronounced this morning, Ruby is a bit surprised that she isn't getting any thoughts at all from the pittie. Unlike her human clients, Ruby doesn't want to fake it with the canines. They are sitting in the living room of the owner's split-level house. The dog has been willing enough to let Ruby put hands on him, but all she feels is a cloud of silence. The dog does seem sad, his stubby ears cocked backward as if he wishes to hide.

The owner, a young guy with a man-bun and a full sleeve of crimson and green tattoos, waits patiently for Ruby's diagnosis. Like any good doctor, she begins to gently question the fellow. "Any changes recently in your life?"

"Same old same old. Work, workout, go out."

"Is he alone here a lot?"

The guy shrugs. "Maybe. I guess so."

"How long have you had him?"

"Well, let's see. A year, maybe a little more. My ex and I . . ."

As soon as he says that, Ruby gets a quick pulse of thought from the dog. "Wait. You said 'your ex.'"

"I did."

"How long ago, if I can ask, did you split?"

"You think that had something to do with his mood?"

"I do. Was he close to her? Does he see her?"

"Him."

"Him. Is there any kind of contact between them?"

"No. Philip bailed and went out to Seattle."

Ruby rests her cheek against the dog's head, waits. There it is. A fine mist of grief. And a scintilla of anxiety.

"He's afraid you'll let him go too."

The client rubs his face. "Is that what he thinks? That I *let* Philip go?"

"I could be interpreting it a little broadly, but in Max's view, you didn't tell Philip to stay. Like you should have given the command: stay."

"What do I do?"

"Short of finding another boyfriend, try to give this guy a lot more attention. Take him with you more often. Play with him."

The young man kneels beside the dog and wraps his arms around him. "Max, I'll never let you go." He looks up at Ruby. "Do you think he understands what I'm saying?"

"Not by words, my friend, by actions."

The second dog, the Xolo, whose name is Maggie, is a marked example of beauty is in the eye of the beholder: skinny, hairless, and a mottled black and gray. But the dog has a sweet nature and seems eager to meet Ruby halfway in her quest to figure out what's bothering her. Gingerly, Ruby places her hands on the dog, finding that the bare skin is baby soft. The dog snuffles at Ruby's face. "What are these dogs meant to do?"

"Guards, companions."

"And why did you choose such an unusual dog?"

"I always wanted a cool dog." The owner is a balding middle-aged man, very typical of the men she's seen around this upwardly mobile town. A little podgy, nice shoes. Likes status symbols like the Lexus in the driveway and the Rolex on his wrist.

Ruby strokes the dog's naked body. It feels like a bald scalp. The dog looks into Ruby's eyes and she sees that she isn't sad, she's bored out of her mind. "She's pretty intelligent, would you say?"

"Yes. She was housebroken pretty easily, and her trainer thinks that she could do obedience."

"So, you didn't train her yourself?"

"Oh, I don't have time for that."

Except for the Turcott's unhappy Great Dane Ruby hasn't yet suggested re-homing a dog, but she is tempted in this case. "Do you have a family? Or anyone who takes her for walks?"

The owner shakes his head. "I see what you're getting at."

"Dogs aren't accessories."

"Is that what you think I'm using her for?" His face is growing flushed, not an attractive look.

Ruby backs down a bit. No sense pissing off a client. "She's a sentient being who is telling me that she very much wants to be a bigger part of your life." Ruby thinks about the Hitchhiker and how enormous her role has become in her own life. Which brings the threat of losing her to mind. She closes off that part of her brain. Ruby's job right now is to make this unusual-looking dog happier.

"How do I do that? Make her happier?" He sounds sincere and Ruby relaxes a bit.

"Look, you've taken the first step, recognizing that she isn't happy. You called me. That's a big deal, the fact that you noticed her mood.

Now talk to her, take her with you for rides to the gas station. What kind of games does she like to play? Tug, chase the ball?"

He shrugs. "I'm not sure."

"Get some toys. Find out. Call me in a week and let me know how she's doing."

"I will." The client fishes his wallet out of his back pocket, pulls out a hundred-dollar bill.

"I don't have change for that."

"Keep it. Please."

Ruby has never been one to argue a customer out of a nice tip. "Thank you. Remember: play, walk, ride. Call me."

It being too hot to let her sit in the van, the Hitchhiker is waiting for Ruby at Bull's house. When she pulls into the yard, she spots Bull in his usual lawn chair, sucking down a Mountain Dew. The dogs are stretched out on either side of him. The Hitchhiker jumps up and runs to meet Ruby climbing out of the van. As always, her exuberant greeting makes Ruby feel like the queen of the world. Beloved. How could she stand to lose her?

Ruby gets to the restaurant a little before the first guests are meant to arrive. She wants to scope out the space, see where best to hold her little readings. The wait staff are finishing up the cheese station and two young women in cocktail dresses are arranging centerpieces. Ruby guesses that they are the bridesmaids, doing the best that they can on such short notice.

Ruby joins them. "It looks beautiful."

"Thanks. Thank God for Pinterest." The blonder of the pair smiles, but Ruby can see the tension, the pressure to make this event a happy one. "You must be a sister." No one has told her the bride has a sister, but Ruby is certain that this thirtysomething is.

"I am. And you must be the fortune-teller."

"I am."

They agree on a spot to the left of the head table. A little discreet but not out of sight. Part of the success of the entertainment will be attracting the nervous to partake. Not unlike getting the reluctant to join in Karaoke. Suddenly it looks like fun.

Ruby unpacks the tools of her trade, the wooden box with the set of tarot cards. The tiny teacups. The teapot. She gives it a perfunctory wipe with the soft cloth she keeps it wrapped in.

The guests have begun to arrive. Gifts are piling up on the gift table. The signature drink is being dispensed, something pinkish and sweet and Ruby isn't remotely tempted. She doesn't mingle, but circulates, listens, an intelligence-gathering exercise. That one is complaining about a husband, the other one her kids. Someone else is talking about a sick mother. A new job. Finally Rachel Bergen shows up and spots Ruby. They agree that she'll start doing readings after the toasts. Ruby thinks that's perfect, they'll all be loosened up with that pink drink and ready for fun.

Not a guest, Ruby takes herself to the bar of the restaurant and orders dinner. She'll earn back the cost of the pricey burger in her first reading. She gives the party an hour before she ducks into the ladies' room and changes into her caftan. Undoes her hair and shakes it out. Puts on a redder lipstick. Adds a bit more mascara and eye shadow. Voilà—everyone's idea of a fortune-teller. A few minutes after she hears the last toast, Ruby steps through the kitchen door and asks for a carafe of hot water so she can begin brewing the tea.

Rachel makes the announcement that Ruby Heartwood, Psychic and Seer, is open for business. As usual, it takes one brave soul to venture over and within a few minutes, a line has formed. The girls, for they are mostly young women, queue up with drinks in hand and blatantly listen in on one another's readings. Ruby fashions her insights for the maximum of entertainment for the crowd. In an hour and a half, she's promised fortune, fun, and romance to a couple dozen now fairly inebriated girls and soothed the mother-of-the-bride's qualms about her choice of dress for the wedding. And then there are two left. The bride and her future mother-in-law.

As Ruby taps the deck of tarot cards into alignment, she feels a shiver run from the nape of her neck to her waist. Not the kind of shiver that suggests the air-conditioning is set too high; it is the kind that old wives used to say was the result of a goose walking over your grave. A portent of things to come. She splits the deck and shuffles the large cards again. The frisson dissipates.

Everyone has decided that the bride must go last. So it's the future mother-in-law who is forced into the chair next. Cynthia Mann.

The shiver down Ruby's spine suddenly makes sense.

The first thing Ruby notices is that Cynthia, unlike the rest of her guests, is not the least bit softened up by the signature drink. Indeed, it looks to Ruby like Cynthia has been abstaining. She files away that bit of intel. The second thing that Ruby perceives is that Cynthia, far from being a good sport about this, is seething. And her most belligerent glance is not at Ruby, but the soon-to-be daughter-in-law. Who is giving it right back. Okay, add a touch of family divisiveness to the blend. Sweet. The third thing Ruby gleans in the fifteen seconds before Cynthia turns her scathing attitude toward Ruby, is that Cynthia doesn't wear any jewelry except for a tiny pair of diamonds in her ears. For her this is no celebration, but a wake.

"Well, hello, Cynthia. Congratulations on the upcoming nuptials." Might as well poke the tiger, get it over with, thinks Ruby Heartwood.

"Don't be ridiculous," Cynthia hisses.

Ruby leans over, whispers, "Don't worry, we both know this is just for show. You don't want to go down in family history as the mother-in-law from hell, do you?"

"I don't think it matters."

"I think it does. You want to keep your son close, be nice to his wife."

"Is that your idea of a fortune?"

"No. Just a little advice from a fellow mother-in-law." What Ruby doesn't say is that she happens to be the mother of a daughter, who happens to also adore her son-in-law. No point in mentioning that. "They could be married a long time, and once kids come, you don't want to be on the outside."

"I think it's a little too late for that."

Both women sit back. The few girls still lingering around the fortune-teller's table pause in their chatter, all eyes on the psychic, wondering what she will say, what she might reveal about this woman they all understand to be against this marriage.

"Tea leaves or tarot?" Ruby still has a little hot water left in the carafe. "It's Earl Grey."

Cynthia shrugs with a delicate gesture, signifying her utter disdain. "Tea. I suppose. Why not? But please don't expect me to swallow your hogwash."

"Not in the least."

Ruby goes through the ritual as if she was entertaining the queen. A spoonful of tea, hot water, gentle swirl to ensure the leaves are spread, pour with care into the teacup. She hands the fragile cup to Cynthia, asks her to take a sip. Cynthia looks as if she's been asked to drink last year's Beaujolais. She comes away with a flake of tea on her upper lip. She seems unaware of it and Ruby doesn't point it out. With a frigid hauteur, Cynthia puts the cup down and slides it to Ruby.

Ruby studies the scrim of tea leaves plastered to the bottom and sides of the tiny cup. She is perfectly willing to make up a palatable plate of prognostication for this woman, but something else happens. "May I ask a couple of questions?"

"Do I have to answer? Isn't that how you glean enough information to make a prediction?"

"When you go to your doctor, do you answer his questions so that he can make a proper diagnosis?"

"She. And of course."

"Same here."

A voice from the peanut gallery: "Oh, come on, Ms. Mann, play along."

Cynthia doesn't take her eyes off of Ruby's face, doesn't deign to respond to the soused bridesmaid in the circle.

Ruby notices that the bride herself is standing at a distance. She's got a lei of ribbons around her neck, the bows from her gifts. She looks to be falling down exhausted, less enthusiastic about her party than her friends, probably because she's had to abstain from the pink drink. Ruby will give her a generic fortune and send her on her way, confident that she's going to be all right, that her mother-in-law won't always hate her. Although that won't exactly be accurate.

"Let's get this over with. I'd like to get out of here."

Ruby studies the tea leaves, and a wash of magic floats through her. It doesn't happen often, but when it does, it's like a jolt of adrenaline straight to the heart. "You've decided something recently."

"Everyone makes decisions."

"I see a long quiet period in your life."

"When? I could almost look forward to that. I'm so busy. It's wearing me out."

Mindful of the gathering around them, Ruby leans across the table and whispers into Cynthia's ear, "You've decided not to run for reelection."

Cynthia blinks, sits back, says, "I haven't told anyone that," thus confirming Ruby's intuition.

"You've had a lot on your plate in the past year or so."

"It's been harder than I thought." Cynthia looks away, says, almost to herself, "I don't think I could get reelected."

"For all its sophistication, this is really a small town and I get why you might think that you wouldn't have the support you once enjoyed."

"I've said no too many times."

Ruby nods. She's heard from her townie friends that Cynthia is known as the Queen of No, voting down pretty much everything brought to the board. It hasn't endeared her to those who would like to see a little less gentrification and a little more affordable housing. But there is something else that the constituents of Harmony Farms aren't keen on, the fact that her husband, albeit now ex, was convicted of animal abuse. In some minds, Cynthia is tainted by association. Particularly with her antipathy toward the animal control department, holding that tiny department responsible for the upheaval in her life.

Ruby dribbles a little more water into the teacup. Just enough to float the dregs so that she can take another read on Cynthia's fortunes, but the magic has passed.

"You won't tell anyone, will you?" This is a different Cynthia.

"No. Like with your doctor, this conversation is confidential."

The bride has been pushed toward Ruby by her sister. "One more, Madame Ruby!"

Abruptly, Cynthia regains her hauteur, stands up and flicks back her hair. "Ridiculous. All for show." She looks at the few guests still lingering around the bride then back at Ruby. "You, like all your kind, are a fake."

"You make yourself sound almost racist when you put it that way. All my kind?"

"Charlatans, frauds, preying upon the naïve and ignorant. The vulnerable."

"I don't see you as the least bit vulnerable, ignorant, or naïve, Cynthia. But you are clearly taking me too seriously."

Cynthia turns away from the round table. As she does, her hip hits the edge and the beautiful purloined little teapot hits the floor, smashing to bits.

23

The Hitchhiker noses the fragments of china that Ruby has laid out on the table. A spout. A handle. This piece looks like the miniature masterpiece of a portrait of a violet. There's the bulge of the teapot; there's the finial from its cover. Ruby doesn't know whether to feel sad, or maybe relieved. Has this object been the long lingering reminder of a most painful moment? Surely there have been times when she's used it without thinking of Madame Celestine. Without thinking about the hurt inflicted when the woman she had come to think of as a mother betrayed that affection. Surely over forty years the teapot has become just a teapot. But looking at the shards of the thing, Ruby knows that a kind of spell has been broken. She collects the pieces. She has a square silk scarf she used to wear around her head, turban-style. She's had it almost as long as she's had the teapot. She places the pieces into the scarf and gathers the ends together to tie it. None of the shards will fall out. Done, Ruby folds back the table, climbs into the driver's seat of the Westie. She knows just the place to ceremonially inter these remnants of her second oldest decision. If she was anywhere near the ocean, she'd given them a burial at sea where the porcelain shards would be smoothed into beach glass, eventually heaved up on the shore to be found by a delighted beachcomber. Lake Harmony will just have to do.

The morning sky is hazy with the promise of a good hot summer day. It is still early enough that the parking lot is empty except for a yellow-vested town worker stabbing litter with a stick, stuffing his booty into a plastic trash bag. Ruby doesn't particularly want to be observed tossing her bundle into the lake, so she makes like she's just there to walk her dog, ostentatiously dangling a ready poop bag from the hand not grasping the silken bundle. They are quickly away from the sandy beach, following a well-trodden trail up and through the skinny woods. On this, the public side of the lake, the trail will double back, respecting the boundary with the very much private side. Ruby has been along this path enough times with the Hitchhiker that she has figured out how to boldly trespass. Just look like you belong there.

They come to a low pier, a flotilla of tiny sailboats bobbing alongside. Ruby has seen these little craft out on the lake, children who look too young to be sailing alone piloting them in varying degrees of ability. The Harmony Farms Yacht Club learn to sail program. There is always a motorboat in the vicinity and she's never actually witnessed a capsizing.

Ruby strides to the end of the pier, the dog right at her heels, her little brown eyes fixed on Ruby's face, wondering what's going to happen next. Before she launches her bundle into the drink, Ruby reconsiders losing the scarf. It is pure silk, a pale orange sherbet struck through with threads of emerald green. No reason to heave that out of her life too. She unties the knot and begins flinging the teapot shards one by one into Lake Harmony. The water here is deep enough, she hopes, that no kid, having fallen overboard, will step on the broken pieces. In time, perhaps even without the tidal wash of the sea, these broken bits, these remnants of her fractured life, will turn harmless.

The breeze has picked up so Ruby ties the scarf around her head to keep her hair out of her face. From her vantage point on the end of the pier Ruby sees that the town worker has left. In the distance, she hears the sound of children's voices and she knows that she had better beat it out of there. But still she lingers. The dog presses herself against Ruby's knees, so she scoops her up. The vibration is strong, clear, and Ruby allows herself to breathe in the scent of the dog's thoughts.

"This is a good place. I like it here."

"We can't stay."

"Stay. Yes. We are home here."

And Ruby realizes the dog is thinking not about the pier upon which they are trespassing, but the place where they found each other, where they have become partners. And, Ruby thinks, it's Friday and she is still nearly $1,000 shy of the $2,000 she needs to secure that partnership. Time to get to work.

Avoidance is a skill and Ruby is displaying that skill by leaving her phone on Do Not Disturb. If Mrs. Cross has tried to call her, she's failed. Ruby is also displaying her resistance to temptation by not checking the damn thing anyway. What was that expression? Good news will keep, and bad news won't go away? She's set up her round table and two chairs under an oak tree in the park, not too far from where she sets her tent up at the Faire. She's displaying her busker's license prominently. If her profession is somewhat suspect, her legitimacy isn't. She's close enough to the foot traffic exploring the shops on Main Street, now in full August sale mode, to attract the random tourist who might not be around for the Makers Faire on Saturday. Lots of people pass through Harmony Farms on their way to the Berkshires, finding it a good stopping place for a lunch break. It's been Cynthia's mission to get them to stay long enough to spend some money in town.

As a final touch, Ruby unfolds the sandwich board with her menu of skills. Psychic readings: palm, tarot. She has taken a strip of masking tape and covered "tea leaves." When she gets a chance, she'll poke around in a thrift store and see if she can find a new teapot. But, for now, her most prominent offering is written in large letters: Animal Communicator. It is a sign of desperation that Ruby has also modified her fees, upping the palm and tarot readings to forty dollars from twenty and animal communicator to a flat sixty bucks. It will either work or she'll do a fire sale at the end of the day.

The Hitchhiker is doing her bit, wagging and wriggling in joy at the approach of every stranger. She has this amazing ability to make you think that you are the most special person in her life. It would make Ruby jealous, but she knows that the dog is somewhat of an actor. True affection is the way she speaks to Ruby alone.

Two hours, four customers later and Ruby is doing mental calculations. This must be what it felt like during World War I when success on the battlefield was measured in inches, not yards.

I really enjoy being a hostess, greeting passersby and asking them to join us. It feels as though that is my purpose, at least as long as we enjoy the park and the lovely heat of the day. Ruby is very pleased with my unsubtle friendliness. I know others of my sort who distrust, but I have never been one of those. It is my feeling that all human beings deserve a chance to be befriended. Sometimes two chances. As I've said, I don't dwell on the past, but I will say this, the night that I bolted from my former home, it wasn't so much that I was running away, as toward. I knew that my purpose there had ended with my elderly companion's life. I was also crazed to get out, to run, to stretch, to burn off the anxiety that had kept me company for however long it was before other human beings came to open that door. I was less hungry and thirsty than I was bored. I don't know how long I kept moving, except that, at some point, I knew that I needed to keep going in the direction in which I was headed. Going back wasn't possible.

The storm that came up had me seeking shelter under the porch of a building near the lake. As that white van pulled in, I was jolted by the certainty that it was now my new home. That inside of it I would find someone who would be mine. I knew, without knowing how, that the woman in there would be able to understand me, understand my language well beyond the common words a dog uses: *eat, out, water, ball*. I asked to be admitted and Ruby opened the door.

In the last few days there has been a darkness to my companion's spirit. At first I thought that the object with the papers in it, pungent with the scent of a dark damp place, was the cause of her darkness. But now I wonder. I think it has something to do with me.

Ruby knows that her fallback position on raising the money to purchase the Hitchhiker is to ask Sabine for a loan. She just wants that loan to be as small as possible. A far better thing to owe your daughter $500 bucks than $1,000. Even better, to owe nothing at all. Sabine has already offered, and Ruby declined as quickly as she could. She really doesn't want Sabine to have proof that her mother is living as close to the financial vest as she is. Sabine surely has few memories of the belt tightening Ruby inflicted on her during her earliest childhood. The thrift store shopping, the soup kitchens. No, Beenie was a little child, a toddler. She couldn't possibly remember those horrible years. Living not in a Westfalia, but in shelters and motels far less clean than the Dew Drop. Ruby had been a child herself, so young, that she often pretended that she was the babysitter, not the baby's mother. Did Sabine hold some vestigial memory of eating stolen baby food? Ruby remembers one day, a hot Florida day. She'd taken them down south so they didn't have to worry about staying warm. There were only a few bucks left from the bus trip down. There they were, sitting on a beach, watching a woman throw perfectly good bread crusts to gulls. The urge to fight off the birds and give those spent crusts to her child horrified Ruby. Instead, she left Sabine sitting on the beach, playing with a shell, digging in the soft sand. "I'll read your palm, ma'am. I'll tell your fortune."

The woman had looked at Ruby, looked at the baby playing on the sand. The annoyance quickly changed into worry. "No, thank you. But here." She pulled five dollars out of a pocket. "Get your baby a meal." She pulled her hand back before Ruby could take the money, reached into her other pocket, pulled out a ten. "And yourself."

Ruby shakes the thoughts off. The dog has her paws on Ruby's lap, her spaniel eyes downcast, the tip of her white tail fluttering in the hope that Ruby will snap out of it. At least she hasn't had to steal dog food. Things are better. By the time Sabine was seven, Ruby had figured it out.

"Okay, enough for today." Ruby folds up the sandwich board and the table, the two chairs. All in all, it hasn't been a bad day; she's got another $200 in her purse. Another inch of territory toward her goal. Best part, she hasn't heard from Mrs. Cross. Maybe, if she's able to eke out another week before the son shows up, she can make the goal and win the war. As Ruby gets into the van, she notices a yellow envelope under her windshield wiper. A parking ticket.

Polly Schaeffer is waiting for Ruby in Bull's yard. She's out of uniform, but she has an official expression on her face. A displeased expression. Out of uniform, Polly favors tent dresses, what might even be called caftans if they were less floral, espadrilles on her feet. As Ruby backs into her spot on the worn grass, Bull comes out of the house bearing a plate of uncooked hamburgers. The Hitchhiker licks her lips. The scent of charcoal fragrances the air and, like the dog, Ruby feels the urge to lick her lips. Her lunch of a peanut butter and jelly sandwich is but a distant memory.

"Join us for a burger, Ruby?" Bull flourishes his spatula, gives Polly a fretful side glance.

Polly stands her ground. "I got a call from Mrs. Cross."

"Yes," Ruby says.

Bull takes it as yes to a burger. Polly takes it as yes, she knows she's been avoiding the inevitable.

24

Ruby slips her phone out of her back pocket. She's resisted the temptation to check it to the point she's nearly forgotten to. Unlocks the Do Not Disturb. Three missed calls, two of them with Mrs. Cross's number. One from Sabine.

"If I had answered her call, would Mrs. Cross have reached out to you?"

"She did say that she couldn't reach you. She's apparently not the sort who likes to have to keep trying. Twice was enough she said."

"Have I screwed myself over by not answering?"

"Ruby, I don't know. She only said that her son would be on his way to pick up the dog."

"Mrs. Cross told me I could buy the dog."

"She didn't say that."

"She didn't tell you our deal?"

Polly looks out to the middle distance, not meeting Ruby's eyes. "She mentioned something about how you would like to buy the dog, but not that it was a done deal. Ruby, she thinks you aren't able to keep her, keep her properly." Polly hears herself and has the good grace to look distressed. "I told her that you were the perfect person."

"I am. I thought we had an agreement. She promised me."

"Did she?" Polly grabs Ruby's hands. "Look, whatever you think she promised you, she's changed her mind. You see, Mrs. Cross is fixed on the dog having a secure home. Fenced in yard, et cetera."

"How does she know that I'm not planning on being that person?" Ruby feels herself break out in a cold sweat. "We agreed that if I could come up with the money, I could buy the Hitchhiker."

Polly has heard enough of Ruby's story to know that the promise of staying put is completely out of character. "She knows that you're, how did she put it, nomadic."

"Who talked to her? She was perfectly at ease with the situation a few days ago." Even as Ruby asks the question, the answer comes to her. "How did Cynthia get involved?"

"I don't know. Word gets around, you know how it is."

"I don't think I do." Ruby makes herself keep her hands away from Polly. "How did Cynthia find out?"

"She was on my case about unregistered dogs. Yours might have come up."

"I still don't see how she made the connection to Mrs. Cross from that." And then Ruby does see. A nervous Polly, an overbearing Cynthia. A slip of the tongue.

Ruby looks at Bull. "No thanks on the burger. Hitch, come."

The dog, blatantly begging in front of Bull, ignores Ruby.

Bull ignores the dog. "Ruby, don't say no to a real good dinner. I've made coleslaw."

How Bull imagines coleslaw can heal a broken heart, Ruby can't fathom. He's been good to her. She can't be rude. "All right. Let me just go freshen up." Meaning sit alone for a moment to collect herself. The perfidy. The outright meanness of that woman, Cynthia. Who never even apologized for breaking Ruby's teapot. Who just walked away from the table without a word, never mind bending over to help gather the pieces. Well, Ruby is in pieces now.

The dog follows, although she gives Bull a sorrowful look. She jumps into the van with Ruby, recognizes what her job is at that moment and gets to work trying to jolly Ruby out of this black funk.

She rolls over, exposes her belly, pokes at Ruby with a hind leg; grabs Ruby's wrist gently between her teeth. Her antics only serve to make Ruby lose the battle with tears. "What am I ever going to do without you?"

When Sabine was in first grade, Ruby had settled for the winter in a mid-sized city. She made sure that Sabine was dressed neatly every day for school, that she was clean and that she never told the officials that their home was a squat. Nonetheless, someone figured out that the little girl was wearing the same two outfits and that she had drawn a picture of that squat, complete with the gang that hung around the stoop. Ruby had never had any trouble with those men; they had made a pet of Sabine and occasionally slipped Ruby a sawbuck for Sabine's needs. Drug money. Maybe. Welcome when the telling of fortunes was running dry, yes. A city welfare officer showed up. Two cops flanking her although the gang members had quickly vanished into thin air. Ruby didn't answer the door. That afternoon she and Sabine hit the road again. The next town was smaller, and Ruby got a job waitressing so that their next home was acceptable enough to the next set of officials who worried about the little girl with two dresses.

When threatened, leave.

"Let's go."

This was all wrong. My feeling has always been that we *stay*.

The dog jumps down and scratches at the closed sliding door. Whimpers as if she's suddenly possessed with the urge to relieve herself. She throws Ruby a look over her shoulder, whines and scratches, whines and scratches.

"Go sit." Ruby points to the passenger seat. She climbs into the driver's seat. Drops the keys in her haste to get going. They bounce and go under the seat. She can't quite reach them without getting out of the van to retrieve them. Stretching, Ruby bangs her cheek against the steering wheel which does nothing to make her slow down or stop crying. The dog jumps into the space between the seats and puts her paws up on Ruby's knees. For the first time, Ruby looks the dog in the eyes and gets her message loud and clear. "Stay!"

"You don't understand."

"I do." And to prove it, the spaniel licks Ruby's teary cheek. Licks the other one. "Only prey runs."

A knock on the slider. Bull's shaggy head appears in the window. "Ruby, your burger is ready. Don't let it get cold."

"Eat first," says the dog. "Meat makes everything better."

Ruby wipes the dog-licked tears with the back of her hand like a little kid. Sniffs. Reaches for a tissue. "All right. But we're not done here."

As Ruby heads toward the grill, Polly comes up and takes her arm. Ruby flinches slightly, confused into thinking Polly is there to arrest her. "Ruby, I'm sorry. We can work this out, I just know it."

They sit in silence as Bull serves up his surprisingly good coleslaw. He doesn't own a picnic table so the three of them balance their paper plates on their laps, which only encourages the Hitchhiker to beg. Ruby points the dog to a safe distance and tells her to stay. They take turns tossing tiny fragments of food to the dog in return for her continuing to "stay." Who is training who? Ruby wonders. For his part, Boy has positioned himself behind Bull, yellow muzzle just inches from Bull's shoulder. He doesn't have to work for his treats. Bull fingers nearly half of his juicy burger into the dog's mouth. If the Hitchhiker resents the difference, she isn't saying.

Her own aura bleak, Ruby cannot distinguish those of her dining companions. Or maybe it's that they are all sitting within the same unhappy atmosphere. Half dread, half disappointment. The light is fading, the crickets tuning up. A cicada grinds out the day's last alarm about tomorrow's heat. In a moment Ruby will get up and dump her empty plate, say good night to these two, who have been good to her while she's been in Harmony Farms. Polly's loose lips notwithstanding, she's been a good friend. Once Bull's lights go out, she'll drive away. It's what she's always done. It will feel good to get back on the road, to hear the singing of the tires beneath her, to look for a new place to park her van. North, she thinks, it's late enough in the summer that the big agricultural fairs are starting. She'll hook up with the Benini Brothers. And, as soon as she can, she'll send Mrs. Cross the money for the Hitchhiker. It feels good to have a plan. She has lingered far too long in this town.

"Thanks for dinner, Bull." Ruby doesn't have it in her to say more than that, doesn't want to tip her hand. "I'm done in. Good night, Polly. And it's okay. I'm not mad."

Polly pushes herself out of the low lawn chair, drops her empty plate on the ground where Boy grabs it faster than anyone can tell him not to. She throws her arms around Ruby, whispers in her ear, "Don't be foolish."

"Never."

And over Polly's shoulder Ruby sees a car slow down on its way by, pause, reverse, then stop. It blocks the driveway completely.

"You should have told me he was coming now."

"I lacked the courage."

As a large man climbs out of the car, Ruby wonders, if she had listened to Sabine's message, would she have been warned to make her escape hours ago? It wouldn't be out of the question that Sabine might have divined the imminent danger.

"Am I in the right place? I'm looking for . . ."

"Ruby Heartwood." Ruby sees the man taking in the scrubby yard, the loose dogs, the paper plate sticking out of one dog's mouth while

the other, *her dog* teases him for it. Surely he's noticing the lack of
fencing, the rotted front porch, and the Westfalia parked like a fugitive
against the scraggly hedges, its sliding door open, revealing her caftan
flung across the back of the bench seat, the chemical toilet without its
discreet daytime cover. "And you are?"

"Dougie Cross."

A grown man who calls himself Dougie is going to take away her
dog?

At this point the Hitchhiker has given up wresting the paper plate
from Boy's mouth and taken notice of the newcomer. In her typical
fashion, she darts toward him, back end wriggling, and Ruby has to
wonder if the dog remembers this guy, if she has had history with
him. She is greeting him with the same unabashed exuberance she
does every stranger, but then, perhaps he is not a stranger but an old
friend.

Dougie bends over and scoops the dog into his arms, accepts her
kisses and laughs. "Well, well, another standoffish Cavalier, eh?"

"I have almost all the money," Ruby says, knowing that "almost" is
a relative term. She is nearly $400 short—$425 short if she pays that
parking ticket.

"Money? Oh, hey, Mom isn't cool with that idea. She's checked
references, and, well, sorry. No go."

"References? The ones I gave her?" Polly, the vet, Carrie Farr.
Which one of them would say she wasn't the best person for this dog?

"An outside reference. People always say nice things about friends."

"Cynthia Mann no doubt."

"Maybe, I don't know. Just that she pointed out your, um, transience,
and Mom takes that sort of thing seriously. Stability is everything."

"I'm not a bum, if that's what was implied. I have a business. Like
any traveling salesman." As if that profession still existed.

"But you call the dog the Hitchhiker."

"And your mother called her Roundelay and sold her off when she
wasn't perfect in the show ring."

"Gave her. Dotty was an old friend. She'd had a couple of Mom's retirees over the years." Dougie's voice has yet to match the pitch of Ruby's, he's keeping a cool head. Probably has removed dogs before, she thinks. Probably enjoys it.

"She promised me if I could come up with the money . . ." Ruby lets her sentence trail off, recognizing the futility and the way she now sounds like a petulant eight-year-old.

Ruby and Dougie are still standing beside his car, Polly and Bull both keeping their distance from the scene unfolding in the twilight of a hot August day, but not their attention. Dougie sets the dog down on the ground. The Hitchhiker immediately moves to Ruby's side, sits against Ruby's feet, her feathery tail tucked around her own, her ears flattened. Ruby knows that if she puts a hand on this dog's head, she will be cast into her thoughts, and the idea of never getting to do that again brings a fresh assault of tears to Ruby's eyes. She fights them back. "She's happy, Doug." She won't use his diminutive, neither will she address him as Mister Cross. "Don't break her heart."

"Cavs are happy wherever they are."

"Then why did she come to me? Out of all the people she might have chosen? She chose me, Doug. Me." Ruby is aware that her own aura is sliding from dull to brilliant. She can't see it, but she knows the feeling. She's had it half a dozen times when she has had to fight for what she needed. Leaving the convent. Cursing Buck into a future of despair. Keeping her child when sense would have suggested another path. Some would say that fighting for ownership of a small dog doesn't compare to the last example, but Ruby would not. "Partnerships are chosen, and this dog chose me. I will not turn my back on that honor." Ruby scoops the dog up into her arms. Leans slightly toward Doug. "Please take the money and tell your mother, with all due respect, that we had a deal. That her so-called reference has a vendetta against me for reasons that defy reason."

Dougie takes a half step back.

"I just need . . ." Her righteous anger begins to deflate. "A couple more days."

Ruby is suddenly aware of Bull standing beside her. "Hang on for a sec. Don't go anywhere." He dashes back to the house, or more accurately for Bull, lumbers like a bull elephant heading for a fight.

Polly is also at her side. "It's true, Cynthia Mann is weirdly antagonistic against Ruby. She's also very persuasive, so I'm not surprised she could turn Mrs. Cross around from what is a perfectly reasonable decision."

Dougie puts up his hands. "It's not my decision, ladies. It's my mother's."

Ruby is about to say something that she knows will not advance her case when Bull huffs back into the group. "How much you short, Ruby?"

"Give or take four hundred."

"Here. With my compliments." Bull fishes five hundred-dollar bills out of his pocket. They are pristine. He doesn't wait for her to protest, he takes her hand and puts the folded bills into her palm. "Take it, Ruby."

Ruby won't even pretend to object. "Give me a moment, if you will." Before Dougie can say anything that will blow a hole through her hope, the Hitchhiker glued to her heels, Ruby heads to her van, pulls her purse out from under the passenger seat, and finds the envelope containing $1,550. All of the money in it is well used, mostly twenties, tens, a baker's dozen of fives, an even number of ones. Some filthy, some crumpled, one marked with graffiti, every one of them precious. She lays the five pristine hundred-dollar bills behind the smaller denominations. The Hitchhiker is up in the van, her curiosity about Ruby's every movement evident in her eyes, in the tilt of her head, the wriggle in her little black nose. Ruby leans in and whispers, "Pinky to paw promise, you're mine and I'm yours." If Doug rejects the money, she'll lock herself and the dog in her van until he leaves.

When Ruby turns around, Bull has managed to drag Dougie over to the lawn chairs and is plating a cheeseburger for him. "Coleslaw is there; Polly brought the potato salad and you shouldn't skip that." If Ruby had ever wanted a brother, she would have wanted him to be Bull.

Dougie takes the plate, spoons on the sides, not being shy about amounts. "This is awfully nice of you."

"Don't want to see good food go to waste." Bull has his third burger on a new paper plate. "You know what I mean?"

Around a mouthful of coleslaw Doug agrees. He's a big guy, fifty-ish, gray streaked throughout dark hair, and has the look, in Ruby's eyes, of a guy who might be a former jock now coaching kids in some fashion. She doesn't know why that idea pops into her head, but then, she is a psychic after all. Despite the contention between them, Ruby sees in Dougie's aura a strong decency of character, and that is why she doesn't drag her feet going back to hand him the envelope of money. She is certain that he will accept it.

"My mother is a formidable character and she isn't going to like this."

Ruby takes the plate from Dougie, hands it to Polly. Takes his hands in her own and turns them so she can read his palm. They grow hot in her hands, and he blushes. "You are a good son. You take good care of her." She runs a forefinger along his life line. "And your mother loves you and will listen to you." She folds his fingers around the envelope.

Dougie doesn't say anything for a moment. He slides the envelope into his breast pocket without even counting the money. Then, "Can I have my plate back?"

The man stays until dark, and the picnic begins to feel like a party. I like chasing fireflies, and Boy thinks that I'm deranged. He prefers a siesta after eating. The humans talk well past when I think it's time to go in and cuddle. Finally the new man gets up and I am quite intrigued as he and Ruby, who challenged each other earlier, walk arm in arm to his car. I follow at a close distance. Their verbal farewell is inflected with the sense that they might see each other again.

25

When Ruby finally thinks to listen to her messages, the one from her daughter is indeed a warning that she should be prepared for disappointment. Sabine has been picking up a threatening vibe. It makes Ruby proud to think that her daughter's skills are so developed, even as Sabine pretends she doesn't have any. It's late, really too late to call, so Ruby thumbs a quick text to let Sabine know that, for now, things seem to have worked out. The Hitchhiker is curled up on the end of the unfolded bench seat, her eyes closed but her woolly bear caterpillar eyebrows reveal that she is not asleep by the way they rise and fall with Ruby's every move.

The high anxiety that has been pressing down on Ruby for days now has vanished and she feels in danger of floating away. Imagine Bull Harrison handing her $500 as if he was pulling spare change out from between the couch cushions. Ruby smiles thinking of the look on Polly's face, something between shock and suspicion. After Dougie had driven off, Ruby caught Bull by the arm and pulled him into a hug. He resisted, then gently patted her on the back.

"Where, Bull? Why?" She knows that she's being inarticulate, but he'd known what she was asking without asking. Where did he ever get such money and why did he give it to her?

"I had it. I'm not going to use it."

"Well, I'm paying you back."

"It's blood money. Please don't."

"Then you have to explain."

"You know that my son Jimmy died."

"Yes."

"He was a drug dealer."

Ruby stays perfectly still, aware that if she so much as makes a consoling comment, Bull will shut up.

"I found that in the house, a couple bundles. I found it long after he was dead. At first I felt like it was kind of a gift from him. Something to keep me going. But that idea just didn't stick. I could have turned it in, probably should have. But . . ." Bull pauses long enough to light a cigarette. "I didn't."

Polly chimed in, "Nobody has missed it. You weren't taking food out of a kid's mouth by keeping it."

"No, but I coulda donated it. Anonymously, like."

"Is there more?" Polly again.

"I've been chipping away at it. But yeah."

Ruby patted Bull on the arm. "It was a gift. Jimmy did leave it so that you could find it, use it when you needed to. I believe that."

"He was a good kid when he was little. No one remembers that."

They sat in silence for a bit longer, each in their own thoughts until Boy got up off the ground, shook himself violently, and suggested to Bull that it was time to turn in. The August humidity had thinned, and muted stars appeared overhead. A nimbus-frosted quarter moon.

Polly pulled her car keys out of her caftan pocket. "I'm heading out. Thanks, Bull, for a very nice evening. And, Ruby, I couldn't be happier for you."

Ruby wrapped her arms around Polly and the two women held each other for a long moment. It was such a rare event, this affection for another person. As they let go, they simultaneously put out hands to bring Bull into the circle.

•　　•　　•

The file folder and its contents has been shoved aside for the past few days, almost forgotten what with the more immediate realities. Ruby pulls it out now, having no particular place to go and no particular reason to drive off. Bull and Boy have headed off to hold up the wall of the Cumberland Farms. Polly is hunting down a missing cat. The Hitchhiker is getting her beauty sleep in the passenger seat, biding her time until Ruby pulls on her Skechers and takes her for a walk. Ruby pops up the folding table, sets the folder on it, pours a second cup of coffee. This time she lays her hands on the unopened file, divining what, if anything, it might tell her psychically. The palms of her hands grow warm, a little damp. She picks them up and there are faint imprints of her hands on the folder, quickly evaporating in the day's warmth. Ruby is given only minute flashes, impressions, nothing dynamic. A taste of school macaroni and cheese. The scent of glue. Nothing more than any adult gets thinking about elementary school. She does not see the face of her mother. Nor of this stranger named Estelle Williamson.

Where did her mother go? Like all the rest of the girls at the convent orphanage, Ruby had secretly hoped for a long-lost relative to come claim her, to right the wrong that had been done in leaving her there. What if her mother had gone back to reclaim her, but Ruby had disappeared? Was she still looking for her?

The questions have become a little foolish, and Ruby grabs the dog's leash. Not that she won't stop thinking, now that she's opened the floodgates, but at least she'll be getting some exercise in the process.

The Hitchhiker acts like she had been expecting to be disappointed. Jumping and dancing, all jolliness and frivolity. Ruby doesn't even have to touch her to know that the dog is hoping that their walk will take them to the lakeside. She just loves it there.

"Okay, let's go to the lake." This time they won't wander over to the private dock. This time they'll stay on the correct path and just enjoy the scenery. The dog will paddle about at the water's edge and Ruby, who has never learned to swim, will try to keep her feet dry.

•   •   •

The stroll around the lake leads to its logical terminus, the Lakeside Tavern. Ruby's recent economics prevent her from even entertaining the notion of stopping for a bite. She's got to rebuild her fractured finances, which means, of course, another Saturday at the Farmers' Market and Makers Faire. Checking her watch, Ruby picks up the pace, time to retrieve the van and get over to the park. With all the emotional commotion of last night, she'd forgotten that today is Saturday.

Emily Hippy Chick greets Ruby with a beaming smile that belies her surprise that Ruby has shown up. "Oh, I wasn't expecting you. Cynthia said you had left town."

"Did she now? Wonder why she thinks that."

"At any rate, I rented your space to someone else."

"It might be good to have a different space today. What's left?"

"Nothing."

Ruby absolutely knows that Emily has been given firm orders. "It's a big park, and I have a small tent."

Is that a bead of sweat forming at Emily's temple? The beaming smile begins to quaver. "I think we're supposed to keep within the boundaries the town has given us."

"Boundaries can be flexible. I don't see any yellow tape. Border walls."

"Um." Emily pulls out a folded diagram of the area. Thin numbered rectangles are described on the paper. She runs a forefinger along the diagram. "Maybe here?" She's pointing to a block that seems to abut the phalanx of porta-potties.

"Why not?" Ruby looks at this not as an insult, but as an opportunity. Everyone who needs the comfort facilities will pass her way.

Ruby hands Emily the day's fee. This continued animosity from Cynthia Mann has become puzzling in the extreme. After their ses-

sion at the bridal shower, after the woman broke her teapot and never
said boo, after smearing her to Mrs. Cross, how much more hate has
this woman got in her? It's almost like Cynthia took one look at Ruby
and hated her on sight, the polar opposite of someone falling in love
at first sight. Maybe it's the same thing, an emotion driven by pher-
omones and not by logic. Maybe there's something about Ruby that
speaks to a deep turmoil within Cynthia's psyche. She only wishes
that she'd been able to suss it out when the opportunity had presented
itself at that shower. If she'd grabbed Cynthia's hands instead of using
the tea leaves, maybe she could have divined what it is that drives
this loathing.

Ruby drives the van across the field and up to her space on the
outer edges of the Faire. Fortunately, the blue and white outhouses
are freshly delivered and odor free. She manages to set up the tent far
enough away that she doesn't look like she's selling tickets to use the
potties. The Hitchhiker bustles about, knowing what their day will
look like, happy to be of assistance. She parks herself beside the sandwich board, ready to leap into action.

It's too hot to let her hair down, so Ruby keeps it in its twist, takes the
silk scarf and winds it around her head, turban-style. In her hand mirror, she looks authentic and Ruby tries not to allow that this might not
be the most flattering style for her. And then wonders at that thought.
She prides herself on being a woman without vanity, or at least having a controlled level of vanity. She knows what colors are best for her
skin tone, keeps herself trim. But other than that, who is she trying to
impress? Enough of that. She dabs on a little more lipstick. Open for
business.

The morning clips along, a nice stream of clients stopping by, and
for the first time, Ruby has some repeat customers. Mostly dog people.
She needs to make a determination if a rescue pup will accept another
rescue pup. Yes, the dog says, as long as I am alpha. Another owner is
curious about a new behavior, facing the wall and barking. The dog
explains to Ruby that there are mice in that wall. She recommends

seeking out a good exterminator. The humans are the common garden variety of should I seek a new job, boyfriend, apartment, vacation. All in all, this awkward spot is turning out to be lucrative. People seem less hesitant to chat with a psychic as they wait for an open porta-potty and Ruby begins to suspect this space offers a comforting discreetness. Although, she could use a little of the scent of lavender emanating from her last neighbor's herbal booth, instead of the cloying scent of urinal cake.

There is a lull in the action and Ruby takes advantage of it by taking the dog for a little walk around and using ten dollars of her replenished cash to buy a Caesar salad wrap and an iced tea. The day has gotten progressively hotter and she feels sticky beneath her caftan. She can't afford to bag it now; she's got to stick it out till two. Despite what Bull has said, she's going to pay him back even if it's in twenty-dollar increments.

With the wrap gone, and one tiny piece of chicken accidently dropped in front of the patient dog, Ruby collects herself and gets back to business. The dog, feet pumping up and down, starts yipping as if she's spotted someone she knows, which is basically how she greets everyone, but this time Ruby hears her thoughts.

"I know him. He's a nice guy. He let me lick his plate."

Ruby looks up to see Dougie Cross coming across the field. "Oh, shit." All she can think is that his mother, the redoubtable Mrs. Cross, has sent him back to return her money and take her dog. Ruby jumps to her feet. Wishes that she wasn't dressed as a fortune-teller, but in her ready-for-battle jeans and T-shirt. She unwinds the turban. Stands up, fists clenched. She can grab the dog and jump in her van and be off in a heartbeat. She's done it before.

Dougie spots her. Smiles. Would a man about to break her heart smile so broadly?

The Hitchhiker, oblivious to the danger, runs toward him and he scoops her up.

"Hi, Ruby! Bull told me I'd find you here."

"Good afternoon, Doug. What brings you all the way back to Harmony Farms so soon?" Like he'd never left. The idea that he'd driven all the way to Stockbridge and then turned right around the next day and driven another two hours to give her the bad news is frightening.

"Oh, I don't live that far away. I live in the next town over, North Farms."

"So you didn't go to your mother last night?"

"Oh, no. I called her." Doug looks a little embarrassed. "Of course I should have said that first. She's okay with letting you have the dog. I told her that you made a great impression on me and that I think it's the best thing."

The fight or flight instinct quickly settles into relief. The weight of the caftan is suddenly smothering. "Thank you, Doug. It means the world that you were willing to go to bat for me."

"I couldn't live with myself if I hadn't."

Ruby sits down, gestures to Doug to do the same. The dog is in his arms, licking his face. Ruby's curious now. Why didn't he just call her with the news?

"Just here for the Farmers' Market?" That's such a couple thing to do that Ruby supposes he's left his spouse/girlfriend/partner at the herbal booth.

"No." Doug keeps his eyes on the dog, now wriggling free of his lap. "Um, look, I don't do this often, so bear with me."

"Okay. A reading, then?" The Hitchhiker takes a lap around the table, sits beside Ruby.

"Actually, no. I mean, not now. Maybe some time." Doug draws the folding chair up closer to the table. Under his big frame, the chair looks incredibly vulnerable. "Would you ever consider . . ."

Ruby doesn't even have to use her psychic powers on this one. "Going out with you?"

"Yeah."

"Sure. But I don't know how long I'll be in town." Ruby phrases this very carefully so that she doesn't make him regret going to bat for her. "I have an engagement in New Hampshire in a week." There she will join the Benini Brothers Carnival on their travels for the next couple of months.

"Then how about tonight?"

"I'd like that very much."

26

It's not like Ruby hasn't had a date before. When Sabine was little, she refused to date, too busy trying to keep one step ahead of child protective services and poverty to pay much attention to anyone else. After Sabine went off to college and effectively never returned to the family bosom, Ruby did enjoy an evening out, a movie, a little making out. She even dated one of Sabine's neighbors, Arthur Bean, for a little while during her brief period living with Sabine in Moose River Junction, attempting to convert herself into a stay-at-home human. Ruby is pretty sure she doesn't have a string of broken hearts left behind her. Nor has she allowed herself to have her own heart broken apart. Another reason to keep the wheels on the pavement and the steering wheel in her hands. So she'll go out with Dougie. They'll meet at six at the Lakeside, her recommendation. Although there are plenty of other better restaurants in the area, the Lakeside has become something of a habit. The food is good, the view nice. And she's bound to have an acquaintance wander in, so she can establish a certain amount of stability in a subtle fashion. If you can say hi to someone across the room, you've got a string or two holding you down. Just enough to bolster her case that she is a stable person, worthy of keeping the Hitchhiker, even if she can snip that string with a pair of nail scissors when she's ready.

In the meantime, the Makers Faire is over for the day and Ruby is packing up. It's been an unusually good day; she's pulled in twice what she did on her last best Saturday. She's desperate for a shower, so will head to the Dew Drop for the night. It is such a relief to be able to spend a little and not fret that it will cost her what she holds most dear. Another couple of days like this and, fingers crossed, the Westfalia doesn't act up, she's out of Harmony Farms.

Ravi greets Ruby with his usual grace, happy to give her a room. This one is a different room from her usual end of the complex space and lacks a little of the charming crookedness. Her moisturizer stays put where she sets it on the shelf, however the wall art is exactly the same as the other room. It both feels different and feels like home.

The Hitchhiker sniffs around, looks a little puzzled that, at least scent-wise, this isn't her familiar digs. Then she jumps on the bed and circles three times. Burrows her nose beneath her hind leg. Sighs. Sleeps.

First date. Local tavern. Ruby pulls out her best jeans and her white button-down shirt. Another good reason to take a motel room today is that she is sure that there is no iron in Bull Harrison's possession. Much less an ironing board. The motel room ironing board squeals in protest as Ruby sets it up. She heats the iron, presses both the jeans and the shirt, and then jumps in the shower. She almost feels decadent. Ravi's selection of bath products is quite nice. He may run a slightly seedy motel, but he doesn't skimp on the quality of shampoo and soap.

Refreshed, Ruby pulls out the file folder once again. Alongside it on the desk is her laptop. On television, all you have to do is look someone up on the internet and all will be revealed. She opens the laptop, boots it up. Opens up her Facebook account. Ruby scrolls down, cheered by the humorous memes and pretty travel pictures posted by the sundry "friends" she's attracted, mostly through Sabine, and the few real friends she's left in her wake. An ad for a special kind of dog harness pops up. Algorithms are more psychic than she is, and Ruby sometimes wonders when she'll be automated out of a job.

The fussy air conditioner grinds out an atonal tune, shudders, rests. Ruby goes to the search bar. Types in "Estelle Williamson."

Ruby thinks that if she can just locate her that there might be a trail of breadcrumbs leading toward her mother. Predictably, there is more than one: young, old, black, white, fat, thin. Living from sea to shining sea and across the ocean. And those are just the ones with a profile picture, the rest are blank-faced silhouettes. "Where do I start?" Ruby closes the laptop. Would a woman as old as Estelle must be even have a Facebook account? A thought that gives Ruby another idea. This time she simply googles the name, adds approximate age and sits back. She'd have better luck throwing a dart blindfolded. So many like-named women in the world. The name pops up in genealogical paragraphs, obituaries, and come-ons for pseudo-scientific products. Ruby gears herself up for a prolonged hunt, reading every fragment of information available via the search engine. If she promises herself an hour a day, she should get through this in a week. Maybe two. Already she sees that fragments lead to other fragments. And then she wonders, even if she lands upon the right woman, what in these fragments will connect *her* to Estelle Williamson? Maybe answers aren't to be found in genealogies or obituaries, but news articles. Holy moly!

Ruby closes the laptop, flops back on the bed, bouncing the little dog from her siesta. The Hitchhiker regroups and presses her back against Ruby's side. In moments they are both asleep.

Ruby startles awake. The dog is standing on the edge of the bed, looking at the air conditioner, which is spurting water all over the floor.

Ravi, all full of apologies, cannot move Ruby to another room as the Dew Drop Inn is full for once. He mops up the water. Offers to bring her a fan. Ruby waves off his offer of a refund; he's already giving her the friends and family discount, plus honoring her AAA membership; she can't expect him to do more. She knows a shoestring operation when she sees it and a desk fan will be enough to cool her off. After all, her van only offers open windows and a battery-operated fan, so she's used to roughing it.

It's nearly five-thirty, so Ruby pulls on her freshly ironed clothes, does her hair in a neat twist, and dabs on a little makeup. Nothing like her fortune-teller persona. This is the conservative Ruby. She adds the little hoop earrings that the kids gave her for Christmas a couple of years ago, a pair that says its wearer is a regular gal.

Ruby looks at herself in the mirror, smiles. Her distinctive little freckle winks back at her. Presentable.

The sun is setting prettily over the lake when Ruby takes her seat at the outside table for two where Dougie Cross waits for her. He is all gentleman as he stands and offers Ruby the seat with the best view. It puts the lowering sun right in her eyes, so she shifts a quarter turn to the right so that they are now adjacent instead of opposite. Fortunately, the table for two is big enough to manage a certain comfort zone between adjacent nominal strangers. They chit, they chat, they pore over the menu, listen to the recitation of specials, order a glass of wine each. Choose the same entrée, buttermilk fried chicken with garlic mashed potatoes, and seasonal vegetables that both of them will leave on their respective plates. They will not order dessert, but both will have another glass of wine.

Ruby guides the conversation with the skill of a fortune-teller, easing from Doug the salient facts of his life without planning on giving away too many of her own. But Doug is not without conversational skills of his own and applies his training as a school counselor to good use, easing Ruby's reserve. With half the chicken gone, too much really for one meal, they settle into a conversation more typical of a third or fourth date. Ruby knows that Doug is Dougie because he is a junior. He's in this part of the state because he went to college in Boston, and didn't want to go back to Western Mass. And, as she intuited about him at first sight, he does indeed coach high school sports. Baseball in the spring and basketball in the winter.

"Did you play as a kid?"

"Sure did."

"And you went to college on a sports scholarship?"

"Yes." Doug smiles at her. "Are you doing your psychic thing?"

"Not without permission. But let me guess—you found education as rewarding as the trophies."

"Got a nice one for debate club. Yeah. That and the fact that I tore my ACL and put an end to any serious hopes for a future in professional baseball."

"That's awful."

"I would have made an okay fielder for a triple A team, but I'm a great counselor."

"Things happen for a reason."

"I've heard that said before, but my own philosophy is that you have to make lemonade out of oranges." Doug laughs at his own joke and Ruby kind of likes that.

"What about you? Any broken dreams?"

Where to start? Ruby knows that her particular story lends itself to pathos. Runaway teen, teenage mother, homeless, making a living reading tea leaves and palms. Yuck. Usually she just tells a sanitized version: "Independent" at an early age. Romance of the road. That sort of thing. But there is something about Doug that pushes a desire to tell a more complete version of her story. Maybe it's that all this recent interest in locating her origins has cracked open a door in her reserve that she's kept shut. She's on a new journey toward finding out her history; the old journey, away from it, has come to an end.

"I was left in a Canadian orphanage when I was a newborn. I guess you could say that my only dream was to be retrieved, but that dream never came about. I'm not sure it qualifies as 'broken,' but it has certainly impacted my life."

"Jeez."

"When the nuns took aim at my, um, unusual skills, I ran away. I hooked up with a carnival, learned how to use those skills to make a living."

"How old were you?"

"Fourteen." Ruby pauses, chews a piece of chicken. Sips from her water glass. She likes that Doug waits, doesn't immediately pepper her with questions she may not answer. "I was raped and ran away again, this time pregnant."

"Sweet Mother of God."

"She didn't listen to my prayers, I can tell you that."

"What happened?"

"I have a daughter, a most beautiful daughter, who has two of the most beautiful children. Sometimes dreams come to you before you're ready but end up all right. It wasn't easy, and I'm not proud of some of the things I've had to do, but it worked out. So, Doug, I don't look back on what I might have hoped for. I got it. A life I enjoy, a nice family when I need them, and now, thanks to you, a really wonderful companion."

"And now? Do you have anything you dream about?"

Ruby sits back, folds her napkin. The sun has slipped behind the hills and the afterglow of sunset is radiant in golds and reds. "I want to find my mother."

Doug lays his hand on hers where it lies on the edge of the table. He doesn't say anything, doesn't press to find out what she's done so far, what she's planning on doing to accomplish this needle-in-the-haystack quest. The feel of his large hand gently encompassing hers gives Ruby a curious sense of calm. She looks to read Doug's aura and sees only the sunset.

"Crazy, huh?"

"No. Not at all." He lifts her hand away from the edge of the table and holds it gently, as if it were a small pet. "When he was a young man my father discovered that the man he thought was his grandfather wasn't. It was a revelation of a deeply held family secret, something so embarrassing, as only family secrets were in those days, that of course no one would tell him the truth. His mother claimed she had no information; his grandmother was dead. His aunts and uncles maintained radio silence on the subject. So, he embarked on a quest of his own."

"Did he have a starting place?"

"He did. Letters with vague references, neighbors who could be encouraged to talk."

"I've no starting place except a document assigning custody of me to the convent and a Baptismal certificate giving me nuns and a janitor for godparents."

"That's a paper trail."

"It's more of a dead end." Ruby extricates her hand from Doug's, excuses herself to use the ladies' room. This is quite enough of soul baring for her.

When she gets back to the table, Doug has settled the bill. He stands at her approach and now is the moment of extending this pleasant sojourn or calling it a night. Ruby has had a good time and wishes she could suggest a walk around the lake, but it really has grown too dark. Instead, Doug suggests, as they haven't indulged in the Lakeside Tavern's signature molten chocolate cake, that they head into town to find some ice cream.

"Capital idea." Ruby gathers her purse.

"Could I ask an indulgence?"

"Of course."

"Would you be willing to drive? I've always wanted a ride in one of these." He points to the Westie, waiting in the parking lot like a faithful cow pony outside the saloon.

"Sure, but I have to warn you, there's nothing smooth about it. It's a bit like riding in a washing machine."

Doug hauls himself into the passenger's seat. Ruby figures that a man whose mother raises dogs wouldn't care about a bit of loose dog hair on his clothes, so she makes no apologies for what the Hitchhiker has left on the seat.

As they reach the main road, Ruby shifts into third, asks, "So, in the end, did your father find out the secret?"

"He did. Kind of a sweet story in its own way. Apparently Great-grandma got herself in a little trouble with a charming scoundrel and Great-grandpa stepped up to the plate and married her."

"Your great-grandfather sounds like a decent, kind man." Ruby signals to turn onto Main Street. "I suspect you take after him. I mean, philosophically."

"I'd like to think so."

Ruby insists on paying for their cones, hers maple walnut, his butter pecan. They stroll along Main Street like tourists, window shopping and admiring the street art. Carrie Farr drives by, toots her horn, and Ruby waves. Emily Hippy Chick comes out of the Country Market and asks Ruby if she's planning on doing the Faire this weekend. "If I can have the same space, yes. I think I'll stick around." That potentially less-than-perfect spot had proven to be quite perfect.

"I know that you consider yourself a wayfarer," Doug says around a mouthful of butter pecan, "but you sure seem to have made friends here."

"You can make friends and still move on."

"Is that so?"

Ruby waits for the inevitable pitch to stay put. She's heard it often enough that she can recite the lines from memory. It is one of the gravest dangers in making friends. They don't cotton to abandonment. But Doug just finishes his cone. Subject dropped.

"I should be getting back. The Hitchhiker will need her evening potty break."

They head back to the Lakeside Tavern to collect Doug's car. There is a space beside it and Ruby slots the van into it. Handshake or peck on the cheek? Ruby wonders. "I've had a lovely time, Doug. Thank you for dinner."

"Thank you. Thank you for taking pity on this guy and saying yes to a date."

"I usually don't. Almost never."

"Then I consider myself very lucky." Doug presses a hand to his chest with a dramatic flourish.

"How much Irish do you have in you?"

"None that I know of, why?"

"You seem to have the gift of blarney."

"Well, maybe that charming scoundrel who seduced my great-grandmother was Irish."

"Maybe you should get one of those DNA tests done."

And in that moment, it strikes Ruby that *she* should take a DNA test.

27

"So, how was your day-yate?" Sabine knows better than to treat a dinner out with a new friend seriously. In her whole life, Sabine has never been threatened with her mother's falling in love with anyone other than herself and her family. And, now, the Hitchhiker. Oh, there were times in her young life when Sabine *encouraged* her mother to look elsewhere for affection, but Ruby never took that seriously either.

"Very nice. Great buttermilk fried chicken."

"Skip to the chase, Mom. Did he kiss you?"

In fact, he had.

There is just enough of a pause in replying, that Sabine jumps on the implication. "Good for you."

Ruby forestalls the next remark. "And, no. He drove off in his car and I drove off in mine."

"You know that saying . . . If this van's rockin.'"

"Nothing rocked."

"Not even your world?"

"Stop it." Ruby is laughing. In fact, that good night kiss was quite nice. A little zizz of interest was definitely felt. "But there is something that came up that I want to talk to you about."

"Okay." Sabine takes a moment to redirect a child toward the chore he is tasked with. "Shoot."

"I'm going to take a DNA test."

"And that will do what?"

On television, swabs of DNA become markers to find criminals, or reveal nationality, prove paternity. What will knowing if she's Scottish or English or French or Lithuanian actually tell her? "It will be a starting place. If I join one of those databases, it may show me that there are living relatives. To me and to you."

There is the sound of a door shutting. "Molly came home yesterday crying because she divined that her friend Amber is going to move. Amber knew nothing about it and got mad. Then her mother called me to ask if I wanted any of their houseplants because, you guessed it, they're moving."

"I don't know if the genetic marker for being a psychic is possible, but wouldn't finding out that somewhere in our history there were others like us be a good thing?"

"You mean your mother?"

"Yes. If taking a swab of spit out of my cheek will in any way lead me to the woman who left me behind, then I'm doing it."

"But it may not lead you to the reason."

I cannot decide if I like living in the rolling house better or living in the place where lots of other people live. In the one, it's just me and Ruby. In the other, there are so many lovely scents to follow. In the rolling house—the van—we get to be with Boy and his person. Here, where we are now, I get to meet so many nice people. I get pats and treats. What could be better? Plus, it's cooler here, or at least it was until the thingy that blows cold air stopped blowing cold air. And I get to stretch out on the bed. In the van, we are sometimes a little more scrunched together than I like. Especially when Ruby doesn't open up the bed.

I have read the signals and I can see that it is time for us to go back to sleeping in the van. Ruby has packed up her things. She's borrowed the horrible machine that scares me a little so that I have to bark at it, and she cleaned all the dirt that she brings into it out of the van. Sprayed it with that nasty stuff that takes away all the good scents of last night's dinner and my own lovely doggy smell.

I am surprised when we don't follow our usual route into town, or toward the lake, where I hope to get a nice run in, or to Boy's place. Instead we get on the fast road, with the cars that go around us instead of keeping patiently behind us. I sense that this is going to be a long ride, so I curl up on the seat and close my eyes.

The wonderful thing about living in your transportation is that you never leave anything behind. Ruby could point this van in any direction on a whim and never have to go back and pack. She gooses the Westfalia up to sixty miles per hour and feels the fetters of a settled life break away. If she chose to, she could leave Harmony Farms in the dust, leaving behind her the haunting legend of the psychic who, for a time, made life better for the animals within the town's borders. Apropos of that, Ruby is on her way to a farm to analyze what has been described to her as a performance horse. She's known *performing* horses, so she's actually not sure if this is a circus horse or an athlete. Carrie Farr is sending her to Peterborough, New Hampshire, to a friend of hers in the horse world. This will be the first time that Ruby has had an opportunity to practice her animal communicator skills outside of Harmony Farms and she's a little nervous. What if, as she has thought before, this weird skill is restricted to the borders of a little affluent Massachusetts town? She'll fake it, that's what she'll do. This is a premium job requiring a premium price which, apparently, the Peterborough horsewoman is willing to pay.

Ruby signals for her exit off the highway and heads north on a secondary road. Her directions seem to be leading her around and around, but eventually she comes upon a large Colonial-style house. A red barn is situated at a bit of a distance from the house, and between the two buildings, two horses doze in a large white-fenced paddock. A third horse paces in a small enclosure attached to a smaller barn. She figures out right away that one is going to be the beast in need of interpretation.

A woman comes out of the house, waves Ruby toward a second driveway that ends in front of the red barn. Predictably, she's dressed in haute equestrienne couture including really interesting boots adorned with a surfeit of buckles. The whole shebang smacks of wealth and privilege and Ruby immediately thinks of Poor Farm Estates and the unfortunate Great Dane. "Oh dear," she says to the Hitchhiker.

The dog has moved from the bench seat to the passenger seat and has been inspecting the view with her tail drifting slowly left to right. Interested, but not excited. Ruby shuts the van off and puts her hands on the dog, a little test to see if she's going to be able to carry this off.

"What is this place? You aren't going to leave me, are you?"

"Whatever would give you that idea?"

"It happens."

Satisfied that the psychic vibe is there and assuring her buddy that she is safe from abandonment, Ruby gets out of the Westie and greets the client.

Prudence is the client's name and she sticks out a firm hand for shaking. "Carrie thinks very highly of you."

"I think the world of her." Through the proffered hand, Ruby picks up a quick suggestion of competitiveness, and a little dash of nerves. She also gets the vibe that Prudence is a woman betting the proverbial farm on the outcome of Ruby's visit today. She gets a real sense of someone in the background, perhaps a husband, and the aura of a last chance.

Prudence leads Ruby to the big horse in the small paddock. She sees that the horse has a choice, in or out, which seems like a good idea except that the "out" area seems nearly as small as the "in" area. And this is the biggest horse she's ever seen. Every muscle ripples beneath a bronze coat, ears at attention. He is still for only a heartbeat then goes back to circling the twenty-by-twenty pen clockwise, pawing and snorting, shaking his head before trotting off counterclockwise. He is absolutely gorgeous, like an Elgin marble crossed with a dragon and come to life.

"He seems agitated. Is he usually kept in this small space?"

"He doesn't play well with others." Prudence inclines her head toward the pasture where the other two decidedly less spectacular horses are dozing on their feet. She puts a hand in a pocket and pulls out carrot chunks, which she shares with Ruby. "Besides, at the price I paid for him, I can't afford a self-inflicted injury. He may look big and strong, but he's as fragile as porcelain. You probably know that horses are about as accident prone as any of God's creatures."

Ruby decides that acting like she has horse experience is better than not. "Yes."

The horse doesn't approach the two women standing at his fence; he doesn't want their puny offerings. Ruby doesn't need to lay hands on him to know that he is claustrophobic and holds humanity in utter disdain. Carrot bites aren't going to make him docile. "What do you do with him? Carrie said he was a performance horse."

"Eventing."

"Which is?"

"Cross country, stadium jumping, and dressage."

"And cross country is . . ."

"Big fixed jumps, water jumps, ditches, et cetera. It's meant to suggest what you'd find in the hunting field, only bigger."

"Sounds a bit daunting."

"Oh, it is."

"So, you need a big, brave horse."

"Yes. And that's what he's supposed to be. He's been bred to do it."

"Does he know that?"

"We haven't discussed it." Prudence shakes her head. "The thing is, if I'm not brave, he's not. And, frankly, between you and me and don't you say anything to Carrie, he fucking scares me."

That doesn't come as a surprise. "So, what do you want me to help with?"

"Look, this is nonsense, no offence, but if you can let him know that I'm on his side . . ."

"Can you get him to stand over here?"

"I'll get him." Prudence goes through the little barn and comes back out in the paddock with a halter and a lead line with a long chain attached. The horse doesn't resist being haltered, but the cast of his eye suggests that he's already anticipating unpleasantness, exacerbated by the fact his owner has laced the chain around the nose band of the halter, effectively putting the brakes on his ability to resist. "Come on through. He won't hurt you."

Indeed, the horse is standing stock still. There is nothing relaxed in his immobility. He looks like a powder keg about to go off. Ruby mentally girds her loins and walks toward the horse, neither slowly, like a predator, nor quickly like a jerk. "Hey, big guy." She offers one of the carrot chunks, balancing it on the flattened palm of her left hand. The gelding doesn't even lower his nose to where he could sniff it. Everything about him suggests distrust.

"What's his name?"

"He has a long complicated registered name, but we call him Brando."

This animal is so tall that Ruby could fit beneath his chin and he wouldn't even notice she was there. With her right hand, Ruby carefully reaches up to touch the horse's shoulder. Unlike Carrie's troubled mare, she's not about to put her face close to this one. "Okay, Brando. Will you talk to me?" She lightly glides her hand from his shoulder to his neck, which is nearly rigid beneath her fingers. She wonders if she would hear a heartbeat should she rest her ear against his chest, which is just about level with her ear. Some instinct keeps Ruby moving her hand gently up and down his neck, over his withers, which she scratches. Suddenly she is rewarded with a heavy sigh, a puttering of his nostrils. Prudence looks surprised. Ruby keeps scratching.

Images begin to flood into Ruby from the animal, memories of mutual grooming with another horse, playfully rearing, bucking, running side by side with a pal. The taste of grass. The images are so strong that Ruby falls into something like a trance, a state of mind she rarely experiences. Eyes closed, she presses her forehead against the horse, breathes in his rich scent. She lets the images and equine thoughts float until she understands what this beast needs to tell her. Finally, Ruby feels something soft and moist against her cheek and then the touch of the cold metal chain. In a split second, Ruby is shaken out of the trance-state.

"He's never done that with me," Prudence says. "I've been waiting for six months for him to acknowledge me like that."

In the distance, the other two horses have roused themselves and moved under the shade of a tree. Ruby says nothing, watching the pair scratch each other's backs in the same way she had "seen" it in her trance with Brando.

"You need to start over with him. He needs to be a horse first, a competitor second."

"I don't have the time. I mean, we've got to be competing this year. I bought him for that purpose, not to be a lawn ornament."

Ruby pats the horse, whispers to him, "I'll do what I can."

She places her hands over Prudence's. "He's told me that he is claustrophobic in this little barn all by himself. He needs companionship. He is happy to jump big things, but he doesn't like his saddle. He doesn't like the bit. He is fighting both. He doesn't like that you are afraid of him. He needs you to spend more time just being with him with no saddle, no bit. He is willing, but he needs some accommodation, especially time to run around and, yes, he might hurt himself, but he craves it. He calls it free run. To run around without weight, bit, saddle, or human direction." She lets go of Prudence's hands.

Prudence reaches up and pulls the halter off the horse. Brando shakes his head, relieved of the restraint. He doesn't immediately move away. Prudence strokes his neck. "Okay, let's see what we can do to make your life better."

Back on the road, Ruby pulls off at a farm stand. She takes the dog out for a quick break, then treats herself to a cup of coffee and a freshly baked muffin. Sitting on a redwood bench, Ruby reflects over the events of the last hour. The Hitchhiker is doing her best I'm-not-really-begging-but-if-something-fell-from-your-lips-I'd-clean-it-up act. Ruby finds a carrot chunk in her pocket and drops that. Always game, the Hitchhiker snaps it up, mouthing it in a sportsmanlike way.

Free run. The horse had been filled with a desire Ruby herself has known. The need to be unrestricted. Unencumbered. To get back into the Westfalia and spin the metaphorical compass to see what direction she should take. Put some distance between herself and Harmony Farms and regain that wind in her hair feeling of life on the road. There is nothing and no one holding her back from doing that. Everything she owns is with her.

The dog spits out remnants of the carrot. Stands, shakes, bows, and points her nose at the van. "Time to go home."

"That is home." Ruby points her own nose at the Westfalia.

Yet, at the end of the day, the horse expressed a willingness to work, to, in effect, be fettered if only with the right equipment and with the right attitude from his owner.

"We aren't done yet," says the dog.

28

There is one good reason to stay put, if only for another few days. Ruby ordered her DNA kit and had it sent to Bull's address. Once she's got the kit and has sent off her sample, then she'll get back on the road. She'll give Joe Benini a call and see where they're headed, hook up with the carnival for a few weekends. The Farmers' Market and Makers Faire continues into early October, but she has no intention of sticking it out that long. By September she wants to be gone. She's always had itchy feet, always obeyed an instinctual call to migration, and fall has always been the hardest season to be still.

Doug called last night. Ruby filled him in on the DNA ordering, emphasizing that she'll send in the sample and be gone; as the results will be emailed, there is no need to sit tight to wait for an envelope to arrive. The conveniences of modern life. He countered by asking if she'd like to go on a picnic. She said yes.

Doug is still on summer break from the high school, so they choose Wednesday afternoon for their picnic. The day is, as promised, clear, less humid, and not as hot as it's been over the past couple of weeks. The little beach at the lake is packed so they venture farther on to a grove with an available table. The Hitchhiker approves and scampers about as if they have planned this day for her.

Without benefit of a kitchen, Ruby's contribution to the meal is from the Country Market, a selection of deli salads and cold cuts.

Doug has made fried chicken and potato salad. Fresh lemonade. Ruby thinks, but doesn't say, he'd make some woman a great husband. Probably has. There is a suggestion that Doug is one of those divorced men who married too young, or to the wrong woman, or both. He doesn't mention kids.

Plates filled, Ruby and Doug settle on opposite benches of the picnic table. The Hitchhiker stations herself under it, ready and willing to clean up should something edible fall to the ground. Conversation is easy and they bat opinions and observations around for a bit, mostly touching upon favorite television programs and bands. They laugh a bit about eighties styles, high-waist jeans and high hair, boxy jackets and mullets. Grunge bands and *Star Wars*.

"It really doesn't seem that long ago." Doug snaps a lid on the container of potato salad.

"I know. And yet it seems a lifetime ago. My daughter's first decade of life. I was eking out a living and then I kind of hit my stride, figured it out and made it work." Ruby slides the ham back into its deli bag, reaches for the roast beef and "accidentally" lets a slice drop toward the ground. It is gone before it hits the dirt.

"How did you do it?"

"Most people ask me *why* I did it. Short answer is because that's all I knew. I was given a gift, of sorts, and I exploited it."

"So, and don't think I'm trying to be insulting, you really are a psychic?"

"Most of the time. It comes and goes."

"And the animal thing?"

"I'm hoping that it's here to stay." Ruby reaches down and the Hitchhiker licks her hand. The vibe of connection is pure and quick. "You taste like meat," says the dog.

"Do you think your mother was a psychic?"

Ruby doesn't remember mentioning this to Doug, only the fact of wanting to find her, or find out what happened to her. "I don't know. I want to assume she was. I am, and my daughter is, and it's beginning to look like my granddaughter has some ability. That's something I would really love to know."

"That and why she left you?"

Ruby reaches across the table and takes Doug's hand in hers. Not as a psychic, but as someone who is growing fond of him. "Absolutely. I've lived with this mystery all my life and I'd like to solve it."

"When you get the results back from the DNA company, you should let them post them. There's a whole world of people trying to find their relatives out there. Who knows, maybe she's looking for you."

Isn't that exactly what she has been hoping? "I've been hiding in plain sight, Doug. I can't imagine that she couldn't find me if she had wanted to."

Doug comes around to Ruby's side of the picnic table. He sits beside her so that they are both facing the lake. The Hitchhiker takes stock of them and then wanders down to the water's edge. Ruby waits for him to tell her that she was a runaway, with an assumed name and no permanent address—how could she be found when she worked so hard not to be? He doesn't. They sit quietly like that for a moment until Doug slaps his knees, pushes to his feet. "Let's take a walk."

There is a lot of food left and, as Doug is heading to his mother's in Stockbridge for the rest of the week, Ruby has the leftovers. It's too much for her tiny cooler fridge, so she thinks that maybe Bull would like a nice dinner of leftovers and she'll keep what she can fit. She's on her way to his back door when the mail truck shows up. She pauses. Watches as the lady mail carrier pulls down the door of the dented mailbox, leans through the mail truck window, and slides in a day's worth of junk mail, bills, and, lordy, could it be? A white box.

It's not her mailbox. Ruby feels a bit sketchy to just help herself to Bull's mail even if there is something in there for her. She's always been a stickler for obeying the law, parking tickets, theft of personal property, and begging on the streets notwithstanding. It's not the eighties any-more. She has scruples. She turns her back away from the mailbox and marches up Bull's back steps. His bike is gone, as is Boy, so she braces herself and opens his unlocked back door.

As unkempt as the outside of the house is, the inside is no sur-prise. A short hallway is more coat closet than passageway, coats of the Army/Navy variety hang from pegs. Boots and sneakers are kicked to the wall in a mismatched helter-skelter fashion. Entering the kitchen, she notes a massive old wood-fired range takes up most of one wall. It is piled high with all manner of things, papers, pots, a mitten. Ruby makes her way across to the yellow-hued fridge, not certain if it's vin-tage seventies yellow, or just yellow from decades of Bull's cigarette smoke. She hesitates before opening it, imagining all kinds of science experiments that lie behind that rusted door. Surprisingly, it is nearly empty. Cans of Mountain Dew and a single plastic container. She has plenty of room to insert her contribution to Bull's nutrition.

Ruby goes back outside to wait for Bull, sitting on the top step of his sagging back porch. The Hitchhiker joins her, staring off into space as if she is thinking deep thoughts. For fun, Ruby lays hands on the dog and listens to what's going on in her head.

"I could have enjoyed more meat."

"Maybe for dinner."

"Is there a cat nearby?"

"Why do you ask?" This is interesting. Ruby looks around to see if there is a feline stalking the sparrows pecking at the leaf mold beneath the bushes.

"You are quivering inside, like you want to chase something."

"Anticipation. That's what that is called."

"Like hoping for a treat?"

Ruby runs her hand down the length of the dog's back, marveling at its softness. Marveling at the perceptive nature of this little beast. Marvel-ing, most of all, at this gift of canine interpretation. That the concatena-tion of scent and sound and senses form such clear thoughts in her own mind and in that of the dog. "Yes, like hoping for a treat." Ruby digs into her pocket and pulls out a Milk-Bone, fingers it into the dog's mouth, and is rewarded by a wagging tail. Is there anything more gratifying?

It is only a few minutes later when Bull pedals into the yard, his faithful yellow dog at his side. Ruby notes that the dog isn't even panting, but his owner is. Ruby stands up. She holds back from running up to Bull, urging him to quick! quick! open his mailbox, extract that white box that she is certain will contain the DNA kit. Ruby makes herself calm down. In her whole life, this is as close as she has come to being a kid on Christmas morning. And this is only the first step, it's going to be waiting for the results that will truly test her patience. The Hitchhiker knows that something is afoot, and she leaps and cavorts and yips as if she's the one encouraging Bull to mosey over to the mailbox, never mind lighting up that cigarette, and pull out the mail.

Bull finally notices Ruby standing there, eager-eyed. "Oh, hey, you check the mail?"

"No. It's not my box."

"So? You're the only one around here expecting anything."

So much for scruples. Ruby dashes to the box, yanks open the dented door and pulls out the mail. Nestled in the valley of a folded grocery store flyer, there it is. Family History Labs.

"That it?"

"It is. Now what do I do?" Ruby surprises herself by saying that out loud.

"Go stick a Q-tip in your mouth, I guess." Bull does that coughing/laughing thing.

Ruby studies the directions, pulls out the swab kit but doesn't open the package. She holds the swab kit in her hand and wonders if it behaves like a crystal ball or more like tarot cards that look backward instead of forward. Is she falling for a different kind of fortune-telling than that which she has practiced for forty years or more? Will this little object give her any answers at all to her questions? Should she ask it not only what it sees in her past, but in her future? She shakes off the thought as a bit of a stretch. Focus. A good cheek scrub and a run to the post office and she's done. Gone. Free to hit the road. Goodbye, Harmony Farms, hello . . . where? Ruby sets the kit down, pulls out her phone. Scrolls through her contacts looking for Joe Benini's number and can't find it. She could have sworn she'd saved it, but maybe not. She'll have to hunt the carnival down online and hope that Joe meant it when he said she could set up with them. And if it doesn't work out, then maybe she'll do something else.

My friend kept that odd little object in her hand, studying it sort of like how I study a stuffed toy, trying to determine the best way in to get the squeaky out. Finally she opened the packaging with a delightful crinkling sound. Made my teeth just want to gnash at something. Then she did exactly what I would have done had I been given the chance: she stuck it in her mouth. Oh, but I was mighty curious about that, and very much wanted her to let me have a taste. I have found those little white sticks that fall to the ground and bear a hint of sweet and more than a hint of human. I thought perhaps that's what this was. Imagine my surprise, then, when she took it out of her mouth and carefully inserted the little stick with its bulbous tip, into a thing and then into another wrapper and sealed it up. "That's that," she said, and I thought that it was really about time for dinner.

The post office in Harmony Farms is a typically New England–style sturdy brick building, foursquare and two stories. The handrail is bronze, and the black shutters are held back by wrought iron straps. It could have been a bank at one time, or a jail. Ruby doesn't really have to go to the post office to mail her package back to Family History Labs. It's in a pre-paid envelope; she could drop it off at any of the free-standing mailboxes around town. But she feels as though this particular piece of mail is so weighty as to need special consideration. This isn't some RSVP to a party; this is her essence. As if in welcome and encouragement, there is a parking space right in front of the building.

Inside, Ruby slips the mailer into the brass slot, hoping for a satisfying thud but hearing nothing. She turns to find Polly Schaeffer right behind her.

"I hear you're going out with that guy, the breeder's son."

"'Going out' is a fraught term, Polly. We've had a date, well, two, I guess you could say."

"And . . ."

"You and Sabine. Honestly, we're two middle-aged people enjoying a meal or two. That's it."

"Humphf."

"Humphf yourself." Ruby shoulders her purse. "Nice to see you. Have a lovely day." She won't tell Polly that she's finally about to drive away from Harmony Farms. She has avoided goodbye scenes all her life. Appear and then disappear. Leave them wanting more.

"Hey, can I ask you a big favor?"

Ruby's purse slips off her shoulder. "Sure."

"The volunteers at the shelter have come up with an idea for a fund-raiser."

"Go on."

"Would you be willing to read pets for an owner's contribution to the shelter?"

"And when would this be?"

"Well, they wanted to get your commitment before they set a date, but probably the end of the month."

Two weeks.

"Would a new washing machine be the target goal?"

Polly grins. "Yes."

Ruby thinks of that beautiful horse, his desire for being unfettered. His willingness to compromise. "Of course. Set your date."

They walk out into the August sunshine arm in arm. Ruby's van is just out front of the post office. The Hitchhiker sits in the passenger seat, patient as always. On the windshield, tucked neatly beneath the windshield wiper, is yet another parking ticket. Somehow Ruby has neglected to notice that that handy parking spot was designated a handicap space. As she has done with all the rest, she tucks it into the glove box to deal with later.

29

By now, Ruby has developed a routine, three days at Bull's, two at the Dew Drop, staying away from weekends when Ravi has to charge more, and then back to Bull's yard. The other day Ruby located a lawn mower in the side yard. She has never mowed a lawn in her life, but she got it started and pushed it around the front yard to see if she could do anything with the overgrown grass. Turns out, although the mower started, the blade was so dull all she succeeded in doing was matting the grass down and chipping away at the dandelions. She rolled it back to where it had been living happily, out of sight, out of mind.

Every day, even though she knows it's going to take time, she hopes for an email from Family History Lab letting her know that her results are available. She's opened the requisite account and studied the several ways she can maximize the information she will receive based on the raw material of her cheek cells. She schools herself: It's only been five days. Barely enough time for the mailer to have gotten to Ohio. Patience, she tells herself. Fifty-five years of not caring has been supplanted by this sudden urgency to know what she is made of. If not from whom.

Every night Ruby takes the file folder Sister Bea had sent her and ponders the imponderables of some information but not enough. She chides herself for imagining that she would have opened up this folder and found a clear document with the reason for her abandonment writ large. Instead, she has only the impression that—perhaps—her mother was overwhelmed or coerced. The question that won't go away is: Who the heck was this Williamson woman? An aunt? A grandmother? A friendly stranger? Surrendering agent. Ruby feels a thin trickle of psychic vibe work its way from hands to heart. The Hitchhiker has nosed her way under Ruby's elbow and set her chin down on the file.

On impulse, Ruby hunts down her phone and dials the number for the convent. She has a question, probably unanswerable, but she's going to ask it anyway. Although it's after five o'clock, Sister Beatrice Johnson picks up. "Sacred Heart, how may I help you?"

Ruby plows right past the niceties. "Do you think you could find out if an Estelle Williamson brought other children to the orphanage?"

There is a moment of silence so perfect that Ruby thinks she's been hung up on. Then, "Hang on." There is the sound of a door gently shutting, the lock being engaged. "Ruby, I've been here my whole life, as a child and as an adult." Sister Bea's voice is one level up from sotto voce. "There are things buried in the past that would curl your hair."

Ruby lets her former classmate talk without interruption, understanding that this is likely the first time that Karen Johnson as she once was has spoken these thoughts out loud. Suspicions and facts.

"After I sent you that file, I started getting a little curious about myself. I knew what I'd been told, accepted it, and never gave it much thought beyond the usual adolescent bouts of self-pity. Once I found that I had a vocation, it was more that I was deeply grateful that God had placed me here. I was meant to be here. But not all of us were. I kept a handful of files from that box where I'd found yours. The rest were sent away for shredding. Of the six or seven files I've pulled, five of them had Estelle Williamson's signature as the relinquishing agent. Including mine. Including yours. The dates go from mid-fifties to mid-sixties. Three of us are still here at Sacred Heart. One died before high school graduation. It's unclear of what cause. And then there was you, who eloped."

"Was that the official term, elope?"

"Yes. Better than AWOL or escaped, I suppose."

"Do we know anything of Estelle? Where she was finding these babies?"

"My gut tells me that she was running an unofficial safe haven for unwed mothers. Abortion in the United States wasn't legal at that time, girls had to disappear for a few months."

"So, girls in trouble were going over the border to find help?"

"It's one theory."

"That would explain the lack of a birth certificate in the file."

"None of the files contained a birth certificate. I feel so safe here in the convent because I exist here. I don't exist elsewhere."

"I don't exist on paper either. At least, not real paper. I've a bit of the manufactured sort."

"We all do what we have to do."

"You've been really helpful, Sister. I'm really sorry about predicting your fall in the playground."

"Funnily enough, that may have been the beginning of my vocation."

"How so?"

"Remember old Sister Clementia?"

"Maybe—little apple doll face, wimple always slightly grubby?"

"That's her. Well, she got me to my feet and took me into the nuns' cloister to wash my knee. It was the first time I'd ever been where they slept, where they ate when they weren't with us. It was hushed and the light through the big windows was so lovely. I was awestruck by the beautiful bathroom they had. Then Sister Clementia took me into their private kitchen and gave me two cookies from the nuns' stock of Oreos and a glass of cold milk. On our way back to the schoolroom I saw that each sister had a room of her own. Tiny, to be sure, a cot, a prie-dieu and a crucifix. But private. I wanted in from that moment on."

"But haven't you ever wondered about your mother?"

"Of course. And I thank God every day in my prayers that she gave me to Him."

When Ruby is done with the call, she notices that the Hitchhiker has draped herself across her lap. Ruby has been stroking those long curly ears while she's listened to Sister Bea's story. She reaches for the file one more time, reads the intake report with a different view. It should be a lot easier to find an Estelle Williamson if she isn't looking for her as her mother. She's looking for a former midwife.

The laptop takes a moment to boot up. She types in Estelle Williamson again, but this time adds "midwife," "nurse" and the name of the province she likely operated in. A couple of hits, but they are all too young. She tries adding an age range that could work. Nothing. Ruby removes the province. Listens to an inner voice, types in Niagara County, NY. Bingo.

Death Notice: January 4, 1990, Estelle Williamson, age 83, of Easter Village. Former nurse. Owner/operator of a private home for delinquent girls, 1951–1964. No survivors.

Ruby clicks on the fragment and finds out little else about the woman who transported her over the border and denied her the privilege of being an American citizen.

Delinquent indeed.

"I've got something for you." It's Dougie Cross, fresh back from his visit to his mother.

"What?"

"Your dog's papers."

"Oh." Ruby hadn't given the idea of the Hitchhiker's papers a single thought. All she had worried about was being able to keep the dog. This is just gravy.

"How about I bring them when we have dinner tomorrow?"

"Oh, are we having dinner tomorrow?" Ruby lets a little flirtatiousness into her tone. Just a smidge.

"I'd like to, if you'd like to."

"I would." Ruby adds, "I have some interesting news."

"What's that?"

Because her discovery is so new, Ruby says, "It'll keep till I see you." She wants to think about it a little more before she tells anyone this intriguing clue to her origin story. She hasn't even told Sabine and she certainly should hear this before a new friend does.

"Can't wait to hear it. Now, would you be interested in Italian food?"

"Absolutely." Ruby thinks that there isn't a decent Italian restaurant in Harmony Farms; the closest is the Pizza Palace which is, technically, Greek. "Where?"

"North End of Boston. I'll pick you up at five, if that's all right."

"Nothing too fancy, Doug. I don't have dressy clothes." She's already worn her best blouse and jeans on their first date. Her space is so restricted that Ruby has always made it a practice to keep her wardrobe to a minimum. Some people know how to pack for a weekend, she knows how to pack for a lifetime on the road.

"Totally casual. Promise."

What with all the summer activities, the regularly scheduled FaceTime call with their grandmother has been marginalized in the kids' lives, but tonight she gets the call even before she realizes that she should have been waiting for it. The kids look tan and tired. Summer is almost as much work as winter. Molly is showing off new braces. When did she get old enough for braces? Tom pushes his sister aside, his own dental news to share, another lost tooth. He looks positively jack-o'-lantern. They talk a moment about the generosity of the tooth fairy and Ruby can see Molly in the background rolling her eyes, clearly no longer a believer.

Sabine shoos the kids away from the screen and off to find their shoes so that they can go get ice cream. "Okay, I'm getting a bunch of vibes about you. What's going on? I'm getting a sense of discovery."

Ruby tells her about her conversation with Sister Beatrice.

"And you've found this woman? So you have a starting place."

"Yes. I do." A starting place, what a lovely description. Ruby is no longer fumbling around in the complete dark. She's got a keyhole letting in a bit of light.

"That's really exciting. What do you do next?"

"I'm thinking that I'll go there, to wherever this Easter Village is, poke around, see if anything comes to me."

"Well, my other sense is that you aren't ready to leave where you are just yet. Do I detect that you have another date coming up?"

"I do, but that's not what's holding me back." Ruby tells Sabine about the animal shelter fund-raiser. "Every time I think I'm going to leave this place, something or someone prevents me."

"Then stay. Maybe you have accidentally found your home port."

This is the point in the week when Ruby is parked at Bull's house. The Hitchhiker is welcome to stay with Bull and Boy while Ruby and Doug head to Boston for the evening so Ruby needn't worry about it getting too warm in the van while she's out. The August day has been thick with humidity, and there is the promise of rain later on.

Doug pulls into the yard at five o'clock on the dot. Taking Ruby's request for casual to heart, he's dressed in cargo shorts and a baby blue polo shirt, shirt tails out. Teva flip-flops complete the ensemble. She's also in shorts and wearing her favorite ruby-red T-shirt. Ruby carries a light sweater anticipating that the restaurant will likely be over air-conditioned. She doesn't own an umbrella, but Doug says he's got one in the trunk in case the promised rain catches them. For the first time in ages, Ruby gets into a passenger seat.

With traffic, it's after six o'clock when they reach the parking garage

closest to the North End. Summer tourists clog the sidewalks, standing in line waiting for their turn at a cannoli from Mike's Pastry or
for a table to open up at any one of the dozen restaurants on Hanover
Street. Ruby and Doug dodge and twist this way and that, and Ruby
begins to worry that they will have gone too far afield. Finally Doug
takes a quick left, a right, and heads up a flight of cement steps to a
tiny place that looks less like a restaurant than a bar. "This is the place.
Best food, no crowd."

Ruby keeps it to herself that no crowd may not be a good indicator
of the best food.

The hostess greets Doug by name and Ruby relaxes. Inside knowledge, isn't that the way to guarantee a great experience? She seats them
at a window table, the view, such as it is, is obscured by the potted
plants crawling up the plate-glass window seeking what sun must be
available for a couple of hours a day, given the shadow of the buildings
opposite.

Settled, Ruby has to ask, "So, you come here often?"

"Every chance I get. I worked here during college. Bussed, waited
tables. Tossed drunks. I stand by what I said about the food. Best in
town. We're not even going to order, just trust in the chef."

They settle down with red wine, dipping pieces of warm bread into
olive oil.

"Before I forget, here." Doug hands Ruby an envelope. "Mom's
signed over the AKC registration to you. The dog's pedigree is in
there."

Ruby studies the Hitchhiker's lineage, which goes back generations.
The superlatives of "Ch" along with a host of other initials that mean
nothing to Ruby are affixed to each name. "Ch, I assume that means
Champion."

"Yup. Your girl comes from great stock; she's even got obedience
champions, agility, certified companion dogs, every degree a dog can
earn except doctorate in her background."

"Guess that's what makes her special." She says this with an odd sense of jealousy. A dog can trace her lineage and all its glory back generations, and she can't even name her mother.

"You said you have some news?"

"A little piece of the puzzle about my mother." Ruby dips another hunk of bread in the oil. "It looks like she was an unwed mother in upstate New York, Niagara County. She went to live with a woman, Estelle Williamson, who was a nurse or midwife running a"—she finger quotes—"*'home for delinquent girls.'* " She would take these unwanted babies over the border into Canada to the convent."

"The convent where you grew up?"

"Yes, Sacred Heart." Ruby sips her wine. "It's like I've finally found a chink in the wall of silence surrounding my origins."

"I'm happy for you, Ruby." He briefly covers her hand in his.

"Naturally the first thing I did was go on the internet armed with this new information and bing bang, I located this Estelle woman almost right away. She's passed, of course, but she was in a little place called Easter Village."

"What are you thinking of doing?"

"I'm going up there as soon as I can." Unfortunately, in the immediate future, she's committed to catching up with Joe Benini and his carnival in New Hampshire. "I want to see if I can get some more answers, make more progress."

Doug raises his almost empty glass. Sets it down, fills it, raises it again. "To progress."

"To progress."

The promised rain comes down as they are leaving the restaurant and Doug apologizes for forgetting the umbrella in the trunk of the car. They arrive at the parking garage soaked but laughing, a little winded from race walking after such a big meal. It is a warm rain. Ruby is a little chagrined to see that she could now be a contestant in a wet T-shirt contest, as could Doug. They politely avoid noticing. Doug keeps the heater on so that they are nearly dry by the time they get back to Harmony Farms. The rain has stopped, or perhaps hasn't begun here yet. The lawn chairs are dry. The van is just too small a space to comfortably invite a man Doug's size in without getting tangled up in each other, and Ruby is not quite ready for that. Not yet.

"Would you like to sit outside for a bit? I can make coffee."

"That would be very nice."

Bull opens his back door and the Hitchhiker runs out to greet Ruby and Doug as if she doesn't have royalty in her background but is just your average mutt. Ruby scoops her up in her arms, nuzzles her and gets the strong vibe of feelings of relief. "You didn't think I wouldn't come back, did you?"

"I didn't know. I like them, but I love you."

"I love you. But I do get to do things without you."

"No."

"Yes."

Doug busies himself pulling the lawn chairs closer to the van, pretending he doesn't hear an apparently one-sided conversation between woman and dog. Ruby still doesn't know if he considers her profession legitimate or just a charming quirk of hers.

PART III

30

There had been a time in Ruby's life when she fantasized about her mother appearing incognito in her fortune-teller's tent. The fantasy woman would hold out her palm for reading and Ruby would be filled with the knowledge that this was her mother, she was holding her mother's hand. She would reveal herself to the woman, who was, of course, beautiful and exotic. One of two things happened in this waking dream: either the woman ran away screaming or she embraced Ruby and begged her forgiveness. Ruby had no control over which way the daydream went. It was a childish thing, this delusional hope. Magical thinking. After Sabine's birth, Ruby stopped doing it. Fantasy was crowded out by reality.

In the days since her discovery of what was likely her mother's story, Ruby had the old fantasy running free in her imagination. This time it wasn't her mother visiting the tent, it was her finding her mother sitting on a park bench in a town called Easter Village. With a name like that, Ruby was certain it would be a tiny place with a lovely park, maybe even a bandstand. Her mother would be there, maybe feeding pigeons, and there would be something so familiar about her that Ruby would sit down and reach for her hand. And there the fantasy stalled. Ruby cleared the idea out of her head. What she was doing was envisioning Harmony Farms.

• • •

Because the animal shelter is a bit out of town and there is limited parking, the planners have decided to hold the fund-raising event in the park on Labor Day. Ruby thinks this isn't the best idea, not about the park, but the day. If parents consider Labor Day a high holy day of summer—that is, the end of summer vacation, the kids back to school tomorrow— then they aren't likely to be interested in dragging their dogs to the park. Most need to still get school supplies. Besides, if people believed in her abilities and had problem dogs, hadn't they already consulted her?

Turns out that there are any number of folks willing to slap down ten bucks for a reading for Fido, even when they don't believe in it. They are out there to support Polly. Ruby is amazed, and humbled. The organizers quickly arrange a queue in front of Ruby's tent. A number of pet supply stores from the surrounding area have set up booths of their own, as have the Etsy crowd with handmade dog coats and blinged-out collars and leashes; others are shilling all-natural flea remedies and shampoos. Others are offering doggie Halloween costumes because it's never too soon to plan your dog's Halloween party. It's a bit like the Makers Faire except that the entire thing is devoted to animals. Polly Schaeffer will have her new washer . . . and maybe even a dryer.

The Hitchhiker sits on Ruby's left. She greets each of the dogs with an appropriate hello, then returns to Ruby. Dog after dog allows Ruby to spread her palms against its head, stroke the length of its back. But it is the Hitchhiker who is communicating, her chin firmly pressed against Ruby's knee. "She doesn't like being alone." "He is hoping for better treats." "No complaints." "Entering her first heat. Confused." Ruby relays the report, keeping it to herself that she isn't reading their dogs so much as she's listening to her own. She's getting the vibes from each canine, but the rapidity with which her little dog comes up with the other dogs' thoughts speeds things up considerably.

There are all manner of dogs, and several are repeat customers. Their people are enthusiastic about letting Ruby know she's helped them out with the behaviors they had wanted changed. Ruby thinks that it really is more about getting better training advice, but hey, who is she to discount her own usefulness? She is particularly delighted to catch sight of a massive fawn-colored Great Dane. Gulliver is attached to a very different person than the haughty Mrs. Jane Turcott. The dog is accompanied by a family. His ears are up, his tail is wagging, and he has a goofy Scooby-Doo look on his face. Rather than wait for the family to reach her, Ruby asks the next customer to take a seat, she'll be right back.

"Gully!"

"Wow, you are a psychic. How'd you know his name?" The apparent father of the group looks bemused, and a little suspicious.

"Gully was one of my first clients." She gives Gully a kiss on the head and is rewarded with a quick message. "I love my people. I have games."

"He's very happy with you. He loves playing with you. Thank you for making him a part of your lives."

"We were so sad to have to give him back to his owner. We knew he was well cared for, but we all had the feeling he wasn't happy. He didn't wag his tail when he was reunited. How sad is that?" The mom of the group has joined the conversation. She keeps one hand on Gully's head, resting it there like it was a tabletop.

"Very. Did Mrs. Turcott realize it?"

"Not right away. Took about a week and then we got a call from Polly. Yada yada, did we want him?"

Ruby grins. "I'm so happy. I felt terrible leaving him in that lonely place."

The dad recalls his manners. "We're Mo and Jess Shute. These rug rats here are Caden and Delilah. We'll wait our turn for a reading."

"Nonsense. I've already read him and he's beyond happy. Nothing else to add. Go make a contribution to the shelter and thank you."

The event is only supposed to go from ten to noon, but the vendors and Ruby are so busy that no one remarks on the fact it's long past noon. The food trucks that were serving breakfast suddenly start turning out sandwiches. Not willing to break momentum, Ruby doesn't leave her tent and is starving. As if he could read her mind, Doug shows up with lunch. She hasn't seen him in a week or so, what with school about to begin and freshmen to orient. She hasn't told him that she's leaving today after the event. She's already missed this weekend with the Benini Brothers Carnival; she can't really afford to miss another.

It feels like I'm back in the show ring. One dog after another to greet and converse with. The difference is that we are not being made to compete against one another. And no one is aggressive, all are enjoying quality time with their people. As am I. Although Ruby and I have been in communication since the beginning, today it feels like I'm faster at it. Or maybe she is. I'm not all that happy with her touching all these others, but I am happy to tell her their concerns. What she isn't aware of is that I can hear her concerns as well. Loud and clear, she is determined that today is the day we depart from this place. I know that I should consider any place where Ruby is, and I am, home. But my instincts are telling me that happiness isn't found in going; it is in staying.

The crowd has suddenly dispersed, as if by magic. Ruby lets Doug help her fold up the tent, notes how carefully he packs it into its canvas sheath, ties the ribbons—not too tightly—to hold the whole package together. She hasn't set up the table, of course, just the two folding chairs—one for herself and the other for the owner, so that's that. Doug puts the tent over his shoulder and grabs both chairs in one big hand. They walk to the van, and Ruby is struck with nerves, her mouth gone dry. Her usual departures are done without anyone to see her off. She doesn't know if she can just drive off with Doug thinking that she's simply going to the grocery store. He's been too nice to ditch like a bad date. Neither can she tell him she's leaving and have him expect, or hope, that she'll be back. She's not sure that he understands her shark-like need to move. She says nothing, wishes she could take off her caftan because she's desperately hot. She can't; beneath it she's only in her underwear. Her plan was to blast out of town, pull off for one last look at Lake Harmony, and quickly change into shorts and a tee. Doug has complicated things, for sure.

Ruby shows him where to stow the tent case and the folding chairs in the rear of the van, moves around to the front. Doug joins her. "Well, it looks like you're not going anywhere."

The left front tire of the Westfalia is sporting a wheel clamp, a parking boot. Ruby's unpaid parking tickets have caught up with her. To add insult to injury, another ticket graces her windshield. There is nothing she can do but laugh.

It being a holiday, the office of the parking clerk is closed. It being a holiday, Ruby wonders how it is that she's gotten a ticket. Monday through Saturday there's a two-hour limit, Sundays and holidays are not restricted. What cop on a holiday beat is going to boot a car when the owner of that car is freaking doing a fund-raiser for a town department that works out of the police department? The only cop she has seen all day is the nice young fella who gives the Hitchhiker cookies when they run into him walking his Saturday beat at the Makers Faire. The only car with a ticket is hers. Ruby's intuition is going into overdrive.

Ruby climbs into the Westie, closes the curtains, and changes into her street clothes. Doug waits outside, entertaining the dog by playing tug-o-war with her rope toy. Emerging from the van, Ruby shoulders her purse like a soldier shouldering his rifle and marches in the direction of the police station. "I'll get to the bottom of this."

Doug comes alongside. Ruby stops. "You don't have to come with me. This is my problem. I'm sure you have other things to do."

"No. I came to see you. So, I'll see you to the police station."

"You don't have to do that."

"I have a feeling I may have to bail you out."

Ruby gives Doug a playful poke in the ribs. "Ain't my first rodeo; I can handle myself."

"I'm sure you can. I kind of want to watch."

Lev Parker is the chief of police of Harmony Farms and, by extension, Polly Schaeffer's boss. He and Ruby know each other a little, at least by sight. Ruby blasts right by the sergeant at the front desk and walks into Lev's office. He, being raised well, gets to his feet and puts out a hand. "Ruby, thank you for what I'm hearing was a really good event. Polly tells me that you helped raise enough to cover—"

"That's not why I'm here. What do you know about my vehicle, my home, being clamped?"

"Clamped?"

"You know, one of those boot things. Keeping me from driving away."

Lev shakes his head. "Hold on a moment. Stay here." He leaves the small office to speak with the duty officer, returns. Ruby is still standing, and the Hitchhiker, being ignored by the humans, is sniffing around the corners. She comes away with a dust bunny on her nose.

The chief picks up his phone and makes a call, asking someone to please see him. While they wait, he types something into the computer on his desk. "Okay, three unpaid parking tickets. No moving violations. Registration in order. I didn't know you live in Moose River Junction. I have a cousin there."

"I'm rarely there." An understatement. One of the benefits of having a rooted daughter is being able to use her address for things that require a residency. Hence Ruby's Massachusetts license and the Westie's registration.

"I really don't see any of this as problematic. It usually takes a year's worth of tickets and a serious violation for us to get the boot out."

"Will you see that it gets removed?"

At that moment a young woman knocks on the open door. She is dressed in plain clothes, but Ruby knows right away that she's a traffic cop. There is a dent in her hairline to suggest the shape of her cap.

"Officer Milcharsky, do you want to explain to me why you felt the need to put a wheel clamp on the vehicle owned by Ms. Heartwood?" Lev's tone is neutral, neither putting the officer on the defensive nor inviting a lie.

"Sir?"

"You were on traffic this morning, correct?"

"Yes, but I didn't boot anybody's vehicle. I directed traffic. No tickets. No violations."

"All right, officer. Thank you."

"One thing, though." The young traffic cop looks at Ruby. "A couple of the guys have been a little inaccurate with chalk marking. Like, maybe it hasn't been two hours since they marked that white VW. Very specific. They think it's a joke."

The chief dismisses Officer Milcharsky. Looks at Ruby. "I guess we got a rogue out there."

"My guess is that selectperson Cynthia Mann is throwing her weight around. Bullying young police officers into harassing me."

The chief doesn't bite, and the look on his face suggests that he will be taking care of the in-house problem in his own quiet way. "I don't suppose you noticed a tow company name on that boot?"

Ruby shakes her head. No. All she saw was an orange abomination.

"I did. Turner's Towing." Doug has leaned into the room. "Little gold sticker on the base."

"Right. That's our town towing company." Lev grabs his phone and hits a speed dial button, rocks back in his swivel chair. "You folks head back to the vehicle. I'll take care of this."

Ruby really wants to wait around to hear the police chief lambaste his tow guy for being a dupe in a malicious game of revenge, but Doug gently takes her by the arm and guides her out of the office, out of the building.

"Why do you think this woman is doing this to you?"

"That's what's so frustrating; I have no idea why she has such animus toward me. I'm a hair across her ass, and I don't really know why. I do know that if she'd just leave me alone, not hold me up with wheel clamps, I'd be out of her hair."

"So, you are leaving?"

Ruby links her arm through Doug's. "Yes."

"Today?"

"If I can get the clamp removed." She likes that he doesn't protest. Doesn't try to hold her back from her urge to go. He only holds her arm securely against his side and says nothing.

31

Ruby and Doug and the Hitchhiker sit on a park bench under a tree and stare at the hobbled Westfalia. Lev Parker called to say that, what with the big travel weekend, Turner's Towing is very busy with breakdowns and won't be able to fix their mistake for a couple of hours. Or more. It's already almost four o'clock. The day has begun to cloud up and the day's heat is cooling down with a lovely light breeze from the west. It would be pleasant to sit here and contemplate pleasant things, but Ruby is seething. Her getaway plans have been trashed. Her quiet and unheralded departure, her hope of slipping away, shot to hell.

"Will you be going to Easter Village?"

"I wish I was. No, I have to catch up to Joe Benini's carnival. It's a commitment I made and he's giving me good terms." A commitment that seems like a lifetime ago. "I'm just going to have to be patient. I'll get to Easter Village in due time."

"Sounds like a good plan." Doug swings an arm around Ruby's shoulders. "Would you consider spending the night at my house? You could get a good start in the morning."

In much the same way as she feels the vibrations from touching the dogs, Ruby gets a sense of Doug's life from the touch of his hand against her. She leans in. He is uncomplicated. She envisions his life as moving from one benchmark to another: elementary school, Eagle

Scout, high school athlete; of being disappointed by a forced change of hope, of becoming determined to pursue a new course and giving his all to it. She sees, too, an old pain. He's asking her to sleep with him and she knows nothing about his history with women. So, she asks.

"I came close to marriage. Close enough to have rented the tux." Ruby waits for him to continue without prompting. "Turns out she had a few wild oats left to sow. With my best friend. Trite, huh? It was like a twofer; in the course of one ten-minute conversation I have no fiancée and no best friend."

Ruby takes his hand, flattens it, and runs a finger along his lines. "I see that having been in that situation has tainted you. You haven't trusted anyone since."

"Is that your professional opinion?"

"Am I wrong?"

"I have come close to trusting you."

Ruby lets go of Doug's hand. "I don't think Turner's Tow is ever going to come release my van, so how about you take me home with you."

Ruby put some of her things in a bag, and some of my things in another. I watched, making sure that my favorite stuffed toy was among the things we brought with us to Doug's house. This I wasn't expecting, but Ruby explained it to me. We were going to den with him for the evening, and the next day, early, we would be back where we left our rolling house. But then, she said, we would be off. I didn't understand what she meant. In my parlance, "off" means not "on."

Before we reached Doug's house, they left me in his car and went into a store and came out with food. Then, much to my delight, Ruby did something I had never seen her do . . . cook!

I was allowed a nice taste of the food she made and got to lick the plates. Heaven. The two people settled on the couch and I heard that word again: off. They eventually moved to where Doug sleeps and shut the door. I decided that I shouldn't be offended. That couch was pretty comfy. I forgot about the "off" word and settled in for the night.

Doug had told Ruby that he had school in the morning, so they needed to scoot back to Harmony Farms really early so that he could be back and in the building by the seven-thirty bell. Wouldn't do to have the school counselor be late on the first full day of school. So, it is with a degree of horror that they both wake to find it already six forty-five. No way can he get her back to Harmony Farms and be on time.

Making the best of it, Ruby sends Doug to the showers and she makes the coffee, scrambles some eggs. She isn't looking forward to a whole day of waiting to get started on her journey. This one step forward, one step back is driving her crazy. By the time she gets back to Harmony Farms and retrieves her van, it could be five o'clock. It's not that she won't start a journey that late, it is just harder to do at this point in her life. Long gone are the long hours of night driving.

Still damp from his shower, Doug stands at the counter to eat. Ruby sees that this is his habit and thinks about her own single-person patterns. "Why don't you drop me off at school, take my car, and go deal with your van?" Doug puts his dishes in the dishwasher. "I don't need it. I'm out by three, three-thirty at the latest if the staff meeting doesn't get bogged down in some circular argument about grades."

"That's very generous of you."

"Well, you've been a bit generous with me."

The Hitchhiker reminds Ruby that she hasn't been fed yet, or maybe it's a little jealousy making her wriggle her head between them.

Ruby drops Doug off at exactly seven twenty-five.

Ruby rolls up Main Street, noticing that the little trees planted along the sidewalk have begun to take on a fallish hue. The deep green of summer is faded, and each little tree—maple?—has a smattering of red leaves woven within the green. How is it she's been here so long that she's gone from new leaves to nearly autumn? That hasn't happened in a very long time. Well, time to move on. Finally. She signals for a parking space close to where her van was. Was. Should be. Isn't.

Choice words fly from her mouth, epithets and garment-rending fury. She is glad that there is no one walking by, glad to jack the air conditioner up to full and the radio to blasting. She will not be contained or prevented from her more than deserved tantrum. Ruby's patience has been ground down to dust. "Cynthia! Why? What have I ever done to you?"

Ruby suddenly realizes that she's cowed the dog. The Hitchhiker is drooping on the passenger seat of Doug's car. Her dark brown eyes are little orbs of sadness, of fear. She must think that Ruby has lost her mind. As quickly as Ruby lost it, she pulls herself together, shuts the car off, and reaches for the dog, who backs away. "Oh, baby, I'm not mad at you." She scoops the dog onto her lap. She is struck by the connection, a powerful odor of fear and confusion, the tingle of an old memory of running. "You're my good girl. I'm so sorry."

The dog's thoughts are primal, wholly organic. "Don't be separate from me."

"Never."

The dog rests her chin on Ruby's shoulder. Sighs. The odor of fear, the tingle of unease begins to fade until there is only the lingering taste of confusion.

Ruby and the dog get out of Doug's car and walk around the park. Ruby needs the motion to formulate her next step, and the Hitchhiker needs to move to regain her usual joi de vivre. Calmed down, Ruby pulls out her phone and looks up Turner's Tow. She's not going to bother to call, she's just going to show up and demand her van back. There is no doubt in her mind, and this isn't due to some psychic vibe, that far from removing the boot, they have towed her car and impounded it at the behest of that witch.

As Ruby and the dog get back into Doug's car, it dawns on her that she needs to find out why Cynthia is so antagonistic. Yes, she's kind of known for it around town, but to be so pointedly antagonistic specifically to Ruby is a mystery that it was high time Ruby solved. It is no longer enough to leave Cynthia in the dust, to leave Harmony Farms and never give her another thought.

Instead of heading right for the towing company lot, Ruby goes around the block and turns up in front of the town hall. If Cynthia isn't there, she's going to find out where she is. Ruby beats back the "and then what" in her mind. Ignoring the NO PETS sign on the town hall front door, Ruby and the Hitchhiker march in. There is no receptionist, only a hallway with a sign indicating various town offices and their room numbers. The place reminds Ruby a bit of a school. There's the same scent of paper and ink. Dust. Butcher's wax. Each office door has an opaque glass window and old-fashioned black lettering designating it as Town Clerk, where Ruby had applied for her busker's license; Tax Office; Board of Health. The Selectperson's office is upstairs. "Let's go." The pair don't bother with the elevator. Ruby is too ready for battle.

It is an ordinary weekday, but to Ruby it feels monumental. The two individuals sitting in the office as she barges in should understand that she is there to demand justice. That their ordinary lives are about to take on a brand-new story, something that they will tell their children . . . the avenging angel of Ruby Heartwood come to demand satisfaction from the self-appointed Empress of Harmony Farms, Cynthia Mann.

Ruby looks at the pair, a skinny man in a short-sleeved white shirt and chinos, ugly tie dangling over a pot belly. He is holding a file folder. The other guy is in a workman's green uniform, a plumber's logo on his pocket, and his name, Ralph, embroidered over it. He's sitting on the edge of a large wooden desk. Both look at Ruby with only mild interest.

"Where is Cynthia?"

"Out at the moment. Can I help you with something?" The guy in the plumber's uniform pushes off the edge of the desk.

"It's personal."

"Well, she'll be right back if you want to take a seat." The ugly tie wearer gestures to a chair pushed up against the wall. He notices the dog. "Um, I assume this is a therapy dog?"

"Attack dog."

It takes a beat, but then both men chuckle, but say nothing more about the dog's illegal presence in their office. The desk sitter resumes his position and the ugly-tie-wearer opens the folder to show him something therein.

Cynthia Mann enters the room wiping her hands with a piece of paper towel. She doesn't look in Ruby's direction, is oblivious to her presence. Ruby stands up, the dog behind her. Cynthia lobs the balled-up paper towel into a wastebasket with a playfulness Ruby would never have expected. "Okay, gentlemen, what's on this week's agenda?" She's reaching for the file folder.

"Ahem."

Cynthia turns, sees Ruby, and smiles. "Oh, so sorry. My colleagues didn't say we had a guest."

Ruby does not smile back. She is gobsmacked at Cynthia's cordiality until she realizes that Cynthia doesn't recognize her, that she's never seen Ruby not in her fortune-teller's garb.

Then Cynthia spots the dog, Ruby's highly recognizable familiar. "Oh."

"We have a problem."

Cynthia looks at her two colleagues and they leave the room without apology. She shuts the door behind them. "You really didn't have to come here. All you need to do is pay your fines and collect your vehicle."

"Oh, no. I could do that, but I want to hear it out of your mouth why you are so against me. What in heaven's name have I ever done to you that you've made it your mission to torment me at every turn?

I even gave you a pretty nice reading. And, you broke my teapot and I still didn't get mad."

"That was unfortunate, and I do apologize for that."

"And the rest? Why, Cynthia? Why?"

"You're the psychic, can't you tell me?"

Ruby studies Cynthia standing in the dusty office. Dust motes shimmer around her, sparkling in the sunlight eking its way through the high window. Ruby watches Cynthia's aura, the greenish smear of self-satisfaction, deepen into a bruised yellow of old hurt. "A bad experience?"

Cynthia leans against the desk. "Yes."

"A bad reading?"

"If you could call it that. Look, I've never told a soul about this; why should I tell you?"

"Because you're blaming me for something that I had no involvement in and costing me a ton of money in the process."

Ruby waits, thinking about a lion tamer she once knew, a skinny Austrian with a pencil moustache who could make his cats bend to his will with the flick of his whip. They would, like Cynthia is doing right now, stare at him with defiance, and then, growling, do whatever it was he was asking for. Grudging but obedient. Hoping, like the Hitchhiker does, for a reward. Ruby keeps her eyes on Cynthia until she pushes away from the desk and sits in one of the guest chairs, gesturing for Ruby to do the same. "All right."

Ruby wonders if she should offer Cynthia a reward.

"I was dating two guys. I couldn't decide which one was the better choice. They were awfully similar on paper, if you know what I mean. It was kind of like the old song, if you're not with the one you love, love the one you're with, but I don't think that I really loved either of them. Not in the way I had hoped, you know, all agog and fluttery."

"Cynthia, I can't imagine you ever being all agog or fluttery."

"Well, I wasn't, and that concerned me. A woman showed up in town, worked in a little shop that sold hippy stuff, beads and hookahs and Tibetan flags, that sort of thing. On certain days, when she felt like it, she'd give psychic readings behind a curtain in the back of the store."

"What did she use? Palms, tea leaves? Cards?"

"Just touch. She'd hold your hands and look into your eyes and ask questions and make up answers. All fake."

"And you know this how? That it was all fake."

"Because she pointed me in the worst possible direction. She said I would be with the man who next asked me out."

"Who was?"

"The man who is now my ex-husband."

"Let me guess, he wasn't one of the two suitors?"

"No. And the fact that he wasn't and asked me out almost within twenty-four hours of this pronouncement, well, I did feel a bit agog."

"She never said that you were meant to be with him forever, did she? She said 'would,' not 'should.'" Splitting hairs, perhaps, but a distinction in the trade. "What else did she say?"

"I don't remember. I just know that my life, my reputation, even my sanity was compromised by that decision based on her advice." Cynthia studies her knuckles. "You know about him, don't you? Arrested for animal cruelty. But he was cruel above that as well."

"To you?"

"In many ways. The more power he got from his job, the more competitive he got with his peers, the more controlling he became. In the end, he tried mightily to leave me with nothing from the divorce. Said I was disloyal. Faithless because I couldn't make myself take his side. How could I take his side? I knew that he was more than capable of doing what he did. Shooting that poor dog."

"You're okay now."

"I have a good lawyer. But, as I said, I won't run for office again. People can't get past my bad decision. A decision that was prompted by a fortune-teller more than thirty years ago."

"No one put a gun to your head." Ruby blushes. "Oh, sorry. That was insensitive."

"A little." The bruised yellow aura is fading, a slightly rose tone rising, signifying to Ruby that speaking of these things aloud has helped Cynthia.

Whoever this mystic lady was, she had given Cynthia an accurate fortune. Cynthia had chosen the next man to ask her out. Ruby has no doubt that there was more to the message, any fortune-teller worth her salt would have added some decoration to a rather ordinary prognostication. *You will be with the next man who asks you out.* Be for life, or simply be in the same room? It's all in the interpretation. It's all in the desire that colors the hearer's understanding.

Cynthia gets to her feet. "I'll call the impound lot, get your vehicle released without fines."

"Thank you. And, Cynthia. I'm out of Harmony Farms right now, but I don't want you to think for one moment that you had anything to do with my departure."

"Of course not."

Ruby snaps her fingers at the dog who has been watching this conversation like a line judge at a tennis game.

"Ruby, here's the thing: I know you aren't that long-ago misguided fake, but you sure do look like her. That's why, well, why I first thought you might be her. But, of course, that would mean that you're a lot older than you look."

Ruby takes her hand off the doorknob. "Cynthia, tell me, where was this, where did this reading take place?"

"Right here. Harmony Farms."

Ruby resists the slightly swoony feeling, forces her fingers to not tremble. "One more thing, Cynthia."

"What's that?"

"You should run again. Give the animal control office a better budget and I predict that you'll win reelection."

32

What should she do with this information? Should she imagine that Cynthia means that she, Ruby Heartwood, in skinny jeans and a plain T-shirt, tinted moisturizer her only makeup, hair bundled into a twist, resembles this long-ago seer? Or that she, Madame Ruby, draped in gold brocade and stage makeup does? After all, Ruby modeled herself after Madame Celestine, who modeled herself after Madame somebody else in a long line of traditional psychics and seers all dressed like a dime novel depiction of a fortune-teller. *Let's face it, we do all resemble one another*, she thinks, and shrugs off the shaky feeling of being on the verge of an important discovery. Cynthia could just as easily be yanking her chain. "Okay, let's deal with the situation at hand and dwell on the possibilities later." Ruby gathers the dog's leash in her hand and pulls the keys to Doug's car out of her pocket.

The dog presses her forefeet against Ruby's thigh. "Sit. Stay." She looks pointedly at a park bench.

"No, we need to get the bus back." Ruby gives her a pat and points the key fob at the car to unlock it.

As they drive along Main Street, Ruby can't help but look at all the store fronts and wonder which one had been the hippy head shop, which one might have offered the services of a part-time fortune-teller. Could it be the card shop? Or the gourmet cookware store? The froufrou baby clothes place? Or the corner store that has paperback books and bins full of plastic toys spilling out of its doors?

At the impound lot, Ruby braces herself to be told that her car has either disappeared or been wrecked, such has been her last twenty-four hours. But Cynthia has been true to her word and the guy behind the plexiglass window slides Ruby a release form to sign. "Got the keys?"

Ruby slides him her set. It gives her the willies to let anyone into her "house" without her, but she knows that he's just doing his job. She can hear the Westfalia before she sees it, a bass note just a little noisier than usual, and she rolls her eyes. Can she please keep it on the road for just a bit longer before attending to the exhaust system?

Ruby is now one driver with two vehicles. The Dew Drop is close enough to the impound lot that she will ask Ravi if she can leave the van there until she picks up Doug in his car after school and they return to collect it. She'll walk back to the impound lot, giving the dog a nice outing, pick up Doug's car, and then meander over to visit with Polly. It's on her mind to ask Polly, who has lived in Harmony Farms forever, if she has any recollection of the woman Cynthia claims to have encountered. If not Polly, then maybe Bull has an idea. He's quiet, but well attuned to the goings on around town.

There are no cars parked in Ravi's lot, and Ruby has to hope that the emptiness suggests only that the guests are all out enjoying the area. His vacancy sign is lit, but she refuses to look at that as a bad sign. After all, it is a weekday and unofficially the end of summer. Surely he'll be full over the weekend if the weather continues to be as beautiful as it has been.

"Ruby, hello. Welcome back." Ravi is alongside the well-trimmed edge of the circular garden, which now boasts a heavy concentration of begonias, a broom in hand. Leaf and plant detritus gathered in a neat pile. "I have your usual room available."

Ruby is about to say that she's not there to stay, and then thinks otherwise. It is for sure going to be too late to start off for New Hampshire by the time she accomplishes all the steps involved in sorting out the complications of having two cars. It was lovely last night being with Doug, but she's not about to make that a habit she'll have to break. "That would be perfect, Ravi."

The room in all its slightly askew affect is comfortingly familiar. The dog jumps onto the bed as if arriving home after a long absence. She immediately flops onto her back and looks at Ruby expectantly, clearly a belly rub is in order. Ruby accommodates her, and the fluffy white tail sweeps back and forth in her ecstatic delight. "Okay, enough indulgence, my dear, get your sneakers on and let's go."

The Hitchhiker really only understands the word *go*. She jumps down from the bed and barks at the closed door, hurrying Ruby, having no idea where they might be going, but happy to be included.

The walk back to the impound lot doesn't take long and the two of them collect Doug's car. Ruby points it in the direction of the shelter, about ten minutes from where they are. Arriving at the shelter, the Hitchhiker balks at getting out of the car, turning gimlet eyes on Ruby.

"Sweetheart, don't you know by now that I'll never leave you anywhere?"

"Everyone in there believed that about their people too."

"No, some of the animals in there got lost on their own."

"No. Their people got lost. They forgot to find them."

Sometimes this Vulcan mind meld of what passes for conversation between Ruby and her dog is exhausting, like arguing with a three-year-old. Which, if she thinks about it, is exactly what she is doing. "If you come in with me, there's treats."

Finally, a word that penetrates the little dog's stubbornness. "Okay. Two."

"Two."

Ruby is pretty sure this whole reluctance thing is an act meant to earn the treats.

Polly puts the tea on the moment Ruby walks in the door. She is still beaming with the success of the fund-raiser. "Cramden's Appliances will be delivering the washer and dryer tomorrow. I'm going to have a field day. Look." She points to a Mt. Everest of dirty towels and bedding.

"Funny the things that make us happy."

"You bet. I remember when I was a new bride, a new umbrella-style clothesline was the joy of my life. Can you imagine?"

"Not exactly." Ruby doesn't mention that having enough quarters for the Laundromat to wash Sabine's two school dresses was often joy enough. "Hey, question for you . . ."

Ruby gives an edited-down version of the past day, leaving out her overnight with Doug for the moment, leading up to the question of Cynthia's real or imagined fortune-teller. "Do you remember a hippy shop? What we used to call a head shop? With a psychic?"

Polly sets the mugs of tea down, reaches for the sugar from the shelf behind her. "Maybe. There was a shop with incense and candles, Indian print skirts. That kind of stuff. I suppose it might have been a head shop, but I never went in there. I'm well past the era of hippiedom. I was raising kids in the seventies. And they all wore clothes and shoes."

"I sometimes believe that I should have been a part of the counterculture, but as my whole life was counterculture, I never felt the need to celebrate it."

Full-figured Polly admits, "I did go braless for a bit. I didn't like it."

Ruby laughs, dunks her teabag up and down. "Where was that hippy shop, if that's what it was. Do you recall?"

Polly considers the question. "I'm thinking the same block with the hardware store. Bet they'd remember. Heralds Hardware has been there since Harmony Farms was founded." She shakes some sugar into her tea, tastes, shakes in some more. "Course, I bet Bull Harrison would know. He was very active around here in the late sixties, early seventies. If you know what I mean."

"A bad habit brought back from Vietnam?"

"For a long time."

Ruby glances at the wall clock; it's after two. "Oops, I've got to go." It wouldn't do to be late picking Doug up from school after he's been kind enough to loan her his car.

Polly walks Ruby out and notices the car. "I thought you got the van out of jail."

"I did. But, well, long story. That's why I'm in a hurry, I've got to return this car to its owner."

"You mean Doug Cross?" One Volvo might look like another, but Doug's is a distinct shade of red.

"Yes."

"You're a dark horse, Ruby Heartwood."

Ruby arrives in the circular driveway of the high school a few minutes after three. She has a ready excuse for her tardiness: the highway had been bogged down by road work seemingly every three miles. Ruby wishes that she'd taken the longer, much more scenic back roads and will say so, but then she gets a text from Doug apologizing in turn for being caught up in a meeting he cannot ditch. She finds a parking space, switches to the passenger seat, lowers the seat back, and settles in to wait. She hasn't waited for anyone in a very long time. The dog climbs over the console and onto Ruby's lap. It isn't unpleasant, this forced stillness. Ruby entertains herself with watching the students on their way to various after-school activities, being picked up by parents, slinging overweight book bags over their shoulders. They look so young for high schoolers. She wonders if she would have seemed that young had her life not taken the route that it did. At fifteen, Ruby was no child. She was a survivor and a summa cum laude graduate of the school of life.

Before long, her eyes begin to droop and Ruby finds herself drifting into a doze, not quite asleep, not quite awake. She is aware of the sound of cars starting, traffic in the street, voices of students grumbling about assignments, but all of that seems muted, an understory to her own patternless thoughts. She dreams voices speaking softly. *She looks like you.*

It's what they always said about Sabine; but who, then, could she have possibly looked like if not her only parent? On very bad days, Ruby could sometimes see a shadow of Buck in Sabine's jawline, the rise of her cheek.

She looked like you. Everyone says Molly looks like Sabine. Auburn hair just wavy enough. Green eyes, just a shade more turquoise than hazel. Brownish flecks. But Ruby can see her daddy in her lean athletic body, her single dimple.

She's looking for you.

"Sorry I'm late." Doug's very real voice startles Ruby out of her suspended animation.

Ruby pushes the seat back upright and hands Doug his keys. "I was actually enjoying the break. It's been a busy day."

Through the open window, the Hitchhiker greets Doug like a returning hero, or maybe like she thought she'd never see him again. Her hind legs on Ruby's lap, her forepaws on the open window, her tail fans Ruby's face. She shoos the dog back into the rear of the car. Doug climbs in, pushes back the driver's seat, and off they go, once more to Harmony Farms.

"So, how was your day?" Ruby hears herself ask this most couple-ish of questions. As if they've been together since forever.

"Good enough for a first day. No crises."

"Nobody complaining about their class schedules?"

"That's not my bailiwick. I tend to their emotional needs. Broken hearts. Broken homes. Bullying."

"When you said counselor, I naturally thought guidance."

"Nope. I'm a psychologist."

"Should I call you Doctor?"

"Only people I wouldn't lend my car to have to do that." Doug knows detours around the worst of the road work, and they are on back country roads passing lovely old homes and farmland. Ruby sees the pretty little yellow house with the maple trees, now commencing their autumnal transformation. She points it out to Doug. "I noticed that place the night I arrived in Harmony Farms. Just perfect."

"Oh, I've always loved that place. I tell you, if ever a for sale sign went up . . ."

"I was hoping it might be a bed and breakfast."

Doug comes to a full stop at the T-intersection. Looks left and right. "You got your van out all right?" Turns right.

"Almost without incident." Ruby lays out her confrontation with Cynthia. "It's hard to imagine someone having that much animus for a complete stranger based on an experience so long ago."

"So, she really said that you looked like this fortune-teller?"

"She did. But I think that she's conflating me with this likely charlatan."

"Why charlatan?"

"Because she was so specific. At least according to Cynthia. That's hardly a true psychic's stock in trade. We keep to shadowy pronouncements. No one wants to be blamed."

"Pitchforks and torches?"

"Exactly. Who among us in the profession hasn't been accused of witchcraft at one time or another?"

"I've never dated a witch before," Doug deadpans. "That could explain a lot."

"About what?"

"*You put a spell on me . . .*" Doug sings in a pretty serviceable baritone.

"Ha-ha."

"The bigger question is, are you thinking that this woman might be related to you in some way? Based on what Cynthia said."

Ruby waits; a left turn and then a right. The Dew Drop Inn is in sight. "Yes. I can't help but wonder . . ."

"If she's who you've been looking for?"

"I thought I was the psychic."

"I'm pretty good at reading people. Kind of my job." Doug pulls into the parking lot and into a place beside the Westfalia. "Can you bear another trip back to my place?"

"Well, you see . . ."

"You're booked in here?"

"Yes. I think it's best."

Doug nods. "Of course. Wise." He leans in and gives Ruby a friendly kiss. "Thanks for picking me up."

"Thanks for lending me your car. And for, well, for last night." Ruby gets out of the car, opens the rear door for the Hitchhiker, who immediately runs around to her favorite rest area. As she shuts the passenger door, Ruby leans in. "Do you have to rush back?"

"No, ma'am."

33

Ruby pulls into the Cumberland Farms gas station to fill up her van. The Hitchhiker puts her paws on the dashboard, little spaniel nose pointed in the direction of the wall that usually sports Bull Harrison leaning against it like some kind of urban mural. There's no sign of him or his dog. Normally that kind of thing would hardly be worth noticing, but at this time of day, Bull, a creature of habit, is notably missing. Ruby was hoping to see him this morning so she could ask him if he has any memories of a psychic in a local head shop. Now there is a trickle of premonition zizzing into Ruby's heart.

She's on her way. Finally. If she can get a decent start this morning, Ruby plans on catching up with Joe Benini and his crew late today. He's already in Maine, but not too far up. Doug fiddled with the muffler and the rumbling has diminished, so she isn't that worried about the Westie being up to making the journey. Ruby taps the last drop out of the nozzle and locks in the gas cap. That blank wall seems so much bigger without Bull leaning against it.

"I need a coffee," she says to the dog. "Hang on a minute."

"Treat?" thinks the dog.

Inside Ruby grabs a Farmhouse blend and a granola bar. She adds a package of Pup-Peroni, an indulgence for sure, but it's going to be a long ride.

"Is that all today, ma'am?" The usual clerk is behind the counter.

"It is." Ruby puts a ten on the counter. "Have you seen Bull around lately?"

The boy hands her her change. "Can't say that I have. Not for a few days anyway. A week maybe?"

Ruby sets her coffee in the cup holder, opens the package of Pup-Peroni for the dog, who is yipping in excitement at the scent of the fake jerky. She's thinking about the last time she saw Bull herself and cannot. Was it in the Country Market? Pushing his bike along County Road? She and Doug went to the Lakeside last night and he wasn't there, nor had she seen him there the first time they went out. Ruby pulls out her phone and calls Polly. She'll know what's going on.

"Nope, can't say that I've seen him either."

"Is this normal? It seems to me that he's always around. Does he go anywhere?"

"Not that he's ever said. His son Cooper comes up and sees him from time to time."

"Maybe that's it. Maybe he's had company." But even as she says it, Ruby knows that's not the case. "Maybe I'm a worry wart, but I'm going to swing by on my way out of town."

"Good idea. Out of town, huh? For long?"

For long. Forever probably, but Ruby doesn't say that. It's why she never says goodbye. And then she thinks, she's never really had anyone she'd needed to say goodbye to before. And now she seems to have collected a trio of them. "I don't know. At least through the fall."

"Will you come back?"

Ruby says, "I don't know. I usually go south in the winter."

Doug hadn't asked that question, not the one of *how long*, or the other one, *will you be back.* Doug had been nonchalant about her declaration of intent. All he'd said: "You'll keep in touch?" And all she'd said was "Yes."

•   •   •

Boy is sitting outside on the back steps. No sign of Bull in the yard. The dog fairly lopes over to Ruby as she gets out of her van. He and the Hitchhiker nose each other briefly before he reaches Ruby. He sits, waits. Knows that she will touch him and what he has on his mind she will understand. Ruby does, cupping both hands over his skull, over his eyes, along his cheeks. Her mind is filled with the sour sweet odor of fever. The images coming from the dog prompt her to run to the back door, shoulder it open when it sticks, and call out Bull's name.

"In here."

Ruby finds Bull in his one soft chair, the television on but muted. Mountain Dew cans litter the side table, surrounding an ashtray full of butts. Dressed in stained sweats topped with his favorite Patriots sweatshirt, he is more gray than usual and clearly gasping for breath.

"Pardon me if I don't get up."

"What's wrong?"

"Just a bug. Nothing." But the look on his face belies this attempt to downplay the pain he is obviously feeling. He suddenly looks at Ruby with panic on his face. "It hurts."

The dogs have followed Ruby into the living room. Boy sits with his head on Bull's lap, his powerful nose pressed against Bull's middle. He moves away, sits in front of Ruby to tell her something. "Deep sick. Inside him."

Ruby has heard that there are dogs who can sniff out illness, cancer, epilepsy, diabetes, but they are trained in what to look for. She doesn't discount that the dog might have an instinctive sense of trouble within, but she cannot imagine that he has diagnostic capabilities. "You need a doctor, Bull. Let's get going."

It is no mean feat to haul a hefty guy like Bull out of a soft chair, but Ruby does. She points him toward the back door, grabs his wallet sitting on the counter, and guides him toward the van. He is wobbly and stops every few steps to bend over in pain. She struggles to counterweight him when he leans too far to the right. Just when it begins to seem like an impossible effort and she's going to have to call an ambulance, she manages to get him into the van, not into the front seat but up onto the bench seat where he doesn't fit. His feet are still on the floor, but he can presumably be more comfortable in a mostly reclining position. The dogs jump in, Boy to lie on Bull's big feet and the Hitchhiker to take up her usual passenger seat position.

There is no hospital in Harmony Farms, so she heads to the local urgent care facility. By the grace of God, she gets him out of the van and into a wheelchair and into the building. The dogs stand in the open doorway of the Westie, and she points a finger. "Stay, do not move."

Bull is quickly taken out of Ruby's hands. She can answer no questions, she knows nothing more than what she has seen, so they quickly dismiss her as the good Samaritan and the hiss of automatic doors concludes her part in the drama. She goes back to the van and is pleased to see both dogs framed in the open slider. And then it hits her. If something happens to Bull, if he's hospitalized, what is she going to do with Boy? She can't leave town with him. She can't leave now at any rate, not until she knows what's going on with Bull. Once again, Ruby finds herself trapped by circumstance. She looks at her watch, relieved to see that it is only just past ten o'clock. If she can get on the road by noon, one o'clock at the latest, she can still get to Maine by nightfall. She and the Hitchhiker can sleep in the van, meet up with Joe Benini in the morning. "Okay. We'll just head out a little late. No biggie." She strokes Boy's head. "It'll be fine, big guy. He'll be fine." Even as she says this to the dog, she has a hard time believing it herself, and he picks up on her doubts, heaving a great sigh and a soft whimper.

Ruby sits on the edge of the van between the dogs and calls Polly to let her know what's up. Polly is on patrol, so within a few minutes she shows up in the animal control vehicle. "Any word?"

"Not yet. You know how these things are. Besides, they aren't going to tell us anything. Do you have a way to get hold of that son of his?"

"I already did." Polly settles her utility belt around her broad hips. "Unfortunately, he's not going to be able to get here any time soon.

He's on a missing-persons search with his K-9. I promised we'd keep him posted."

"This could be serious, Polly." Ruby is thinking of Boy, of how he pressed his nose into Bull's belly, how he spoke of "deep" sickness.

Polly's radio crackles and she reaches into the cab of the truck to pull it out. Ruby doesn't pay close attention to the back and forth, keeping her hands on the dogs, reassuring Boy that she's there for him. Letting the Hitchhiker know that she's a good girl.

"I've got a dog versus car incident, so I've got to go. I'll come back as soon as I can. Call me if, well, just call me if you need to." With that, Polly heaves herself into the truck and speeds off. Boy raises his head to watch her go. Ruby checks her watch. Still only a little past ten.

Herein lies the rub of being in one place for too long, the complication of other people. The complication of human decency. She could just drop the dog off at his house and get going, but Ruby knows that she won't. These are no longer strangers. After leaving Madame Celestine's camper van lo those many years ago, Ruby has not allowed herself to become attached to anyone other than her family. The clinging strings of friendship serve only to contain her forward movement. Case in point, sitting here in the parking lot of an urgent care facility with a dog not her own, miserable in his separation from his person, dashing any escape plans for today. Ruby cannot leave without knowing what is going to happen with Bull and she hasn't got even the slightest glimmer of psychic intuition—good or bad—to release her from this vigil.

Occasionally, she has dealt out a pattern of tarot cards suggesting a bad illness to come or one already there and unknown. She is not a doctor, a shaman, or a healer, and predicting an early death is not her style. She might suggest a visit to the doctor but couch it in terms of maintenance, not bad news. The one thing she has come to accept in her business of reading the futures of other people, almost no one ever lets her know if she's been right. Never any follow up. She is left to sit at her table and wonder if that man with the card pointing to death will heed her advice and seek medical attention. Or, even if getting help, will die anyway.

Ruby shakes the grim thoughts out of her head. "You stay put." She slides the door mostly shut, not confident that the pair of dogs won't get out of the van. She notices that the wheelchair she had commandeered for Bull is back in its place as she walks up to the reception window, taps to get the attention of the woman behind the glass. "I'm here to check on Bull Harrison."

"I'm sorry, who?"

Ruby realizes that she has no idea what Bull's real first name is. "The older man, gray sweatpants, Patriots sweatshirt. Great pain? I brought him in an hour ago."

"Are you a relative?"

Why not? "I'm his cousin." It just pops out.

"You can wait in chairs." She points at the rank of chrome and blue vinyl chairs.

Ruby doesn't care for the grammatical construct. "But I'd like some information."

"The nurse practitioner will come out to talk with you."

"So, you do know what's going on?"

"No. I didn't say that. I have no information. You have to wait."

Grumbling to herself, Ruby chooses a chair as far away from the rest of the waiting patients as she can get. She drops a quick text to Polly to get Bull's actual name so that she can play this fake cousin game a little better. *Barton,* Polly quickly replies.

A nurse comes out, calls a name, and a sniffling sneezing young guy goes in. Another nurse, another patient. And another. Ruby shifts in her seat, studies her nails. Waits another beat before going back to the window to get the same response. At least this time she can ask for Barton Harrison. It is to no avail and she is sent back to wait it out in the seating area. It strikes Ruby that all this waiting is not a good sign, that Bull Harrison isn't going to come out from the back of this place with a prescription in his hand. What is she going to tell his dog?

When she is just about to give up, a nurse practitioner comes through the door. Ruby knows that, this time, it is she this woman is looking for, so she quickly gets to her feet. "I'm with Barton Harrison."

"Are you a relative?"

"Cousin." Fingers crossed that this woman doesn't actually know Bull and who he's related to. It is, after all, a very small town.

"We are having him admitted to U-Mass Medical. We're just waiting for transport."

Ruby doesn't ask what's wrong, will he be okay, or any of the usual responses to this sort of news. She just asks if she can go in and see him. Ruby really doesn't want Bull to think he's been abandoned, or, more important, to worry about Boy.

There is a definite reluctance, but the nurse finally nods. "For a minute. Maybe you can collect his things, take them home for him."

Ruby is led to where Bull is lying in a mechanical bed, tilted up at a mild angle. He looks pale and gray but no longer in pain. He also looks frightened. "How are you feeling?" It's such a silly question.

"Nothing a little Jack and a Marlboro can't fix." He wants to laugh, but he manages only a grunt.

"I don't think that there's a prescription for that. They're pretty set on you going to the hospital. I can take your stuff home, if you want."

"And Boy? Where is he?"

"He's with the Hitchhiker, in the van. Don't worry about him. He'll be fine for a couple of days without you." A couple of days.

"You're a good friend, Ruby Heartwood."

"Actually, these folks here think I'm your cousin, or else they wouldn't let me in."

"Hey, who knows. You ever get that DNA stuff back?"

As a matter of fact, as she's been sitting and waiting, Ruby has gotten the email from the Family History Lab. She didn't want to open it on her phone, or in a public place, so she's letting the anticipation build until she can settle in for the day. Settle in at Bull's.

Before Ruby can answer, a pair of young men in dark blue uniforms with the ambulance company logo on their shirts come in and take over the room. Ruby steps out as they begin the transfer of Bull from hospital bed to gurney. As they roll him out of the tiny room Ruby reaches out and takes his big mitt of a hand. "Polly's been in touch with your son. I'll take care of Boy and you get better."

"You got it." But the strained look on Bull's face suggests that he might have a hard time keeping up his end of the bargain.

The touch of Bull's hand in hers floods Ruby's intuition with unwanted vibes, an unwanted psychic message that Boy is right. There is disease deep within Bull.

Ruby reports back to Polly, who will relay the news to Cooper Harrison. She backs the van out of the parking space and points herself back to Bull's. Boy remains on the floor in the back, the Hitchhiker in her usual shotgun position. It's after two o'clock. Time enough to get partway to Maine before dark, but Ruby knows that she's not going anywhere. When she got into the van, Boy had come up to her and put his great big head in her lap, crying out for reassurance that this upset in his life was temporary. Since the day that Cooper gave the dog, only barely rehabilitated from his traumatic weeks as a semi-feral runaway, to his father, the pair have been inseparable. She understands exactly how that feels. What would she do if she had to be hospitalized, heaven forbid? Who would take care of her dog while she was away? This is something Ruby hasn't considered in her wholehearted conjoining with this happy beast. And yet the worry is familiar, and she recognizes it from her very early days with infant Sabine. The dread that something would happen to her and her child would be left to strangers. Much as she had been herself.

Ruby backs into her space in Bull's yard, lets the dogs out. She scrolls her "favorites" and hits Sabine's number.

"If anything happens to me, will you take my dog?"

"Hello, is this my mother?" Sabine at her wittiest. "Of course, but is there something you need to tell me?"

"No. It's just that a friend of mine . . ." She relates to her daughter the past few hours, and how it has made her think of potentialities. Made her think of her time being the only person responsible for a child.

"You never told me this before, how afraid you were. I only knew about your anxiety about having me taken away from you, not you from me." Sabine pauses. "You don't have to worry; the kids would love nothing better than to add a dog to the family, but we'd really like it if you came along too."

"I know, I owe you all a visit and I will, once I get back from fair season."

"And yet you haven't left Harmony Farms."

"Don't tell me about it. I was literally on my way out of town when I had this premonition to check on Bull. It was a good thing to do, but now I'm stuck for yet another couple of days, at least till we know what's going on and what I should do with his dog, Boy."

"Has it yet occurred to you that you're supposed to stay?"

"Is this a prognostication?"

"Maybe. It's odd, but I've never been to Harmony Farms, but I picture you there perfectly. When I think of some future event, like Christmas or Molly's birthday, I see you coming to us from there."

"Well, stop it."

"By my calculation, it's the longest you've stayed put in many a year. How many weeks? Two months?"

"Three and a half, four almost."

"A record for you."

"Change of subject. I got the DNA results back."

"And?"

"I haven't looked. I will, after I hang up with you and grab a bite."

"How can you wait?"

"I guess maybe because I'm afraid of disappointment, that nothing in the report will lead to answers."

"Call me tonight when you've digested the information. Let me know if I have to add long-lost relatives to my Christmas card list." Sabine signs off as it is suddenly school pickup time, which makes Ruby think of Doug. She should really let him know she's not on the road. And even having that slight suggestion of common courtesy gives Ruby pause. She has never before considered someone else having a need-to-know position in her life. Sometimes, not even Sabine.

Still in school, Doug doesn't answer so Ruby leaves a message. "Unavoidably held up. Still in Harmony Farms. Give me a call and I'll explain."

34

My friend Boy is very upset, and I try to make him feel better with shoulder bumps and shoving my toys in his face, but he is inconsolable. His person is absent. His person was in a strange place with strange smells and stranger people and then he wasn't and that is the part that Boy is having the hardest time with. Where did they take his person? Boy also knows that his person is sick. Not the sick of having eaten carrion unadvisedly, but sick from something deep within. Boy's person, for the size of him, is very fragile.

With Boy preferring to sit on his own porch, I have gone back to my person, my Ruby. I let her know that Boy will not leave the yard, that he won't leave the steps until his person, Bull, returns. He may not even eat, which is troubling for me, although when Ruby sets down a dish of kibble in front of him, he does pick at it and reminds me that it is *his* dinner, not mine. No big deal. I prefer my kibble to his anyway. He laps at the big bowl of water and he does allow me to share in that with him. For a short time, the three of us, Boy, Ruby, and I, sit on the back steps and say nothing to one another. But Ruby's right hand comforts Boy with ear scratches, and her left hand admires me with broad strokes. As surely as she hears mine, I hear her thoughts and I worry that this staying put is temporary. Ruby has this constant hum of wanting to be in motion that I have tried hard to neutralize with demonstrations of immobility, especially after a long walk when immobility is so pleasant.

"Boy, do you want to go in the house?" Ruby stands up, dusts her backside, and opens the screen door for the dog. She really doesn't want to leave him outside all night, but she's ready to pack it in for the day. The dog casts her a baleful look then slips past her into the house. She shuts only the screen door, if he needs to get out, she'll hear him. She really doesn't think Bull's tumbledown place is much of a security risk.

She and Doug have played a little back and forth with messages. He'd had meetings after school, and tonight is his bowling league, so he'll give her a call later if that's okay. She texted back, *any time is fine,* and then wished she hadn't. She's beat. All this worrying about someone is such hard work.

Ruby's laptop is open on the pop-up table. Bumping the table wakens the screen and the unopened email from Family History Labs, still dark with "unread" status. She sits on the bench seat, not yet unfolded for sleeping. She sits forward, feet on the floor, hands hovering. Click. A cheery welcoming paragraph, and a request to enter her ID and password. Miraculously, Ruby remembers both, which doesn't always happen, and taps the information into the login screen.

What appears before her now is a lovely pie chart, pretty colors in varying percentages, but mostly of a lovely green hue that identifies Ruby's ethnicity as primarily Scottish, Irish, an infusion of French, and a healthy dollop of Welsh. Jones. A quintessentially Welsh surname. So, maybe that really is her name, Mary Jones. Another segment of the pie indicates a flavor of Scandinavia. Ruby knows enough history to figure this has something to do with the Vikings raiding the English shores.

It's like looking at history through her own lens. Really, there is nothing surprising here. "So, where does the fortune-telling gene come in?" The Hitchhiker looks at Ruby, decides that the human speech isn't meant for her and closes her eyes. It would have been nice to see a line of pink, say, or gold to indicate this special trait.

Ruby's phone chimes with an incoming call, Doug. She fills him in quickly with how her plans for the day have been scuttled.

"Almost sounds to me like divine providence."

"How so?"

"Being in the right place, knowing what to do. Being curious about that other psychic enough to seek out Bull on a day when he really needed you."

"I think it was just plain old bad karma."

"Don't sell yourself short. You had a feeling and you followed up on it. And if your escape plans have been delayed, that's maybe all right."

"Doug, you have no idea how trapped I feel."

"Why is that, Ruby? You are as free a person as I've ever known. A will o' the wisp of a person."

"What you're saying is that I am one of the few people in the world who has no responsibilities. No connections. No roots."

Doug doesn't answer right away, one of the things she has noticed about him, he thinks before speaking. She supposes it's part of his training as a psychologist. Let the patient do the talking. Interject little if nothing to turn the conversation. She decides to turn the conversation herself. "I got the DNA results."

"And?"

"Nothing particularly exotic, mostly what you'd expect. Heavily British Isles with a bit of cross Channel mixing. A soupçon of Welsh and Viking." She clicks on one of the pie segments; it expands to zoom in on a more select section of northern Britain. "If there had been a bit of Spanish or Middle Eastern, I might think that's where the mystic in me originated, but it kind of looks like that's not the case."

"I'm pretty sure there are plenty of solidly British fortune-tellers. After all, tea is solidly British and only the British wrap their teapots in blankets." He's teasing, of course, but it does remind Ruby of the broken teapot. Maybe she should have been protecting it with a quilted tea cozy against the depredation of Cynthia's bony hips.

"So now I have to buy into the database. I know what I am, but not who else might be out there with the same genetic material. What if no one related to me has ever gotten the test?" She knows she sounds a little defeatist, a little petulant, but Ruby is a bit disappointed that all of this waiting has really answered nothing.

Doug counters, "Oh, I don't know. Seems to me that getting your DNA test done is becoming all the rage. In the thousands of possibilities coming from your genes, surely you'll find one."

"I only want to find one." Her mother. That's what all this has been about. Finding her mother.

It's getting late and Ruby has had enough of the topic. It seems only polite to ask after Doug's day, but he sounds done in too.

"School was fine, only one meeting. Dowling was fine, I didn't embarrass myself. Will you leave tomorrow?"

"I wish I knew."

"That seems like an odd thing for a psychic to say."

"You're right. I'm going to pull out my tarot cards right now."

"Call me if you do. Or don't. Either way."

"I will." *And maybe I won't,* she thinks.

Ruby has left the van's windows open and in the middle of the night she feels the breeze ramp up, a tinge of fall in it. She pulls up her extra blanket. The Hitchhiker stirs, sits up, listens. Ruby hears Bull's screen door being pushed open, the dry squeal of a hinge, and a sharp slam. Boy has let himself out of the house. She slides out from under the covers and opens the sliding door. Boy clambers in, jumps uninvited onto her bed, and flops down. "Hey, move over." He's three times the size, maybe more, of her usual bedtime companion, who has now planted herself on Ruby's other side. Boxed in by canines, Ruby no longer needs the extra blanket.

Maybe it's the extra weight of the big yellow dog, maybe it's the circumstances, but Ruby dreams vividly of being boxed in. She literalizes her current sense of entrapment with a dream of walls closing in. This is a dream that she has had before, always in the wee hours of the morning, and, upon waking, she has made her decision to leave. It has happened so many times in the past that she is surprised when she wakes up this time and the decision to go has been neutralized. She feels calm, unhurried. And then she understands that she is not really awake. Ruby's dream self has emerged from the box and is standing at the crest of a gentle hill. In the distance is a figure, familiar in its etherealness, its facelessness. Ruby the dreamer cannot tell if the figure is advancing toward her or if it is moving away.

Ruby awakens abruptly. Someone has distinctly said: *Find me, find you* but there is no one there besides the dogs who are both sound asleep.

My prey eludes me. I dash and grab, shake and growl. Vermin, fuzzy, I will gut you. I am a mighty hunter. I lose my grip and it moves through the air, but I am fast, as fast any anyone and I pounce, grab, and shake. Growl. It resists and I tug and yank and growl. I dig my hind legs into the dirt and pull for all I am worth, and suddenly my prey is in my mouth, so I shake and growl. Chomp down until it squeals in agony. I am so satisfied until it leaps off the ground and up into the air, arcing as Ruby tosses my stuffed fox into the basket. We are making our house back into a ride.

As her "mother" dreams do, this one has lingered long past the point it should have dissolved into the mists of dreamworld. *Find me. Find you.* Who is being sought, who is looking? As soon as it is a decent hour on a school day to call, Ruby calls Sabine, who has just dropped the kids off at school and is on her way to work. "I've got ten minutes, Ruby, so let's have the interesting stuff first."

Ruby quickly gives her daughter the results of her DNA test.

"What about cousins, aren't those things supposed to reveal that?"

"Yes. But I haven't bought into the database yet."

"Well, do it. This is only part of the story."

"There's something else I'd like you to think about." Ruby outlines her dream, still vivid, still puzzling. At least to her.

"Basic stuff, you're searching for your origins. Your mother. Your dreams just suggest that you should keep on. Ergo, buy into the database."

"But what about the words: the 'find me, find you'?"

Sabine considers the question. "Because if you find her, you have found yourself."

"That seems like a simplistic interpretation."

"Jeez, Mom, it was a dream. It is simplistic." Sabine laughs.

"So, what would you tell a paying customer who'd come to you with such a dream?"

"Oh, I'd dress it up in woo-woo, of course. It's what's expected." Sabine rarely uses her gifts, preferring to keep that part of her under wraps. The one thing Sabine is that Ruby is not, is a medium. Sabine sees ghosts. That's a much more intense kind of psychic talent. One that Ruby is glad not to have, one she assumes Sabine inherited from Madame Celestine, who often took on the role of medium, passing along messages from the dead at the behest of paying customers. Ruby hadn't believed Celestine's shtick until her own daughter developed the sixth sense.

Sabine has arrived at work, selling advertising for the local weekly. "Gotta run."

"Sabine, do you think anyone related to us has bothered with a DNA test?"

"Just do it. Even if it turns out that we have no curious living relatives."

Ruby has prepped the van for travel. All the loose objects, for instance, the half dozen squeaky toys scattered around, have been stowed. The bed put back into its bench seat configuration and the table put away. The cupboards are latched, the chemical toilet covered in its day wear. The Hitchhiker has assumed her shotgun position. It is only Boy who remains uncertain. His anxiety is palpable in the way he keeps yawning, the way his tail is down and tucked. The way that his eyes have been following Ruby as she's performed her tasks. He's standing in the middle of the yard, halfway between her van and the house.

Polly called this morning to fill Ruby in on Bull's status. Although there are more tests that the medical people want to perform, the initial diagnosis is an infection, most likely in his gallbladder. This almost sounds like good news. You can recover from gallbladder surgery. Antibiotics can perform miracle cures. Polly mentions hepatitis and it no longer sounds quite so encouraging.

"Cooper says that he'll be in the hospital for a while longer. A week or so. Depending on how tough the infection is. Where it is. If that's what it is."

"What about the dog? What about Boy? Will Bull's son come and stay here?"

"No. It's an easier drive to Worcester from where he lives. He's going to go every day after work."

"Oh." *Thwarted once again*, she thinks but doesn't say.

Polly must have heard the dismay in her voice. "Boy can stay at the shelter, guest of the town. Don't worry about the dog if you're set to go. There's no need for you to wait around. He'll be fine with me."

The heavy weight of being thwarted is lifted. "Polly, that's great. Thank you. I know that Bull will be happy to know he's with you."

So that's that. Ruby opens the sliding door of the van. "Okay, Boy. Hop in." A quick run to the shelter and merrily, merrily, off to Maine they go.

Boy doesn't move. The dog backs away, ears pinned against the side of his head, his humped posture is stiff, unyielding. He gives her a sideways look and Ruby, even without touching him, knows that he's beside himself with fear.

"Oh, sweetie, you're just going to go visit Auntie Polly. She'll give you treats and belly rubs." Ruby approaches the dog, who goes even deeper into a cowering crouch. She gently places her hands on his head, hoping to communicate what *she's* thinking.

"No. No go. No go. I want my person now. If I go, he won't find me."

"He's sick, Boy. He needs to know that you are safe with Polly."

"Safe with you."

"I can't."

"Safe with you. Please stay."

All of this comes through her fingertips and into her mind like a thick white sheet of dread. Her sense of smell is clouded with the perfume of fear—rank and foul flavored. Sour. Bile rises up in her throat. She lets go of the dog.

The Hitchhiker approaches with caution. A fearful dog is a dangerous dog. Just the tip of her white tail moves, her head is low, and she licks her chops acknowledging Boy's apprehensions. Slowly she presses herself against his hunched body, rests her chin on his neck. She looks up at Ruby and the thoughts in her head are loud and clear. "We can't leave him."

In tears, Ruby drops to the ground and both dogs climb into her lap, acknowledging with gratitude her capitulation.

· · ·

The table is opened up and her laptop is booted up. Ruby types a quick email to Joe Benini to let him know that she has been unavoidably delayed but not why. *Will maybe be able to catch up in a few days, a week at most. Let me know where you are or will be.* She is only aware of the qualifying "maybe" as she hits Send. She's hardly ever this dithering. Ruby has always prided herself on her quick decision-making skills, her strength of resolve in the face of difficulties. Yet, ever since accidentally landing on the shore of this lakeside town, she's been reduced to hesitancy. To dithering. To caring about other people and their doggoned dogs.

Even though it's during school hours, Ruby texts Doug to let him know she's hanging around a bit more. Does the same for Sabine, with the addition of saying that, now that she seems to not be in a hurry, she's buying the second level of the Family History Lab's services and should shortly have the database available to her account. The website suggests setting up a family tree. Ha-ha. Ruby fiddles around and decides that she can work backward from Molly and Tom, Sabine, to herself.

This little exercise reminds her of the year that Sabine, maybe fourth grade, possibly fifth, had been assigned to do a family tree. Considering that the neighborhood where they had ended up was hardly an example of suburban family stability, half the kids had stepparents; talk about a teacher being tone deaf. So, she and Sabine had created what Ruby laughingly called their artificial tree. Sabine was appalled at first, but then got into the fun of making up names, choosing outrageous combinations like Mariella Frizzella—great-grandmother—and Dibley Dubious—great-grandfather on the other side. Aurora Boreallian, a distant relative on her mother's side. They'd never had quite so much fun doing homework. Even if Sabine was given a B for the drawing and a C for content, they couldn't prove a thing.

Ruby closes out that screen and notices that she now has a View All DNA Matches button on the dashboard. Oh boy.

•   •   •

Boy, trusting in Ruby's word, happily climbs into the van so that they can go get a few groceries. How the dog knows that she won't just drop him off at the shelter, she doesn't know, except that it is possible that the Hitchhiker has made him that promise in their language and will hold her to it. Ruby just doesn't have it in her to break her word to this damaged, fragile dog. Through the cloud of his anxiety, as she has done before, Ruby caught a glimpse of the trauma that had turned a happy-go-lucky youngster into an emotional wreck. Cynthia Mann's ex. The drunken brutality of anger. Buried in there, the scent of pond and duck.

Ruby lets Boy sit in between the front seats, while the Hitchhiker assumes her usual position. Every time she shifts gears, she pats his head. He's a little slobbery around the mouth, but Ruby looks at that as a good thing, he's relaxed now. Now she's the one with anxiety. The Makers Faire is still going on, but she hasn't signed up for a spot. She could set up her van and do busking in the park, but the weather is predicted to be lousy this week. Already the clouds are thickening up and the taste of rain is in the air. The fact is, she needs to earn a few bucks right now. As wormy as it makes her feel, she hasn't been able to pay Bull back, having to use the few dollars she's managed to raise for her own subsistence. Despite his insistence that the money was a gift, she really wants to pay him back. Although, Ruby now thinks, maybe this business of taking care of Boy will be a fair trade. Ease her mind from this overwhelming sense of obligation. Obligation, like attachment, a state of being she avoids.

She's so judicious about using a credit card, but she's stormed that barricade in paying for the DNA match button. And she's about to use it in the Country Market. She needs, among other things, dog food.

35

Ruby drives slowly along Main Street. It is a relatively short drive, six uneven blocks, if that, anchored on one end by a bank and on the other by the library. In the middle, the park and the municipal parking lot. At this hour, a midmorning weekday, the town is fairly busy, mostly moms in Lululemon, holding Starbucks cups and pushing racing baby carriages, and women of a certain age, shopping bags hanging from angled elbows. Here a workman, there a pair of Mormon boys on their mission work, white shirts and black ties, backpacks perfectly aligned on their shoulders. Everyday people on their everyday errands. *Are you my cousin?* It makes her think of that sweet children's book: *Are You My Mother?*

Ruby opened up the DNA Matches tab on her computer and discovered that she has cousins all over New England. Up into New York State and beyond, all the way to California and even in Hawaii. It was a knee-weakening moment, seeing those little marks that indicate someone shares a part of her, not just a trait, but possibly even a history. That maybe one of these markers shaped like little green trees leads to someone who can tell her what she wants to know. If she has the courage. The website suggests treading lightly in cases where there might be a potentially explosive—her word not theirs—family dynamic. Ruby is pretty certain that dropping herself and her mystery origins into some distant cousin's life could be a delicate process and fraught with all manner of emotion. She has to choose her first contact wisely. In her mind, Ruby composes a possible message to an unknown, unsuspecting relative: *My name is Ruby . . . no Mary Jones, I was dropped off at a convent orphanage in Canada fifty-five years ago. Know anything about a knocked-up teenager in the family? On either side of the border?*

As Ruby drives along the street, she finds herself looking at all the small businesses that line either side. Harmony Farms has managed to preserve most of the look of Main Street since the early twentieth century, in that the facades and doorways are mostly original or good reproductions. There are even a few buildings that date back to the nineteenth century, preserved by Harmony Farms' twenty-first century discovery of how to be trendy. Ruby can fault Cynthia Mann for her attitude and snooty behavior, but she knows that Cynthia has long been a part of Harmony Farms' revival. So, which one of these storefronts once held a head shop? A place where a middle-aged hippy prognosticator might have practiced her dark arts and advised poor Cynthia into picking a cruel a-hole for a husband? Ruby wishes that she could get a vibe, a feeling of connection, but so far, not so much. All she feels right now is the heavy head of Boy as it rests on her lap, making shifting gears a tad difficult.

With so much whirling around in her mind and imagination, Ruby decides that she should just focus on the task at hand, getting in a few groceries for herself and the dogs. Sometimes there is great relief in thinking only about the quotidian.

Elvin the proprietor is in his usual position, behind the meat case, chatting up the old boys. It seems odd not to see Bull there among the green pants and Carhartt jackets. When he's not holding up the wall at Cumbie's, he's here jawing with his cronies. Assuming that none of them know what's going on with Bull, Ruby approaches the group to fill them in. As Ruby has discovered, in the way of small towns, they know who she is, how she fits into Bull's life: The lady with the Westfalia, parks it in Bull's yard. Reads dogs' minds or something. That's Ruby Heartwood.

"Oh jeez," says Elvin.

"That's a shame," says the nonagenarian of the group, Deke Wilkins.

"Them cigarettes. I told him time and again. Gonna kill him," says a guy whose name Ruby doesn't know.

As Ruby steps away from the group, she is struck with a thought. "Any of you gentlemen remember a kind of a hippy store in town, late seventies, early eighties?"

"Like with incense and those ugly woven ponchos?"

"Exactly. Except that this one had a psychic in the back, did people's fortunes, tea leaves, that sort of thing."

Elvin sets a package of pork chops on the counter for a customer and then rejoins the group. "Like you do?"

"Yes."

"Deke, who was that who ran that weird little place over by Heralds? Long-haired guy, skinny as a rail. Always wishing you 'peace, man' even when you just walked by." This from the guy whose name she doesn't know. "Far out, man." He does a credible hippy accent, although, thinking about it, Ruby believes he's exactly the right age himself to have been of the counterculture.

Elvin says, "Oh, yeah. Glen and Lucy Atkins's kid. Antiwar protester. He ended up in real estate. Done well for himself. Why the question, Ruby?"

"I'm trying to track down who that psychic might have been." Ruby hopes she doesn't sound foolish.

Deke pulls a phone book out from behind the counter. Thumbs it open. "Here you go. Robert W. Atkins Real Estate. Huh, same location. Fifty-one Main. Go visit him."

And just like that, as easy as pie, Ruby is gifted with a breakthrough.

The long-haired skinny-as-a-rail hippy has become a bald, stout man dressed in a blue blazer and beige chinos, a popped collar on his light blue polo shirt. He looks the image of a real estate salesman. Ruby realizes that she's seen his image in advertising all over town so meeting him is almost like speaking to someone she knows.

He is alone in his office, although there is a messy desk on the opposite corner from where he is sitting when Ruby comes in. Robert W. Atkins leaps to his feet at her entrance, hand already extended, as if he's been waiting for her, and she thinks that maybe he has been expecting someone, just not her. "Robert Atkins, welcome. How can I help you today?" Ruby gets it then: This is his persona. He greets everyone this way. She likes him.

Ruby introduces herself. "Well, this may seem a bit strange. . . ."

"Please, have a seat." Atkins gestures to a pair of comfortable-looking chairs set up in the window, a window that is plastered over with listings for homes and land in the area. As she sits, Ruby is startled to recognize the Dew Drop Inn as one of those listings.

"What can I do for you, Ms. Heartwood? We get all kinds of strange requests in here, so don't feel shy."

"Was this once a head shop? A hippy store?"

If he's surprised, Atkins keeps it together. "Well, you might classify it as that. When I was younger, I did have a little store here, we sold some goods that might be considered a little outré. But it didn't last long. I got my real estate license." That is, entered the mainstream, Harmony Farms style.

"While you had it, did you also have a woman here who read tea leaves?"

Now Atkins sits back. Rubs his chin. "It's been so long, but I did have someone come in from time to time to work for me. If she did that kind of thing, tea leaves, it was without my knowledge. I was a hippy but not interested in mysticism. I'm a Catholic."

"Well, it's not necessarily mysticism, but it is fortune-telling. Do you remember her name?"

"Wow. Gosh, I don't think that I do. Why are you so curious?"

Ruby stands up and hands Atkins one of her old business cards.

Madame Ruby, Seer and Fortune-teller. Tea leaves, Tarot and Palms.
"If you should think of her name, would you please give me a call?"

Outside, Ruby feels such a weakness in her knees that she thinks she's
going to have to sit on one of those benches that bear Robert W. Atkins Real Estate advertising images. So close. So very close. Was it her
imagination, her suggestibility, that she felt the presence of that other,
long-ago psychic in that room? As clear as day, Ruby remembers the
moment she knew that she was pregnant with a child conceived out
of violence.

She'd thrown up the meager breakfast she'd had, a cheap McDonald's
breakfast sandwich that had turned vile almost as soon as she'd choked
it down. Since her sheltered orphanage life, she had been educated in
the ways of the adult world and knew what a missed period and a vom-
ited breakfast indicated. She sat down on the curb, wiping her mouth
with the back of her hand. Still inside were her traveling companions,
two of the girls from the carnival who had decided to hitchhike west to
Las Vegas, try their luck at working casinos. Ruby foresaw a different
kind of working life for them but kept her mouth shut. She wasn't ready
to travel alone just yet. That morning, in some town she can't recall, the
sky had turned a different color, a gauzy mauve, the air around her felt
saturated with a novel hope. Against all logic, all sense, this new reality
felt like magic, like inspiration, not the worst that could befall a young
girl. This was her miracle. This was her chance to get it right. This was
her chance to show her absent mystery mother how it could be done.

Just as Ruby gets her van settled back into its space in Bull's yard, her
phone dings with an incoming text. Much to her surprise, it's Doug,
texting during a lull in his meeting schedule. She guesses that the no
cell phones during the day rule does not apply to school staff. *Can I tell
you that it doesn't break my heart that you're still in HF?*

That brings an unexpected warmth to Ruby's cheeks. She's not sure what to answer. If she should answer. But then she does. *It's not such a bad thing.* 😊

Thumbs-up from Doug.

What, are we fifteen? Communicating in emoticons?

Considering that's the age group I mostly hang out with . . . I speak emoticon pretty well. You should see my TikTok.

What if you just dialed me?

Can't now, later this afternoon?

LFTI

??

Looking forward to it.

Xo

Ruby doesn't hesitate, does her own xo. No hearts, no kissy face. Just a nice sign off between friends with a little skin-to-skin history.

The dogs play for a bit in the yard and then Boy asks to go into the house. Ruby follows behind, mostly to make sure that he has fresh water in his bowl, and maybe to see if Bull's washer works. Considering she's only ever seen him dressed in the same or similar clothes—sweatshirt, workpants, ball cap—she's a bit skeptical that he might even own such a thing. But with her current state of finances, she could use a free wash and dry, so she looks around. She's in luck—tucked into a nook off the kitchen is a stacked washer and dryer, and, hallelujah, even a bag of detergent pods. Fabric softener. It seems odd to think of Bull as someone who thinks to buy fabric softener. How little we know one another until we peek into one another's homes.

Laundry started, Ruby finds herself tidying up the kitchen. She's sure Bull won't mind someone doing the dishes, wiping the counter, the table, the floor if she can find a mop. She won't do enough to imply the place is a health hazard, but enough to feel comfortable maybe eating her lunch at the table instead of in the van. The rain has started in earnest and the van can feel dank and cold on such days. She'll bring in her laptop and fiddle around with an opening paragraph in her query message that she will send out to selected green tree matches. Something benign. But compelling. Interesting, but not shocking. Casual, not pleading.

Ruby sees that she's got a reply from Joe Benini. He's not encouraging.

"Heading to Presque Isle tomorrow (Friday) will only be there two days, then heading back through Vermont and points south."

Timing sucks. She won't be able to catch them in Maine before they head to Vermont, and she may not even catch them there. By that time, the agricultural fairs will pretty much be done with.

The email ends: "Not to worry. Maybe next year, Ruby. Say hi to Sabine for me, Joe."

If it's a disappointing message, it also has the effect of releasing Ruby from an obligation. Enough with the distraction of carnivals. There is a growing sense of closing in on her quest and that bears far more weight than her compulsive desire to keep moving. For the first time in her life, Ruby doesn't balk at staying put. For the first time it feels like the right thing to do. That this is the right place to be.

As if reading her mind, the Hitchhiker runs up to Ruby and drops her forepaws on her lap. "Yes. Stay. Happy." Her tongue is lolling and her woolly bear caterpillar eyebrows bounce up and down her dark forehead. Her tail beats so hard Ruby can feel the breeze on her ankles.

"Yes, we'll stay. For now." Ruby kisses the dog on the head. "For now."

36

By Saturday morning, Ruby has spent most of her time composing the query letter she hopes will encourage perfect strangers with shared DNA into pointing her toward the answers she craves. She's run it by Sabine and by Doug, and both have offered, from their own particular perspectives, edits and suggestions. Sabine's from being tied to this quest by blood, and Doug by virtue of his profession. A message laden with delicacy and provoking of curiosity is hopefully what she has crafted.

> My dear genetic cousin. My name is Ruby Heartwood, but I was christened Mary Jones. Christened in a Canadian convent and orphanage, Sacred Heart near Ottawa. As with so many who have questions about ancestors, I too have come to Family History Labs to see if I might locate my ancestors. However, I am most interested in locating my nearest relatives, not the more distant. Your green tree suggests that we share xxx amount of ancestry . . .

Ruby will plug in the exact amount for each cousin she contacts.

> . . . I am hoping that you might be willing to share your family tree with me as I have no starting point. Should you have

family stories, rumors, anything that might shed some light
on my origins, and be willing to share it . . .

This is where she's gotten stuck. Doug suggests starting with the
family tree and leaving the quest out of it. Sabine thinks she should
just ask bluntly for family scandals. No one suggests that she mention
her peculiar gift of fortune-telling. Giving the letter one more quick
scan, Ruby closes it out, still not quite satisfied.

She's wangled a spot at the Makers Faire and is running a little late.
This morning she's going to press the animal communication skill a
little harder with a view to getting a few house calls during the week.
She's got a new placard for her sandwich board with "animal communicator" at the top of the list. Polly mentioned that Carrie Farr has been
talking up Ruby's talents to her horse community, so maybe something
will pop up. She unabashedly charges more for equine readings than
canine. A couple of those this week and she'll be able to relax.

Boy gets a little stressed as Ruby packs up the van. He leans against
her, putting himself between her and the van. "It's okay, Boy. We're just
going to the park."

"Forever?"

"No. Till after lunch. Then we'll come back."

"What's a lunch?"

"Eating for humans. Not for dogs. You get dinner."

If she thought conversation with the Hitchhiker was frustrating,
conversation with Boy is worse. He is still skeptical of her promise
that Bull will come home. She knows why; even she's not entirely sure
she's speaking the truth when she makes that promise. The infection
is stubborn. Despite his size, Bull is not robust, years of smoking and
Mountain Dew have exacted a toll. The dog picks up on that as if he's
the psychic. She gives the Labrador a full-body hug. "Hop in. I don't
want to leave you home by yourself." She thought it might be better to
let him be in his own house but has changed her mind. He might feel
abandoned and she can't put him through that.

Reluctantly, the dog gets into the van, stretches out on the bench seat. The Hitchhiker joins him, as if offering her own version of a full-body hug. Then rolls over and playfully nips at his chin, his paws, until he pushes her off the seat. Ruby thinks that this van is beginning to smell like dog. And not in a good way.

The Farmers' Market is in full harvest mode, luscious vegetables, fruits, and baked goods fill the boxes displayed on each table. The coffee guy is enjoying a long line of customers on this slightly cooler Saturday. After a few slow weeks during the dog days of August, the event has ramped up; it is September, the kids are back in school, and fall is in the air. Ruby can tell from the crafts now on offer, that vendors are already looking forward to Christmas sales. Are those ornaments on a fake tree? Shop early, shop local. On her way by the knitters consortium, she can't help but pick out a pom-pom hat for Molly and a pair of mittens for Tom but then blanches at the price for the hand-made items. A little embarrassed, she has the vendor set them aside with a promise to come by after the Faire to pay for them, hoping that she will be able to afford them after a successful day. If not, she really shouldn't be buying Christmas gifts anyway and she'll explain herself to the woman. Or barter a reading for the hat.

The day has gone better than she had hoped for and Ruby lays another twenty into her cigar box, squishing the lid down against the growing stack. She's on a roll. This is one of those rare days when she doesn't have to make much up, just dress up the images and impressions and inspirations she's receiving in the language of her trade. Back in the very old days, Ruby used to use a fake Bohemian accent, mostly because she was so young, no one would believe a girl like her could possibly interpret the signs accurately. Once Sabine hit middle school, she persuaded Ruby to drop it. "It's, like, so embarrassing. People think I'm from Transylvania." Heaven forfend that she embarrass her daughter. Ruby smiles at the memory.

Another customer comes up to the table. Tea leaves this time. Ruby has just enough hot water in the thermos to do one more reading. She's replaced her smashed teapot with a cheap little ceramic pot she found in the thrift store for two dollars. It is so plain that she almost didn't spot it on the shelf among the oversized souvenir mugs adorned with witty slogans or resort names. Plain as can be, off-white, holding only a pint of water. Surprisingly, it has poured out some nice fortunes today.

By the end of the day Ruby can pay for the knitted hat and mittens and put some away to pay Bull back for his kindness. She's got three house calls to read dogs, one barn call to see about a mini donkey's behavior problem, and a birthday party all arranged. It has been a very good day. If it wasn't for Boy, Ruby might consider a night at the Dew Drop, which makes her think of the listing she saw in the window of Robert W. Atkins Real Estate office. Impulsively, she turns the Westfalia toward the motel. Sure enough, there is a real estate sign poked into the ground at the edge of the circular garden. Just looking at it makes Ruby think that Ravi has lost heart and that is very sad to her. He's given up. Was this his American dream? Where will he go now? Should she have stayed more often?

Ruby spots Ravi coming out of the office, dressed, as always, in his crisp white shirt, black pants. He sees her van and waves her into the circle. "Hello, Ruby. Will you be staying with us tonight?"

"Oh, I can't. I'm, uh, dog-sitting for Bull Harrison. He's in the hospital." She assumes Ravi, like most of the town, knows who Bull is, even if he's not personally acquainted with him. Bull is, after all, a fixture.

"I am so sorry to hear that. Wish him well for me when you see him." Ravi stands away from the side of the van to let her move off.

"I was just passing by." She doesn't really need to explain her random arrival, but she does. "I saw your For Sale sign. I'm so sorry."

"Oh. That. Well." Ravi's smile is a little sheepish, a little less pretty than usual. "The owner is selling. He's been selling the place for fifty years."

"I thought you were the owner."

"Oh, no. I am the latest in a long line of South Asian desk clerks."

"But you treat the place like your own."

"I will take that as a compliment. I do take pride in my work."

"Would you want it to be your own?" Even as she asks this question, she sees that Ravi's aura has changed from its everyday pleasantness to a shade of blue that she associates with ambition.

"Perhaps. I'd want to make some big improvements, of course. A new pool, for one. Create suites instead of single rooms, efficiencies with kitchens. Attract families. Maybe even put in mini-golf or a rock-climbing wall."

Ruby is charmed by Ravi's ideas. She can't imagine what it would take to accomplish, what kind of capital. This is not her area of expertise, but fortune-telling is. She reaches out and takes Ravi's left hand. Turns it over. Runs her finger along his life line and the four little branches off of it. "I see success for you down the road. But you have to take the first step."

"My grandmother back in Sri Lanka is a fortune-teller. She has said the same thing." He grins at Ruby, gently takes his hand back and pats the side of the van. "Nice to see you. Give my regards to Bull."

It has been a busy day, meeting lots of people, not much time to nap. Boy doesn't rest, not really. He's not playing much either, which is disappointing for me as I have come to depend on his being on the other end of my tug toys. I keep telling him that his person will be back, because my person has said so, but he is what the people call a skeptic. He has trust issues. I know he scented out the disease that took his man away, and that he can't get that scent out of his nose, but

I do believe that things will be okay. I love the word *okay*. It is deployed only when things are good. Along with *good girl*. I must tell Ruby that she needs to tell Boy that he is a good boy. She forgets sometimes. She is distracted too. She doesn't smell of disease, thankfully, but she does emit a curious scent of disquiet. She sits and studies her box things and then pulls out that really interesting pack of objects that smell so delightfully of a myriad of hands touching. People who have just eaten popcorn and people who are freshly exercised. Walkers and strollers and baby holders. Young women in heat and young men in rut. Ruby has to push me away when I get a little too close and the objects scatter all over the floor. I pounce, but she shoos me away, gathers the objects and puts them back in their little wooden box.

Ruby gathers the scattered tarot cards, taps them into alignment and puts them back into their little wooden box. It had been a pointless exercise; they had revealed nothing more than what she already knew, had given no direction or guidance. She had wanted them to point the way to sending those email missives to unknown cousins, giving her a sense of authority, of a predetermined success. More specifically, she had wanted one green tree to be designated the best choice. But of course, cards can't do that. A flip of the coin is a better technique for such indecision. There are three potential contacts. Each one is a second cousin, meaning that she and they share a set of great grand-parents. Any first cousins haven't shown up. That would be too easy. No hint that one of these strangers is actually closer in relation than another. A sister perhaps. Maybe something will appear in the next wave of Family History Lab results. They add information as more people climb onboard the DNA railroad.

Well, she could do an eenie-meenie-miney-mo thing, but instead Ruby decides that she'll feed the dogs and eat the other half of her lunchtime sandwich. As they climb out of the van to go into Bull's kitchen, a car pulls into the yard. Boy immediately does his hiding in the bushes thing that he has taken to doing since Bull disappeared. As a young man gets out of his vehicle, the dog bursts out from the hedges and fairly knocks the guy over with his exuberance. His tail is whipping back and forth and suddenly the big dog is in the guy's arms. Ruby knows instantly that this must be Bull's son Cooper.

"I hope that you've got good news."

"Pretty good. First of all, thank you for getting him to the hospital. Secondly, yes, Bull is doing much better. He'll be in for a few more days, but they've got the infection under control. And, thank God, it wasn't hepatitis after all."

"That is good news. Boy will be overjoyed to see him."

"Well, that's why I'm here. Bull's doing better, but I think that if he can see the dog, he'll really improve. He's down, you know."

"Being sick is hard work. It's depressing."

"I'm going to pull a little fast one on the medical community and bring Boy to see him. Don't you think he'd make a great emotional support dog?"

"I think that's exactly what he is." Ruby can hear the dog's thoughts even as she stands three feet from him. Cooper carries Bull's scent on him, and the dog is crazed to figure out what it means. "He just needs a vest."

"I just want you to know that I don't hold with faking therapy dogs and the like, but in this case, I think that it's the truth."

Cooper seems like a nice young man; seems like he cares for his father. But Ruby also gets the sense that this is a reborn relationship. That it hasn't always been so. She shakes the impression off. What is important is what is happening right now. "They need each other."

Man and dog are gone in ten minutes. Cooper will keep Boy with him until his father comes home. All of a sudden, Ruby is free to go.

Well, given her appointments coming up in the next week, not so free to go far, but certainly free to not be living in her van in Bull's yard. She grabs her leftover turkey sandwich, locks Bull's back door, and she and the Hitchhiker head out of Harmony Farms to spend the night with Doug.

Doug sets a glass of wine in front of Ruby, just to the side of her open laptop. When she'd called him, Doug had made her promise that she would show him the latest iteration of her query letter after a shared meal of leftovers. His, yesterday's chicken tacos, hers, the turkey sandwich from lunch. She'd had one of his tacos, and he'd had half of her half sandwich. All in all, enough for both of them and a dropped piece of turkey for the dog.

"You've got no reason not to send this to all of them. What's the worse that happens? No response? Just do it."

And so she does. Pressing the send key to launch the three missives into the unknown. It is an anticlimactic act. If this was a movie, there would be an appropriate sound track with French horns bleating. "Do you suppose they all know each other?"

"Could be. Although I can't tell you who my second cousins are. My mother's cousins' kids. Well, maybe one. Okay, two. Most of them grew up in the same neck of the woods." Doug grins. "It is legal for second cousins to marry, right?"

Ruby twangs out the *Deliverance* banjo motif.

Her feet are very cold, and Ruby realizes that she's standing in snow. The Hitchhiker is dragging her by the leash through dirty snow piled up on streets. The dog seems in a great hurry to get somewhere. She hears, but doesn't see, Doug, who is telling her that they have tickets to a play and that they are going to be late. Another voice speaks to Ruby. An older woman with permed hair, threaded with gray. This woman gives Ruby a gentle hug. "Hi, Auntie," Ruby says. She's never had an aunt before, so she is delighted when this dream aunt offers her a cup of coffee saying, "You need to visit your mother." The coffee spills down Ruby's front but doesn't burn. It melts a gap in the snow, and the Hitchhiker laps at it. "Where do I find her?"

Doug wakes her up when he rearranges the tossed bedclothes over them, tucks the blanket around her bare feet.

Like the rest of her mother dreams, this one is vivid hours into the day. The dream aunt is so real that Ruby assumes she is a composite of women she already knows. She wishes that Doug hadn't woken her, that her aunt had given her the answer to that question: Where do I find her?

"I'm no Freudian," Doug says. "I don't interpret dreams, but I think that all this one was is a result of your sending that message to potential relatives. It's so much in the forefront of your thinking that naturally your id is going to rejigger it to sort it out for your ego."

"Id? Ego? You forget I only had an eighth-grade education."

"You're one of the smartest women I know, Ruby Heartwood. You can't throw me that line. You forget I've seen the contents of your Kindle."

For some reason that makes Ruby blush a little. She's an autodidact and she's proud of that fact. From the time Sabine was little, Ruby worked hard to never be in a position where her daughter would be embarrassed by her lack of education. Her weird profession, that's a given as an embarrassment, but not a lack of education. She may not have a college degree, but she does have a G.E.D. Every high school lesson that Sabine brought home, Ruby studied as well in the guise of helping her daughter with her homework. If Sabine had ever cottoned onto what Ruby was doing, she had the grace—or perhaps the maturity—not to mention it.

It is late Sunday afternoon when Ruby cautiously opens up her laptop. They've had a lovely quiet day, a nice walk, a casual lunch. She won't stay tonight. Doug has work in the morning and she has her first appointment at eight-thirty to read a mischievous puppy. She doesn't want to risk getting stuck in commuter traffic. It's getting dark earlier these days, so she'll head back to Harmony Farms after she checks to see if the chum she's tossed out onto the sea of family research has been bit. Expecting nothing, she is completely surprised to see a message in her Family History Lab inbox. She feels Doug's big hand on her shoulder. "I'll be in the backyard with the dog."

37

It's a chatty little message:

> Hi Ruby, so glad you reached out to me. I am your second
> cousin. I have been collecting family history for many years
> and this is the first time I've been approached by your branch.
> It sounds like you have some questions about your history,
> and maybe I can enlighten you a little bit. Having said that,
> there is a lot we don't know. I suggest that we communicate
> via regular email instead of the FHL."

It is signed: Your 2nd cousin, Sarah Grace Devereaux (married
name Bidwell) with her email address. Ruby immediately taps in a
cordial reply and her email address and cell phone number.

It's a start.

Ruby arrives at the front door of her eight-thirty appointment a few
minutes early. It hadn't taken long to find the place, and Ruby realizes
that she's become quite well versed in the highways and byways of
little Harmony Farms. This place is on one of the offshoot roads that
thread themselves around the lakeside. The house is a tiny renovated
lake house, with a six-foot chain link fence surrounding it. She gets

a ripple of foreboding. This is the kind of fence you use when you want to keep something very big inside of it. Sure enough, she hears a thunderous bark and a massive Rottweiler bounds out from behind the house and crashes into the fence, upright on its hind legs. Ruby's first impulse is to jump back into the Westie and book it out of there, but she doesn't. She waits for the dog's person to shout at him, grab him by the collar, and haul him away. None of which happens. Maybe this isn't the right house, but according to the address she has written down, it is. "I'm giving it one minute," she says under her breath. She also thinks that this is the stupidest arrangement, the way the fence surrounds the house, instead of allowing for access to the front door by UPS drivers and psychics. There is no way to ring the bell. Surely the owner can hear this commotion. Surely this is the reason for the consult in the first place. Ruby has no intention of laying hands on this dog who is now banging his massive forepaws against the chain, biting at it and growling. "Hey, I'm here to help," she yells. And the dog shuts up. Mischievious puppy? Interesting description. Clearly the owner has understated the issue.

"I'm so sorry, I was in the bathroom." A tiny middle-aged woman comes out of the house. Ruby instinctively shuts her eyes against the carnage as the dog bounds up to the woman. "He's really a peach."

"So I see."

The dog is rolling around on his back, begging for a belly rub two seconds after he was threatening Ruby with dismemberment.

"I'm Ruby Heartwood, I'm here to consult with you about your dog."

"Yes, I know. Again, sorry for his behavior. He really doesn't mean anything by it, but it's making it hard to have anybody over."

Ruby waits at the gate as the woman coaxes the dog away from the fence and into the house. "I have to be honest, I don't really think I can help you." She makes no move to open the gate, step onto that property.

"Once you're in the house, he's fine."

In her mind's eye, Ruby sees a chorus of Polly, Doug, and Sabine all screaming, "Nooo!"

"Let's talk out here for a moment first. How old is he?"

"Ten months."

Ruby begins peppering the owner with all kinds of questions about the dog's routine, origins, preferences, and when this behavior became apparent. All without going through the gate. She can see the dog's big head in the picture window. He's standing on the couch and facing them, a gargoyle of a dog. She detects a string of drool going from his lips to the windowpane. He flips his head and a spray of saliva paints the glass. And suddenly she gets right into the dog's mind. "He's bored. He's in need of a job. He would enjoy meeting other people, but he has all these feelings of superiority. What I think he means is that he's become a mature dog. He needs to be neutered."

"He thinks that?"

"No, he thinks he needs to mount, that is, dominate, everything and everyone."

"I've been meaning to get an appointment but . . ."

"I know, he's hard to manage without the fence. Get help."

Ruby walks away with her fee in her hand wondering why in the world such a small woman would have such a dominant dog. Companionship or protection? Ruby thinks that she'll ask Polly to find a trainer for this lady before it's too late.

The next appointment is a cake walk in comparison and comes with a nice cup of tea offered by the poodle's owner. They sit chatting long after Ruby has translated the little dog's reason for recent anxiety: the owner's new boyfriend is a cat person. Détente is possible if the boyfriend will bring special treats when he comes to visit. She's thinking of Doug when she recommends this; he always has something special for the Hitchhiker whenever he's around. Last night, in the end, Ruby hadn't gone back to Harmony Farms to sleep in her van in Bull's yard but had again stayed the night with Doug. It has become awfully easy to do. Ruby thinks that there is some danger in this, but

Doug makes no call on her to stay put. He never asks why she insists that she needs to move on. He never tries to argue her out of it. Even if she is experiencing some difficulty in actually leaving, he never says anything—like it must mean she isn't really ready to go.

Well, tonight she'll get a room at the Dew Drop Inn. Tomorrow she has the barn call and then one more house call. After that she is hoping to book herself into another Renaissance Faire. There's a good one opening up this weekend on the South Shore that she'd done a few years ago. First, though, Ruby needs to make another repair to the rip in the tent, it's migrated north in the fragile fabric. That and she noticed on Saturday that her little pennant is horribly faded and should be replaced. It's always something, she thinks. Always something.

When Ruby pulls into the parking lot of the Dew Drop Inn, Robert W. Atkins is escorting a couple of men dressed in the uber casual style of slackers, although they seem a tad too old for droopy black pants and hoodies, horn rimmed glasses, and stubble. Investors, Ruby decides without guessing. Harmony Farms is laden with such folks, people who telecommute to jobs with inexplicable descriptions and eat kale. Earn more money in a week than she does in a year. She sighs. What will be will be. Que sera sera. She envisions the Dew Drop demolished and rebuilt to include all the amenities of a resort. Concierge service and a spa menu. Something entirely out of her price range. Ruby parks the van and hustles into the office, the Hitchhiker on her heels. Ravi has taken to keeping biscuits in his office for the growing number of dogs staying at the Dew Drop and she knows where he keeps them.

"I notice that your real estate man is here." Ruby signs the registration sheet. "I wouldn't be deceived by the look of the pair he's got with him."

"Oh, I'm not. I'm quite encouraged." He makes the Hitchhiker sit before giving her a treat. "The scruffier they are, the more money they tend to have. It's a cultivated look." Ravi fishes out another treat for the dog. "This place is crying out for an infusion of capital."

Ruby has to admire his optimism, and then she thinks that maybe it's a brand of hope, that he will either benefit from the new ownership or be forced to move on.

As Ruby slips the key into the lock to her usual room, Robert Atkins and his companions come around the corner of the building. "Hey, it's Ruby, isn't it?"

"Indeed it is."

"I'm here showing the property to these two gentlemen," Atkins says, stating the obvious, but Ruby is too polite to mock him.

"It's a nice place, I'm very comfortable here. The management is quite good." Plug Ravi where she can. "Very nice place." They've been in every room but her little crooked one, so she hopes she's not overselling.

"I'm sure." Bob turns to guide his clients in the direction of the laundry room, then pauses. "You know what? I just thought of that name you were looking for the other day."

"Oh?" Knees begin to weaken, and Ruby collects herself. It means nothing. It's just a name. Of a woman in her line of business. Bet it's someone she already knows. The thoughts stream through her mind in a rush. "What is it?"

"Probably made up, but she called herself Aurora."

"Just Aurora?"

"That's all I can recall."

It must have been the late sixties, early seventies. Hippies and free love. Names as made up as her own. Was Aurora self-inventing or hiding? Drifting through life as an itinerant soothsayer or focused on earning enough of a living to settle down?

"Now that you remember her name, do you happen to recall what she looked like?"

Robert W. Atkins, once of the skinny hippy longhair leaping gnome stage, now stout and bald and successful in business, blushes a teensy bit. "Actually, now that my memory is jogged, I recall that she was gorgeous, in the way of girls in that era. Thin, long red blond hair, ethereal. Floated into my shop for a few weeks and then floated away. Couldn't catch her. Couldn't pin her down."

He is describing Guinevere drawing pentagrams, as in the old Crosby, Stills & Nash song.

"Do you know about how old she might have been?" It is important that this creature of his memory and of Cynthia's be the right age. Ruby has thought a lot about this. If her mother had been in some kind of home for unwed mothers, then she would have been a teenager when Ruby was born. If she appeared in Harmony Farms in the early seventies, then she might have been at most in her early thirties. If this woman in Cynthia's memory and Bob's is too old, well, then it can't have been Ruby's mother. Likewise, too young wouldn't work.

"Gosh, I'm no judge of a woman's age, but definitely on the good side of thirty."

"Thank you, Mr. Atkins. That helps."

Ruby lets herself and the dog into the motel room, flops onto the bed, and stares up at the ceiling, which has a spider on it. The dog jumps up beside her and circles, happy to have a quick nap if that's what Ruby is suggesting. "Aurora. What a great name. Wish I'd thought of it for myself." Ruby starts to laugh. "Wait, maybe I did." That long-ago fake family tree. Hadn't they made up the name of a putative grandmother, Aurora Boreallian?

The dog has no reply, tucks her nose beneath her hind leg and lets her eyes close slowly into pure relaxation.

Ruby, however, cannot relax. She gets up, disturbing the dog, who, after making sure going back outside isn't on offer, just closes her eyes again. Ruby looks at her phone, sees that she has a couple of email messages, but prefers to check them on her computer. Booting up seems to take forever, so she peeks at the phone to see who they are from. If she was a superstitious person, she would cross her fingers, hoping that her new cousin Sarah Grace has sent her some information. Confirmation that somewhere in the family history is a hippy chick named Aurora. She wants a message from Sarah Grace so badly that she is shocked when she actually has one. No, two. Both email messages are from Sarah.

The first is another chatty message with lots of names that don't seem to add up to anything remotely useful. Second cousins and third cousins once removed, twice removed. Seemingly all human beings who arrived on these shores from the British Isles appear to be related.

The second gets down to brass tacks. Females prevail in this family. Grandmothers have sisters and mothers have daughters. The last paragraph of the rather long, complicated email is the one she should have started with.

"I believe that you may descend from my great aunt Lidia's second daughter's second daughter, who supposedly ran off. I don't know much about that part of the family, so let me do a little rooting around, make some calls. However, I'm off on our long anticipated Alaskan cruise, so if you don't hear from me right away, don't lose hope."

38

It is too hard to wrap her mind around the various generations and how they may fit against the framework of the last fifty-five years. Was this missing daughter lost in 1964 or 1934? Is the allusion to females "prevailing" in this family a coded message on a particularly female tendency toward fortune-telling? Ruby taps in a quick thank-you and a promise to be patient. "So many questions!" she writes, again including her cell phone number in the reply.

The Hitchhiker rests her chin on Ruby's knee as Ruby sits and ponders the imponderable. The dog sighs. Yawns. Wriggles her chin deeper against Ruby's leg, exerting an attention-getting pressure. Woof. "It's time for dinner. Feed me."

"You think that it's always time for dinner."

"It is."

"No, it is not." Ruby has to be firm with this little muncher. "Maybe time for a cookie."

"Okay. Many."

"One."

"More than one."

"Two."

The dog agrees in principle and moves to allow Ruby to get up and fetch the box of Milk-Bones. Ruby's wooden box holding the deck of tarot cards is beside the box of dog biscuits. She feels a strong need to consult them on her own behalf, although she is never quite sure if her self-interpretations are of any use. She should get someone else to do it for her, but there is a critical shortage of psychics in town. Instead, she thumbs through her contacts list. Maybe Lily Parmenter or Sylvia Truelove would be willing to do her a favor. Ruby has never been a fan of remote readings, but any port in a storm, as they say. Lily answers on the first ring, "Ruby Heartwood! As I live and breathe, I just knew you were about to call."

"Right. And the same back to you, you old fraud."

They laugh. Lily was always fun to be around. Not a true psychic, Lily is a wizard tarot interpreter. She can weave a fortune like nobody's business based solely on what the cards reveal. Ruby and Lily bring each other up to date enough on their lives to allow Ruby to get to the point of her call. "I'm looking for someone. I need to know . . ."

"Uh-huh. Don't give me ideas. Do you have FaceTime?"

In a moment, Ruby and Lily are virtually face to face. Lily shuffles her cards, a nice set that looks fairly new. Ruby compliments them. "Got them from a retiree. Barely used them."

"Only on Sunday, that kind of thing?"

"Sort of. Hey, I think you knew her, way back."

Ruby can watch Lily lay out the cards. "Who?"

"Celeste Fox. Went by Madame Celestine back in the day."

"Yeah. I knew her." Ruby hopes that Lily is too busy with her cards to see the look of surprise on Ruby's face at the mention of her erstwhile mentor, but Lily is too good at her job not to make sure she looks up at exactly the right moment.

"History?"

"You could say that." Ruby has never told anyone the circumstances of Sabine's conception, only that she had learned the trade from Madame Celestine (who knew that her real name was Celeste Fox?). But now Ruby is riven by curiosity. What had become of Buck, he who she had cursed so potently?

Lily's eyes on the tiny screen bore into Ruby's. "What do you want to know?"

"Tell me about her."

Lily describes an elderly woman with a bad dye job, dressed in a velour track suit that might have come from the eighties. "A little lady. Not over five feet tall, I bet, although most of that was hunch."

In Ruby's memory, Madame Celestine towered.

"She handed me the box of cards and I handed her the money. She was clearly lonely and wanted me to stay for a cup of coffee, but I had to go."

"Did she mention her son?"

"In passing. I felt bad about leaving her alone, but she said that she was expecting her son to visit, that he came every Saturday. But, Ruby, I had the feeling that this was a lie."

"How so?"

"The screen door needed fixing, the grass in the yard was in dire need of cutting. Little things a devoted son would take care of. You know what I mean?"

"I do." Ruby then thinks to ask, "When was this?"

"Oh, gosh. Maybe a year ago."

"Where?"

"Providence."

Ruby can't believe that. The last place she pictured Celestine was in New England, much less an hour or so away. Celestine seemed much more the type to end up in Florida.

"At any rate, how can I help you, Ruby?"

"You know what, give me Celestine's address if you remember it and let's forget the reading."

"Okay." If Lily thinks this odd, she doesn't show it.

Ruby is never going to trust a deck of tarot cards that once belonged to Buck's mother.

She forgot my other cookie. She doesn't think that I can count, but I can count when I haven't gotten more than one. Those little boxes that people cling to are so distracting, much like finding a new scent on a blade of grass when you are on a walk. Suddenly that scent grabs your nose and you can't think of anything else until . . . squirrel! At any rate, Ruby is so distracted by the little thing that she must be reminded of my missing treat with a sharp yappy bark. I accept her apology.

Polly called to let Ruby know that Cooper has brought Bull home, that the old guy is doing pretty well, and taking his medicine and keeping away from the cigarettes and Mountain Dew. Ruby says she'll drop in on him after her appointments. Déjà vu again. Leaving Harmony Farms Part II, or III or whatever it is. Stop at Bull's and keep going. That was the plan a week ago, that is the plan today. She's settled up with Ravi, wished him luck with the sale of the motel, called Sabine to let her know that she's heading to the South Shore to the Ren Faire near Plymouth. Doug says he'd kind of like to join her there, spend the upcoming weekend. He's even offered to find a nice hotel, what he laughingly said might be a step up from the Dew Drop. At first Ruby balked at the idea of company. She's working, not sightseeing. But even before she objected, Ruby realized that the idea of having someone to eat with, to talk to about the day and the foibles of the gullible masses would be kind of fun. When Sabine was her constant companion, even during her cranky adolescence, it was nice to sit down to a meal and tell stories. Having another person across from her made her life seem close to normal. So she's told Doug, sure. They won't get a ton of time together, what with a ten-hour day in the tent, but some.

What she's also thinking is that Providence is about forty-five minutes from where she'll set up her tent under the pines on the grounds of the Renaissance Faire. The weekends-only event itself stretches until Columbus Day, and Ruby is hoping to be able to keep her tent up, avoid any more wear and tear on the fabric. She'll have lots of time for a visit with Madame Celestine. Assuming she can gin up the courage.

Ruby finds the hobby farm with the unhappy miniature donkey with little difficulty. It's a tidy little place on the outer edge of the posh Upper Lakes Estates where Cynthia Mann lives. A twenty-by-thirty pen delineates the creature's space. A groove ten inches deep edges the interior perimeter of the circle. The pen itself is made of neat post and board, a scrim of green cage wire obviously intended to keep the animal within the confines of its space. Surrounding this corral are gardens of both the vegetable and floral variety. Stone walls outline a curvilinear cinder path that leads to a koi pond. All in all, more in keeping with *Better Homes & Gardens* than *Farm World Magazine.*

Even before she sees the subject of her morning consult, she hears it. A sound more like someone choking to death than a bray. The sound precedes the appearance of a moldy brown foursquare animal with the most enormous ears and the saddest eyes she's ever seen. A black stripe runs the length of its back and a brush of mane sticks up as if it's been electrocuted.

A woman comes out of the back door of the house. "This is Mr. Bates."

"Really? Interesting choice of name."

"Well, there was a Mrs. Bates, but she kicked the bejesus out of him."

"That hardly sounds like Anna Bates." Ruby gets the *Downton Abbey* reference and likes this lady's style.

The woman introduces herself as Madeline and hands Ruby a carrot to try to entice the donkey over to the gate. "He used to be really friendly, practically dog-like, but lately he just paces and brays, paces and brays."

"I'm thinking that he misses his tormentor. Is that possible?"

"Yes. I thought that too, but she really was miserable with him."

"Maybe he'd like another companion, perhaps a boyfriend?"

"Is that your psychic evaluation?"

"Nope, just guesswork. If he'll let me, I'll see if I can get a more professional read on him."

Madeline manages to get a halter on the donkey and rather than drag him over to Ruby, Ruby goes into the pen. She strokes his ears, mostly because she just wants to see how soft they are. His coat is bristly, but his ears are soft. He folds them back and Ruby steps away. Steps back, lays hands on his face, covers his massive brown eyes with her palms. He immediately relaxes. She can feel the long, long eyelashes against her hands, a little tickly, like caterpillar hair. There it is, a gentle rumble of vibration emanating from his skull. Ruby's thoughts are filled with a deep loneliness that reaches right down and into her own heart. Loneliness and boredom. She releases the donkey's face, lays her hands over her own heart. "He's not lonely for Mrs. Bates; he's lonely for someone else. Someone who played with him."

Madeline bursts into tears.

Back in the van, Ruby turns to her dog. "Well, that was interesting." Madeline, between sobs, had told the story of her husband abruptly leaving her. Completely unexpected, although she should, she said, have been reading the signs for months. Off he went, without more than a half hour's warning, off into the arms of a woman he'd met online. Only Madeline hadn't called it plain "online," using a rather powerful descriptive in between "on" and "line" to establish her feelings about such things. Evidently, the miniature donkey missed the son of a bitch. Shocked into retreat, Ruby had given the only advice she could think of: Madeline should either start being the donkey's playmate or find someone who can. It's only when Ruby reaches the main road back to town that she realizes she hasn't been paid. "Crap." She does a quick Y-turn and heads back to the hobby farm.

•   •   •

Now she's late for her second appointment before leaving town.

Ruby is careful not to stay too long at Bull's, not wanting to tire him out and not wanting to find herself on Route 495 as commuter traffic ramps up in the late afternoon. He looks good, as good as a man who has spent a week in a hospital can appear. Boy looks better too. He has that old happy swing back in his tail that she'd missed the whole time she was taking care of him. He won't leave Bull's side even to greet her properly, letting her come to him.

"Hey, can't offer you a Dew anymore, but wanna cup o' tea or something?" Bull has tried to thank Ruby for her help, but she's put a stop to that with a generic "It's what friends do."

"Friends. That kinda sums it up." He gives her his big grin.

In the end, Ruby makes the tea and they sit and watch afternoon television for a bit before she announces that it's time to go.

"See you soon?" It isn't a plaintive question from Bull, but an affirmation.

"You bet." The tentacles of belonging wrap themselves around Ruby's psyche. For once she is incapable of pulling loose. "I'll be back Monday."

Traffic is indeed thick and slow as Ruby heads south on 495, but it gets better and she's to her destination by four o'clock. All the way past Franklin, Medford, and Wrentham, she is mulling over her quick agreement to return to Harmony Farms on Monday. That had not been her intention, not at all, and it's almost like she's been inhabited by some woman who is *comfortable* staying in one place. It doesn't help that Sarah Grace's quick reply to Ruby's last email included her telephone number with a 508 area code, suggesting that Sarah Grace lives in—who'd'a thought it?—Massachusetts. Is it possible, probable, or just weirdly coincidental that Ruby's only known relative lives in the same state? The same state her daughter insisted on settling in. The one she herself seems to be incapable of getting out of lately. Ruby's own area code is proudly random, having bought her first cell phone while passing through New Orleans: 504, signifying three wildly successful days during Mardi Gras when everyone wanted magic.

The grounds of the Renaissance Faire are unchanged from the last time she was here a number of years ago. Cranberry bogs bordered by a forest of tall pines, within which is a collection of permanent buildings that, when open, will house a blacksmith shop, a costume emporium, crystal sellers, dungeons and dragons–themed souvenirs and, of course, food. Less permanent structures will include the stages for acrobatic acts and the storytellers, the booths for mini archery and games of chance. On the outskirts, the grandstand that will host the day's big event, the make-believe jousting. She can hear the horses stabled beyond the palings, one calling to another. Somewhere out of sight, two combatants are practicing their choreography; she can hear the chime of metal against metal. There is the oh-so-familiar scent of pine chips that are freshly raked over the paths that, in a little while, will be trampled into pulp.

The Hitchhiker at her heels, Ruby heads to the administrative offices located upstairs from the costume shop. There is nothing the least bit Medieval about the offices. Two women are sorting through file folders and a youngish man with close-cropped hair presides over a computer. He looks up as she comes in and Ruby gets the immediate sense that since the last time she worked this gig, there is new management.

Ruby introduces herself and her services.

"Oh, gosh, Ms. Heartwood, we've had all our acts lined up since last year. We don't generally take anybody on this late in the game, and generally nobody new. We open tomorrow morning."

One of the women fiddling with folders puts in her two cents. "Besides, we have a fortune-teller already."

"Oh? May I ask who?" Ruby is surprised at her own lack of

foresight. Of course it might be too late to get in on the action. She's been stuck in Harmony Farms at the Makers Faire while the rest of the world has been making plans.

"Um, let me see." The woman moves to a spot on the office wall where a map of the area is pinned. Squares, rectangles, and ovals each have a number within, and she finds the one she's looking for, checks the number against a hand-printed key, pulls out a file folder with the corresponding number, and opens it. "Okay, here it is. Her name is Annie Felton."

Hardly the name of a practicing psychic. "And what's her professional name?"

"Doesn't say. The business is listed as Clairvoyant and Seer. Pretty generic. Probably uses different names for different gigs."

"Yes. Probably." A suggestion that makes Ruby think this interloper—as she can't help but view her—is a lightweight. A weekend dabbler. A fraud. "Well, if she doesn't work out, please"—Ruby hands the youngish man her card—"call me. I'm not far." Not far at all, having no place to go. "And I'm not new. I worked this Ren Faire for years." She doesn't get as snarky as she feels and keeps the "before you were born" out of her riposte.

Back in the van, Ruby fires off a quick text to Doug to let him know that her weekend plans have opened up. She gets one back almost immediately letting her know that he's gotten a booking at a pet-friendly Airbnb in Sandwich, just a hop, skip, and a jump over either the Sagamore or Bourne bridges. He'll meet her there in time for dinner. He's made reservations for them at the Dan'l Webster Inn.

"Well, Hitch, looks like we get a mini vacation."

The Hitchhiker seems to approve.

After a lovely dinner at the Dan'l Webster, old-fashioned Yankee pot roast for her, the special of the day for him, Ruby and Doug stroll around Sandwich village, admiring the antiquity of it and the pond

with its old mill. The Sandwich Glass Museum is closed, so they plan
to visit it the next day. Even as they make plans, Ruby keeps thinking
about the relative proximity of Madame Celestine. Providence is less
than fifty miles away. But the idea of a gentle adventure, a visit to the
Heritage Gardens and Museums, a walk on the beach with the dog
seems so much more attractive than facing down an old, what? What
was Celestine to her now?

Doug takes her hand as they walk. "What's on your mind, Ruby
Heartwood?"

Had anyone ever asked her that question before?

So, she tells him. About Celestine, about Buck. Somewhere along
the line, they find a bench and sit down while she digs back into old
memories. "And now, all of a sudden, I know where she is. I've had her
relegated to the past for so long it's shocking to think that she actually
exists."

"Why do you think you need to confront her?"

"I'm not sure if confrontation is what I'm looking for, Doug.
Maybe just see for myself that this woman is, like all of us, capable of
bad judgment. That denying that her son was anything other than a
monster was simply parental blindness."

"Did she think you were lying? About what he did?"

"I think she told herself I was. She simply couldn't see what was in
front of her eyes."

"Can I ask you something?"

"Of course."

"She's never known about Sabine? Never known that she has a
granddaughter?"

"As far as I know." Ruby pushes her hair away from her face where
it's caught in the light breeze and pulled free. "I suppose she does know
about Sabine, in general. Not that she is who she is. It's an interesting
world, that of carnies and people in our profession, lots of gossip."

"Everything hits the grapevine?"

"Something like that. People move from place to place and join this carnival or that circus. They regroup, find old friends, talk about who's alive, who's dead, and who's hanging on by a thread."

"Do you think Sabine wants Celestine to know about her?"

"You must be very good at your job."

"I am. What I'm working around to, obliquely, I agree, is that it really isn't Celestine you want to confront."

39

Doug leaves the Airbnb in Sandwich first. Before he goes, he lets Ruby know that she's welcome to bunk in with him if she has no other plans. Ruby likes his turn of phrase. No other plans. She could go back to the Dew Drop, or back to Bull's, or, as she thinks she should, just get on the road and simply go. Drive until she gets free of this sticky sense of belonging. South is appealing. But she'd have to go through Providence to go south. Fifteen minutes on I-95 and she'd be through it. She can point her van and her nose toward Connecticut and not look left or right, not look for an exit sign that announces, "This Way to Celestine Fox's House." Yes, she's looked it up.

Or she can take Doug up on his offer. Spend a little time being domestic. Catch up on her laundry and exercise her cooking skills. She could even take a quick trip farther northwest and visit her family in Moose River Junction. Ruby recognizes stasis when she sees it. For so many years of her life she's practiced the art of cut and run, pick up and go, blow this pop stand. Never looked back, never let the dust of one place adhere to her feet. Until now. Now she can't seem to work up the energy. Maybe energy isn't the right word; it's more the *imperative*.

Ruby suddenly is weak in the knees. The imperative. She no longer feels the urge, the need, to move. Whatever has been pressing down on her all her life has all but vanished.

We are on the move again. I was happy while the direction in which we were going was toward the place I like, the place I feel we are at home. It's not a particular den, more like a territory. Doug's house is in it and Boy's yard. The little room we den in every few days where Ravi has good treats. The street where we stop and chat with humans and dogs we know; the park where Ruby touches other people and other dogs to understand what they need. This mobile den. That's our territory. Not where we are going now; now we are headed in the completely wrong direction and nothing smells right. Ruby is exuding her worry scent, her nervous scent, and that makes me nervous too. If she is apprehensive, then so am I.

It doesn't take but one wrong turn before Ruby finds the neighborhood where Lily visited Celestine. Celeste as she is now. The house is much like every other house around it, a tiny Cape style, faded green aluminum siding, a sentry box entryway with a cement walk leading to it. Scraggy grass, foundation plantings that have become overgrown and reach to the lip of the picture window, itself framed unevenly by heavy draw drapes, the left side far wider than the right, making the window look off-kilter. The plot is tiny, and the driveway abuts the neighbor's driveway, the pair divided only by a strip of dirt. There is no car on either side.

Ruby pulls up in front of the house, shuts off the Westfalia, and sits. The dog climbs from her seat to Ruby's lap, licks Ruby's chin. Asks loudly what is going on. Ruby rests her chin on the dog's head. "I'm going to visit an old friend."

"Doesn't feel like that."

"No. I suppose not. We were close once but had a falling out."

"You fell out of what."

"Affection, I suppose."

"I smell hurt. Did she bite you?"

"Sort of."

Suddenly the Hitchhiker stands on Ruby's lap, growls. "I will protect you."

"You will stay in the car."

A flicker in Ruby's rearview mirror catches her eye as a car lumbers into the driveway on Celeste's side. A beat-up landau-roofed coppertone Oldsmobile very well suited to an old woman. As Ruby watches, the driver's door opens, but no one emerges. After a moment, a leg comes out, the foot shod in a camo green Croc, followed by a barrel-shaped torso. A thin gray T-shirt rides up and grimy chinos ride down. The driver yanks at the pants, then reaches in and pulls out a brown paper bag. There is absolutely no resemblance between the hulk that makes his unsteady way to the side door of the tiny house and the God's gift to women that Buck once was. There is every resemblance to the image she conjured of him on that long-ago day when she cursed him into wreckage. He has become the monster she shrieked into existence. Troll-like he leans heavily against the railing, hauling himself up the steps. As he gains the landing, Ruby sees his face. She has been holding her breath, and now can release it. There is nothing of Sabine in those bruised-looking eyes, those sallow, withered cheeks. To her he looks haunted, defeated. And then Celestine comes to the door and opens it for him, and Ruby sees a softening, a flicker of a smile and a vestige of humanity.

Cars must park on this street all the time because no one has so much as noticed her distinctive white Westfalia sitting in front of their house. Buck has gone in and straightened the crooked curtains. Ruby puts her hand on her ignition key, but neither turns it nor pulls it out. Now or never. The dog, back in her own seat, has her eyes on Ruby, her little eyebrows expressing a near perfect perplexity. Reflecting Ruby's own mixed feelings.

A surge of an old combative spirit rises. The same spirit that allowed a teenage girl to stay out of reach of authorities who would take away her child; the same spirit that enabled her to raise that child, to provide for her.

What Buck did changed the course of Ruby's life. But she cannot imagine it any other way. Forty years ago, this man inflicted himself upon her, violated her. But she has gotten the better of him. She has Sabine. She has Molly and Tom and, yes, Dan, her son-in-law. If evil was done, she has received a greater good. She stepped out of Madame Celestine's RV and made her own way, made her own life.

"What do I do?" Ruby presses her hands on the dog's head.

For once there is no response, no connection. The dog is just a dog, her thoughts inscrutable.

Ruby jerks the key out of the ignition, pops open her door and slams it behind her. It bounces, the latch not clicking, but she doesn't notice. She slips the key into her jeans pocket as she stands on the sidewalk, facing the house. Now she's been noticed. The newly straightened drapes move slightly; clearly, they think she might be some Jehovah's Witness going solo. She wonders if neither Celestine nor Buck will recognize her. Is she someone so far in their past that they may need her driver's license to believe that this avenging angel is who she will tell them that she is?

At her knock, Buck swings the windowless front door open, keeping the screen door between them. He studies her face. She doesn't like the look now any more than she did back then, when his predator eyes felt like they were scraping the skin right off. "Can I help you?"

"Buck."

If he is surprised at her using his name, he doesn't show it.

She waits a beat, maybe two, long enough to see if he *will* recall her, remember the fourteen-year-old star boarder in his mother's RV who he violated.

From behind Buck, "Who is it?"

"It's Ruby Heartwood, Madame Celestine," Ruby calls through the closed screen door.

She hears, "Who?"

It is hard to imagine that two people who had such a profound effect on her life would have forgotten her so completely, as if *she* did not have an effect on their lives. At least, not yet.

Ruby puts her hand on the latch. "May I come in?"

"What do you want?" Buck keeps his hand on the other side of the latch, holding the door closed as if she is an invader.

"To tell you something." Ruby is not shaking; she is not trembling with nerves or with righteous anger. She is calm and knows exactly what she must do. She is no longer a child, a foundling, a runaway. She is a grown woman who has followed her own path and made a life. "I can do it through this door." Ruby lets go of the latch. "But I'd like to talk to both of you."

"Let her in, Buck."

Buck stands aside, lets Ruby pull the squeaky door open for herself. There is a fist-sized tear in the screen. A fillip of trepidation lights in her belly. Is this really such a good idea? Maybe she should have looked him up, Buck, to see if he has a criminal record, a rap sheet, a prison record. She wrangles her momentary doubts into submission, walks into the house.

Madame Celestine is exactly as Lily Parmenter had described her. A widow's hump has pressed her posture into a gnomish crescent. Just the sight of it makes Ruby stand up straighter. Celeste has to twist her head sideways and look up to see Ruby's face. There is a hint of recollection in her wrinkled face. It's like watching a thought blossom, the way she begins to nod, a faint smile developing, quickly replaced by the full memory of Ruby's ignominious departure and, of course, what she took with her.

"You stole my teapot."

"I did. Actually, let's be clear, I took it as payment for services rendered."

"You also took my money."

"Again, payment."

"I can't stand here trying to see your face. Sit down." Celeste has reverted to Celestine. "There." She points to a lonely dining room chair separated from its partners still grouped around a maple table jammed into an alcove. Sitting, Ruby is now eye to eye with Celestine, who stands in front of her. Close up, the formidable fortune-teller's age falls away and Ruby can see the woman as she remembers her. It's a bit of a shock to think that she herself is now older than Celestine was when they first met. She'd seemed so old to those very young eyes, a right and proper age for a crone. In fact, Celestine could only have been in her midforties. Now Ruby looks into faded blue eyes surrounded by a lacework of wrinkles, and the image of the woman Celestine was is subsumed by the woman she is now, Celeste Fox.

Would her own mother be more like this, an old woman, rather than the ethereal dream woman who inhabits Ruby's mother dreams?

"Why are you here? Are you going to give me back my teapot?"

"I wish I could. I would, in fact, if it hadn't recently met with disaster." Ruby is speaking the truth, as suddenly as the idea has come upon her. She *would* have given the old woman her teapot back. Maybe she should have saved the shards and handed them over, a fine metaphor for the smashing of her youth. "It served me well, Madame Celestine; it helped me to support my daughter."

"Well, fine. It was a good teapot. I got it from—"

Ruby wonders what kind of seer this old woman is if she doesn't put two and two together. She interrupts, "My daughter, who is forty now." Come on, do the math.

Buck has left the room.

"Why are you here? Do you want me to give you a reading? You should know that I don't do that sort of thing anymore. I sold my tarot cards."

"I know. Lily told me. It's how I found you." As easily as that, she found the woman she had no intention of ever seeing again. She cannot find the one she wants, but she has effortlessly found this woman for whom she has harbored nothing but hate for forty years. A hatred predicated on Celestine's brutal rejection, a hatred born of hurt. She looks the old woman in the face and is shocked by the fact that she has no feeling toward her at all. The simmering, decades-long anger hasn't boiled to the surface; it's gone lukewarm.

"What do you want to know? You seem to have everything in order. You don't have a confused aura."

That seems unlikely. All Ruby feels at this moment is confused and betrayed by her own sudden inability to tell Celestine what she needs to say, what she came to say. As unlikely as this reunion had seemed just days ago, Ruby has envisioned shattering this old woman's world with a life-changing announcement that . . . that what? That Buck's evil action means that Celestine has Sabine to call her own? Of all the scenarios that have floated through her imagination, Ruby hasn't given thought to the idea that Celestine might *want* to claim a relationship with Sabine and her family. Ruby really should have run all this by her daughter before this impulsive visit.

"Let me help you, Ruby." Celestine reaches behind herself to find the edge of the couch. Sits down. "You have come to tell me that my Bucky violated you and left you with child."

"Yes."

"You're not the first. You'll get nothing from me."

Ruby almost laughs. "What would I possibly want from you? It's far too late for reparations."

"An abortion, of course. It's what all the others demanded."

"Celeste, this was forty years ago."

"Ruby, leave her alone. She gets confused this time of day." Buck is standing in the archway between the living room and the dining alcove. "And, just for the record, there have never been any others. You were it. My only . . ."

"Victim?"

"If you insist."

Ruby takes a good look at Buck now. He looks almost as aged as his mother, but he can only be in his sixties. He has the pallor of a man who has endured ill health. "I would like to know if there is some illness that I should let my daughter know about. Diabetes? Cancer?"

"Chronic pain. No known cause."

"For how long?"

"Since the day you cursed me."

The screen door squeaks. All of a sudden Ruby feels the wet nose of the Hitchhiker thrust into her palm. The dog has nosed herself in through the unlatched screen door. Ruby scoops her up into her arms.

The dog's thoughts are clear. "She is no threat. The man is no threat. You are done here."

Ruby starts the van, pulls away from the curb and tries to remember how to get back to the highway entrance. She sees the sign for Interstate 95 South. The Hitchhiker issues a low rumble in her throat, not quite a growl. Ruby remembers the cards she dealt to herself weeks ago, which pointed her in the direction of north. At the time she thought it meant go to northern New England, join the fair circuit. Now she understands. Her destiny lies north of this moment.

Ruby gains the highway, merges into northbound traffic. She is heading back to Harmony Farms.

Content that we are heading back to our territory, I jump onto the backseat, circle three times, and tuck myself into a little package, nose under hind leg. I need to sleep. My person has more to accomplish today, and I will need to be helpful. It is very hard work listening to a human. They are never as clear as they could be, their thoughts are so full of noise and words. They never just let things be. All you really need is a nice place to curl up. A bowl of decent kibble. Fresh water. Toys, of course. Play is good work. But humans prefer to gnaw at their thoughts instead of bones. If only they would nap more. My person has the extra problem of worrying for other people. Like some dogs take on their person's fears. It makes her weary.

It would be easy to keep going a little farther, knock on Doug's door. It would be just a little farther than that to go all the way to Sabine's. But Ruby is weighed down with an exhaustion that limits her to getting only as far as the Dew Drop Inn, where she throws herself on Ravi's mercy and gets her familiar room key. All she wants to do is sleep. Every muscle hurts, and for a moment, she wonders if she is actually physically ill.

When she plugs her phone charger into the wall outlet, Ruby sees that she's missed a call from Sabine. She doesn't have the energy to talk to anyone, much less her daughter, so Ruby turns off her phone and climbs into bed. It is only five o'clock. She'll nap and then see how she feels about revealing all that has happened. Maybe she'll be fresher. Maybe she'll be braver. The Hitchhiker tucks herself into the bend of Ruby's legs, gives her left ear a good scratching, then sighs. Settles. Sleeps.

Three women are sitting at a table. Their hands touch the table, and the scene resembles a séance. They are talking animatedly, but Ruby cannot understand anything that is being said even though she is, in the way of dreams, one of the women. A nimbus surrounds the woman opposite Ruby, as if the sun is rising behind her, and Ruby squints. The woman to her right is in shadow. She cannot see their faces, but she knows who they are. They have appeared in her dreams all her life. Sometimes they came as angels when she was under the influence of the convent's teachings. Sometimes they came as clients, seeking her advice. Sometimes they were random figures standing in a line waiting for something to happen. Today, in this dream, they seem particularly corporeal. She can see the threads of DNA dancing around them like multicolored atoms around a nucleus. She can feel their touch as the women reach and clasp hands around the table. The one to her right side speaks clearly now: *Mom, for goodness sake.* The voice is so clear, the dreaming Ruby wonders if Sabine has arrived in her room. Ruby resists waking to the sound of that voice. She is waiting for the other woman to say something. The features are obscured by the light, but Ruby can see that the woman is opening her mouth to speak. Nothing comes out and the woman places a hand over her own mouth, then reaches across the table to touch a finger to Ruby's, as if to shush her. Finally, frustrated and impatient, Ruby says: *Talk to me, for goodness sake.*

The sound of her own voice wakes Ruby up. She is filled with the sense that she has woken up too soon, that the woman, her dream mother, was finally about to speak. To tell her what she wants to know.

Although she's only been asleep for less than an hour, Ruby is refreshed. Maybe it's the lingering sense of the dream that buoys her spirits. There is an implied optimism in the idea that her dream mother was on the verge of revelation. Equally, Ruby has awakened with the notion that Celestine and Buck are truly in her rearview mirror and will no longer be a factor in her life. And, on the basis of that, she decides not to mention the visit to Sabine when she returns her call.

But first, a bowl of kibble for the dog and a microwave burrito for herself.

"How was your trip to Rhode Island?"

Damn that Find Friends app. Ruby chides herself for not shutting it off. "Fine."

"What made you turn around?"

"What do you mean?"

"You were heading south, and now you're back in Harmony Farms."

"Are you spending your entire day following me around? What about your kids, your husband, your life?" Ruby is reduced to an adolescent kvetching.

"They're just fine, thank you. It's you I'm concerned about." Sabine drops her voice. "I'm getting a sense." Sabine doesn't admit this often. "You have been up to something that has been difficult, yet, I don't know, rewarding? Is that the word?"

"No. *Relieving*. That's the word." And Ruby breaks down and tells her that she has confronted Sabine's father. Her grandmother. That they are now mere cobwebs to be dusted away.

Sabine takes in the information without giving away her own feelings about the matter of her biological father's proximity. She will have to digest it, and in some later conversation she and Ruby will discuss it. This is how they operate. "That doesn't explain why you turned around. With the Renaissance Faire not working out, why not shoot toward warmer weather?"

It's a fair question. It's always been Ruby's pattern that, as soon as it gets uncomfortable to live in a poorly heated van, she goes where the "weather suits her clothes." "I wish I knew."

"Is it Doug?"

"I'm not settling down, if that's what you're getting at."

"Heaven forfend, of course not." But there is a teasing note in her voice.

"I'm not done here. That's what keeps me here, and what won't let me go. There is some business near at hand that I must take care of first."

"And you have no idea what it is?"

"Not for sure. But, Beenie, I think it has something to do with finding my mother at last." There, she's said it. "She may have been here. A very long time ago."

"So, you're on the scent?"

"In a manner of speaking. I am intuiting that if I am to finally find out who she was, or is, I need to be in this area for a little while longer."

"Works for me. Would you consider bringing your friend Doug to our place for dinner next Saturday? I promise not to make you stay."

"I would like that very much."

After her conversation with Sabine, Ruby gives herself an hour before calling Doug and letting him know that she'd done exactly what he felt she needed to do with Buck and Celestine. She needs the time between conversations to regroup, to sort the story out so that it is suitable for who Doug is in her life, occupying the territory of being neither fish nor fowl. Not family, but something.

It was easier than she'd imagined it might be; he listened, made a comforting remark, and then let her decide if the subject was now closed. Which, she was surprised to find, it was. Then she asked him about having dinner with Sabine and her family and he didn't hesitate to say yes. "You bet. I'd like nothing better. Can I bring dessert? I've got my mother's recipe for Death by Chocolate cake." Clearly Doug viewed this dinner as a step forward in their relationship. After she hung up, Ruby spent a little time probing herself for how *she* felt about this next step. She simply couldn't find anything to fear in it. She didn't feel entanglement; she didn't feel the threatening web of connection. She just liked the idea.

40

So here she is, not exactly where she thought she'd be, but all in all, it feels right. Ruby makes a deal with Ravi to stay on at a greatly reduced cost. He's pretty excited that the slacker clients of Robert W. Atkins seem to have a genuine interest in the place. What's even better, they seem to have a genuine interest in him and his ideas for upgrades. "Deep pockets, Ruby, deep pockets." He grins and hands the dog a cookie. "Can you imagine a saltwater pool and a hot tub? They're even talking about a tiki bar."

Ruby agrees that she can. "Just don't lose the charm." She isn't quite sure if she means the crooked little motel's charm or his.

Next stop the Country Market where Ruby runs into both Polly and Bull. It is so good to see Bull back at his post, leaning against the meat counter, jawing with the boys. He's a little thinner, but otherwise seems none the worse for his illness. Outside, Boy and the Hitchhiker wait patiently for their people, keeping each other company. Polly is in the canned vegetables aisle, contemplating brands and prices on stewed tomatoes. She looks up as Ruby approaches. "Thought you'd gone."

"I did, but plans got changed."

"Can't say I'm sorry. I could use a little of your help with a guest of the town."

"Sure. I'll stop by on my way back to the motel."

"Motel?"

"Yes, the motel." Ruby baits Polly's curiosity. "Why?"

"Oh, you know." The look on Polly's face is the sheer dying to ask look of a curious but constrained friend.

"I do." She gives Polly nothing. Doesn't mention the weekend in Sandwich, or the dinner at Sabine's. It's not necessarily a desire for privacy, it's more that Ruby is loath to give this thing a definition.

Ruby has just unhitched the Hitchhiker from her station in front of the Country Market. Boy is wagging himself into a frenzy as Bull has followed Ruby out of the market. As Ruby works at untangling the crossed leashes, she hears her name being called. It's Emily from the Farmers' Market and Makers Faire.

"Ruby, I'm so glad I ran into you. Will you be signing up for Columbus Day weekend? We hold the Faire all three days."

"Three days? I hope that it's not triple the price."

"It's the last event of the season, so all three days are included in the regular fee."

"Sign me up, Emily, sign me up." Yet another excuse to stick around. Ruby prefers to think that she's being held against her will, but that way of thinking is growing a bit thin, almost like the fabric of her tent. Which makes Ruby think that she should pop into the Fabric Cottage and see about something to make a better patch. Her emergency sutures are barely holding together. Doug has offered her his old Boy Scout pup tent, but she's pretty sure he's kidding.

Their dinner last Saturday with Sabine and the family was very nice, and Ruby looks back on it with a certain satisfaction. Sabine played respectful daughter very well, and Doug stayed in his lane as unofficial boyfriend. Plus, the cake was outstanding, and the kids took to Doug immediately. Finding out that he had a history as a ball player, the two kids and Dan coerced Doug out into the backyard, leaving Sabine and Ruby to have a proper catch up as they did the dishes.

Altogether, an ordinary family gathering. And perfectly ordinary for
Ruby to spend the rest of the night at Doug's.

Ruby sets up her tent, careful to respect the silky patch she's hot glued
to the split in the side. She's got the same location she started with
back in the early days of the summer. It still seems impossible that
she's lingered here in Harmony Farms for as long as she has. Except for
the years she needed to spend the winter in one place so that Sabine
could attend school, Ruby has limited her roosting to a few weeks at
most, and only as long as the work was profitable. Lingering too long
eventually means that the stream of clients is tapped out. This time,
though, there seems to be an endless supply of clients, her favorite
kind: the four-legged variety. Even as she sets up her *mise-en-scène*—
the table, the chairs, the sandwich board, placing the thrift store teapot
on a plinth—she's been approached by early birds with their doggies,
all asking if she'll be doing animal communication. In the back of
her mind, Ruby thinks that she'll squirrel away all the animal reading
fees toward pulling up stakes here. And in the next moment she realizes that she's looking forward to that high school football game Doug
wants to take her to next weekend. Homecoming.

Clients are thick on the ground on this beautiful Saturday of a
three-day holiday weekend. Leaf peepers abound, and most of them
are incapable of resisting a craft fair. Ruby highlights the animal communication line item on her sandwich board and sets a fishbowl of
dog treats on her table beside the box of tarot cards. For her part, the
Hitchhiker speaks nicely to each visitor and then leaves Ruby to do her
job after receiving one of those treats as a reward for good behavior.

About lunchtime, Doug shows up and offers to fetch whatever
Ruby wants from one of the six food trucks arrayed around the perimeter of the park. The breeze has come up, her shabby pennant snaps
with a new vigor. Ruby closes her tent flaps and they retire to her van
to pop up the table and enjoy their falafel wraps in comfort.

Having Doug in it makes her van seem a lot smaller than usual. The Hitchhiker moves to the front seat in protest of being squeezed off the bench seat. Ruby has long since removed the two jump seats that would allow face-to-face dining over the table, as it has been years since she was face-to-face with anyone in her mobile tiny house. So, it is side by side that Doug Cross and Ruby Heartwood have lunch. With the slider open, it's a bit like sitting on a porch. The Westfalia attracts a lot of attention from passersby and from acquaintances. Bull sticks his head in to say hi, and then Polly, who looks pleased with this couple-like scene. Ruby would like to shut the slider, but that seems wrong.

As they finish their lunch, passing a container of wet wipes back and forth, Cynthia Mann strolls by. At first it looks like she's going to pretend that she doesn't recognize the utterly recognizable van but then pauses. Raises a hand in greeting, a slight smile breaking free of her lip filler. Keeps moving.

"I think you may have tamed her."

"It's an improvement, for sure."

Sunday isn't quite as pleasant as Saturday, but still a lovely fall day, if overcast. The shabby pennant on the top of Ruby's tent is limp, the fresh breeze from yesterday gone. The crowd is thin at first but then builds as the day progresses. All in all, not a bad day. The cigar box is respectably full. Ruby thinks that she'll make an ATM run after the Faire closes and put that cash in her account. Doug, being Doug, thinks that her security system, or lack thereof, is a problem. Part of her thinks that's kind of sweet, but a larger part of her screams that *this* is why being unattached is preferable. No one to criticize a lifelong habit. In all the years she's traveled alone, she's managed to stay safe. Well, mostly.

The air is so still that Ruby decides it's safe to leave her tent up. Tomorrow is the last day of the event and it would be nice not to have to spend time setting up again, just get down to business. As she ties the tent flaps closed, Ruby's phone chirps with an incoming call. Sarah Grace.

"How was the trip?"

Sarah Grace effuses the glories of Alaska and insists that Ruby find a way to take a cruise. Ruby doesn't mention that doing so is hardly in her budget and gives Sarah a solid "maybe someday" response. Ruby and the Hitchhiker listen to Sarah Grace as they walk back to the van, climb in, and shut the door. She's going to have to guide Sarah back to the actual reason for her call. "So, have you had time since your return to do a little family exploration?"

"A bit. I've gotten emails from two of the second cousins from your branch. Nothing particularly revealing, but I'll send them on to you."

"That would be great. When you say my branch, what do you mean?"

"My great-grandmother's sister's daughters' daughters."

Ruby feels her mind close down. "Any names to go with those?"

"Smith, Green, Watson, Felton, Barr. Common names. It's all on the maternal line, so each name pops up only once or twice."

"It's a jumping-off place." But to where, Ruby can't imagine. "Send me the emails, if you will. Talk soon."

It has been a long day of reading and Ruby feels the tiredness descend. It seems less important to have this sketchy information now than it did even a few weeks ago. What does it all mean? she thinks. A random suggestion that someone who resembled her once worked this town? The idea that she shares blood with people who are strangers and thus might trace herself backward has become a quixotic desire. The list of names are so common as to feel familiar; indeed she can probably come up with people she already knows by those names. Green, Barr, Smith. A client, a teacher, the dentist she went to last year. For goodness sake, her own daughter's married name is Smith. Felton. And yet, there is something niggling at the back of her mind, some pestering idea that won't come clear.

•   •   •

The weather on Monday has turned nasty; rain threatens, and the sweet coolness of fall feels a whole lot more like the rawness of early winter. Ruby zips a fleece vest underneath her caftan and pulls on her Uggs. She doesn't hold out much hope for a good day and promises herself that she only needs to stick it out till noon. The wind, which was dormant yesterday, has picked up and the first thing Ruby notices when she arrives at her tent is that her poor bedraggled pennant has finally given up the ghost and sheared off its pole. She finds it trampled in the grass. She tucks it into the deep pocket of her caftan.

The Hitchhiker ducks into the tent and right into her little bed. This is not her kind of weather, she says. She will selfishly spend the hours Ruby insists on working not being of any help. If there was a bully stick to chew on, that might improve things. Ruby fishes one of the natural chews out of her bag and gives the Hitchhiker a pat on the head. "Stay in bed; it's what an intelligent being would do." If an intelligent human was capable of forfeiting a potential payday just because the weather is sour. Looking around the grounds, Ruby can see that a number of the regulars have indeed forfeited their paydays. She's alone in her assigned row, the lavender lady and the hat seller have literally folded up their tents and booked it.

Even with the fleece vest and Uggs, Ruby is quickly chilled despite sitting inside the conical tent. She pulls out her long-neglected knitting, mostly for the warmth afforded by the wool. The sandwich sign keeps blowing over. Despite all that, there are people strolling, stalwarts in search of the last of the growing season's fresh vegetables, flowers, pies. Fall flowers in bunches, decorative cornstalks and cattails clutched against the wind.

Ruby closes her eyes and lets a curious sensation trickle through her. It is as if the wind itself is speaking through her. It is a sensation similar to that when she speaks to the dogs. Not words so much as images, visions, tastes. She wonders if she's dozed off. She glances down at the sleeping spaniel. There is no other dog in sight. *Felton*. Why is that word—name—buzzing through her mind? It's slipping in like a musical phrase, over and over, without resolution. *Felton*.

A gust of wind tears through Ruby's tent, splitting the mended side, tossing the little tent over, spilling the contents out of it. The table, the other chair, and the sandwich sign are all knocked over. The wooden box of tarot cards hits the ground and bursts open. Cards fly off in every direction as if stirred by a mighty hand. The dog leaps up and bolts. Ruby loses her grip on her knitting needles and pushes out of her chair to try to grasp the tent before it flies away. The chair flies away. *Feltonfeltonfelton*.

As violent as the gust was, it passes and there is a sudden lull. The only thing left standing where the tent had been is the plinth with the little thrift store teapot sitting exactly as she had placed it an hour ago.

Annie *Felton*. That's who took Ruby's spot at the Renaissance Faire. The sudden recollection of where she'd heard the name, why that word has been teasing at her memory, jolts Ruby. Felton in her ancestry. Felton in Plymouth. Ruby scrambles to gather her tent and belongings as quickly as she can. If the weather here is awful, what's to say that the Renaissance Faire hasn't already broken camp? It's the last day of their run. She's got to get there as fast as she can. She's got to get to Annie Felton before she disappears.

"Whoa, Ruby, let me help." Doug gathers the remnants of Ruby's tent into his arms, grabs the folding chairs. "What happened?"

"I have to go. Now. Will you go find the dog? She ran off."

Doug throws everything into the van while Ruby picks up what she can. The cards are a loss. She doesn't care. The knitting is a mess. She doesn't care. She carefully puts the unbroken, unscathed teapot back in the Bubble Wrap and carries it like a holy relic to the van. Doug has the Hitchhiker and all three jump into the van and Ruby slams the gearshift into reverse. "Buckle up."

As they lurch toward the highway, Doug reaches over and pats Ruby's hand on the stick shift. "Will you tell me what's going on? Where are we going?"

"To find my mother."

41

Holiday traffic clogs the highway making progress south a stop-and-go transaction until they cross over the Mass Pike and break free. They also drive right out from under the storm they left behind in Harmony Farms. The squeezing in her chest begins to soften as Ruby sees open road in front of her. If it's clear ahead, both the road and the weather, then maybe she no longer needs to push the Westfalia quite so hard. It likes a maximum of sixty-two, and she's got it wound up to almost seventy. As she backs off the pedal, she can't help but notice Doug visibly relax. He lets go of the door handle, settles his seat belt more comfortably across his chest. Shifts the dog on his lap to a more comfortable position. Ruby reaches over and takes his hand. Smiles. He rubs her knuckles with his thumb. Smiles back.

"You feel as though all the pieces are coming together."

"I do. I have an absolute certainty that this is the moment I have been waiting for."

"What does that feel like? Absolute certainty?"

"I'm not sure I can describe it. I just know that this fairly recent need to solve my deepest mystery is about to be fulfilled."

Doug says nothing. Ruby knows that he's worried she'll be disappointed, or worse, devastated if this woman isn't who she hopes she is. It really is so little to go on: a coincidence of name, a shared profession. But Doug isn't blessed with second sight. He doesn't know the rapture of seeing that which isn't *yet*. But will be. She supposes the closest thing to it is faith in God. Unseen. Real. The mighty wind that blew through her tent, smashing her props, all except the doughty teapot, surrounded Ruby with an enfolding message. Go. Seek. Find.

The parking lot at the Renaissance Faire is beginning to empty out; a long line of cars snake through the rows heading toward the exits. It is late in the afternoon and the event itself is winding down. Ruby skips the main parking lot, heads directly to the back of the grounds to the employee parking area. As she expects, it is full of RVs and equipment trailers, the temporary stables for the horses who act in the main event of the faire, the faux joust. Two are all tacked up, all the trappings of an American vision of Medieval sport hanging from bridles and covering saddles. The third act of the play will commence in a few minutes, the final "joust" between the chosen champions of Lady This and Lady That. The other two acts would have involved the challenges: spiking hoops on a lance, trick riding, dramatic tumbles off accommodating horses. This one will end in clanging swordplay. Ruby glances at the combatants, sharing a bottle of beer, and puts her money on Lord Redcoat. The guy in black never wins.

"This way." Ruby leads Doug and the dog through the employee entrance. Either because it's so late in the day security can't be bothered, or because being dressed in her gold-embroidered caftan suggests she's part of the cast, no one challenges Ruby and her escorts. She gathers the fabric of her caftan in her fingers, keeping it off the dusty path, the wood chips long since dissolved with hard use. Her trajectory takes her around the perimeter of the jousting field, between the blacksmith's forge and the Bard's Corner, right to a small building tucked in between the mud pit comics and the ax throwing game.

The shed is perhaps twelve by ten; a single window sports a solid shutter, now propped open. The door is narrow, a wrought iron latch and curlicue straps give it an authentic antique air. A banner hangs from the eaves: *Mystic Marianna: Fortunes Told ~ Crystal Ball ~ Palms.*

Ruby thinks that she's going to be sick. Doug puts one large hand on her shoulder. "You can do this. I'll be at the picnic tables."

"Thank you. I'll meet you there in a minute."

"Ruby. Certainty."

As Doug makes his way through costumed faire-goers, looking like a modern man cast suddenly back in time, a present-day Yankee in King Arthur's Court, Ruby is filled with a certainty she hadn't looked for. She is certain that she loves him.

"Here goes nothing." Ruby drops the hem of her caftan, shakes out her hair. She can hear the thundering of hooves as the joust begins. The clunk of fake lance against shield. The roar of the crowd cheering on the actors. Her breath is coming faster, as if she is also galloping across a wide field. She remembers the dreamscape of the hillside, the ethereal woman either coming or going. Her palms are clammy with nerves.

Ruby feels a slight pressure below; the Hitchhiker, nose working the air toward the open booth door, presses her forepaws against Ruby's foot. "I am with you."

This is interesting. Although I haven't laid eyes on her yet, the scent of the woman sitting in this tiny house fills my mind with images of Ruby. It isn't quite that they have the same odors, it's that they have the same markers. That is, similar tastes in food and soap. I know that if I am allowed a deeper investigation, I will be able to find many other markers, ones more deeply buried than what appears on the skin. In the way that I immediately recognized Sabine and her playful children as blood to Ruby, I am getting a similar flavor, even as apart as these two women are. I nudge Ruby to go in. I'm anxious to confirm my suspicions.

"Don't be afraid. Come in. Come in." The voice is moderate, a slight accent, much like the type Ruby had used for years. Who would trust a psychic with a solidly New England twang or Southern accent, after all? "Mystic Marianna will help you to get the answers you seek."

"I hope so." This under her breath. Ruby steps inside only as far as the doorframe. A sudden break in the clouds and she is illuminated from behind. The gold in her caftan glitters. The woman sitting in the booth chuckles. "I see we have the same taste in caftans. Broadway Costuming, Toledo, Ohio, I presume?"

Marianna the Mystic cannot be Ruby's mother. She is younger than Ruby. She looks more Sabine's age. She looks like Sabine.

As Ruby lingers in the doorway, the sun goes behind a cloud, she is no longer backlit.

"Oh, my God." There is nothing of the foreign accent in that re-mark. Mystic Marianna jumps to her feet. The two women, both in golden caftans, of an equal height, stare at each other with gold-flecked hazel eyes. Frozen in tableau. "I never thought that I'd lay eyes on you." Marianna takes one step forward. It is a tiny space, and as Ruby steps forward, they are within touching distance. "We've been looking for you."

The dog looks at one, then the other. She sniffs. Her tail wags. Satisfied that she knows what's going on, the Hitchhiker takes an ol-factory survey of the small space, finds a dropped French fry.

Ruby's mouth is dry and she longs for a drink of water. She doesn't know whether to ask questions or give answers. "My name, what I call myself, is Ruby Heartwood. I was given the name Mary Jones when I was left behind."

"And I believe that you are my lost sister."

At that, Ruby's legs give out and her sister helps her to sit down, put her head between her knees. She also pulls the shutter in and flips the CLOSED sign on the door. For a long silent moment Mari-

anna rubs Ruby's back until Ruby feels able to sit up. Mystic Marianna takes her seat opposite Ruby, the tiny round table with a little
white teapot centered on it between them. Ruby feels like a client.
She's never sat on the south side of the table before. "I have been
searching for my mother—who abandoned me as an infant."

Maybe it's habit, maybe its professional, but Marianna puts out
her hands and takes Ruby's. "Which she has regretted every day of
her life since."

"I assume that you are her second daughter."

"Yes. Annie."

"I've been in touch with a genetic cousin of ours. She says that we
come from a long line of second daughters. Who have the gift." This
last is an interpretation of Sarah Grace's more vague remarks.

"We do. Mostly." Annie looks at Ruby. "You're a first daughter."

This isn't the line of conversation Ruby is most interested in, not
by a long shot. "And our mother? I suppose I should know, but I truly
don't. Even Sabine, my . . . your niece, whose gifts are of a medium,
has never been able to tell me if . . ."

"She's alive. She's well. She's been having dreams about you."

"And I of her. But I never conjured you."

"Funny. You've haunted my dreams since I was a little girl."

There is a tingling in her palms, as if Ruby can feel Annie's blood
flowing hot in her capillaries. She pulls her hands away. "We need to
have a conversation without all the psychic trappings. Like regular
sisters suddenly introduced as adults."

"You have someone waiting for you."

"I do. And it would be good for him to meet you. If only to prove
that you exist."

"I like your familiar." Annie reaches down and gives the Hitchhiker
a pat. "I'll close up shop; it's time anyway. Meet you at the beer stand."

"Okay."

·   ·   ·

Doug gets to his feet at the sight of Ruby coming toward him. The look on his face suggests that the look on her face is troubling. And yet, now that the initial shock has died down, she feels a rising tide of excitement.

"And?" he asks.

"You'll never guess. I have a sister. Mystic Marianna is Annie Felton."

"And your mother?"

"I'm about to find out. Will you be willing to get us a couple of beers? My *sister* is closing up shop."

"I can take the dog and go hang out in the van."

"No. Please. Stay at least for a little while. I'd rather have you witness for yourself than have to tell you about it."

"Okay. But I'm a fly on the wall." As if to prove it, Doug waves away an actual fly. The picnic grounds are a mess, bees and flies and wasps are coming in for their late-afternoon forage. The joust is over. The jugglers and acrobats are taking final bows. The Bard has completed his raunchy sonnets. The storm that Ruby and Doug left behind is fast approaching from the north.

Mystic Marianna has become Annie Felton, dressed in jeans, turtleneck, and polar fleece. She's wearing the same Uggs as Ruby has on her own feet. She has pulled her hair back into a ponytail. It may be a trick of the light, or a very good coloring job, but her hair is exactly the shade of auburn that Sabine was born with. She takes one of the beers out of Doug's hand. "Thanks. I'm Annie."

"Doug. Doug Cross. Ruby's . . ."

"Boyfriend." Ruby takes the other beer. She doesn't like beer, but this unique occasion certainly calls for an adult beverage in hand.

"Boyfriend." Doug leans over and kisses Ruby. "I'll just be over there." He slides down to the end of the ten-foot-long picnic table, leaving these weird sisters at the other end, face-to-face.

"He seems nice," Annie says loudly enough for Doug to hear.

"Very. Very nice," Ruby answers. "So, rather than me interrogating you, why don't you fill me in on the basic facts of my life?"

"I don't know about your life, but I do know how it started."

"It's a beginning." Ruby doesn't want embellishment, just the basic truth.

Annie sips her beer and Ruby can see that, despite her seeming calmness, Annie is nervous. "You were conceived in love. But it was a star-crossed kind of love."

"Please, keep it simple. I know how to spin a tale, but you really don't have to do that."

"He was married. She was twenty, maybe a little younger. You see where I'm going with this?"

"She went to a home for unwed mothers. Estelle Williamson's place in Niagara Falls."

"So, you do know a little."

"I don't know why she never came looking for me."

"She did."

"I don't believe that. I was there for fourteen years."

"Where?"

"At the convent, in Ottawa. Outside Ottawa. No birth certificate, nothing but a custodial intake record. I was disappeared."

"She never knew that."

Ruby is doubtful. How could a true psychic not know where her own child was? But it seems wrongheaded to have a fight with a person she has only just met. "What did she think happened to me?"

"She was told that you were adopted. Right from birth. But in those days, adoptions were closed; she wasn't allowed any information."

"Do you know what it was like to be raised in an institution? To live in hope every single day that your rightful parent would come and claim you?"

Annie shakes her head. Her eyes, so like Sabine's and her own, are filled. "She thought that you were growing up a happy little girl in a happy little home. A far better situation than that of her only other alternative."

The alternative she herself had not pursued. Neither had Ruby sent her baby away into the hands of strangers. There had been a third choice.

The two sisters sip at their warm beers and stare at the sticky tabletop. The gathering storm will soon put an end to this conversation. Already the breeze has the surrounding pine trees dancing. A fat drop of rain lands on Ruby's caftan. Or maybe that's a tear. She swipes at her eyes, forgetting that she's in full fortune-teller makeup. "Shit. Sorry."

Annie pulls a clean tissue out of her vest pocket. Hands it to Ruby. "What's her name?"

"Aurora."

There is a sense of being pinched between past and present.

Ruby takes a deep breath. "Not her fortune-teller's name, but her real name."

"Her real name is Pearl."

Pearl. "And where is she now?"

Annie, Mystic Marianna, hands Ruby a card with an address penciled on it. She has been expecting this question. "This is where you will find her."

A bubble of laughter rises in Ruby's chest, impossible to suppress. "Of course it is."

42

Ruby asked Doug to drive them home. He tried to keep the pleased look off his face, being graced with the privilege of driving Ruby's beloved Westie, but she caught it. Smiled back at him. "Wow. What a day."

"Do you want to go now? To see her?"

"No. I need to regroup. Annie says she wants to give her a little notice anyway. She's in good health, but the shock of seeing her long-lost child might be hard on the heart. So, tomorrow."

"Will your sister, Annie, be there?"

"I thought she would, but believe it or not, she's a second-grade teacher; school day tomorrow."

"I'd take it off. If you wanted me there."

Ruby puts her hand over his. "Thank you, but I think this first meeting needs to be just us."

The Hitchhiker settles herself into a curl on Ruby's lap, puzzled but pleased to have Ruby in that seat instead of in the lap-forbidden driver's seat. She makes the most of it, letting Ruby know that she likes the new relative they found. "Me too, little dog, me too."

The yellow of the little Hobbit house is warm in the fall sunshine, more butter than lemon. Details of the decorative gingerbread trim, picked out in bright white, reveal curlicues and animal faces hidden within its pattern. The maple trees that front the yard are at the peak of their colors, even though most other foliage has faded by now. Red, gold, orange. Ruby pulls her rumbling Westfalia into the driveway of the house she has so often admired. She remembers the expression: heart beating like a trip hammer, but this is the first time she understands what that means.

The Hitchhiker is staring at her. Brown orbs reflecting her own face back to her. Ruby slides a moist palm across the dog's domed head. Waits for the connection to kick in. She is not disappointed. "What you have been hunting for is here."

In her mind's eye she detects all the things that this little dog considers good: the heft of a marrow bone, the scent of meat, the feel of a soft cushion against which she can tuck herself. The satisfaction of catching a mouse even if it is actually a stuffed toy. But, most of all, Ruby detects the calming of a gentle hand stroking her back as she is now doing to the dog. She is calming now. Her heart rate is slowing. You cannot really die of getting your most fervent desire.

Last night, when she called Sabine to tell her the news, Sabine had cried. Cried in happiness, Ruby knew, pleased to tears that Ruby had finally gotten the central mystery of her life resolved. A thought comes to mind, as strong as any psychic vibe: They are now four generations. Her mother, Ruby and Annie, Sabine, and now Molly.

The dog pulls away from Ruby's hands. Stands on the passenger seat to give herself a good shake. "Go. Now."

The woman who opens the door before Ruby can even reach for the bell is as Ruby has seen her in her dreams; as if the faceless ephemeral spirit has become corporeal. She is an older version of the rest of them, at least in height and eye color and faded-to-gray strawberry blond hair loosely knotted. No longer faceless, she is so very like Sabine or Annie or Molly down to the same little freckle decorating the corner of her mouth as it does Ruby's.

"Hello, Pearl."

"Hello, Ruby."

Far from being a mystic apparition from an imagined past, this woman is very much a creature of now. No fortune-teller's mother here, simply a woman whose own most intense desire has been fulfilled. Ruby looks into her mother's eyes and sees her own longing fulfilled.

While the Hitchhiker watches from the open van window, the two women, mother and daughter, step into each other's arms.

What I know is this: when human beings grow up, they do not leave behind their littermates or progenitors. It is a curious thing, this attachment they have based on the content of their blood. That my Ruby had not had her own mama close by is apparently unusual. Now that they have reunited, they are often in company with each other. I like Pearl's little house. It has enough of a yard, especially way out back, much more than Doug's little yard, or Boy's. We all go for long walks. The humans keep up a steady patter of talk while I follow along or precede them so that I can make their way safe from vermin. Bunnies!

If I understood the concept of time, I would tell you how long it has been since that morning when Ruby pulled our van up to Pearl's house. But I can only say that the seasons have gone from cool to cold to rainy to warm to hot. We have observed the weird day when children get treats by simply knocking on doors, the really nice feast people enjoy that accords even pups like me a nice dinner not involving kibble. Then the day when even the adult humans get excited about shredding paper and tossing it so that I had mouthfuls of it to shake and rend. Right now the air is redolent of fertile dirt, which is fun to bury things in, although neither Pearl nor Doug approve when I choose to bury things in their gardens.

We live with Doug now. An arrangement I am mostly all right with, although I do sometimes long for the days when it was just Ruby and me. But, well, she's so much easier to read these days. The mystery that had kept her moving has gone away. She still jumps into the van and we go spend a day or two as we once did, meeting people and their pets, talking and solving problems. But we don't stay away. I can trust Ruby to bring us back to our territory. And that's what I know.

ACKNOWLEDGMENTS

To my readers opening this book in the summer of 2021, I think that it would be remiss of me not to acknowledge that, as I was deep in the final weeks of completing this manuscript, the world as we knew it utterly changed. We are enduring a pandemic; a renewal of the Civil Rights movement; and economic freefall. We are experiencing a presidential race like no other in terms of consequence. As I write this on August 3, 2020, you, my reader of the summer of 2021, will know how it all ends.

What you are holding in your hands, or listening to, or scrolling through, is the result of a tremendous amount of work and I don't mean mine. I had the easy part. The rest of those named below not only had to create a book out of my words, but they had to do it at home while quarantined. All of this, from cover to copy edits, to design, was accomplished remotely. And it felt seamless to me. It also gave me the chance to learn how to use electronic tracking. Thank you to Sallie Lotz, Alexis Neuville, Maria Vitale, Lisa Davis, Donna Noetzel, Crystal Velasquez, and Young Lim. And at Macmillan, Abigail Starr, Matthew DeMazza, Samantha Edelson, Katy Robitzski, and Alyssa Keyne.

Without the team at the Jane Rotrosen Agency, none of this would ever happen. Thank you, Annelise, for your wise counsel, and Andrea, for sticking with me. Thank you also to Donald Cleary, Chris Prestia, Julianne Tinari, Michael Conroy, Sabrina Prestia, Hannah Rody-Wright,

Ellen Tichler, and Hannah Strouth for keeping all the bits and pieces together.

My deepest gratitude to my extraordinary editor, Jennifer Enderlin. It means the world to me to continue to have your confidence in my work.

This is a book about finding family, and I have my own family to thank for helping me give Ruby a crash course in family research. Thank you to my cousin Deborah Thayer and to my husband, David, for their insights and guidance into what DNA and family research can (and cannot) reveal.

Lastly, to Cora, my furry little muse.

ABOUT THE AUTHOR

Bob Gotlard

SUSAN WILSON is the bestselling author of many books, including *One Good Dog*, *Cameo Lake*, and *Beauty*, a modern retelling of *Beauty and the Beast*, which was made into a CBS TV movie. She lives on Martha's Vineyard.